No Art Without Sin

BY THE SAME AUTHOR

Nothing Disappears

Missing Persons

Bunny, a romance

NONFICTION

*The Cartographic Imagination in Early
Modern England*

No Art Without Sin

D. K. Smith

Cedar Point Press

KANSAS CITY   RIDEAU LAKES

Published in the United States by Cedar Point Press
www.cedarpointpress.com

Library of Congress Control Number: 2023912259
p. cm.
1. Unrequited love—Fiction. 2. Fathers and daughters—Fiction.
3. Separation (psychology)—Fiction. 4. Revenge—Fiction.
5. Romance—Fiction.

Smith, Donald Kimball
No Art Without Sin / D. K. Smith. –1st paperback ed.
ISBN 979-8-9851941-1-1

cover by CPDesign
vector image: Marek Tr/Shutterstock.com

For Annie once more

"All beauty comes from God, but there is no art without sin."

–Simon Motherwell, *Giorgio Vasari and the Pattern of the World.*

Prologue

He would have invented the aunt if he'd had to he tells her, and she laughs.

This is four hours into the drive and they are just entering the Adirondacks, heading north. The landscape is so harshly beautiful, so starkly uninhabited, there is clearly no turning back. He would have stolen the car, he says. He would have made up the whole trip on the spot. And she says with a widening smile, Well, I'm glad you didn't have to.

She had been standing in front of the Ride Board dressed in overalls and a flannel shirt, as if debating between a day in the fields or floating down a river on a raft. In that first glimpse she looks like an adventure already underway. Her dark hair is curly and cut too short, turning her jaw stubborn and her nose into a dainty thumb. She is looking for her destination. Northeast. Far northeast. The map doesn't really go that far; it stops with New York State. So she lets the label hover over the blank wastes of Ontario, and the boy says, "Oh. I wouldn't go up there alone. It's a wilderness."

Half-turning she smiles. This is all part of that moment in her life when everything is on the verge. "I'm not planning to go alone. I'm planning to find a ride."

"Well," he says. "This could be your lucky day."

He doesn't tell her he has only just arrived on campus. That he's never done anything like this before. He has come halfway across the country to spend his junior year in upstate New York, not just for a new town but a new life. And here he is, suddenly, a completely different person.

"How far are you going?" she asks.

"All the way," he says. "I'm visiting my aunt. She lives beyond All Expectations."

And now she eyes him appraisingly. "She sounds like a remarkable woman."

"It's a town," he says. "Up there." And he lays a finger on the blank space north of the border, not so very far from hers.

"Isn't that something," she says. And if there isn't actually a smile on her lips, that certainly doesn't detract from them.

"And what is your destination?" he asks with a new touch of formality.

"I'm heading beyond my wildest dreams. Do you think you can drive that far?"

"I think maybe I can."

"It's near a town called Pont-de-Galliard, Ontario. Ever hear of it?"

And surely he can be forgiven for thinking he is simply putting himself in the hands of fate. "The very place," he says. "I'll introduce you to my aunt."

He has borrowed his landlords' car, an ancient red Saab. He met them the week before—a brother and sister—and the town being empty, they have become friendly. "How long will you need it?" the sister asks.

"Not long. A day or two."

They drive for seventeen hours through light and then darkness. They talk easily from the beginning, lapsing comfortably into silence. As the fatigue and caffeine kick in they grow punchy, laughing over nothing, and periodically they get out and stretch, walking among the trees and picnic tables as if they have never seen anything so primly beautiful. He never wants to stop. He'd have driven on forever, if he could; put everything but this behind him.

They come to the border, and that, too, is a kind of omen— rising out of the darkness like a roadblock and then opening like a gate. The last stretch is down a gravel road winding through cedars and spruce. They follow little flashes of color painted on the tree trunks: a number 4 in a shade of blue made famous years before at the Venice Biennale with a painting called Blue Spruce Sunset—a graceful, self-absorbed woman climbing into a claw-footed tub while, through the wide window, a distant scrub tree catches the last of the light.

"Four what?" he asks.

"The Gang of Four. Don't you know anything?" She speaks gaily, nervously, because they are coming to the end and because she, too, thinks her life is about to change.

The edge of a lake. The headlights die away. Water shines pale as mercury through the black trees. Climbing out they stand vibrating from the road, the blank surface endless in all directions but one. In the middle distance the rounded hillside of an island lies perhaps a hundred yards off shore.

There are no phones on the island. No electricity. No reception. She is glancing around. "There's supposed to be a bell."

"There."

With a smile she reaches up and lifts a large copper cowbell from a broken branch. The night seems much too silent for such a thing. The breeze makes him aware of his skin, and then of hers—a sharp peppery scent after hours in the car. Almost without thought he steps behind her and gently slips his arms around her waist. Over the warm flannel shirt, beneath the loose bib of the overalls.

"So that's how it is," she murmurs. "What are you going to do? Are you going to fuck me right here?"

And, of course, he is undone, suddenly reduced to himself. All bluff and dry throat. "I would," he says, "but you're holding a cow bell."

"I could put it down."

It's a joke, of course. Of course it is. Though the further he gets from that moment the more he wonders. The years will go by and he will imagine himself back there, again and again, replaying that moment. A different person with an entirely different life to follow.

But now, with an instant's hesitation that places all the burden of disappointment squarely on his timid, pounding heart, she laughs. And turning, she slips out from under his hands and rings the clanging, clamorous bell as if determined to wake an entire town.

From across the pale expanse comes the thump and rattle of a boat. And like a snake on the water a length of rope cuts the surface, pulling taut against the trunk of a tree. They are still waiting for the sound of rowing when the boat appears. There is a small cloaked figure in the bow, a woman, drawing herself forward hand over hand as if gathering all that motion out of the air. "Is that you, Beatrice? We were expecting just the one of you."

"This is my friend Ash. He gave me a ride. He's on his way to his aunt's."

"Is he? Well, isn't that lucky."

The boat shifts on the water. The boy steps up. "Should I do anything?"

"Just the bags, and then yourselves. I'm Professor Chalmers. Once we get to the island you can call me Margery."

He steadies it while Bea climbs in. Then he tries to shove off as he steps inside, but the rope snags against the tree and he stumbles.

"Is this your first time in a boat?" asks the woman.

"No."

"First time on an island?"

"If you don't count North America."

"Well, hold onto something. No, not like that. We're facing this way, now. Do be careful! I've never yet met a man who could move with any grace."

"Sorry."

"Take the rope. Gently," she warns. "Have you ever milked a cow?"

"No."

"Good. She would have hated it."

There is one main house and two out-buildings, all masked amid the trees and night. The stove and fridge are propane, the lanterns are kerosene. During the day it looks like an ancient encampment, smoke-stained and low. At night it glows like a dream.

Margery opens the door, pouring out its lamplight, and steps inside. She removes her cloak. She wears a loosely flowing dress of silver and rose as if she's come from a garden party a hundred years ago, though the fingers of her right hand are smudged black and she holds them away from her dress with unconscious care. "Come in. Sit down. Leave your bags on the porch. No talking now. It's the sketching hour."

It is a vast room of fire light and ancient pine walls, with a stone hearth like a monument at one end. There are five easels arranged in a wide circle. Margery takes possession of one. At the others, four men—no, three men and a woman—in evening dress: black pants, black dinner jackets, white shirts. Two are short, one is tall, and one is in the middle. They lean forward over their sketch pads while, in the center of the circle, a naked woman stands frowning into the distance. Her hip is cocked, one knee bent, one hand reaching up to the opposite shoulder. Her thighs are lean, her hips square, her skin pale as marble in the golden light.

"All right. One more minute." And there is a little flurry of finishing.

"I think classical this time," says the woman in the tuxedo.

"All right." This is the man who is neither short nor tall. "Classical please, Joan. And now. Change."

Pages turn. The model stretches like a runner before a heat, bringing each knee up to her chest then bending low, straight-legged and hugging her knees to her breasts. The artists watch impatiently. When she straightens up she steps into the pose of a striding athlete, caught mid-motion like one of Degas' dancers.

Margery clears her throat. "Classical please, Joan."

"Sorry."

The model reaches down and peels off what turns out to be a little merkin of dark pubic hair, leaving her body smooth as a statue. For a moment she stands uncertainly as it clings to her fingers, wispy and dark. Then she holds it out to Bea. "Careful," she says with a smile. "It's delicate."

Bea is transported. How could she not be? The firelight. The soft sounds of water in the distance. She is eager for her life to change, and, of course, it does. It already has. Though not in the way she hopes. Each time she remembers this night it will mean something different.

PART ONE

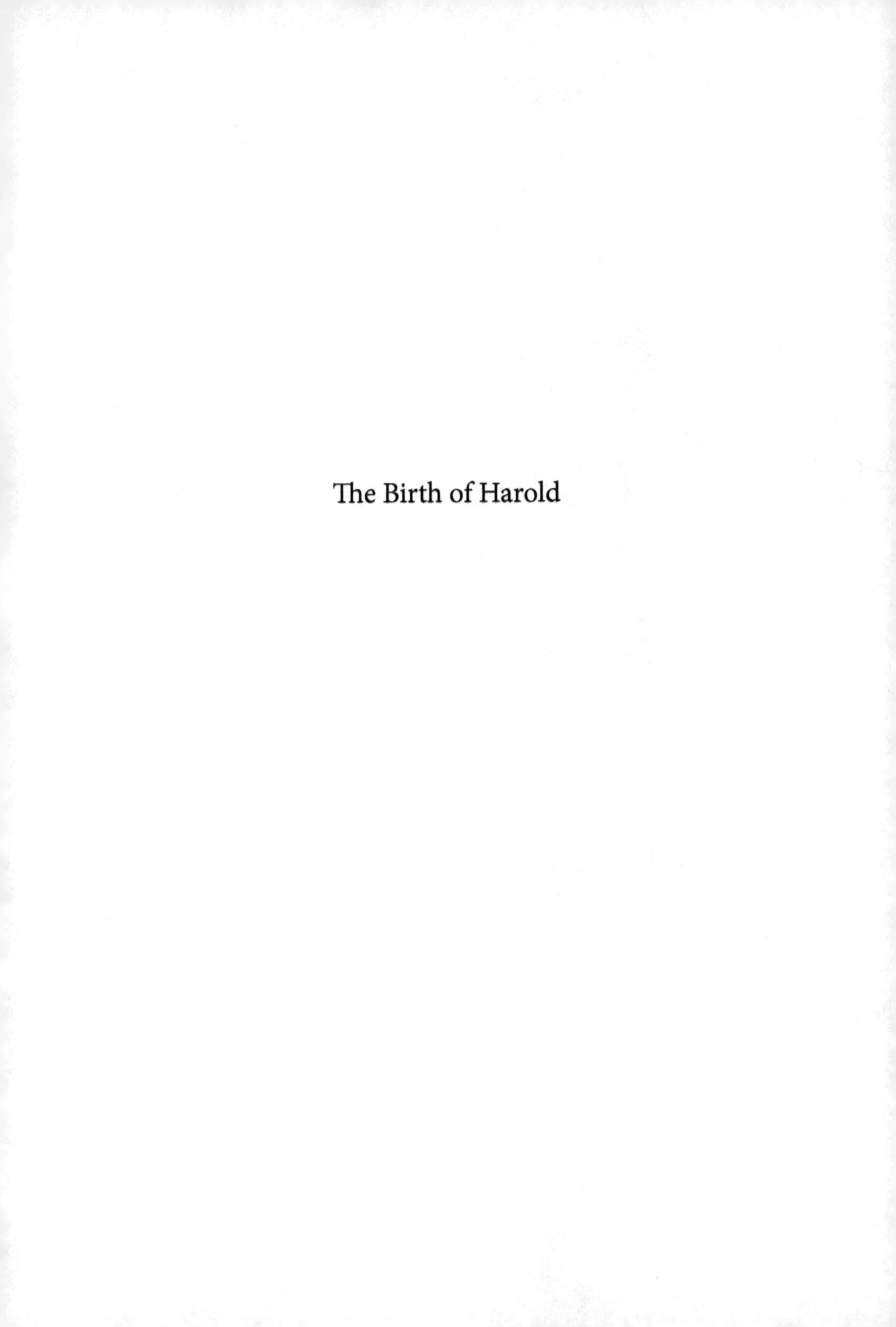

The Birth of Harold

1

Like any great work of art the Taft Hotel Bar in Ashdown, New York was more fantasy than real and more ego than either. An ostentatiously large room of wood-paneling and gilt, it had once been part of the great New York hotel—temporary home to presidents and kings since 1891. But over the years the Taft had come down in the world, and then abruptly it was just coming down.

Francis Buckton Bennett, whose father, also Francis, had been the Baking Powder King of Milwaukee, was having one last lunch. He was dining with Garry Wilson, chair of the Ashdown College Art Department, and an up-and-coming painter Garry was trotting out for potential donors. Weland Tilyard ("just one 'e' and it rhymes with zeal") had won a prize at the Venice Biennale though that made no impression on Francis. He was facing unresolved tax issues and thought the time had come to complete his father's proposed bequest to his alma mater. He wanted the result to be impressive, but not overly so. His feelings for his father were as unresolved as the taxes.

"You should give us this place," Weland suggested without so much as a blush.

"What would you do with a hotel? Paint it?"

"Not the hotel." And he gestured around at the elegant bar. "This would make a splash."

In the years afterward no one knew whether he'd expected to be taken seriously. Certainly the Ashdown Development Office turned collectively pale at the prospect of a $20 million donation going to such a thing. But by that time the idea had taken hold.

They took the restaurant apart like a baroque cathedral, transporting it to the wilds of Southern New York and reassembling it among the trees and dairy farms. The bequest made the front page of the Times and then—over the course of its installation—every Arts Section in the country. The building was a trick of the mind. A simple stone box, in the dim light of an overcast afternoon you'd be forgiven for thinking it was a modern eyesore amid the brick and clapboard quaintness of the town. But it became more magical the closer you drew.

A two-story cube of honey-colored granite inset with marble panels translucent as mother of pearl—in the daylight you wanted to walk up and touch it. But, oh, at night. The interior lights glowed through the eggshell walls, turning the whole stone box into a lantern. Step inside the big bronze doors, and you were back in the Gilded Age.

It won three major prizes the year it opened; fifteen less lofty awards from all around the world. And though no one remembers the architect, it nestled the little town of Ashdown into the gently curving hands of the world's awareness and made Weland the object of hushed reverence among foundations, philanthropists, and students of beauty up and down the country. It didn't move the college any closer to the city. But it shifted its gravitational center toward the heart of the art world and carried Weland right along with it.

Though that was a long time ago.

Now, it was 4:55 on a Thursday afternoon, and the bar was nearly empty. Two men sat in the midst of all that grandeur, too far apart for conversation. One had arrived five minutes before, the other had been drinking for hours, though you wouldn't want to guess which one. The older man was beautifully tailored in a grey silk suit and somber bowtie. His hair was carefully cut, greying to an almost perfect match for the suit. His mustache had been grown to make him look older, back when it was necessary, and now he didn't want to change the brand.

The second man might have been sleeping outside the bar

until it opened, though in fact he had only just arrived in town. He was dressed in black—pants, vest, jacket—all grown a little shabby with time. His hair was lank, his face desperately unshaven. He sat reading a book to distract himself from the glass of beer standing perfect and untasted before him.

Across the room Weland—for of course it was Weland—took another sip of his martini and, like a man unaccustomed to quiet, said, "It's not going to drink itself."

The stranger didn't bother to look up. "Three more minutes and it won't have to."

"I haven't seen you in here before."

"First time."

"Beautiful place, isn't it?"

"Beautiful."

"It took me a long time to get it just right."

The man considered that for a moment. And with the final tick of the clock above the bar he picked up his beer and drained it as if pouring it on a fire.

Weland considered the desperate face, the shabby clothes, the faint scent of smoke clinging to him like the memory of some disaster. On the bar beside the empty glass stood an old cardboard shoebox. Weland loved a telling detail. "What's in the box?"

"What box?"

"You look like a Degas. *The Absinthe Drinker.* All the world's dreariness made flesh. Or even Manet. Such a tight-ass, but what a line. Don't tell me. You're a traveling salesman, but you've fallen on hard times."

The man looked up at the clock and signaled for another beer.

Weland leaned forward. "No, wait. An out-of-work actor. No, an undertaker."

"Close enough."

"And what a nice surprise in this day and age. A reader."

The man tilted the book in his hand as if he'd forgotten. A modest battered volume with a cover the texture of a brown paper bag and a title that might have been typed across. *The Wide Bed* by Childe Harold. "I picked it up at the Inn."

"How do you like it? The book, that is. Not the inn."

"Too early to say. Why?"

Weland smiled. "I'm just surprised you haven't read it before. It made such a splash… what? Ten years ago? Twelve? People could not stop talking about it."

The man regarded the cover as if trying to locate the source of such tidal enthusiasm. "I suppose you wrote it."

"Oh, no. Well. In a manner of speaking. I think it's a book almost anyone could write."

"And you're going to tell me why, aren't you?" He picked up the second beer and drained it, then held out the empty glass. "Would you mind? I have a schedule to keep."

"Childe Harold is, of course, a *nom de plume*."

Two martinis had arrived, and the man considered his for a long moment as if comparing it in size to what had come before. Weland thought he might drain it like the beer, but instead he took a maidenly sip and set it down. Then he straightened himself for the task at hand. "The hell you say."

"Don't get me wrong. Some parts are hot. But in the end, it's just another story about sex."

The stranger eyed the unremarkable cover. "You'd think they might mention that."

"Eventually they did. In later editions there was a beautiful cover that told you everything you needed to know. But at first I think they were trying to give it a little cachet. Plain brown wrapper. Type face. You've got to admire them: trying to make sex dirty again. But there's nothing much to it. A man and a woman. They fall in love. They have a frantic summer of passion. Then they break up."

"Don't give it away," the man said mildly.

"Don't be silly. That's every story since *The Odyssey*."

"So it's not worth reading?"

Weland took a complacent sip. "It was when I got through with it. That's the thing about a book. There's almost nothing to it. Words on a page. But by the time I was finished, it was the hottest thing in America. Cover of *Time, Art Forum, Entertainment Weekly*."

"I'm not a big reader," said the man, "but I don't remember your face."

"My painting. You'd remember that, I guarantee it. The most famous image in the world that year. Well," he said modestly. "The most famous art image. Posters, cards, magazines. And the cover of the book for its second printing. And third and fourth and fifth. I forget how many."

"So you're some kind of illustrator."

"Oh," said Weland. "So much more. I discovered it. And as soon as I read it I knew: this could be great. I was looking for something to make our mark. To bring us together."

"Us?"

"The Gang of Four. You've heard of us."

"I'm assuming you're not a band."

"We were the biggest thing since Warhol. *The next great voice in representational art*. I can't remember who said that. They all did, in the end. And I was the one who brought them together. Made them what they were. Though they won't thank you for telling them so. If you can find them, that is. If they haven't disappeared off the face of the earth."

And he seemed to consider that for a moment, as if enjoying the prospect.

"I've always been ambitious. I'm not ashamed to say so. But this was more than even I could have imagined. And built on what?"

"You're going to tell me 'talent', aren't you?"

"Oh," said Weland brushing it aside. "Talent, vision, drive, charisma. All that goes without saying. The Gang of Four? They'd still be painting their terrible landscapes if it weren't for me. Well, not Jonathan, of course. But the rest of them. They needed me. But what did I need?"

"You cannot imagine," said the man, "how desperate I am to hear." He held up his empty glass to the bartender.

"A chance," said Weland. "That's all. A fluke. A twist of fate. And I got it. Hell, I made it. I picked up that ridiculous book and made it great. It was nothing when I found it. A cult hit. A bit of elegant porn the literati could enjoy with a clear conscience. Even the author was embarrassed by it, hiding behind that ridiculous pseudonym. As if even the ghost of Lord Byron could save it. But I saved it. And I sure as hell didn't hide behind anyone else's name."

"I believe you."

"I read it and I thought, this is my *Elegy to the Spanish Republic*. My Campbell's Soup can. I knew it just like that. *Just like that*. And every step after. My God. It was like a flower that just kept opening and opening. People could not get enough. We were the light in their eyes, the word on their lips. When Joe from Peoria thought about art, this is what he thought. And then, just like that, it was over."

He sat frowning as if, even after all this time, the ending still caught him by surprise. "How is that fair? That you only get one chance? How can that even be possible? Sometimes I think I'd give anything, a leg, an arm. Not my right arm, of course."

"Your soul?"

"Of course my soul. If the devil walked up to me right now and said, Weland. You can have it all again—."

"Weland, you can have it all again."

He blinked. "How did you know my name?"

"Don't be silly. You just told me."

"Did I?" And turning, he took in the unexpectedly steady gaze, the funereal suit, the lingering smell of smoke. Even a man less drunk than Weland might be forgiven for the thoughts that came to mind. But he didn't take it back. "Do you know what it's like to be part of something so important? To be at the head of a wave sweeping the country? To know that everyone in the world is thinking of you?"

"It sounds exhausting."

"It's magnificent. It's like you're filled with light. When was the last time you were filled with light?"

"It's been a while," the man conceded.

"You think I wouldn't sell my soul to have all that again?"

"I think you should be careful what you say. Nothing goes unheard." But wearily, reluctantly, as if he knew he was going to regret it: "I suppose you have a picture."

All they had to do was walk down the bar. It was up there on the wall, a little smaller than expected and even more beautiful: a nude woman, golden and sunlit, reclining across a storm-tossed bed. A blue robe hanging over a chair provided the only color that didn't seem drawn from the warmth of her hair and skin. She was tumbled into sleep, as if she had given herself up to all that must have just occurred. You could feel the rumpled dampness of the sheets, the heat of her skin, the wide pervading tenderness of a long summer afternoon.

The stranger stood, his glass forgotten, looking even shabbier and more bereft in the dawning light of wonder.

"You'd read a book with her on the cover, wouldn't you?" said Weland.

"I think I might."

"You can see how she might change your life?"

"Maybe so."

Weland was smiling now. "How would you like to meet her?"

2.

They walked unsteadily through the uncertain night until a high white house glowed in the darkness beside a driveway roofed with trees. The back door was unlocked. Out of a cool evening smelling of pine needles and mown grass they stepped into the bright, fragrant world of breakfast.

The kitchen, old fashioned as a parlor, seemed to have made its journey unfaded from a world before television and frozen food. A long scuffed table, grandmotherly chairs—an ancient sofa, for heaven's sake—all hemmed in by cupboards and appliances. And as if rebelling against all the antique comfort, a woman stood by the stove at the grumpy center of all that needed to be done.

She was grey-smocked beneath an elaborate white-ribboned cap and apron—a refugee housekeeper from some Orwellian past where work was freedom. But despite the weight of servitude, her face was shiningly composed: cheeks foundation-smooth, lips bright red, eyelids roundly shaded with an iridescent pink as glamorous as a tropical fish. She stood at the counter between a low basket of rumpled laundry and a wide frying pan, breaking egg-whites into a bowl.

"Be warned," Weland murmured. "It's a house of women." And stepping forward with a widening smile, "Good evening, Miss Isabel. How are you today?"

She glanced up peevishly. "Oh, no, Wheedle. Ar' you here fo' dinner? I'm gonna need mor' eggs."

The voice was sharp but softly unfinished, as if the words couldn't hold their edge under the force of all her scorn. But Weland was untroubled. "Not to worry. We don't eat much. Where is everybody? It's the shank of the evening."

"Mrs. Holliman is still asl'ep," she said, as if that were the last straw.

"And, uh, Ms. Cooper?"

"Up in th' studio."

"Thank God," he breathed. "I told you this was our lucky day." And making his way to the liquor cupboard he said, "Now what do we have that's open?"

His companion was less at ease. Cowed by the brightness of the room he hovered in the doorway like a mouse caught suddenly in the open. Isabel frowned. Sooner or later people always made her impatient. "Ar' you coming in or not?"

He looked startled to be addressed, but drunk as he was, his hands made a little swoop of movement, palms brushing together, two fingers bumping. "Nice to meet you," he said.

Her glare turned cold, and one hand rose to adjust her cap over the little crescent shell of the hearing aid. "Don' do tha'!"

"What?"

"It's impoli'."

"What?"

"I'm no' deaf!"

She turned huffily back to her eggs, though out of the corner of her eye she followed him as, hunched and cautious, he moved toward the table. She felt a pang at her response—he looked so woeful. Was he hurt? Crippled? Something wrong with his back? Though as he sat down she realized it was only that he carried a shoebox hugged against his chest. He set it on the table.

After a moment she relented, her enunciation growing momentarily taut under the weight of good manners. "I like your suit."

"Thank you."

"It looks old fashioned."

"It belonged to someone before me. And maybe before him. I'm not sure."

"Have you had it a long time?"

"Long time."

"Thos' are nice buttons."

"Are you a fan of buttons?"

She shrugged, but she considered the idea. They were small, fabric-covered, crowded a little fussily along the placket of the vest. And she saw that if you buttoned them all the way up, the vest formed its own little collar: a low black rim with a gap in the front. "Ar' you a priest?"

Weland choked on his wine, his eyes bright. "A priest? Oh, please tell me it's true."

The man looked pained. "I've never liked that term. It's always sounded so harsh and unbending." His hands spelled the words in the air.

"You don' have to do that," Isabel said, more gently this time.

"I don't mind. I like it."

"Unbending," she showed him two fists straining to be straight.

"This is so much better than I could have hoped," said Weland. "I don't think I've ever met a priest up close."

"I prefer the term parson."

"I like that, too," Isabel agreed. "It sounds cozy."

"And I'm not anymore."

"A defrocked priest," murmured Weland.

"Unfrocked, maybe. All but frocked."

"Did they fire you?" asked Isabel.

"In the end I think they did."

"You must have done something really bad."

"Oh, yes."

She weighed this for a moment. "What's in the box?"

He gazed down at it, nestled between his curled hands. "It's my conscience."

"You carry your conscience around?"

"Of course."
"Can I see?"

Reluctantly he raised the lid and slowly upended the box as if prepared to surprise even himself. An enormous spider, black-furred and huge, slid plumply onto the table top and sprang to its feet.

"Jesus Christ!" Weland splashed his cabernet like a trail of blood as he jerked away. "What the hell?"

"Wheedle! I jus' mopped that floor!"

"Don't tell me. Tell him!"

And to be fair, it was appalling.

Dark legs drawn up big as a fist, the spider crouched for a moment as the whole cozy kitchen adjusted to the sight. Then it leapt into motion, legs churning, racing to get away from such a bright expanse of space.

"Jesus Christ! Jesus Christ!" Weland was almost gleeful with terror. But the man sat helpless and undone. He started to reach out clumsily with the lid to corral the frantic creature, but Isabel slapped his hand away.

"Don't! You'll hurt her."

"For God's sake!" cried Weland. "It's going to bite you!"

But Isabel was unmoved. She reached for the box and set it upright on the table. Then slowly, like a delicate grappling hook, she lowered her fingers and picked up the spider—eight legs slipping free of the table like an ice-skater swooping into a fall. With nothing beneath, it scrabbled against the air.

The man flinched, but he was ready with the lid, and as she set it down within the box he hurried the cover into place.

"Oh, lord." He leaned back, pale and drained. "Thank you."

But Isabel was outraged. "That was so stupid!"

"I'm sorry."

"You can't just let her run aroun' like that!"

"I didn't mean to."

"She's terrified. If she fell off the table she could hurt herself."

"I'm sorry. I didn't know." But her anger seemed to steady him. "How do you know it's a she?"

"The females are always bigger. And braver. Like in Charlotte's Web."

"And how do you know that?"

"Miss Isabel works in a pet store." Weland had, by this time, stepped around the red puddle on the floor and was refilling his glass. "How many jobs do you have now?"

She frowned at him. "Not that many."

"The thing is," said the stranger, "I thought I might have just imagined her."

Gently Isabel raised the lid. The spider hunched forlornly in the corner, pressing as close as she could to the featureless walls. "What have you fed her?" she asked.

And to her horror the stranger began to weep. Hunched and sagging into his tears he said, "Nothing. I haven't fed her anything. God help me. I didn't know what to do."

3.

A sound carried to them—the sudden impatient creak of footsteps on the stairs—and Isabel glanced angrily at the clock. "Nuts!"

"What is it? What's happening?"

"We're in for it now," said Weland and he topped up his wine.

Hurrying to the stove, Isabel turned up the heat under the frying pan. She gave the eggs a final frothing stir and dumped them into the pan just as a nearly naked woman came stalking through the door. She had short blonde hair, peroxide bright, and her skin was tanning-booth gold. She wore (and Izzie was grateful for the chill in the air) a short silk robe that left her long legs bare and hung like parted curtains from her thighs to her chin. "Is that my dinner?"

"Two minut's."

 "I'm getting off schedule!"

"Almos' ready."

"I'm right in the middle! I'm going to lose it!"

Startled into silence the man's first thought was of the painting in the bar: the golden woman on the golden bed. He waited distantly for the first squawk of embarrassment—eyes going wide, hands clutching the robe closed. But the woman just scowled at them like a stripper between sets. "You again, Weland?"

"Always me," he said cheerfully. "And look. I've brought company. I wanted to introduce him to the famous household."

But her attention had wandered back to the stove. "How are we doing there? It's after eight."

Isabel didn't bother to reply. The egg whites were scrambled dry and pale as wax. Tilting the heavy pan she scraped them onto a plate. Salt and pepper, a dusting of turmeric for antibodies, fresh ginger for energy and vascular health. Then she banged a fork down beside them. "Done."

"Is that six eggs?"

"Yes."

"No yolks?"

"Jus' the whites."

"I don't like cumin."

"It's tu'meric."

She accepted the plate. Then, leaning forward, unmindful of the robe, she pressed a quick kiss on Isabel's cheek, "Thanks, doll." And she turned and padded up the stairs.

Weland stood with the bottle in one hand and his empty glass raised high as if he had saved them both from shipwreck. He was smiling benignly. "Isn't she something? I knew you'd enjoy that. Who's ready for another drink?"

But the stranger sat motionless, as if he had expected almost anything else. Isabel gave him a sympathetic frown. "She was jus' hungry. She gets a little grumpy when she's cutting weight."

"I'm sure." But then, more hesitantly, "She looks taller in the painting."

And Weland started to laugh. "Oh, no. No, no, no, no, no. Good lord!"

"What do you mean?"

"Absolutely not! Don't even think of such a thing. Different woman entirely."

But the man seemed unreassured. He was peering uneasily around, as if the kitchen itself might transform before his eyes, until Izzie caught his attention and traced a complex knot on the air with her fingers.

"Use your voice," said Weland testily.

But the stranger relaxed into a smile. "*What do you want for dinner.*"

"Brw'avo."

"I think those are the nicest words in the English language. But aren't you tired of cooking?"

"I've got to make breakfast now."

"Wasn't that breakfast?"

"That was dinner. Mrs. Holliman works nights at the bakery. She usually gets up around now."

"And what about you?"

"Henry and I will have something."

"Good." He considered the woman—the studied drabness of her uniform, but eyes like an Egyptian queen. "I think maybe I should give you a hand."

He seemed to grow steadier with an apron round his waist. "Oatmeal first," she instructed. "Then eggs and bacon and toast."

"Your boss is a big eater."

"She works hard."

"And for you?"

"Hot dog. Mac and cheese. It's what Henry and I usually have."

"And is Henry coming down, too?"

"She's just waking up."

She turned to the laundry basket just as the pile of rumpled orange flannel raised its head with the expression of one who has seen this program before but is just too tired to change the channel.

"That is one big cat," he said.

Izzie smoothed a hand over the broad head, and the sleepy eyes closed. "She might just have the hotdog tonight."

"Hot dog it is." He turned to their audience of one. "Mac and cheese, Weland?"

"Absolutely not. I've got to keep my girlish figure. I could manage an egg or two."

Izzie's hands said something impatient over the egg carton.

"Sorry," he said. "All spoken for. It's hot dogs or nothing."

From upstairs came the rush of water in the pipes and once again the sound of footsteps on the stairs, sleepy this time and slow.

With an impresario's smile Weland raised his glass. "Now this is our gal."

The woman was taller than the first, and much more ordinary. She wore a terrycloth robe over the rumpled comfort of pink pajamas, and in her hands she carried a little bundle of eyeglasses like the clumsy remnants of something fallen to pieces. She had glasses for distance, for reading, computer, highway (though that was a joke these days), studio, eating, and sex (a different joke). Each in turn offered its temporary relief—a momentary glimpse of clarity. Other than that, she was a fish swimming through murky seas.

It was something called *bird-shot uveitis*—both random and rare. Little white dots that spread over the retinas and warped them out of alignment. No one knew what caused it; some sort of autoimmune response—the eye attacking itself. And that, Bea knew, made its own perfect sense. If the eyes were the windows of the soul, then her soul was getting exactly what it deserved.

"Ah, dearest," said Weland. "Aren't you looking lovely this evening."

"Not now. Please. I haven't even had my coffee."

"We have it right here." And he gestured to Isabel, who handed her the mug with an ostentatious curtsy.

Bea sighed. "This is not a good time."

"Nonsense. We're on the verge of a great adventure."

"Of course you are. But you have to be quiet. Joan's working."

"We just saw her."

"Oh no."

"Don't worry. We were gentle as mice. She's back in the studio, and all's right with the world." He raised the bottle. "Now join us for a drink, why don't you. We have much to celebrate."

She frowned and sipped her coffee.

She was an old hand at the business of Weland; she'd grown adept over the years. Tonight she put him in the four-martini range, and the first flush of annoyance was so familiar it was almost a comfort. She should just throw him out. Long gone were the days when she would simply bend herself to whatever he could imagine. And she pictured it now: shoving him out the door, slamming it behind. It had a kind of cartoon drama. But like most of her satisfactions these days it was entirely hypothetical.

"I've got to get to work."

"Not yet. There's plenty of time. Come on, dearest. Just a little one. Look, we're making breakfast. You've got to eat."

So it's going to be that kind of a night, she thought.

Though truth be told, there was part of her that didn't mind. She had been on the straight and narrow for a long time now. Joan didn't drink, and they rarely saw anyone else. After all the disasters of the fall, their circle had shrunk to nothing. And though the cupboards were filled with wine—theirs had always been the departmental party house, even before they had lived here—she worked hard to ignore it. One more test, masking itself as an invitation.

"Besides," said Weland. "I want to introduce you."

Only then did she notice the figure by the stove, a blurred vision in rumpled black, hunched in an air of unsteadiness. "I'm sorry. I didn't see you."

"Probably for the best," he said.

Weland smiled. "We've just been talking about our long ago success. Our collaboration in the pursuit of beauty. And I know I speak for all of us when I say: it has made me think. Because here, in this moment, we have an unexpected opportunity. Tonight we have the chance to welcome a man returning to the heart of his life."

The man glanced up at him hollow-eyed. "What? What did you say?"

But Weland had found his rhythm now. "A man who is all but broken by circumstance, but who raises himself for one more attempt."

"Stop it. You need to be quiet. You don't know anything about me."

"Nonsense. Do you think I can't recognize the depths of human suffering? You think I can't see it in your face?"

"Just shut up!"

"We are two of a kind."

"For God's sake! We are nothing alike." But he seemed somehow exhausted by the thought.

"Of course we are. A pair of anguished souls who would give anything to get our lives back. Tell me you don't know what it's like to have your heart broken. Tell me you haven't lost everything that's made your life worth living. Go ahead. Tell me you wouldn't give anything in the world to have it back."

"Please stop."

"And now tell me you don't think we can help each other. Tell me you don't feel it. Tell me you don't know exactly what I'm thinking right now."

"Jesus Christ, Weland. I don't have the slightest idea."

Though afterward he could almost swear he had seen it coming—that it had somehow caught him leaning in, like a plant toward the light—as Weland turned with a beatific smile and said, "Beatrice Holliman, our lady of *The Wide Bed*, I'd like you to meet Childe Harold. I'm sure you remember his work."

4.

In the silence all eyes turned to the stranger—as if perhaps they had simply misunderstood. As if they were waiting—even Weland—for some point of clarification. The man's face was pale and unmoving. All those martinis, of course. But the rest of it, too: heartbreak, disappointment, such a long and terrible year. A life so withered and sere there was nothing to return to. *Tell me you wouldn't give anything in the world to have it back.* How could he not? And here was something, at least, as if in return. The warmth of the kitchen, the smell of bacon, the woman's face turning toward him with a look of surprise that seemed, itself, a kind of hope. Really, how could he resist?

"How do you do," he said.

Beatrice sank into a chair. "Jesus, Weland. You can't do this. You can't just make things up."

But Weland held up an admonishing finger. "Just give it a moment; let it sink in. Think about what a wonderful opportunity this is. A chance to have the author here."

"He's not the author."

"You're missing the point. Here we are, talking about old times, you and Childe and I. About his wonderful book. You know, we're coming up on the twelfth anniversary of that first show. And we were thinking, wouldn't it be something to make a fuss? Now that we have the author with us. Emerging from years of anonymity. Isn't that a wonder? Isn't that bound to spark new interest? Wouldn't people, who were so fascinated by the story, by the whole beautiful pageant of it all—wouldn't they be excited to relive those moments? Wouldn't that make them sit up and pay attention?"

"This is insane."

"Is it? Because it feels like a celebration to me." And he set a glass before her.

So it's going to be that kind of a night.

Spread over the table the combined meal looked like a riot. Toast and hot dogs, macaroni and cheese, scrambled eggs and bacon, a bowl of oatmeal that nobody seemed to claim. Weland dug in with enthusiasm, helping himself to the eggs and bacon despite Isabel's glare.

Bea sighed and reached for her wine. "So you're Childe Harold," she said drily.

"I'm told it's a pseudonym."

"I've always imagined it was."

And then, because it was the truth, after all, and she was tired, and the wine, against all reasonable expectations, was hitting the spot. "Your book meant a lot to me."

"Thank you," he said modestly. "That's always nice to hear."

And that made her smile. "What should we call you? Childe?"

"I don't think anyone's really named Childe. I guess you'd better call me Harold."

"Isn't this exciting?" Weland raised his fork like a conductor's baton. "Beatrice, I wonder if you have your copy of *The Wide Bed.* The good edition?"

"In the living room somewhere."

He sailed out of the room and returned with a book, the same book, but the plain brown wrapper was gone. The now-familiar painting glowed across its cover. He set it down on the table. "Beautiful, isn't she?" And Bea felt a flush of the old anger.

Your book meant a lot to me.

That didn't overstate it.

Weland used to say he had given the gift of sex to the heartland. Paintings whose erotic charge was subdued to such beauty and warmth that it became a kind of innocence. As photographs they would have been irredeemable. It was only the brushwork—that surface of such dreamlike softness—that offered viewers a chance to stand before them without self-consciousness or embarrassment. To let the full charge wash over them.

That had been the achievement. And when Weland had cranked into motion the whole elaborate machinery of public attention, she had been carried along. Transformed into a figure of such beauty and erotic power that it took years for people to realize she was none of those things. And far fewer years to find herself back where she began.

"Raise your glasses, everyone. We are drinking to the second coming. Imagine it. A festival. *The Wide Bed Returns. The Place Where It All Began.* Banners and parties. A show at the museum."

"There's already a show at the museum," said Isabel, visibly underwhelmed.

"Then something bigger. *The Wide Bed Renewed.* All new paintings. A whole new series. Something to reach out and grab the public by the throat." He glanced around. "Come on, people. Why do I have to do all the work? We hire actors to pose as living paintings. We put them here and there around the town, so you turn a corner and there's a painting in the flesh."

"That's a lot of flesh," murmured Bea.

"Body stockings, then, if you're suddenly so prudish. And an exhibition. Paintings on every street corner. The whole town becomes our canvas. And more. A festival. Imagine it. *Childe Harold Days.* Oh, I like the sound of that. The man and the myth. The secrets behind the phenomenon. Who wouldn't want to cover that? *The Times? Art Forum?* It's news, isn't it? A seminal figure from our cultural history rising from the dead. How does that sound?"

He tilted the wine bottle over the man's empty glass. Reflexively the stranger put up his hand, but then he let it fall. "That's the spirit," Weland said and poured with a flourish.

"So, let's say a month. Two months. Just to give ourselves a deadline. Get the museum organized; all the festivities. And you know what would be perfect? A sequel. *The Wider Bed. The Wide Bed Again.* Something like that. A whole new story for a whole new series of paintings. What do you think?"

The man regarded him for a long moment, glass hovering in the air. "I think you do not lack for balls."

And Weland laughed. "No, sir. I do not."

It was, Bea knew, a ridiculous idea. But it had been a long time since she'd be drinking with Weland, and she had forgotten the bright, unapologetic gleam of his enthusiasm. Even the stranger hesitated. Perhaps he was beginning to foresee all that it might entail. But then he tilted his glass and drained it, as neatly as closing a door.

"That's the spirit! Oh, you're going to enjoy this, padre."

"Enjoy what, exactly?"

"Everything. Just imagine. A parade. Speeches. A barrage of news. NPR, *The Times*, all the big magazines. An opening here, and then around the country. *A Writer Comes Home. The roots of a romance that thrilled the nation. A passion so big it could only be expressed in paint.*"

Weland's eyes were shining, as if the whole vision were right there before them. "The old favorites on view again. We'll get them back from collectors. Every image. We'll put them all under one roof. All the old paintings. And the new ones too. So when the world comes calling again, we'll be ready."

"And what, exactly, am I supposed to do?" said Harold.

"You? You're the lynchpin. You're the center of everything."

"Yes. I see that. But what's in it for me, exactly?"

Weland stopped, momentarily dumfounded. "What do you mean? You'll be famous."

"A famous pornographer."

"A famous romantic. A writer of passionate prose."

"I don't think I'm really seeing that part yet."

"You've read the book."

"I've started it."

"Then you know. You're the beating human heart at the center of all this. You and Bea. Reliving old times. Retelling the whole romantic story."

"Yes," said Harold. "I guess that's the part—"

"It's all in the book. Your book. It's all right there. Love. Passion. All you ever wanted. Everything within your grasp. You meet a woman. A beautiful, sensual, passionate woman. And you love her. And she loves you. And though the rest of your life is falling apart—your father dead, your mother dying—you clutch hold of this blazing love and you cling to it. Through all that long, passionate summer it builds for you, layer upon layer. Your heart growing fuller and fuller. Your cock growing harder and harder."

"Language, Weland," said Bea.

"There's nothing dirty about passion. It's the center of everything that makes us great. It's the center of this book. Your book. Love and life exploding like a volcano out of your chest. But then, tragically, after the whole long summer—a summer you thought would never end—it's over. You don't know why. There's no explanation. Love fades. Life intervenes. You return home to your mother's death. And the spell is broken. It can never be mended. You can never go back again."

For a moment Harold sat without a word. "It sounds heartbreaking." He held out his glass, and Weland refilled it. "Why would I ever want to do that?"

"Why? Because it's the fountain of youth. To have it all again. Love. Art. The tragedy of it all."

"See. It's the tragedy part…"

Weland waved him away. "It' has to be a tragedy. That's the point. There's no great *happy* art. Art is suffering. That's what it is.

But in that suffering—that whole boiling caldron of tragedy and passion—there's a chance for redemption. A chance to taste it all again. To make something lasting and magnificent out of the pain. And this is you, Harold. This is you I'm talking to. If you've fallen on bad times. If life has not been all you would have wanted. I offer you this. This one true beating heart. This summer of passion. That you can build from the very fabric of yourself and found yourself upon. That's what you get out of this. You get to be an artist. You get to feel what an artist feels. You get to know what it's like to have a whole world of people feeding their hearts from your heart. Their loins from your loins."

And from the height of his imagination Weland looked around. "What is wrong with you people? This is no time for gloom! This is our moment of greatness, once again thrust upon us. I need all your enthusiasm. All your passion. Miss Isabel? Bring out the Macallan."

"I don't know, Wheedle. I don't think that's a good idea."

"And fresh glasses. Come on, woman. Bring us the scotch."

Reluctantly she retrieved it from the cupboard.

"I've got nothing to mix it with," said Bea.

"That doesn't matter. There's no room for moderation in art."

As Isabel set the three smallest glasses she had down on the table—her final effort to slow this train—he filled them each to the very top, until the scotch was shivering against the rim. "This is the test," he said. "No spilling. No carelessness. This is a time for concentration. We fix our eyes upon the object of our desire, and we master it! Concentration, grace, and an eagle eye!"

He was as drunk as Bea had ever seen him. But reaching out he picked up his glass, slowly, surely. Not a quiver of trepidation. He brought it to his lips and drank. Then he held up the empty glass like the proof of some unproveable thing. "That is what it's going to take."

And really, what could she do? She picked up her own glass,

cautious and careful. Her hand twitched, and she could feel the scotch running down the side. She hurried it to her mouth and gulped, feeling the harshness in her throat, the catch in her breathing.

"Yes!" said Weland. "That's the spirit!"

And the warmth rushed into her face and she was eighteen again, flushed and rising on the fumes.

"Now Harold. We're back to you."

The stranger picked up the glass and held it before him, as if to give it every chance to spill. But the unbroken surface seemed braced against the whole impending rush. He brought it to his lips and poured.

"That's the stuff!" cried Weland. "That's how you begin!"

And letting his head fall back against the chair he sank into sleep.

5.

In the dim light of the hallway Isabel walked him to his room under the cautious eyes of the two Misses Finley. The sisters had inherited the Inn forty years ago from their widowed mother, and they had maintained it ever since for its nostalgic comfort, sheltering themselves and their guests from an uncongenial world. *Wind in the Willows, Pride and Prejudice, The Secret Garden* were all touchstones in their determined innocence. But even they could tell the evening's drinking had come home to Harold in way rarely seen.

"That's his room there, Izzie. *Elizabeth Bennet.*"

"Don't let him bump his head."

Isabel pushed open the door. "Here you go, father."

"You didn't need to do this."

"It's okay. I have a room down the hall. Better brace yourself."

She turned on the light.

"Oh, my."

The Misses Finley believed if you decorated a room to please yourself it would please everyone. The result was a Victorian clamor of upholstery and curtains, tasseled lamps and figurines that crowded the room to bursting.

Harold stood swaying at the sight.

"Do you have pajamas?" asked Izzie.

"I have a nightshirt. It belonged to my predecessor."

"Don't you have any of your own clothes?"

"They're mine now."

She drew from his suitcase a large, red-flannel garment, faded and voluminous. She took a moment to examine the seams, the placket, the small discrete patches. "This is nice detail."

"I used to think it was ridiculous."

"No. It's pretty." She gave him a gentle shove toward the bathroom. "You put that on. I'll get the bed ready."

She turned down the covers, tugging the corners straight and fluffing the pillows with professional care. She set the water carafe and glass by the bed, and, turning on the bedside lamp, doused the overhead. Harold emerged into a warm and crowded atmosphere of comfort. Draped in red flannel from neck to shins, he seemed a piece of the whole. "Thank you," he murmured as he sank onto the bed. "I don't know what's become of me."

"Don't worry. Everything will look better in the morning."

"I don't see how it can," he murmured, but he slipped beneath the covers. "Oh. This is nice."

"See? What did I tell you?"

At the gentleness of her tone, he began to weep. But sadness was nothing new to Izzie. He so reminded her of Henry that she stroked his forehead gently and watched as a kind of peace invaded his features. "There, there. It's just a feeling. It's just a feeling. You go to sleep now."

But suddenly he started up. "Wait! Where's Bea?"

"What?"

"The spider! Where is she? I didn't lose her?"

"No, no. It's all right." Izzie pressed him back. "She's right here. On the table."

But at the sight of the shoebox the whole long drive, the drinking, the endless year of anguish and grief, it all descended upon him at once. "Oh, God," he whispered. "Oh, my God. What's happened to me?"

Izzie leaned in close. "Wait a minute. You named the spider Bea?"

But he was drowned in sleep.

Harold in Hell

6.

He had wanted it so much to be a dream, but it was true again each morning. Sara gone, Miss Pru dead. And Bea. The church had closed officially by then, but the townsfolk continued to offer him work, small repairs to their houses, fences, barns—the assortment of odd jobs that had been such a part of his life since he'd come. They were offering him continuity, but every object in his life gave off the same lilt of grief.

He would work when he could, but most hours he just sat in the rectory and watched poor Lola fly. Not that she would fly for hours. But she had always been adventurous. It used to be she would hop out of her cage onto Bea's finger, then scurry with a purposeful swagger up the length of her arm and stand nibbling an earlobe, gazing around like a jaded comedian in a half-empty hall, muttering snatches of song under her breath as Sara prepared dinner and he sat re-working one of Father Ben's sermons.

But now when he opened the cage and set his own unsteady finger as a perch, it all seemed so desperately insufficient. She would climb reluctantly onto his hand and, surveying the wide room, leap almost inadvertently into the air, looking more frantic than before, less sleek and purposeful. She would flap convulsively to the top of the fridge and hunch there like a cormorant on a cliff, contemplating an entire house now empty of possibility. In the end she would perch on the high promontory of his shoulder and make a low murmuring sound like falling rain so no matter where he walked through the familiar rooms he carried the sound of weeping with him, right there under the eaves of his ear.

He drove to a pet store, bright and bare as a cafeteria, looking for something to cheer her. He bought a little bird bath, a new seed ball, a perch that jingled softly when it rocked. He bought a cat toy, all feathers and fabric, that he hoped she might mistake for a companion. And he hung them up in her cage as soon as he got home. But Lola didn't notice. And when he let her out for exercise, she swooped through the kitchen and down the short hallway and out the back door that he had left ajar in his hurry to show her what he had bought, and he never saw her again.

Now he slept when he could. But sleep stripped away all the shaky progress of a year-and-a-month, and left him with nightmares stretching from the moment he closed his eyes to the grey light of dawn. In the evening he drank whiskey until he was sobbing at his desk.

And every night before bed he mixed a mug of hot cocoa laced with rum and made oatmeal. He had never liked oatmeal—too glutinous and thick. But Bea had loved it above all things: cocoa and oatmeal every morning at this very table—as if it had been nothing at all. As if it were the most ordinary of things. Stirring it now became a kind of meditation, eating it the only remembering he could bear.

He was lifting down the heavy saucepan, setting it on the stove, when he caught a glimpse of something in the bottom. A dead mouse curled against the side. A dark smudge of fur. He felt a wave of pity, almost more than he could bear! A lost mouse wandering into his oatmeal pot and dying, helpless and alone.

Hesitantly he reached out. To touch it, prod it into motion—to give this whole imagined fairy tale a happy ending—and at his touch it scurried away. But he had expected the liquid surge of mousey movement. Instead it ran on stilts. Too many joints, too many legs. He jerked back with a cry and a pounding heart.

As a boy he had been afraid of spiders. No. Afraid didn't begin to cover it. A tiny silhouette in a distant corner would make him conscious of nothing else. A glimpsed shape creeping on his bedspread would wrack him with sobs. As he grew older he tried to convince himself he was no longer afraid. Interest, fascination, that's what he was feeling. He would rescue them from the bathtub on an overlong staircase of toilet paper, hurrying to the door as they climbed higher and higher. Years ago, gardening, he had pulled his arm out of a crowd of day lilies and felt a tickling presence on his bicep. A green and black orb spider—sudden round body, long splinter legs—was already rappelling down, quicker than he had been and just as frightened. He complimented himself on not having hurt the creature, but all he had wanted to do was smash it.

Now he thought, how fitting. In being reduced to such a fragment of himself, he was reduced to this as well. Because there was no hint of progress, no adult understanding. He stood staring down, heart clenched like a fist, and the only thing that saved him was the dawning realization that it couldn't climb the smooth sides of the pot. So he set it down on the counter and forced himself to look.

As a mouse it would have been large; as a spider it was appalling. Some sort of tarantula, maybe. But less rangy, less prickly-haired than the pictures he had seen. It pressed like the remnant of every childhood nightmare up against the side of the pot.

What should he do? Take it outside? He thought of those long, trailing ladders of toilet paper—so insubstantial and weak. And this was so big. So fast. He could already imagine it clambering up toward his hand.

The whole long day settled on his shoulders. Fear and fatigue. He couldn't think. He put a lid on the pot, then after a moment set it ajar. Even a spider had to breathe. He took a sleeping pill and then another, added more rum to his mug. Then he climbed the stairs and sat in bed sipping slowly, breathing deep. Remembering the instructions Sara's therapist had given him, before therapy itself made him too sad. *Make your mind a basket, and then one by one, lift out every thought and idea until it's empty. Your mind is an empty basket, and you can just close your eyes.*

He thought of the spider, alone and trapped in its pot. He would let it out tomorrow. But right now—and the thought surprised him—it was an unexpected comfort. Another fellow creature in the wide, confining sadness of the house. And with a little glimmer of warmth, the rum and the pills and the sadness—which was itself indistinguishable from the weight of fatigue—carried him down beyond the reach of all but his dreams.

7.

How could he have known that Bea, his time with her, her place in his life, would be only a single chapter. That it could come to an end. She had entered their lives with such a sense of permanence, a tiny infant with such bright, demanding eyes. "She's like Hitler," Sara had said, holding the infant to her breast. And for the rest of the afternoon they had responded to the new range of murmurings and cries, part discovery part demand, with a murmured sieg heil. How could it not go on forever?

But then, in the middle of the night, out of a sleep so deep that everything became a dream, he dragged himself awake to find her standing by his bedside, four years old, thin and swaying in a pale pink nightgown. And even then everything might have been all right. He wasn't panicking. He was even pleased that she had come to him, that she had left her mother sleeping. He wanted nothing but to comfort her.

"Hey, bear. It's okay."

That was the first thing they had learned to say. *It's okay.* Begin with reassurance. And then, just to make her smile, he'd signed, *I can see you.*

It was a game they had played early on when it was all so new. She would laugh at how clumsy he was, her little fingers light as butterflies. But it had made his heart glow each time to see her receive his message across all that silence.

It was something in her inner-ear. A tiny bone she was born with that wouldn't shake loose. They weren't sure what to do. Lip-reading is better in the world outside, but it's harder to learn and less clear. They tried signing and she took to it so fast—like a Bea to honey, Miss Pru had said.

She couldn't use hearing aids at first. There wasn't enough

hearing left. And maybe it was just as well. She liked the quiet better. Though she was never quiet. Sounds, vibrations. She would touch his chest or throat and she would laugh. They had to keep encouraging all the different sounds to keep her in the habit. It was another game they played. Shaping her lips, her mouth. She never cried, but she would sing—just sit there swaying and singing.

And then, when she was three, she had the operation. A surgeon went in and cut it free, that little bone. And just like that, she could hear. She had cried and cried. Too loud, too strange. As if that warm and endless silence was all she had ever wanted.

And so, with his head still on the pillow he signed *I can see you*, and snaked out his arms to encircle her, breathing her in, still warm from her bed. He was already thinking, if he could comfort her quickly, he might still get back to sleep. She was so much like her infant self, so sweet and self-absorbed. And he remembered when Sara would just settle her on the bed between them and let her sleep out her nightmare there, the whole family floating under a blanket of darkness.

But Sara thought she was too old for that, so instead he sat up. "It's okay, bear. It's just a dream." And he was thinking to himself a little proudly that he was keeping his voice low, so his wife might not even have to wake up. And he said again, "It's just a dream." Because there's comfort in repetition.

And she said, "Daddy, I feel funny. Here." And she touched her chest, and the whole familiar night was wrenched away.

Her face went slack, her whole body sagged in his arms. And he couldn't cry out. Every possible sound was trapped in his throat. He lay her on the bed, smoothing her face, her chest, not daring to be rough, wildly hoping he might just sooth the life back into her, because whatever else this was, he knew like a band around his heart that it was bad.

"Sara! Sara, wake up! Wake up!"

And she did, with a suddenness that amazed him. Sound

asleep and then alert. "Call the ambulance."

But he already had. And there was no hope of it being a nightmare now.

The ambulance took seven minutes to arrive. He started mouth-to–mouth, shallow breaths, two or three seconds, her perfect face cupped in his hands. He could feel her thin chest lift and fall, but her expression had already turned patient and still. Sara wanted to take over, but he couldn't stop, so she struck him on the back in rough time to his breathing as if she could force her awake through desperation alone.

But no.

Help arrived. The EMT's carried her out. And for fifteen minutes they were locked away in the huge, flashing bunker of an ambulance, as the two of them stood on the grass pressing all their need into this one moment. And then the ambulance started off. Without warning it lumbered down the driveway and hurried away down the road. And long before they made it to the hospital and found their way through the terrible bleak light of the waiting room to stand by her bedside, she was no longer there.

It was her heart, but not her heart. Something electrical. A sudden flicker of the light in her eyes. There was no pain, they said. And that was what he remembered on her face—not suffering; more like a soft and blossoming curiosity about what this feeling could be. And the tone of her voice, *I feel funny.* So soft. Not frightened. Thank God for that, not frightened. He would always remember it as exactly the sort of voice in which she had asked him about where all the ladybugs came from in the spring when they lined the window panes and wouldn't leave. A question about something important that she knew he could answer.

And that's what they were left with, Sara and he. With that. And with the knowledge that Sara would never forgive him for not having woken her in time. For surely there was something she could have done if only she'd been allowed. But he hadn't. So that, in the end, after everything, and in all the years ahead, it was always only he who might have saved her.

8.

One of the first things he bought when Sara moved out was an automatic coffeemaker so he wouldn't have to wait. It was those first unprotected moments of the day—just rising out of sleep, when memory, dream and hope were all mixed together—that killed him over and over. But now he could come awake to the distant ding of the brewing coffee, and he would drink it standing at the counter, bath-robed and bereft, one mug after another, until the kick of it—strong and bitter as coal—lodged him tight in the grip of the day.

And then a shower. And more coffee as he dressed. The caffeine should have exploded his heart, but instead it just squeezed it tight. That was the trick. Coffee to begin each day and too much whiskey at the end. Every morning he woke feeling nauseated and bent; by the end of the day he was merely exhausted.

But today he opened his eyes to a vague expectation. Something new and strange was added to his life, and it took him a moment to recollect. Only when his eyes landed on the oatmeal pot, standing out of place on the kitchen table, did he fully remember, and then he felt his spirits sag. In his dreams it had been something startling and important. A revelation. But this was just a spider trapped in a pot, and standing there he tried to remember why it had seemed so remarkable. He sipped his coffee, wandered over to the table. Removing the lid he glanced down into the saucepan. It took a moment to realize it was empty.

His first thought was to wonder if he had simply imagined the whole thing. If his mind, in the end, had just given way. And he wondered at the thought. That this is what his mind would create—so freakish and so terrifying—in order to make sense of all he had lost.

As he drank his coffee, though, the uneasiness grew. He found himself glancing into corners, under chairs. He was aware of his naked legs beneath the nightshirt. His bare feet. He tried to put it out of his mind. It was only a spider. It didn't even matter if it was real. It would be cowering back under the stove or behind the fridge, squeezing itself into some tiny crack, thinking its little spider thoughts about bugs and darkness.

But he looked before he stepped into the shower. Peered behind the bathroom door, beneath the mat. Nothing foolish, he told himself. Just a quick glance. He checked the towel before he dried himself, his clothes before he dressed. Shoes, socks, inside his underwear, his pants, his shirt. He couldn't help himself. He shook out his jacket before he slipped it on and turned to the door.

Out of the corner of his eye there was a little blur of movement. A dainty smear. And crouching down he spied in the corner under the kitchen table a small rounded shadow against the white baseboard. Cautiously he moved the chair, and on hands and knees eased his head closer for a better look.

He jerked back. It was appalling. Even in the light of day, pressed against the wall as if trying to make itself invisible, it was the size of an orange, hunched and thickly furred. Horrifying and fierce.

That was the only thing that saved it. It was too big to crush. He was reaching for a magazine, a boot, his mind already calculating the angle of the wall, how to get in close with a clear swing. But the sheer bulk of the creature.... He thought of the mess, the living destruction. He tried to still his heart. But hunched and frozen he couldn't stop staring, didn't dare take his eyes off the thing.

Yet somehow, in its dark compactness, he couldn't see it clearly. Reluctantly he leaned in close to tease it into movement. Christ! It made a wild dash for the corner, and with a bleat of fear he started back, knocking over the chair. A clear shot. He could smash it now. But it had found another corner at the base of the table, and it lurked there, hunched and ready.

He searched for a jar, a glass, but nothing was big enough.

Finally, he emptied the shoebox that held Miss Pru's sewing supplies, dumped them onto the table, and turned back, magazine in one hand, shoebox in the other.

It should have been a disaster.

But the spider was sluggish, distracted, or perhaps just too frightened to budge. And though he moved much too slowly, prodding the creature, easing down the cardboard trap, he had it.

Somehow they had moved, the two of them, out of the realm of a horror movie and into a domestic comedy. He eased a magazine under the box and flipped it over. The spider fell with a disturbing thump onto the bottom. And now he was a bomb disposal expert, the hero of the moment. He set it down on the table, removed the magazine, slipped the lid into place.

And he realized, just for those moments, how far he had been from his grief. He could imagine telling Sara the story—it was suddenly something they could share. But beneath the gleam of appreciation there was something more distant. A faint uneasy feeling, not sharp, but restless and playing about his heart.

He tilted the shoebox, but the spider declined to move. In his mind it was cunning and furious. He imagined it, a creature bent on revenge: sticking to the lid, waiting to leap out and repay him for all his indignities. But when he cautiously cracked the cover, it was sitting on the bottom, hunched and forlorn.

And now he had a problem. He had carried spiders out the door before, and wasps and beetles and even flies. Everybody gets a second chance. They'd all vanished into Miss Pru's garden. But this. The idea of putting it out front, so close to the door and yet hidden…. He decided on the back. All the way back, against the distant property line, where the wild ivy and bushes separated one house from another.

It was a narrow band of wilderness, and he felt pleased that he was giving the creature a whole new world. Though, in the light of day, the property looked shabby and unwelcoming. There were glinting soda cans amid the weeds and a few scraps of white Kleenex matted down into the earth.

Perhaps that's what unsettled him. Perhaps just the memory of the spider hunched against the side. As he leaned down and loosened the cover he felt a gnawing at his heart. There was a rank odor of something decaying in the soil; the sharper scent of dogs— the neighbor in back had two of them, and they were clearly allowed to roam. And as if to make the point, from the back of the house came the muffled sound of barking.

He chose a spot under the spreading leaves of a wild day lily, and as gently as he could he tilted the box, felt the sliding weight, watched the spider land with a gentle bump on the earth. It sat there, frozen, too frightened to move. And in that instant he felt the creature's fear, suddenly so much like his own: abandoned and cut off from all it had ever loved.

He went to work. He was rebuilding Mrs. Oldcastle's shed, carefully re-using the weathered clapboard so it wouldn't look new. During his break he typed into his phone a search, and a dozen videos of spiders presented themselves. He chose 'Monsters of the Web,' and it made him a little queasy to watch. Not the close-ups, so much—the jewel-like eyes and the fangs delicately gathered like an elderly aunt with her knitting needles. No, it was the helplessness of the victims that caught his heart—the bumbling fly, the little moth who wandered into the web. He couldn't watch. Though in the opening scenes of tropical jungles and wild exotic locales, he began to wonder for the first time where it could have come from.

In the evening he carried the uneasiness home with him. He couldn't sit. He was ferociously hungry. But as he reached for the oatmeal pot he hesitated. It wasn't that he expected anything—and glancing in, of course, it was empty. But as he set it on the stove he was aware of a faint keening sound. No. Not a sound, not quite. Something in his chest. An ache. Outside, the dogs were free. He heard them bounding around, barking like a pack on the trail of something soft and afraid. He thought of the moth from the video. He thought of little Bea. *Stop. Lock your mind like a box.* But of course it didn't work. And the fear was building now. Barking, barking. He'd never been afraid of dogs, but now he thought of them differently. Huge and bounding, lunging through the bushes, nosing fiercely through the weeds.

He turned the heat off under the pot and hurried out the door.

The dogs were enraged by his appearance, yelping and fierce. The sky was still pale, but the earth had sunk into darkness. He had his phone out, flashlight on, casting over the tangle of weeds and soda cans. And there it was, still under the lily. It hadn't moved all day. What was it thinking, huddled beneath the overhanging leaves? He bent down, held out the open box. The spider flinched back. The dogs were clawing at the thin wire fence as if he were stealing from them.

He had forgotten the lid. It was back on the table. The spider hunched and cowered under the wide bowl of noise. Cautiously he reached down with his phone to give it a nudge, and it exploded into motion. His heart leapt. He tripped back, yipping with fear, dropping the box. And then he was standing, shaking, casting the light wildly around, imagining the touch of it on his ankle, climbing his leg. He had time to unfurl a whole banner of fears before the swooping light glanced across the shoebox, and he saw it there, braced and substantial, in the bottom.

He slept through vivid dreams, imagining shelves of food around him, pots of food, but every time he went to serve himself it vanished. He woke in the night and ate saltines and peanut butter and drank a glass of milk, but returning to sleep he was hungrier than ever, searching cupboards and closets in his dreams but finding only empty jars. He woke up famished, though his stomach was full. He stopped at the shoebox. He imagined opening the lid and finding it gone, but there it was, solid and peering up at him, shifting on its feet, anxious, imploring.

"Are you hungry? Is that it? What do you eat? Bugs? I don't have any bugs. Milk? Would you drink milk?"

He had a wild thought of the little kitten he had once found in the dark. Too young even to lap, she had drawn milk from an eye dropper as if tied to life by the frailest of threads. She had seemed too tiny to live. So that when Bea started nursing, he had suddenly remembered that kitten again, and he had hovered anxiously over Sara and the child. But from the beginning Bea had shown no sign of flagging.

Now he poured a bit of milk into a bottle cap, but the spider just cowered away. He stirred up an egg, tried a piece of buttered bread; he scoured the house for dead flies and dropped them in. But the spider just sat there amid the litter of scraps looking up at him pleadingly.

And he realized once again that there was no one in this whole wide world that he could not disappoint.

9.

Belief works in different ways—taking root in unprotected corners of the heart and spilling out unexpectedly.

He and Sara had taken their separation almost for granted. There seemed no point in being together. The loss of their daughter made them strangers. Each of them had come to the marriage from disappointment and heartbreak, and they wanted something safer. Cooler to the touch. They were courteous with one another. Willing to be satisfied if not exactly charmed. And she was Miss Pru's niece, so they had that much in common. They used to joke that they were the only two young people in a fifty-mile radius, but Sara hadn't felt young in a long time, and he never had.

She moved out within a week—back to Garnetville. She was postmaster there and might as well be closer to work. The separation felt strangely familiar, like an emptier version of their usual life. But when she began to stop by with a casserole or books to recommend or television suggestions, he realized how completely she was transformed. She had somehow lifted herself into the community of thoughtful onlookers, moving him to the center of their joint concern, giving comfort from a distance beyond the worst of her grief.

So he withdrew further and further. And somehow the worse he got, the stronger she felt, as if increasing his suffering allowed her to slip out from under her own terrible weight. Even after a year she continued to stop by once a week, having completed the transformation from Miss Pru's niece to wife to mother and back to niece again.

So when she gave her quick, peremptory knock and let herself in—a visitor now, coming and going—she found him sitting at the kitchen table with a cardboard shoebox in his hands, jumpy and tense, overfilled with concentration. She had brought a chicken casserole and a little pile of his pressed shirts, and she raised them slightly to draw them to his attention. But this time he didn't move to take them. Instead, when he stood up, he carried the shoebox still.

She waited. It was always the next step in their orderly exchange. Tea? he'd ask. I wouldn't mind a cup. But this time the kettle was cold.

"Perhaps I'll make the tea," she said, with a little frown of irritation. And setting down her burdens she lit the gas ring under the kettle.

"Something's happened," he whispered.
After all the months of bleak exhaustion there was excitement in his voice. And that irritated her as well, because he should know better than anyone in the world that there was no longer anything to get excited about.

"It's a little startling," he said. "It happened last Wednesday."

And that angered her, as well. They had decided not to speak of dates, not to acknowledge each passing milestone, though Wednesday marked a year. She frowned grimly and tried to steady herself back into cold matter-of-factness.

But he didn't notice. "It was waiting for me when I woke up. I thought I had dreamed it at first. It was in Bea's oatmeal pan."

And that angered her as well. The name. Why do that to yourself? As if he enjoyed the pain. She had wanted to throw out all the pans, all the dishes, all the clothes—every marker of daily life. She had wanted to burn down the house. And now to see him clinging to such things....

He saw her irritation. It seemed to make him more nervous, more uncertain. He hurried forward. "Don't scream," he said. As if she would. "Look."

And he removed the cover of the box.

Sara expected nothing in particular. She had trained herself to expect nothing. Though some corner of her mind feared it would be some article of clothing, a doll, some favorite book. She braced herself. But when she saw the spider, it was a relief. So much of a relief that it took her a moment to notice how large it was.

"Well, for pity's sake!" she said, feeling the rage always banked in her heart. "What are you keeping it in a box for? Put it outside."

"I did. But I felt it. I felt what it was feeling. It was afraid. It was afraid and lonely. I couldn't leave it out there."

"It's a spider! It belongs out there!"

And she saw him hesitate. "I don't think it does. I googled it. It's nothing from around here. From the Amazon, maybe. Somewhere tropical. Or the desert. But not even that. It's nothing I could find. Anywhere."

And her fury rushed into flame as she saw where he was going. "Stop it! You're ridiculous! It's a spider. Don't you dare turn it into something else!"

"But look. Look at this."

He sat down at the table and cradled his hands on either side of the box. He started to sing in his low, shaky voice: "The eensy weensy spider went up the water spout. Down came the rain and washed the spider out…"

And her mouth went dry. It was like a fist to her heart. "Stop that! How dare you? Stop that!"

"But look! Look! See that?" And as if it made a kind of sense— as if it could ever be anything more than a cruel, crazy trick—the spider began to bob in place, up and down, as if in time to the song.

All the long, long year of tamping down, shutting down, of putting every terrible thing in a hole dug deep in her heart. All if it was gone in an instant. And she could see him again on that awful night, sitting up in bed, foolish and blinking. A ridiculous man who could do nothing. Not even wake her up in time.

And she swept the table clear, just swept it off—laundry, casserole, ridiculous shoebox. All his crazy foolishness. And she was shouting now, not even words. Just rage. And everything around her, every familiar thing—which he had preserved and made into some kind of shrine to his own terrible failure—it all shattered like her grief: the kettle tumbling, spilling, the pressed shirts a wild blizzard of shapes, and the blue flame of the stovetop catching at the fabric, snapping at it, gobbling it up.

She saw the flame reach up and flicker at the curtains. And there was part of her that was glad. Even his own laundry was sick to death of him. The whole house saw him for what he was. And then she watched as, with a cry, he followed the tumbling shoebox, saw the little black knot of frantic movement, spilling onto the floor. And he was ridiculous. Still ridiculous. Down on his hands and knees like a crazy man, reaching under the table, trying to capture the frightened creature.

And perhaps it was the look on his face—the hint of something like hope sprouting in his heart where hers was all blasted and dry. Perhaps it was just her rising fury that he, who had ruined her life, should have any source of cheer at all. It held her back, kept her stunned and still, for those first few moments as the fire took hold. The curtains became a waterfall of flame, the ceiling smudged and darkened. It spread so fast—an old house dry as grief. The smoke billowed up. And now she was filling a pan of water and splashing it on the flames, utterly foolish and ineffectual, as if he had somehow infected her with his own helplessness.

The fire trucks came all the way from Frontenac and Bullard, but there was nothing to be done. All that could burn burned. And in the end she saved nothing from the house that she hadn't already taken. And he, who had tried to keep everything just as it was—he had come out with only the shoebox clutched like a life-preserver in his arms.

10.

Harold woke to the sounds of a struggle, muffled but dire. Blows landing, a terrible fight. Tangled in the bedclothes he tried to hurry to the rescue, shaking off one set of dreams for another, until even his fears fell away and he opened his eyes. But the room was no better. Crazy with daylight—wall paper, lampshades, frantic upholstery. And the noise continued, a great thumping turmoil echoing through the wall.

He lurched across the room and pounded sharply. "Stop it! Are you all right? What's going on in there?" But the clamor continued. He stood, head aching, air cool against his ankles, the great washed weight of the nightshirt the only familiar thing. He staggered out into the hallway.

The noise was coming from the next room. More subdued, but still—how could anyone bear up under such a beating? He tried the knob. Unlocked. He caught his breath, burst in, and stood in the doorway like a crazy man as the chambermaid, all concentration on the task at hand, trundled the vacuum cleaner around the heavy furniture in a rising crescendo of noise.

"I'm so sorry," he said.

But she ignored him. Hurriedly he retreated, everything turning foolish in the empty hallway. He went to let himself back into his room, but of course the door was locked.

The sound of the vacuum died away. And after a moment, with a few last vindictive thumps, the door opened. Backing out in a cloud of self-absorption, the maid dragged her linen cart behind. As if in keeping with the inn's décor, she was dressed out of a Trollope novel in an elaborate uniform of black tulle, with a white cap and pinafore. Harold waited patiently for the startled cry, but she turned and, at the sight of an unshaven man in a red nightshirt sitting on the floor, made two small adjustments to her hearing aids. "Locked ou'?"

"I didn't recognize you," he said.

"Organize?"

His index finger made a short flight from his temple to his open palm. "Recognize."

"It's the uniform. I'm the chambermaid."

"I can see that." He climbed stiffly to his feet. "I was coming to your rescue."

"Why?"

He considered her air of calm self-sufficiency in the light of all his crowded fears. "No reason."

She looked even more fantastical than the night before—her grey housekeeper's smock grown ordinary in light of this new extravaganza. And her makeup had changed with the outfit. She had paled her face and placed with care a bright disk of scarlet on each cheek. Her eyes were shadowed like a pair of sunsets, orange to red to brown, and her lips caught the brightest russet and held it firmly in a narrow line.

"I'm not sure I've ever met a chambermaid like you."

"I'm not surprised." Briskly she stepped up to his door, her keys on a thin, retractable line. "Can I do your room now?"

"I'm not dressed yet."

"It's my last one."

"I was going back to bed."

"It's eleven o'clock."

"Where am I supposed to go?"

"You can jus' sit down. I'll work around you."

"I haven't even brushed my teeth."

"Well, go ahead. I haven' got all day."

He brushed and washed. He peered into the mirror—haggard and unshaven—marveling that she was so unworried when he was clearly such a fright. He drew on his bathrobe and, emerging like an invalid, found her standing over the shoebox with the lid in one hand and a look of calm concern.

"You probably shouldn't open that."

"You can't leave it closed. She's probably terrified."

"*She's* terrified?"

That seemed to interest her. "You don't like spiders?"

"They scare the bejesus out off me."

"Then why do you have one?"

He hesitated. "I don't like to say. But I think it's important."

"Important to be scared?"

"I think so. Yes."

There was no place to stand that wasn't in her way, so he climbed back into bed. She cleaned as if the room itself enraged her, banging the furniture, roaring over the carpet.

"Do you have a summer uniform and a winter uniform?" he asked during a lull.

"No."

"You look like a Victorian dancehall performer."

She seemed to consider that. Stepping to the mirror on the bathroom door she offered herself a glance. "The skirt was hard," she admitted. "You've got to get that ruching jus' right or it bunches up. The fabric's pretty stiff."

"I can see that."

"But I like the apron. The ruffles are fun to do."

"They look it."

Rubber gloved and be-brushed, she marched into the bathroom and waged a brief and bitter campaign before emerging, in a flush and rush of water, with a frown he was already learning to read as the deepest satisfaction. "That's it, Hen."

And he smiled—he couldn't help it, hungover as he was—that she should address him with such kindness. He was trying to decipher the hen reference—brooding? settled in his nest?—when a low moan rose from the cart, and Harold noticed in the top basket, beside the piled up towels and washcloths, the enormous orange cat. She was gazing around with the look of an opium addict, lifting herself from one dream into another.

Izzie turned to the door and eased it open, her hip braced against the cart.

"Wait!" And from somewhere in his memory came the sign for *Hold on.* His hands felt stiff and unpracticed, but the movement caught her eye. "You two are just going to abandon me now?"

He managed *you two* but *abandon* was beyond him, so he just spread his hands wide in all the breadth of his despair. "You're just going to hand me off to the next maid, who might not care a nickel about my hopes and fears?"

She didn't laugh. She watched him closely, trying to decide how, exactly, he was making fun of her. And Harold wondered if it was merely his own deep sadness that made her eyes look so kind.

"Abandon," she said in that soft, rounded voice, as her fingers tied a mournful ribbon on the air. It seemed to tighten itself around his heart. "So what are your hopes?" she asked, as if his fears were evident enough.

He tried to smile. "What am I supposed to do now?"

"I guess you better begin your day."

"Your cat is very sweet."

"She's not my cat. We're best friends."

"She doesn't say much."

"She doesn't need to." And she turned back to the door.

But something in her seriousness, her deafness called out to him. "How old are you?"

She gave him a startled look. "I'm thirty-five."

"No, really."

But the door had shut behind her, sealing her escape.

Harold in Luck

11.

The house was a narrow Federalist wedding cake with tall black shutters and a too-vivid air. It was handsome but smaller than it seemed, elegant but a little too showy; and the fact that it was perfectly placed to cream off the best of the northern light coming in over the park seemed only an afterthought but wasn't. Harold knocked on the door.

He had been unprepared for such a beautiful morning. His head ached, and the remnant of his dreams were still adding themselves to the weight of another day. The only comfort was knowing that, bad as he felt, Weland would be feeling worse. So he knocked again a little louder. And this time the door opened onto a resolute young woman in a pink apron with the words *Meals by Mindy* embroidered over her heart.

"Yes?"

"I'm here to see Weland Tilyard. Apparently we have big plans. I don't suppose he's awake."

Her gaze traveled over his unshaven face and mended black suit and the battered shoebox under his arm. "It's eleven o'clock," she said.

"So, too early?"

"He's in the studio. He's not going to want to be disturbed."

"I think he'll make an exception for me."

With a shrug she turned and led him through a world of white—hallway, staircase, a glimpse of the rooms beyond—into a kitchen so gleaming it felt like an assault. She drew to a halt at the counter before a pair of brown grocery bags. She'd been removing foil-wrapped trays, making little notes on them in black marker. Now she began loading them into the freezer. "Tell Weland it's 325 for half and hour. He should know by now, but remind him anyway."

"Is that dinner?"

"Breakfast. These are dinner." A second stack of trays. "350. But remember, only half an hour." There followed a series of deli-wrapped parcels—cold cuts, cheese, a trio of perfect tomatoes, and a head of Butter Lettuce delicate as a corsage.

"Thank God," murmured Harold. "I thought you'd forgotten lunch."

She glanced at her watch. "I've loaded the coffee-maker. Cleaned and dusted the house. His clothes are folded, but tell him to put them away this time. It's no good complaining he's out of socks if they're all sitting down in the laundry room."

"Do you do this every day?"

She gave an indulgent laugh. "He wishes. Once a week is all he gets."

And now she was gathering her things, folding the grocery bags, giving the counter a final wipe. "Remember, dishes in the dishwasher. Don't let him stack them in the sink. And rinse the glasses before you load them. Just one capful of detergent. Last time it foamed all over the floor. And watch out for the granite counter. It's overdue for re-sealing and has a tendency to stain."

"Are you Mindy or one of the maids? Just in case he asks."

"Oh, don't worry. He's not going to ask." And turning to the door she said, "Don't make a mess," and tidied herself away.

Harold stood momentarily uncertain amid all that pristine order. Then setting down the shoebox he stepped to the coffee-maker and turned it on. Retrieving one of the breakfast pans from the freezer—*325° for 30 mins*—he peeled back the foil. Scrambled eggs and salsa, sausages, fried potatoes. He found the silverware drawer and helped himself to a fork. Then, picking up the black marker, he turned to the remaining stacks and changed every three to a five.

The coffee mugs were lined up in the cupboard, neat as

Mindy's apron. He filled his mug, then poured a generous splash over the granite counter. It pooled and trickled down the white face of the cabinet. Prowling through the cupboards he found a bottle of Glenlivet and topped up his coffee. Then, tilting down the corner of his breakfast tray, he spooned a generous puddle of salsa onto the spotless tile floor before setting off down the hall.

He found the artist in his studio—though not as he'd expected. Weland was dressed in spotless white coveralls like some nostalgic vision of a furnace repair man, his bowtie bright and jaunty. He stood at his easel, frowning in concentration, like man untouched by anything so mundane as a hangover, and when Harold appeared he barely glanced up, "You can't come in here."

The studio had once been the living room, with high crown molding, a fireplace, and a wide bow-window like the prow of a ship. The walls were white but crowded with paintings, three and four rows deep, and in the center of the room an easel stood, heavy as a scaffold. A stone-topped table served as a palette, smeared with paint and crowded with brushes. And superimposed on the workspace like some illusion of former comfort stood an antique Victorian love seat, all walnut and pink upholstery.

"I helped myself to breakfast," said Harold cheerfully. "I didn't think you'd mind. That Mindy's a dynamo. She wanted me to remind you not to overcook the meals."

Weland regarded him uncertainly for a long moment. "She is a treasure," he conceded. "She used to be a pretty good painter, but decided her heart lay in the service industry." Then, finally, reluctantly, "Have we met?"

"Oh yes."

And the first gleam of worry crept into his eyes. "I don't suppose I invited you here."

"I think it was implied."

"Well, this isn't a good time. I'm working now. I don't like to be disturbed."

Harold sipped his coffee and cast his glance over the studio. Off to the side behind a folding screen two narrow armchairs flanked a patio table like a group of extras waiting for their cue. He set his breakfast down and settled into a chair. "I've thought about what you said."

"Don't sit down," protested Weland. "You can't stay."

"About your proposition."

He frowned. "What proposition?"

"The book?" said Harold. "Childe Harold days? The parade? The speeches? The whole new collection of paintings? You said I'd be famous. Don't you remember?"

Weland sighed and turned back to his easel. "Oh, I always remember eventually. It's my curse."

Before him on the sofa a series of pencil sketches had been laid out in lieu of a model—glimpses of a woman, nude and evocative, but somehow underwhelming in the bright clutter of the room. After a moment's consideration he dipped his brush in a tiny mound of yellow paint, and hesitated. "You know I was only joking about selling my soul."

"No, you weren't."

"I'm not sure what you think is going to happen."

Harold chewed a bite of potato. "You said I'd like being famous."

"Oh, yes. No question. I think you would." He dipped the brush again and with a series of precise strokes sketched in the rounded hillside of a plump thigh. "The thing is, I'm just not sure this is the right time. I don't think we need to rush into anything."

"You said to strike while the iron was hot."

"A fine idea in principle," he conceded. "But I think it might be best if we just let this idea simmer for a while. Just put it on the back burner."

"Well," said Harold, sipping his coffee. "If that's what you think."

"I do. I think it's best." And the relief was evident in the line of his shoulders. "And I wonder if we might just keep this between ourselves."

"Okay. Sure. That sounds fine. But you might want to take a look at this."

Harold drew from his pocket a folded copy of the *Olean County Gazette* and held it out. Reluctantly Weland stepped over and lifted it from his hand. There wasn't much news this week, but there on the bottom of the front page was a boxed announcement. *Weland Tilyard Declares Childe Harold Days.* Not a long article, but surprisingly detailed.

"It sounds very festive," said Harold. "I think everyone's excited. I assumed you made an announcement."

Weland sighed. "That's not impossible. I've been known to do such a thing."

"Well, don't worry. I'm sure nobody reads the front page."

Weland handed it back. "Is there any more coffee?"

"I'll get you some. Cream and sugar?"

"Black as the devil's heart. With just a dash of cinnamon."

12

Harold returned with two fresh mugs. Weland accepted his with a nod, his eyes on his easel, his mind on the prospect of disaster. He took a sip. "That's not cinnamon."

"Scotch."

A moment's consideration, then he took another sip. He started to paint again, quickly but with an air of distraction, the way someone else might start talking to himself under his breath. He barely glanced at the sketches. The solid flesh—sleek and golden—rose out of the blankness of the paper like a bather from a pool of cream. The slope of the breasts, the reclining waist, the hand pressed demurely over the juncture of the thighs.

Harold watched with growing irritation, but in the end he couldn't help himself. "That's amazing."

"I know," said Weland wearily. "Is there more coffee?"

"Of course."

"Not so much cinnamon this time."

When Harold returned he carried the bottle of scotch under his arm. The painting was all but finished, and Weland stood gazing helplessly.

The flesh was warm, the muscles smooth beneath the skin. The blonde hair bright as sunshine. But Weland regarded the painting as if it were already somehow receding into the distance like a bus on a rainy day.

"What's wrong?" asked Harold. "It's beautiful."

"Of course it's beautiful. Beauty's not the problem."

"What is the problem?"

Weland reached out with the tail end of the brush and traced a line from the toes to the hips to the settled lushness of the breasts. "Do you see this? The line here? See the brusqueness of it? So unapologetic. Not graceful. Not quite. Just a little off. A little awkward. But you can follow that line all the way up the leg to the arm, then to the back of the sofa. And it leads your eye on a circuit of the picture, tying it all together."

"It's amazing," said Harold.

"It's Manet."

Weland turned and let his eyes wander over the rows of paintings crowded onto the walls. "See if you can find it."

And now Harold took in the wild variety of pictures: half-familiar portraits, still lifes, landscapes from every corner of art history—all varied and unrelated. Wildly different styles and colors. "Please tell me you're a notorious art thief," he said.

"Of course I am. I stood for hours in front of each one and I stole it line for line. Go ahead. Find the Manet."

But Weland was already crossing ahead of him to stand beneath a woman reclining on a sofa, naked but for a black ribbon round her throat and a glance of such unshirking confidence it felt like an accusation.

Harold hesitated. "That looks familiar."

"Of course it does. The *Olympia*. Imagine the scandal when it was painted. Nothing classical about it. Just a naked woman, daring you to look."

At first glance it looked nothing like Weland's. Dark where his picture was sunny; sharp and nervy where his was languid. "It's not that similar."

"Don't be ridiculous."

He raised his brush again. "Look at that line. And this." He following the reclining figure from toe to hip, and now Harold could make out the idiosyncratic curve of the legs, the strange particularity of solid flesh.

"Okay," he conceded. "It's pretty close."

"Fucking Manet. And look at that." He gestured hopelessly at a sun-drenched landscape off to the side. "Can you imagine? Painting with Cezanne? Setting up your easel next to him on the hilltop over that village. And you paint and paint and paint. You're painting the shit out of that landscape. And it's really coming together for you. You're getting each point, each arc of energy and movement. Every part of the scene is anchoring itself just where you need it to be. And than you turn to find that beside you." He stared at the picture— anything but realistic. Every color flattened, every shape bent away from the world, but bright and vivid as a dream. "And you think, What the hell has he done? You stare at it. You try to memorize every line. And you promise yourself you will never again paint an ordinary landscape. But here's the thing. You do. Every fucking time.

"And that's just Cezanne. There's Monet, Degas, goddam Raphael. Picasso. Fucking Picasso." He was pacing now, but he stopped before a painting of old-fashioned figures in a luxurious room, all burgundy, old wood, and black. It looked medieval in its richness. "Look at that. He painted it when he was a boy. Just painted it, just like that. Just to prove he could. Just to show the world everything he was going to throw away piece by piece. Picasso was fourteen when he painted that. And so was I, when I made that copy. I remember thinking, so that's it? That's all you've got?" He shook his head, shoulders sinking under the weight of it all. "I would pay real money to feel that again."

They were back at his easel, gazing down at the sketch. The nude figure seemed to taunt them with its effortless grace. "Have you seen *L'Origine du Monde* by Courbet?" said Weland. "It's a small painting. Beautiful. Amazing technique. Nude, of course. The most beautiful pubic hair. It shocked the world. They tried to ban it as pornography. But it *is* something to see."

"Do you have a copy?"

"I burned it." He took a swallow of coffee, mostly scotch by now. "I worked for so long on that one. You can't imagine. You know what they say: if it isn't easy then you're doing it wrong? I could not get it right. In the end, there was nothing there. A naked woman, that's all. But there is something so incredible in the original. The light, the texture of the paint. It's vivid. Startling. But mine? It was nothing at all."

He reached out again, tracing a finger over his picture. "Look at the arm, the shadow along the muscle. See if you can find it. Go ahead. It's a test."

Harold started toward the *Olympia*.

"No, no, no," said Weland impatiently. "Nothing so obvious."

So together they walked slowly along the wall, Harold's eye wandering over the images, all the tones and figures and shapes. "I don't know what I'm looking for."

"Sure, you do." Weland went back and picked up his sketch. "There." He held it up beside a scene of ballet dancers. They were just warming up, their bodies roughly textured and awkwardly posed. Every figure caught in the instant just before grace. "That one. Near the door."

One dancer more distracted than the rest, as if she were lost in thoughts of the night before. And looking back at the new painting Harold could see the same shading of mass and muscle, and now it carried with it something else. That sense of distraction. The additional freight of its first associations.

"And the curve of the torso?" said Weland. "Twisting just like that? Go on. Find the line. It's a game." Though he didn't sound playful.

They walked together until they were standing in front of a painted Christ, down from the cross and cradled in the arms of his followers. Exhausted by his trial, pummeled by suffering, he lay graceful and exhausted under the eye of heaven. The line of the belly, clenched with effort, was now finally relaxing into peace.

"Fucking Raphael. If there were a God, He'd want Raphael to do his portrait. And then a little Manet to keep it in check. Tighten it into the everyday. And just a touch of Giotto for the expression.

Blank and underdrawn but brimming with emotion."

Harold would rather have gnawed off his own leg, but what he said was, "That's amazing."

"No," said Weland wearily. "Almost, but no. You want to see amazing?"

They crossed the room to a landscape painting, not large, but vibrant with energy. A study of rough light in some northern landscape—water and a rocky shore at dawn. And in the middle distance, standing out against the darkness, was a ragged tree lit up by a single narrow glimmer of the rising sun. In a landscape of greys and greens, it shone with a bright impossible blue.

"It's good," said Harold grudgingly. "Where did you scavenge the parts?"

But Weland just shook his head. "Every time you look, you see it differently—more and more—just opening up as you sink into it. After a while it's hard to look away. But the thing is, when it first appeared no one paid the slightest attention."

"I'm sorry."

"I'm not. It was years ago. It was my first big break. It was the making of me."

"Well," said Harold doubtfully. "Hardship is supposed to make you stronger."

"So they say. But it wasn't my hardship. It was Jonathan's. He showed it to me. Years ago. After everyone and his brother had ignored it. And he asked me why. And I said, there was no sex appeal. And he said you can't put sex appeal in a landscape." Weland smiled. "So I did. I added a little Claude, a little Bierstadt. And the slenderest bit of Renoir. A woman, fresh from her bath, all but hidden in the shadows, but touched with that same amazing blue. And it was a triumph. The judges at Venice said it took them less than an hour to decide. Less than a minute, one of them said. Do you notice that color? Of course you do. Do you know what's in it?"

"Besides blue, you mean?"

"Nothing turns out to be just itself. There's scarlet and cadmium yellow, and some deepest lapis, and a bit of white. You mix it, but not too much. You leave the threads of color running through it so that up close it's like a mosaic of all that went before. Fucking Jonathan. It took me forever to figure it out. From a distance it's a feeling, an ache of brightness. It's like a little hook that lodges itself in your heart. That's what the jury in Venice was feeling. The woman in the shadows just gave them a way to feel it." Weland turned on him bitterly. "Do you see now why I was so taken by that book?"

"You mean *my* book."

"In the beginning I kept trying to see it as pastiche. All the old familiar bits, re-assembled once again. Love, loss, passion. God knows there's enough pornography in the world. But it kept getting away from me. There was something about it. Something at the heart of it. In its own way, it was original."

"Why, thank you," said Harold drily.

"But you know what the problem is with originality? Most people don't know what to make of it."

13.

The University Art Museum looked like a series of glass and concrete boxes that had crashed together at great speed. The impression on first seeing it was always how beautiful it might have been.

"It's designed so you can't wait to get inside," said Weland holding the door. But the interior was no better: a series of modern living rooms, much too large for their furniture, with pale grey carpeting and high concrete walls.

It was only when you moved into the first gallery—an intimate cul-de-sac at the edge of all that unchecked space—that you felt somehow welcomed. Weland had designed it with three shallow steps down to a series of rooms wrapped around four sides of a glass courtyard. The glass was specially tinted—supposedly to protect the paintings, but in fact to dull the sunshine so that even the natural world became the merest approximation of the pigments within.

They stepped into the warmth and paused. On a wall the color of a sunset the elegant black letters seemed to float unsupported: *The Wide Bed*. Below them, only slightly smaller, *The Gang of Four*, and their names—five names.

"It's a little mystical," Weland conceded.

He was *of* the group, but not *in* it. In a way he was the group. Though, of course, he had the good sense never to say so. But here were the names, five names, with Weland's first among them in a type size that seemed like an optical illusion but was, in fact, just a little larger than the rest.

Of course it was laughable—all that self-aggrandizement. Harold tried hard to be dismissive. But standing in that welcoming room, bathed in light as golden as a summer afternoon, he found himself filled with a kind of longing.

And of course that was precisely the point. The room, a few

introductory paintings, a series of perfect moments caught and preserved in all their warmth and enervation. Or rather—and this was Weland's great insight—a series of moments *just after*. Captured in the glow of remembering. He had taken a book about passion and turned it into a reverie.

"So, what do you think?" he said.

"I think that's a lot of naked people."

"Exactly. It could have been a disaster. Come with me."

Taking his arm companionably he led them into a smaller gallery with walls the color of a thundercloud and a single word in raised letters by the door. *Before.*

"Did you choose the color of the walls?"

"Of course."

"It looks a little bleak."

"Just unfinished. *And the earth was without form, and void; and darkness was upon the face of the deep. And the Spirit of God moved upon the face of the waters.*"

Harold sighed. "Oh, Weland."

Before they became the Gang of Four they were working painters, academic painters—each doing something different, but with this in common: they had all drifted into the backwater of Ashdown University and were just waiting there—"Doing fuck-all" —when Weland arrived.

"They could each have been painting in a closet for all the difference it made."

"It might have made a difference to them," said Harold.

"Artists aren't put on this earth to make a difference to themselves."

Landscapes, still lifes, figural drawings ranged across the wall in lumpy earthen tones as if they'd been carved out of mud and paint. "See what I had to work with? Usually when you form a group it's the similarities that bind them. But here, it was just me. I had arrived on a little cloud of fame, but nothing more was really happening. I needed a change. More than that, I needed a brand. So I took them off to some God-forsaken spot and taught them how to paint. I added just that little something to make those terrible pictures come alive."

"And you're going to tell me what that is," said Harold.

Weland smiled. "See if you can figure it out."

He led the way into the next room—dim and unwelcoming—with walls still grey but growing lighter now.

"I brought them the book, and I said, Read it. This is passion and romance and heartbreak, I told them. This is something we can use. But they missed the point entirely. Look at this. It almost breaks your heart."

They had all gone off and painted a little of everything. There were women and men, sometimes singly, sometimes couples—sitting or sprawled or lying entwined on a thickly impastoed bed. They seemed to be struggling to free their limbs from the paint.

"Can you imagine reading that wonderful book and seeing this? Tell me you're stirred. Tell me you feel that ache of recognition and longing."

It wasn't until the end, in the deepest, darkest corner of the gallery, that they came to something new. A single sketch, quick and insubstantial, oils thinned out to near translucency. It was another species altogether, as if this were the line of evolution and at this point things had taken flight. It was all pale sunlight and skin. A slender woman, slim and boyish—not so much reclining as curled in sleep.

"It killed me to put it here," said Weland.

"I can imagine. Hidden away in the corner. It doesn't seem like you at all. So, what happened? They painted theirs and then you painted yours?"

"Not yet. No. Not at first. This is Jonathan's. I was still trying to determine where the heart of the venture lay."

"Ah," said Harold. "And you can't paint from life."

Weland glanced over as if to assure himself of something—Harold's shabbiness, his despair, his inherent harmlessness.

"I didn't need to. It wasn't what was needed. But I admit it. And I would only tell this to you. I'm not always that original. Not like Jonathan. You can see him reaching into the shape of things, as if he could just lift them onto the canvas. But so slowly. I, on the other hand, paint like the wind. And that's the thing about the wind—it picks things up, blows them around, rearranges them. Because there's more to art than technique and less to technique than you might think. Anyone can see if there's something there. But how many see what's not? That's the trick. To look and find the hollow place in an otherwise perfect form. It's a curse," said Weland complacently. "But not just a curse."

He let them paint all those terrible pictures, just to get it out of their systems. Then he showed them Jonathan's and sent them off again. And this time it was a little better.

They were in the final room now, coming to the point of it all.

It was clear what he was doing. Weland was a showman, and he was building the tension, moving from bad to good to best. But even though Harold tried to hang back, tried to spoil the effect—tried to wait on the threshold just a little too long so it couldn't help but be anticlimactic—it wasn't.

Walls like summer sunshine and a new series of pictures—all recognizably different, but constrained now toward a common goal. And at the center *The Blue Robe* stood on its own short wall, like a *Mona Lisa* in sunlight and skin.

The beauty of the painting seemed to take it out of Harold. He sank onto a leather bench and drew something from his pocket.

"Is that my flask?"

"And your scotch. But the idea is mine."

Weland laughed and sat down.

"How many copies of that picture are there?" asked Harold.

"Not copies. Originals. The museum begged me, and I certainly wasn't going to give them mine." He accepted the flask and took a long sip. "How many times has something wonderful happened to you?"

"Not often. More like a series of almost-wonderful things."

"You have to take charge of your destiny. You can't just accept what comes your way."

"Is that what you did?"

"Of course."

In the end Jonathan had made something remarkable. Starting from his sketch he had created a painting that had gone beyond beauty.

"It had almost everything we needed," said Weland. "The sunlight, the languor, the softness that you almost couldn't believe. And of course that touch of blue. It was stunning. Nearly perfect. It pointed us on our way."

Harold turned back to the crowded wall. "So which one is it, this nearly perfect painting?"

"It's not here."

"Why not?"

Weland hesitated. "It was the key to the whole color palette, the whole feeling of the series. It opened my eyes to all that it could be. The texture, the tone. You could feel it with your eyes. It was like nothing I'd ever seen." He shrugged. "I asked Jonathan not to put it in."

"Of course you did. So, where is it?"

"It burned in a fire. Last fall. His whole studio went up. He lost everything." And Weland sat there with a look of something like wonder. "It was awful. A terrible disaster. It was like the hand of fate."

14.

They strolled around town, passing the flask back and forth like old friends. Weland with a pocket notebook and a few colored pencils was sketching whatever Harold found interesting. What do you see? What catches your eye? The town green is odd, isn't it? How about that couple? That young woman there? Is she beautiful? Do you think she's hot?

Everything had become a question. He could no longer tell something from nothing. And with the last of the scotch Weland turned reminiscent.

"It seems like just last week I came to this town. I made a big splash in Venice."

"I think you mentioned that."

"I was all piss and vinegar."

"You don't need to mention that."

"It's not a bad thing, piss and vinegar. You need to push, in this life. You need to know how to get what you want."

"So you arrived in this town…."

"And the first person I met was Beatrice." He laughed. "It all starts to look like fate, doesn't it? She was in my life-drawing class. First time I ever taught. And life-drawing, for God's sake! Can you imagine me teaching life drawing?"

"And yet, I bet you're going to tell me you did."

"I almost packed my bags right there. But Bea saved me. I walked in, and they were all set up at their easels. The model was on the dais. Joan. You've met Joan. And I could barely remember all that stuff from art school. All the drawing classes. The instructions, the rules. I hadn't paid any attention. So I just told them to begin."

And they did. And he had walked around, looking knowledgeable and important, without a word to say. And Bea stopped him and she said, What am I doing wrong? And she showed him her work. And it was terrible. It really was. But he couldn't, for the life of him, tell her how to fix it.

"Oh, I could sketch a bit of Leonardo for her, or a Picasso nude, or Michelangelo. But I couldn't tell her what to do."

So he said, just keep working. He'd come by again. And he made the rounds. There were maybe fifteen students, and some were very good. By the time he got back to Bea he had plenty he could show her. He gave her little fragments of sketches: lengthening the arm, setting the mass of the thigh, shading the musculature.

From then on Bea was his lucky charm. When the time came to choose an intern for that first summer—someone to do the work, all the cleaning and carrying—she was his first choice. "I wasn't sure what was going to happen. Tell you the truth, I wasn't sure what to do. I chose Joan because we needed a model with some sex appeal, and she was like a generator back then. And I chose Bea because I needed all the luck I could get."

Weland walked for a while in silence, letting the memory fill him like a glass.

"So, how did it go?" Harold finally asked.

"Oh, it was brilliant. I couldn't have done better. A little intense." He offered a rueful smile. "It was a very fertile time for me. But you certainly can't argue with the results. And who wants to lead an average life? Come on. This way. I want to show you something."

They were standing halfway down Brock Street, brick buildings rising around them in modest three- and four-story piles. "Look," he said, staring up at an office building, maybe eight stories high and framed by the lower rooftops. On it a sign was painted, chipped and peeling—*Grainger's Downtown Hardware. Paints. Supplies.*

"And I'm looking at what, exactly?"

"I'm going to tell you a secret I haven't told anyone."

"Why do I find that hard to believe?"

He linked his arm in Harold's and, drunk as they were, they stood gazing up. "I have always imagined my face right there. From the first moment I arrived in town, that's what I thought. I drove in along this street and I looked up. And I could imagine it right there looking out over everything. The whole town built around me."

"What a sweet story," Harold said drily.

But Weland was still gazing up at the sign. "Come on. Let me show you."

They went in the building's main door—heavy bronze and glass. Everything was old and solid. Not so much shabby as indifferent to the newness of things. There was an old-fashioned building directory—law firms, insurance companies, several design firms—but Weland didn't pause to consult. "After you."

The elevator took them all the way up, and they stepped out into a bare hallway: linoleum, plaster walls, and a few old desks piled together. At the end there was a narrow fire door.

Weland stepped out onto a gravel roof beneath the late afternoon sky. Overhead the *Grainger's Hardware* sign, too close to read, was dissolving into flecks of crumbling paint. The town looks its best from here. The early industrial patchwork of buildings, then the wide stretch of trees and houses, and the distant fields.

"Not bad, don't you think?"

"I'm not that big on heights," said Harold.

Weland laughed and clapped him on the shoulder. "Then you're going to love this part."

Reaching down he drew from beside the low brick parapet an old wooden painter's ladder, straddle-legged and tall. "Give me a hand here." Together they leaned it up against the high wall right in the middle of the sign.

"After you," says Weland.

"Absolutely not."

"It's perfectly safe. I do it all the time."

"Then I'll hold it for you."

With a smile Weland set his foot on the bottom rung and waited for Harold to get his grip. "Climbing a ladder is like fame," he said. "It takes some getting used to, but the view is terrific."

The ladder bowed under his weight, a gentle nod with every step, but Weland seemed unaware. He stopped near the middle of the sign, his face against the brick. And now Harold could see how nervous he was despite all the scotch.

"Everything okay up there?"

"Fine. All fine."

He steadied himself and with infinite care transferred his grip, shifting his feet until he turned to face the view, poised precisely in the center of the huge painted ad. "Just imagine," he called a little breathlessly. "My face as big as a house."

But before he could answer, Harold felt a shudder run through the bent spring of the ladder—a movement where no movement should be. And with a loud crack it began to tilt.

He threw his weight against it, but it was already on its way. Weland twisted frantically trying to get a better grip, not quite comprehending that the very thing he is striving to attach himself to was the thing going down. The town stretched out below them; the low brick parapet like the edge of the world.

"Jump!" cried Harold.

"Are you crazy?!"

But Weland's hand slipped. He twisted for a moment as if balancing on the air. Harold let go of the ladder and raised his arms, half catching, half fending off. And Weland landed on him with a terrible weight that buckled his legs and sent a white-hot pain shooting up through his ankle like an old friend.

When Harold opened his eyes Weland was sitting, rocking back and forth with his arms wrapped unbelievingly around his chest, and a wide, frantic smile on his face. "I'm okay, I'm okay. Do you believe it? I'm okay."

15.

Weland told him not to worry, the hospital wasn't far. Though when he learned it was an old injury, he lost any sense of urgency. He propped him up companionably, and they limped along. He, himself, was feeling better—not just better. Great. He took in deep lungfuls of air and looked around as if the whole wide patchwork of the town had never looked so good.

The emergency room doctor bound his ankle—just a sprain, she said. You'll want to stay off it for the next few days. But there were no cabs to speak of in a town this size, so they walked some more. And because every story returns to its beginning, they found themselves back at the Taft Hotel Bar.

The place was packed, but Weland appeared not to notice as he helped the limping man—a clergyman? Is he homeless? Is that Weland Tilyard? What could have happened?—to his booth in the corner. He ordered a double Macallan, a triple espresso, and the usual. "We'll have that twice," he said.

The waiter, a college girl in black pants and a high white apron, seemed genuinely pleased to see him. She wrote down the order, though her eyes, attuned to the drama, kept slipping back to Harold.

"Jessica, this is Childe Harold. The noted author. I'm sure you've heard of him. Mr. Harold just saved my life."

"What happened to keeping it all under our hat?" he asked as the girl walked away.

Weland leaned back with a smile. "Some things are too big to hide."

"I thought I was going over."
"You and me, both."
"I saw my life pass before my eyes."
"Your life is always passing before your eyes."

When the waitress arrived with the scotch Weland picked up his glass. "We're going to need two more of these, please. It's been an exciting day." And he smiled meditatively as she walked away. "You know this means we're linked now, you and I."

"Is that what it means?"

"You arrive in town, out of the blue. You save my life, wounding yourself in the process. I think it's destiny. This work we're doing. I think it's meant to be."

"I don't believe in destiny." Though that was probably a lie. He could still feel the ladder shifting, swinging inevitably toward the empty air.

"My life has been saved for a purpose," said Weland.

"Is that what you're going to tell everyone?"

"I won't have to. I think it'll become clear as we go."

And with the second round of Macallan there arrived two grilled salmon filets, and a salad of arugula, toasted walnuts, and candied cranberries, all so perfectly arranged on the plates the waitress paused as if half-expecting him to paint them.

Weland began to eat. "What happened to the ladder, do you think?"

Harold glanced up. "It's an old wooden ladder. I guess it cracked."

Weland nodded and swallowed. "You don't think it was sabotaged?"

"You were on the roof of an eight-story building climbing a wooden ladder to pretend to be a self-portrait. I don't think sabotage really comes into it."

"It's just that I've been noticing some things lately. Accidents. Little things. My basement flooded a few weeks ago. A window got smashed during that last windstorm. Things keep breaking around the house. Did you see that mess in the kitchen? The spilled coffee and salsa? Mindy's never done that before." He frowned as if noticing a funny taste in the salmon and regarded it more closely as if even this might be something. "I've never been unlucky before. It worries me."

"Maybe you just have a guilty conscience."

He tried another bite. It was fine. He drank some scotch. "I've always been lucky. But for a while now—really, ever since that fire at Jonathan's studio—I've begun to wonder about it."

"Tell me about the fire."

Weland shrugged. "There's nothing in a painter's studio that wouldn't love to burn. He left the space heater on. One of the rags caught fire. Everything went up."

"Just like that?"

Weland sat for a moment with an expression so serious Harold assumed the waitress was coming back. But then he lowered his voice, leaning forward over the table. "He'd been having some trouble at home. There'd been a lot of family drama."

"Drama?"

"There was an episode. The police were involved. It was nothing serious but it began to affect him. He was always a very private person. I think he felt a little exposed. He started drinking, missing classes. I think we all hoped no one would notice, but it just got worse."

The Provost suggested a sabbatical. Perhaps he might travel. What painter didn't want to go to Europe? So Jonathan had given up his classes. But he hadn't left. He worked unceasingly on the dozen or so paintings he had going at a time. Step by step, layer upon layer.

"I don't know how he could concentrate."

And in the end maybe he couldn't. The fire started at night. All his unfinished paintings, a number of older pieces, years and years of work—all of it destroyed. With no classes to teach, no studio to paint in, no comfort to be found, he had left. No one knew where. Weland called him repeatedly, but he never picked up. From time to time he would show up in town, for food and supplies, looking thin, stoop-shouldered, going to seed. Eventually Weland tracked him down: living up north near the thruway on an old Narrow Boat on the Barge Canal. Rainy, bleak. You have never seen anything so dismal.

Weland chewed his salmon. "Art is never easy. No one gives you a thing. And no one's really interested in all that you want to accomplish."

Harold considered the last of his scotch and then drained it. "I wondered when we'd get back to you."

"It's not just me. This is the world. It doesn't care if you succeed or not."

"You're going to tell me about your talent again, aren't you?"

"Talent is good. And hard work. Hard work's even better. But sometimes you just need to be a little tougher than the next person. A little more ruthless."

"A little more selfish?" suggested Harold.

"Why not? Selfishness has gotten a bad rap. If something doesn't happen for you, make it happen. If something comes your way, take it. No one's going to give it to you. I think that was always Jonathan's problem. He's a wonderful painter. But he's just not tough enough. This ridiculous episode, he should have just shaken it off. Put it out of his mind. You need to put your work first. People don't care. That's your job; you need to make them care. Nobody else is going to."

Harold sat back wearily. "So, it's every man for himself?"

"Of course it is. It's always been. Oh," he said scoffing, "people want it to be different. Can't we all just help each other? Can't we all be friends? Sure. Let's help each other. But first we help ourselves. It's like those oxygen masks on the airplanes. First you put on your own mask, and then you help the others. *Blue Spruce. The Wide Bed.* My work has brought something new and beautiful into this world. Something that wouldn't be here without me. Something people would miss. They would be less, their lives would be smaller, without it. I owe it to them, to the world, to be selfish. No matter how hard it is. Jonathan lost his way. I'm not going to. You call it selfishness. I think it might be the purest thing we can do."

Harold in Motion

16.

He always had trouble sleeping, and he hated lying awake. So he ended each day sitting in a bedside chair with a last glass of whiskey and a book. Poetry made him cry. Novels seemed empty—strangers doing things of no importance. So he clung to Father Ben's bible; this he could understand. All those stories without explanation—one tragedy after another and so little sense of why. From there it was a short passage into his dreams.

Tonight though he gradually became aware of a voice in the darkness, low and murmuring—without the grief and weeping of his dreams, but with the same determined quality. Slowly he raised his head and glanced at the spider crouching companionably in its shoebox. That was the thing about dreams; they could be anything. The trick, he thought, was not to be afraid. But the spider remained silent. After a moment the murmuring rose again. Impossible to know if it was real or not, though it was, he noticed, coming from his closet.

Whatever else was true, it was no good trying to hide from your dreams. So he stood up reluctantly and opened the door. He hadn't brought many clothes, so there had been little enough to unpack. But now he saw that he had underestimated the closet. Long and narrow, with plain plaster walls and empty hooks, it was less a cubbyhole than a narrow hallway ending in a long black curtain. He knew the rules of a dream. If there was a door, it had to open, if there was a curtain, you had to draw it back. So he did.

Another hallway running left and right, connecting all the dreams of all the closets of all the rooms. And directly in front of him by an open window, in the faint light of the world at night, stood Izzie wearing a knapsack and a look of pained embarrassment.

"What are you doing in my dream?" he asked.

She wore black from head to toe, but with her signature extravagance—something a young Cat Burglar might wear to the prom. Ruffled blouse, long ballet skirt falling below her knees. Black tights, black sneakers, and—he had to look twice in the dim light—a black cloche hat from a distant era, looking somehow both out of place and perfect for the occasion. Her cheeks were foundation pale, with an elaborate fantail of grey above each eye.

She was braced for escape, one foot on the windowsill, but at the question she turned and adjusted her aids. "You should be asleep," she said accusingly.

"You're in my closet."

"Your closet stops at the curtain. This is the chambermaid's hall." But she was beginning to regard him with something like approval—the ancient plaid bathrobe and the nightshirt from a bygone era—one outfit calling to the other.

"What are you doing?" he asked.

"I'm going out."

"That's a second-story window."

"I know."

"It's late. It's dark. All the good people are asleep."

With a scowl she gave up. Tucking in the too-plentiful skirts, she sat down on the window ledge and swung her legs out.

"Wait! This is bad," he said. "This is a bad idea."

"So?"

"Would you like some company?"

Her glance now seemed to weigh him in a whole new scale.

"Just let me go change," he said.

"It's nothing you can dress for."

"You did."

"I know what I'm doing."

"Well, I can't go like this." He was a study in frantic plaid.

"You need to be unprepared," she said.

"I can do that."

"You need to be quiet."

"I'll be quiet."

She was reaching up, turning down each ear, and he could almost see her slipping into deep water. Her pale hands moved in the dark. *Imagine how you want it to be. Pretend it's your life.*

What? Wait!

The night. Tell yourself how you want it to be.

Stop! I don't' understand. His hands were desperate. *We're just going to throw ourselves out the window?*

"Fire escape," she said, and jumped.

He had been alone for so long. Over the past year, when he had stepped out into the night, it was under a huge black sky with stars like shards of glass—the whole wide world empty and bleak. But now she led him through the night as if she were inventing it step by step. Every street lay bathed in lamplight, and he was caught by the vividness of each tree and house. Even Isabel burst into color. Passing beneath a streetlamp the black of her blouse warmed into burgundy, and the skirt turned a deep green before slipping back into shadow.

She seemed self-conscious at first, too aware of him beside her, as if she already regretted inviting him along. But he stayed silent, and like some exotic tour guide she began to point out the sights. *The Kinneys have a pool in their back yard. The Johnsons have a new car. The Macdonalds are getting a divorce.* Her hands swam like fish through the occasional lamplight.

He was aware of his own clumsiness—the long day starting to tell. His feet scuffed in the slippers, he felt outlandish in his bedclothes, but Izzie moved easily through the silence. Approaching the small downtown she led them along an alley—brick walls patched and stained beneath security lights, steel fire-doors locked tight. In the middle of the block there was a narrow wedge of darkness where she had long ago unscrewed the bulb. From her knapsack came a ring of keys, prickly as a hedgehog. The heavy door opened on oiled hinges. Inside, when the beeping started, she tickled the alarm pad until it stopped.

"Is this the moment when I ask where we are?" said Harold,

Her hands were at her ears, bringing the world back up to volume. "Madame Sophie's Textiles and Alterations."

"Who robs a fabric store?"

"It's okay," she said. "We're only visiting."

17.

They were in a crowded storeroom, but through an archway Harold could see high shelves overflowing with rivers of fabric and beyond them a line of wide windows. As Izzie started forward he whispered, "Wait! People can see."

"I'll show you."

Smoothing her skirt she bent low, moving through the shadows from shelf to shelf until she settled onto the floor behind the main counter.

"You've got to be kidding," he hissed.

"Don' be a scaredy-cat. I brought snacks."

By the time he reached her she had the knapsack open, and as he sank onto the floor she drew out an iPad and set it on her lap. Then reaching in again she brought out two cardboard crowns, festive and bedazzled with glitter.

"This is yours," she said, then drew out a pair of paper noisemakers, curled like ferns.

"I thought we were supposed to be quiet."

"Blow it softly."

It was enough like a dream that he did as he was told. The end unrolled with a little crinkling sound and a thin, plaintive squeak. She removed her cloche hat and adjusted her own party crown. Then she opened Facetime and dialed.

Almost before she was ready the screen filled with the pale thin face of a boy: dark hair, dark circles under his eyes. He wore plain blue pajamas like a cross between surgeons' scrubs and a prison uniform.

"You're not wearing your hat," she said accusingly.

"It's here. I've got it." Listlessly he held it up.

"Put it on. You have to put it on."

He did, dutifully stretching the thin elastic under his chin.

"Have you got your noisemaker?"

He held it up for her.

"Okay. Ready?" She glanced at Harold. "All together." They blew a thin plaintive sound. "That's better. Adam, this is Mr. Harold."

"Just Harold is fine."

"This is Adam. He's my best friend. Wait," she said. "I have music."

She touched the iPad, and a bouncy disco version of Happy Birthday rose on the silence. Harold watched her without a word. In the faint light her eye shadow showed blue—what would turn out to be Adam's favorite color—with matching lips and pale circles on her cheeks. Behind all that straining cheerfulness her eyes looked woeful and young.

"So, Adam," said Harold. "Are you away somewhere?"

"Adam's at school. They're very mean to him," said Izzie. "They give him drugs."

"It's not bad," said the boy. "But I have to keep my voice down, if that's okay. I'm supposed to be asleep." He smiled tiredly. "Are you at Euston's?"

"No. This is Madame Sophie's. See? We decorated." Hurriedly she handed Harold a short accordion of folded letters, and when she stretched it out, there it was. *Happy Birthday!!*

It just seemed to make Adam more tired. "That's great, Iz."

But her smile was determined. "Did you have a good day?"

"It was fine. Not too exciting here. And you?"

"Fine. Good. Did you get my package?"

"It's right here." He reached over and from under his pillow drew a great spilling pile of fabric. "It looks great."

"It's the Blue Bird of Happiness."

"I know. It's great."

The boy turned it over on his lap, and it seemed to glint in the lamplight, bright shades of blue and orange.

"Have you tried it on?"

"I haven't had a chance."

"You should try it on now. I made it specially for today."

"I'm a little tired now, Izzie. Is that all right? They adjusted my meds again."

"Okay. That's okay. You don't have to. Did you get the cupcake?"

"It's right here."

From off to the side he brought out a chocolate cupcake with a single thin candle. "I can't light it. They don't let me have matches."

"That's okay."

"I'll eat it tomorrow," he promised.

"Don't get frosting on the fabric."

"I'll be careful."

And it was clear he was done for the night. Hesitantly she drew out the final moment. "Good night, Adam."

"Good night, Izzie. Happy Birthday." And the screen went dark.

18.

She sat with the paper noisemaker in her hands, drawing out the end and letting it curl back.

"It's *your* birthday?" said Harold.

She shrugged.

"It was a nice party," he said. "I'm sure he enjoyed it. I think he was just a little tired."

"Do you think?"

"Definitely." And he hesitated. "You're not really thirty-five, are you?"

She gave him a weary glance, as if even this was slipping out of her control. "I'm fourteen".

And perhaps it was always obvious. The foundation and blush more mask than adornment. The elaborate eye shadow the oldest thing about her. But what he said was, "I never would have guessed. You seem a lot older."

"I know. Right? I've always tried to be."

She'd gotten her first job when she turned twelve—Euston's hardware store. Ashdown was not a big place, and pretty much everyone knew some part of her story. The poor deaf girl in the crazy family of painters. Mr. Euston hired her eight hours a week to sweep and tidy the shelves and to work the key machine, which fascinated her.

So when Madame Sophie came in because she had locked herself out again, Izzie made a key for her and another for herself. And that night, while Mama Joan was working in the upstairs studio and her mother was fast asleep, she let herself in. She had thirty seconds to bask in the glow of her accomplishment before the alarm went off and she fled. But the feeling of stepping through a door into the hushed anticipation of someone else's life had lodged in her heart.

Over the course of that year without Adam, Izzie had found work at six different shops, in addition to taking over her mother's old job as chambermaid at the Inn. Her range of skills was not great, but everyone knew about the fire and about Adam's breakdown and pretty much everything else. So they found her something to do at a range of shops sweeping, or tidying, or unpacking shipments of books or cookies or mints. And Izzie collected her keys and alarm codes. At night she would come and sit in the silence of one of the stores until it started to feel like a place where almost anything could happen.

"So what was that present you gave him?" asked Harold.

"Just something I made."

"It looked very nice."

She had started sewing years ago. She received a Barbie and Ken doll from her maternal grandmother. And though a life of painted nakedness had made Barbie's proportions unfathomable, she found something reassuring in the smooth and featureless Ken. She began making clothing for him, rudimentary at first but gradually more complex. And as Adam became interested, she shifted her attention. She started out working by hand, but one day in the fabric shop she watched a sewing class get underway and was mesmerized by the hammering efficiency of the machines. It was perfect for her. The complex mechanics required all her attention, and the fabric transformed itself as the rucked and buckled seams of her earliest attempts gave way to smoother and more graceful shapes.

They weren't ordinary clothes, because Adam wasn't an ordinary boy. She found an old Simplicity pattern for a jumpsuit, which he fell in love with—*I must have this*, he announced—and she set to work.

When her mother found out, she was delighted that her daughter had found her art form. But that was the whole point for Izzie. It wasn't art. She hated art. Art destroyed your life. This was just something pretty she was doing for love.

Adam's problem, she had decided early on, was that he was a sperm baby. This was after Mama Joan and Adam had moved in with them—Izzie and Adam were maybe three—and even though they were all one big family, Adam was getting concerned about where he had come from. So their mothers sat them down and explained. Seeing how happy Izzie's father had made Bea, Mama Joan had wanted a baby, as well. So she had gone to a special clinic and had been able to become a mommy without a daddy's help. It all made perfect sense to Izzie. Of course they would go to so much trouble to get someone as wonderful as Adam. Still, she worried how he would take it.

How he took it was this: As they grew older and the family fell apart—as her father moved out to the garage and Mama Joan moved into her parents' room—as Izzie began cooking and cleaning, increasingly aware that it was up to her to keep everything exactly as it had always been—Adam began to feel it as a kind of liberation. It wasn't that he had no father. He had a special father, a remarkable father, chosen from among all possibilities.

And even Izzie began to see it in a positive light. Because if she and Adam didn't have the same father, they were no longer really brother and sister. They were no longer—and this seemed like a new way of thinking about it—really related at all. If Adam decided he could be his own sort of boy, then she could be her own sort of girl. And they, who had been all but the same person since they were born, could keep loving each other without having to worry about anyone else.

Now she searched for a moment on the iPad, and held it up to Harold. The video began. It couldn't have been much more than a year ago, but there was Adam, unrecognizably bright-eyed and laughing, standing before a full length mirror. The camera panned here and there. It was a room at the Inn, the chambermaid's room. A narrow bed, overstuffed chairs, a little square table. But the rest of the space was filled with fabric—piled on furniture, spilling onto the floor. And in the middle of the room, like a mahogany altar, was an ancient sewing machine.

The camera dipped and settled as Izzie clipped it onto a tripod. Then she stepped into the frame. Gone was the makeup, the elaborate concealing costumes. She wore a t-shirt and shorts, with a tape measure draped on her shoulders and a tailor's pin cushion on her wrist. She held a complicated pile in her arms, but with a shake it fell out into a jumpsuit of silver and grey. The legs ended in flapping bell-bottoms, the fabric so gored and pleated it spilled from the knees like feathers of glass.

"You finished *Love at First Sight!*" said this new, delighted Adam.

"Do you like it?"

"Scrumptious."

He turned to the camera, lively and at ease. "Ladies and Gentlemen, you are in for a treat. We're here at the atelier of Miss Isabel Holliman, and we have her latest work. But be warned. It's like staring at the sun. Sometimes you just have to look away."

She frowned with pleasure. "Don't tear it. The seams aren't finished."

Without any further ceremony he began peeling down to his underpants until he stood, skinny and sleek, all ribs and smooth indifferent flanks. Izzie held out the jumpsuit—a complicated sack into which he had to climb. With a balancing hand on her shoulder he stepped in like a soul slipping into its body. Izzie was brusque and business-like, but as he straightened up, she drew the fabric carefully over his hips and smoothed it into place. "Left arm. Point your hand. Slowly now." The suit wrinkled and sagged as they eased it on.

Cautiously turning toward the mirror Adam stood hunched and awkward. "There was darkness over the deep," he intoned, "and all was chaos. And Izzie spoke. She said, let there be love!"

And he straightened up, raising his arms wide, pointing like the hands of a clock. And all the looseness of the fabric went taut, and all the fractured colors resolved into the outline of a heart on his chest, with an arrow running through it from hand to hand. And as Adam stood, delighted with the effect, Izzie frowned over the fabric, straightening the seams, smoothing out every wrinkle, as if not just the jumpsuit but Adam himself were a work in progress she could not bear to finish.

19.

The video ended, and Izzie gazed down at the blank screen. Then slowly she began gathering together the birthday supplies.

"You must miss him," said Harold gently.

"Sometimes."

"Why was he sent away?"

She frowned down at the collection of bright objects in her lap as if they contained some message she had inadvertently jumbled. "We had a club."

Actually they'd had many clubs, long before Izzie started going out at night, back when they were both still in deaf school before the teachers realized Adam was just pretending so they wouldn't have to be separated. They practiced sign language by making fun of all the kids who seemed to fit in so easily, but it was Adam's idea to form a club—just the two of them. So there was dance club, sandwich club, rubber band club, eraser club, macaroni club, and—in a new level of irony remarkable in an eight-year-old—Turkey club. Each lasted a week or two, the time it took for the humor to run down. But with Revenge Club Adam knew he had found his masterwork.

Their first client was Ricky Brill, whose mother was one of the custodians at the school and whose father was in jail. Ricky was small, red-headed, with a knack for drawing and a collection of colored pencils that he prized above all things. Russell Latimer, a twelve-year-old who had been making a life's work out of grades one through four, took advantage of an opportunity to demonstrate his strength by snatching up the pencils in their mylar case and breaking them in half with a karate chop. Izzie was furious. She would have punched Russell right there and then. But Adam—

thinner, lighter, more vindictive even then—preferred an indirect approach.

It was surprisingly easy. Russell's mother had put his address on the lock-screen of his phone, and it was a moment's work to find the house on Google Earth. Russell loved his bicycle—a red and shiny Specialized with toe-clips that, he claimed, gave him an extra five miles an hour. That was the first time Adam and Izzie slipped out after dark. Adam had insisted on the need for reconnaissance— he loved a complicated plan—but in the end it wasn't necessary. The boy had left his bike unlocked at the back door, and it took Adam only a moment to wheel it over to the family's huge Suburban and wedge it invisibly under the back wheels. When Mr. Latimer went off to work the next morning he didn't give it a glance.

The next morning news of the accident spread through the class. Ricky Brill looked worried, waiting for the repercussions, but Adam was delighted. He had found his calling. Like a crusader for justice, he would hear of some iniquity, some casual cruelty or unfairness, and he would create the fitting atonement. He put a broken pen on one boy's favorite shirt during gym glass, creating a stain the shape of South America over the breast pocket. He rubbed the toe of Billy Braeburn's spotless new Nikes against a rust patch in the corner of the locker, and googled Viagra on Asa Clement's school computer so that every site carried graphic promotions for sexual enhancement.

"You sound like Bonnie and Clyde," said Harold bleakly.

"It wasn't that bad."

"Actually, I think it was."

And maybe Izzie agreed. But revenge was something special for Adam. Something he thought he was suited for. Something that lifted him above the norm. And Izzie was pleased to be included. It was something they could both do—another way of being together. Until last fall, when everything fell apart, and even revenge only made things worse.

Harold grew very still. "What did you do?"

She glanced up, suddenly afraid she had said too much, that her loneliness had given her away. But he was lonely himself, she could tell that. His eyes were as bleak as anything she had seen.

"Do you believe?" she asked.

"In what?"

"In everything."

And he seemed to balance for a moment on the broken fulcrum of his heart. He thought of the spider bobbing up and down as he sang his daughter's favorite song, as if anything were possible. As if in a world so harsh and inexplicable, even a tiny, lost spirit might somehow find its way back.

"Yes," he said. "I'm afraid I do, yes."

"Will you come with me somewhere strange?"

But looking at the skirt, the blouse, the pale extravagant face, it seemed to him that he already had.

She turned down her ears and signed, *We've got to be silent.*
I understand.
You'll need to wear something special.

She drew from her knapsack a long strip of pale fabric folded into a band. She hesitated for a moment. *I made this for Adam. For when he got out.*

He held it doubtfully in his hands and brought it to his nose. It smelled faintly of smoke, and that seemed to speak to him as well. She waved him closer, and he leaned down to let her tie it snugly around his forehead. Then she wrapped her own strip of fabric like a band around her hat.

Stepping cautiously to the door, she scanned the empty street. Then with a kind of brisk formality she took his arm.

Are you ready?

And what could he possibly say?

Her eyes were closed. She was murmuring under her breath something long and complex. Then she reached for the knob, and together they stepped out into the night.

20.

The night was cool. He hadn't realized how stuffy the fabric store had become until they stepped out into the breeze and the moonlight fastened them into the crystalline strangeness of their surroundings.

Izzie clung to his arm like a bird to her branch. *Don't move too fast. It can be strange at first. How do you feel?*

Okay.

Different? It's a different world. Do you feel it?

He hesitated, not wanting to spoil whatever this was. *Maybe.*

Every spell is different. You have to be ready for little adjustments.

The air carried a drift of blossom sweetness, and she raised her nose as if to calibrate the effect.

Is it what you expected? he asked after a moment.

She frowned. *This isn't my first time.* But at the sight of him, patient and kind, her annoyance faded. *I don't know yet. It's probably better if we don't meet anyone. Reeve says you have to be careful about interfering with the flow of time.*

He waited helplessly. He wanted to ask What do you mean? but she was looking at him expectantly, as if waiting for something surprising to dawn on him. So he signed, *No, I suppose that's right. But maybe you're hungry. Maybe you need to eat something.*

I've never eaten when I'm travelling, she said. *I don't know what it would do to eat food from this time.*

He signed, *It's your birthday. I'll buy you a slice of pizza.*

As they drew closer to the campus, small knots of summer students seemed to settle out of the air, clustering like bees at the door of Asteroid Pizza. *Don't talk to them,* she signed. *Try not to touch them.*

Harold eased them into line, as Izzie cast a measuring glance around. The students all seemed lost in their own version of the night, and they paid no attention. A few wore bedroom slippers. One girl wore pajamas under a volley ball warm-up jacket

I think they can see us, said Izzie. *But I don't think it will matter. Try not to make eye contact.*

Sounds like good advice. Do you want to eat in?

But instead they walked up and down the streets, eating their slices and sipping from a bottle of Sprite.

So, what's different about this world? he asked.

I think the air is sweeter. It's a happier world. I feel it, don't you? It feels full of possibilities. It's a whole world of things that haven't happened yet.

What sort of things? he signed, but she was looking all around and didn't see.

They finished the pizza, but Izzie was reluctant to part with the paper plates. When they passed a trash can Harold lifted them from her hands and dropped them in. But she hesitated.

What's wrong?

I try to be careful about changing the past, in case it all just gets worse.

Do you think that's going to change anything? he asked.

I don't know. Maybe not.

So he reached in and retrieved the plates. Then, folding them, he pushed them into his pocket.

You'll stain your robe.

It won't be the worst thing that's ever happened to it. Where should we go?

She nodded, as if she'd been thinking exactly the same thing. *Come on. I'll show you when Henry was born.*

They left the college behind. The streets were wide and vacant. *How long have you been traveling like this?* he asked.

Since the fall.

Is it always like this?

It's different each time. Depending on when and where I'm trying to go.

And how do you know it's different?

It just feels different. You can tell. I go around to different places, and I think about how they're different. What they would have been like if things had gone differently. She glanced at him. *Does that seem crazy to you?*

Nothing seems crazy to me.

Reeve says I have real talent. She says I'll make a great witch some day.

Reeve?

She's my teacher. She's very smart. And a very powerful witch. I was really lucky she let me study with her.

He considered for a moment. *That is lucky.*

Izzie led them home. They came to a great bank of spruce trees shielding all but one corner of the high white house. The driveway opened like a cave. She grew hesitant.

We're going all the way back to when I was three. Back when my dad still lived with us. Before my mom was famous. That's my favorite time.

She seemed to be bracing herself. *It's important that you see it the right way. You have to focus yourself on the moment. We had been to a party at Wheedle's. Some friend of my mom's was in town.*

You remember that?

Henry helps me remember. Sometimes I tell her the story, sometimes she tells me.

Izzie started down the driveway, moving through this most

familiar of places as if everything was uncertain. As if even the darkness could be disturbed. They stood by the back door, and Izzie drew close. He saw her hands moving, but it was too dark to read. So she raised her lips beside his ear.

"My mom came home from the party. It was so dark. She walked toward the door, and Henry was calling from the bushes. Though she didn't know it was Henry then. A tiny little squeak. She said even I could've heard it. My mom was frightened. She thought it might be a skunk or a racoon. She thought it might be rabid. But my mom's friend looked in the bush and found Henry. So we brought her inside. She was so tiny. I held her. And we gave her food, and milk. And we became friends for life. And the next week Adam and Mama Joan moved in. And we all became one big family."

Her voice faded, as if that were the end of the story. But standing there in the silence Harold noticed the sharp tang of old smoke on the air. He touched her shoulder. "Is something burning?"

She fastened an insistent grip on his sleeve. "No. Not now. Don't pay attention to that. This is a long time before that. It hasn't happened yet."

But as he turned toward the scent of smoke she followed reluctantly into the deeper darkness until there arose a shape like a big empty box outlined in white. He could make out the burned walls, the sagging roof, weathered and rain-soaked through most of a year.

Izzie sagged at the sight, as if hoping even now it might have been different. "It's my dad's studio."

"Weland told me. What a terrible accident."

"Reeve says there are no accidents."

"Oh," said Harold. "I hope that's not true."

But Izzie just stared fiercely at the hollowed-out building, as if even now it might be possible to change it back to what it once was.

21.

From her earliest years Izzie had made a study of love. Observing it, stalking it, she mapped its every danger. From the start she knew there was nothing important about love that could be asked or answered. No one would tell you the truth about it. But her deafness had bred a kind of invisibility—people took her presence for granted—and unable to listen, she had watched. Her mother, her father, Mama Joan, Wheedle. Standing beyond the reach of explanations, she learned what people did, not what they said.

She followed her mother from her dad to Weland to Mama Joan; she watched what love did to her. That first appreciative glint in Weland's eye, in Mama Joan's, it lit her mother up with happiness. But slowly, slowly—no matter what she did—that glint gave way to something less. Annoyance, irritation, distraction. Nothing in the world could stop it from leaking away. Love was a contest of competing needs, an exercise in selfishness. Because, Izzie knew, that was the thing about love: no one was going to give it to you just because you asked.

Growing up she realized everyone, every adult she knew, had something more important they were doing—something that was taking the warmest part of their attention. Their art, their thoughts, themselves. And really, she told herself, it wasn't as though she cared. If at first it hurt her feelings, she came to realize this was just the way it worked. You had to be careful. You had to be quiet. Love was delicate and fragile and inexplicable. There were no questions you could offer. No argument to make. To ask for something was to lose it. It was better if you didn't breathe a word.

The first time Izzie ran away because of Weland she only got as far as the garage. She was six years old, Henry was three, and her family was breaking up. She wasn't exactly sure how it was happening, or why Wheedle was to blame, but she knew he was. Her father had just moved out to the apartment over the garage. It was a dreary place under a sloping roof, filled with old furniture no one wanted and smelling faintly of mildew. When this had been her grandfather's house the handyman had lived up here, but Izzie thought he must have been sad all the time.

Her father hadn't yet unpacked. He'd carried his clothes out in cardboard boxes, and now they stood on the floor, on chairs, on the bed, like a huge delivery no one had ordered. He cleared a place on the sofa for her and found a saucepan in a low cupboard. There was a sink under one window, a tiny refrigerator under another, and a hot plate on the counter. He made cocoa, and they sat together surveying the place.

"I don't like it," she said.

"Don't worry. I'll get it cleaned up."

"I don't see why you can't just stay in the house."

"This is like an extension of the house. It'll be just the same."

"I don't like that Wheedle is painting mom."

"I know."

"I don't like any of it."

"I know. But not everything is under our control."

And that was certainly true.

Izzie had grown up in a world that expected nakedness. That turned it into nothing at all. Painting naked people was just what artists did, and as a toddler she had simply taken it for granted. Her father painted her mother, her mother painted her and Adam, Mama Joan painted the three of them. And it all made a kind of sense.

But this was different. Her mother had started modeling for each of the Gang of Four, rushing like a traveling salesman, she used to say, from studio to studio. And she used to bring Izzie along for moral support.

This was her first real memory of Wheedle—because he was always there, too. She and her mother would arrive, both feeling awkward and shy. Her mother would joke and fret and braid Izzie's hair, or practice signing or lip-reading in those moments of waiting. And then Teddy or Drexall or Margery would start to paint, and Wheedle would stroll in as if it were his room and they were the ones visiting. He'd glance at the painting, then he'd walk around, looking at her mother from every angle and telling her how to pose.

That was what struck Izzie. He wouldn't talk to whoever was painting. Instead he would explain to her mother what she should be feeling, what the light should be doing, what the muscles in her arms and legs should be doing. And the painter—Teddy, say, or Margery, who had no real interest in women's bodies apart from the paint—seemed to hear in those instructions a kind of message, and they would adjust their work.

And once her mother understood that this is what was going on—a collaboration not between her and the painter but always between her and Wheedle—she relaxed and grew more confident. She began to arrive late. She would find the artist ruffled and impatient—as if inspiration were a bus they had to catch—and she would casually remove her clothes. And, glancing at the canvas to remember where they'd left off, she would take her position as if she were locking every-thing into place. As if she, at least, knew what she was doing.

But when she posed for Wheedle it was different. Never so easy. Never so relaxed. With Wheedle her mother seemed to struggle to find the proper posture. The whole session felt tensed with a kind of invisible effort, as if Wheedle and her mother were wrestling with each other without touching. And though Izzie would turn her ears up all the way, she still couldn't make out the murmured comments back and forth. But her mother somehow understood. Her pose would shift. She would soften into an attitude that seemed to hold something it hadn't before. And Izzie would feel strange and left out, because even though she had seen everything there was to see, the meaning was always just out of her reach.

And then fame descended on their family like an unending cocktail party. Weland was more and more in their lives, always smiling at the chaos that swirled around them. There would be whole parties of strangers—Wheedle loved strangers—crowding into their house, staring at some new painting of her mother as if they could own it just by gazing. And somewhere in this whole busy time, as her mother increasingly became the property of anyone who chose to look, her father moved out to the garage.

Izzie took to sitting in his studio while he worked. And when he made himself little snacks of apple and cheese or carrot sticks he would always make some for her, too. She would turn down her ears and read. And when she looked up, she would see him, standing at his easel, lost in thought.

And it became clear to her that everyone else had somehow adjusted without effort to the changing circumstances. She alone was left to struggle with the way things were. Until the night, years later, when her father was arrested for soliciting an undercover policeman in a park.

22.

It was Wheedle who brought the newspaper over at the end of last summer. He wanted to show her mother, but she was asleep, so he left it with her. "I'm sorry," he said. "But it's better that she knows."

He was always saying things like that. But he never looked sorry.

It took her a while to find the story; the paper covered the whole county, and none of it had anything to do with them. But she knew there must be something—she had seen the look on Wheedle's face—and finally she found it: a short paragraph in the densely set column of the police blotter. *Jonathan Holliman, professor of painting at Ashdown University, was arrested on misdemeanor charges of public lewdness Monday for allegedly fondling an undercover police officer in The Meadows section of Durand Eastman Park. He pleaded no contest and was released on payment of a $200 fine.*

She read it over and over. Then she tore out the article and stuffed the rest of the paper into the bottom of the kitchen garbage pale. For the rest of the week she refused to turn up her ears. Most of the people she ran into wore expressions of concern so obvious she wondered if they were trying to be mean.

Izzie spent weeks trying to imagine the scene in the park. She had googled The Meadows—a stretch of trees and grass so wild that when she imagined her father walking there, she always put him in hiking gear or pioneer clothes. She had just read a biography of Stanley and Livingstone, and all she could picture was her father, on his adventure of exploration, coming upon a policeman in the middle of nowhere. She wasn't at all sure what groping amounted to. It didn't sound like something her father would do. And all she could picture was the scene at the end of her book, the cool-voiced greeting after the long, long search. Doctor Livingstone I presume. And she pictured the two men hugging in relief at the rescue. Though even as she did, it was always the policeman who looked relieved. Even in her imagination her father always seemed kindly and a little distracted.

It was only when they had moved into the first days of autumn—and she could think about it without having to worry that everyone else was thinking about it, too—that she had knocked on the door of her father's apartment and showed him the story.

The small print—which had grown familiar and then strange again as she read it over and over—seemed to have nothing to do with either of them, and she half-hoped he would just laugh. But he recognized the article even before he had taken it from her hand.

She dreaded more than anything his embarrassment, a wincing expression of sheepishness creeping across his face. But he just nodded sadly and looked up at her. "I saw this." Then, handing it back, he had gone to his little hotplate to make cocoa. "What do you want me to tell you, pumpkin?"

And in that moment it seemed even more farfetched. Sitting on that musty sofa in that strange little room that had already become his home, the little scrap of newsprint seemed like just another part of what her life had become: true but utterly unreal.

"Was it an accident?" she asked, and blushed.

He gazed down into his cocoa. "You know that people can love all sorts of different people."

And of course that was true; she didn't doubt that. She had always known that Adam was his own kind of boy. She knew that; she wasn't silly. And she wouldn't want him any different. But not her father, surely. "You love mom," she blurted out, and immediately fell silent—worried that he would give up on her for being so childish.

"I do," he said. "Of course I do. And I love you."

"Aren't we enough for you?"

"Of course you are." But his smile only confirmed her sense that she was getting just a part of his attention. "You know that people are different."

"I know."

"It's a terrible thing to tell people they shouldn't love who they love. A terrible thing to have to hide that."

"I know."

"We mustn't let other people make us feel bad."

And she knew that was right.

But later, when everything had fallen apart, and Adam was gone and her father was gone, and she had Revenge Club all to herself, she began to play a game. If she could go back in time and change one thing, what would it be?

But that was the problem. There was so much. Her father, her mother, Adam. She would walk around at night and think, this thing, or that, imagining herself back in the moment just before. She wished her father hadn't gone to the park that night. She wished my mother hadn't started painting again. She wished that Adam wasn't so sad. But mostly she wished that none of them had ever even heard of Weland Tilyard.

"I left the hose running next to Wheedle's foundation last month. It flooded his basement."

Harold glanced over in surprise. "That wasn't very nice."

"I broke a window during the last rainstorm. Just smashed it with a hammer, and then put a heavy branch beside it."

"That was good thinking."

"I was the one who sent the announcement to the paper. About Child Harold Days."

"Why?"

"He's always coming up with these plans. He always makes a

big fuss and then just wants to forget it. I wanted to embarrass him."

Harold considered that for a moment. "I think it's working." And then, "I poured coffee on his granite counter, so he's going to have a stain the shape of Lake Ontario for the rest of his life."

"That sounds bad," she whispered.

"And I dribbled salsa on the tile floor. It doesn't hurt the tiles, but it ruins the grout. He's going to have to have the whole thing redone. And I changed the instructions on all his meals so they'll burn to a crisp."

She weighed all this for a moment. "One night I tried to bend the downspout on the corner of his house so the wind would pull it off. But it didn't do anything."

"Sometimes they can be stubborn. It depends how they're attached. You can't do it from the ground. You have to get up on a ladder and pry out the nails. But just a few. Then, it will bang against his house, and if the wind is right, it might just fall on his car."

"And then you could fix his ladder so when he climbed to the top it would break."

"Not to the top. We wouldn't want to overdo it. Maybe just the first or second rung. Or you could put sugar in his gas tank. It ruins his engine. Or you could use a screw driver to make a hole in his tire. That's probably better. But make sure you go in through the treads. It'll look like he drove over a nail. And you'll need a hammer to drive it in, because the rubber's so hard. But if you're going to do that, you might as well do two. So he can't use the spare."

She was staring at him wide-eyed. "Should you be saying that?"

"It's okay. I hate him, too. It's your birthday. You should make a wish."

And Izzie thought about the ladder and the gutter and the tires and the sugar in the gas tank. And finally she said, "I wish that we burned down Wheedle's house instead of my father's."

23.

She and Adam had been together for as long as either could remember. They loved each other if anyone did. And that was fine as long as there was only one kind of love in the world. But at some point as they grew older her feelings began to change, while Adam's stayed exactly the same. She thought of what her father had said: *It's a terrible thing to tell people they shouldn't love who they love.* So she just watched and waited, looking for any hint that Adam's interest had been caught by some other boy or girl. But the only admiring he did was of the models in magazine ads—stony-faced and thin, standing awkwardly in their elegant clothes as if they had just jumped from a great height and landed awry. Once she asked him if he liked the boys or the girls better, but he dismissed that airily as somehow missing the point.

But then at the end of last summer Mama Joan had sold her first piece of art. She'd only been painting a few years, and everyone agreed it wasn't very good, but her mother wandered around like someone in a daze. She had always been the painter and Mama Joan the model. But now she had lost her way. She decided to start painting again. She couldn't just leave it alone. She couldn't just leave *them* alone.

She settled on Adam and Eve. Maybe she was reaching back to some better time; maybe she just wanted to match Mama Joan nude for nude. What did it matter? There's never been anything good that art hasn't made worse.

Besides, Izzie certainly wasn't going to take her clothes off for art. There had clearly been too much of that already. But she did think it might be nice to pose with Adam. Maybe her mother would want them to hug. And she always painted so slowly they'd have to hold the position for hours. So she made herself an elaborate costume of fabric leaves that she thought turned out well. She offered to make one for him, but he settled instead on a bedsheet draped loosely around him because he liked the way it felt. And so they began to pose.

But it wasn't at all what she thought. Her mother was so tense and serious. And Adam seemed to absorb her mood. He stood like those models in the magazines, stiff and haughty. When Izzie tried to tease him he just frowned at her impatiently. It's art, he whispered. You shouldn't joke.

And what was worse, he had no interest in her clothes any more. Now that he was an artist's model he didn't want to wear her outfits. He no longer stood there laughing as she pinned and smoothed the fabric. And that made her angry as well. This was her Adam; it was what they had together. But now, every time her mother pored over him, trying to capture some stupid detail, he would stand without a smile, sober and serious And afterwards he would talk about what a great painter her mother was, and the feeling he was trying to express in his pose, and how difficult it was to capture just the right expression for her.

And her mother, too, became her own kind of strange. She brought out the old paintings of her and Adam, a pair of naked babies posing in spite of themselves. It was nothing Izzie really remembered, and it embarrassed her to see them. But then it got worse. In some back drawer her mother found her old overalls, faded and too snug. It was embarrassing; she was embarrassing. Izzie hated it. She wore a t-shirt underneath them but no bra, and you could practically see her breasts. But she didn't care. Painting is about seeing, she said. It's about love. And Adam listened intently to everything she said.

Izzie began to play hooky. She told her mother she was sick and crampy—the sudden start of her period was just one more outrage. And she thought that would break up the whole business.

After all, the painting wouldn't work without her. But her mother just told her to rest with a heating pad. She would just paint Adam until Izzie felt better.

She made a point of staying away. But she would sneak into the studio when they were done. And there was the painting, Adam and Eve still side by side. Her figure plump and awkward—the costume of silk leaves looking so much less pretty that she had imagined—while Adam, with every day, grew more slender and assured.

It was going to end badly. She knew it would, even if she didn't know how. And of course, it did—though in the end, at least, Adam came crying back to her. And for a moment it was all that she wanted. Her mother had done something. Something terrible. Of course she had. He was sobbing, humiliated—clinging to her. And Izzie was instantly furious. What happened? she demanded. What had she done?

Nothing. Oh, nothing.

"Did she hurt your feelings? Was she mean to you?" And Izzie held him, just like that. It was all she had ever wanted to do. Until he spoke.

"Oh, Izzie. Oh. I love her, Izzie. I love her. Oh, Bea. I love her so."

24.

They went to her father. There was no one else. Her mother had suddenly been transformed into a creature of awkward silences, and Mama Joan was absorbed in her work. So Izzie led the way out to the carriage house. Her father was leaning over a small canvas on its overlarge easel, as if it were some tiny creature in need of care. He turned as they came in and, after a moment's consideration, set down his brush. "And what do we have here?"

Izzie had never been so pleased with her father, smiling and gentle but with those pale sharp eyes that missed nothing—though Adam would later remember the jaunty tone and feel it was much less than he deserved. Izzie told her father all that had happened while Adam scowled down at the floor, his face burning.

"How awful for you," her father said. "But that's the thing about embarrassment. You think it will kill you, but it won't."

"I'm not embarrassed," said Adam hotly. "I love her. I love her!"

Izzie felt a little stab with each repetition, but her father was all kindness. "I know, son. We all love her."

"No! Not like that. Not like everybody." And he pressed his hand flat against the hard ridges of his breastbone. "In here! It's deep in here."

"I know it is. I know. But Izzie's mother is very upset about this. It was just a mistake. She's very sorry to have hurt your feelings."

"She didn't hurt my feelings," he cried. "I love her!"

And he was so fierce, so angry, so unrepentant, it was impossible not to believe him.

Her father remained nothing but gentle, and eventually Izzie led Adam away, hugging his narrow shoulders. But he wasn't a boy who could blame himself for long. Even Izzie knew that. And of course he couldn't blame Bea. So he kept returning with increasing fury to her father. So smiling and gentle. So superior. But he hadn't even been able to keep his wife. She'd grown tired of him. Of course she had. He was ridiculous. Stuck up. *He* was the embarrassment—cruising in some park. Fondling some policeman. He called him *son*. But he wasn't any kind of father to him. He had embarrassed them all. He'd embarrassed Bea.

And so began the last official meeting of Revenge Club.

Izzie had a key to the studio, of course. They let themselves in.

Adam raged in the darkness, stalking from one corner to another, envisioning all that they could do. Trash the studio, ruin the paintings, make a horrible mess of his life. He had brought a can of spray paint. They could spray terrible messages across the walls, and everyone would think it was some crazy person who had read the article and broken in. Or they could put a black X on each one. Or they could slash them! Ruin every single painting!

Izzie felt queasy at his rage. She knew he had to do something or he would make himself sick. So she suggested the fire.

Just a little one. They could damage the most recent painting. It wasn't far along. They could leave the space heater on and it would scorch the painting, ruin it, she told him. But it would look like an accident. No one would know it was them. Adam loved the idea.

They turned the heater on high, but it did nothing. The cord was too short to bring it close enough. So Izzie draped a rag over it, and in a second it burst into flames. She jumped back, appalled, but it was nothing. The rag was soaked in turpentine—it burned itself out in a moment.

So Adam took out a cigarette lighter. He'd take care of this! He stepped over to the easel draped in its cloth. But all he could do was shout. The very thought of it frightened him. Cursing and crying, he gripped the lighter, but he was falling to pieces. Winding himself into a fury. So it was left to Izzie, who feared for his heart, who loved him more than she could show, to take the lighter from his hand. In the end life is nothing but choices, and she chose Adam.

The cloth caught at once. Before she could blink the whole easel was a torch licking its way toward the ceiling. And with that—with the sudden terrible understanding of all that was about to happen—they could only run away.

It was almost an afterthought later that night when Adam took a handful of aspirin—the only pills he could find in the house.

So Adam went away, and her father went away, and Izzie moved into the Inn. Young as she was, it was the farthest she could go.

But alongside all that terrible regret there was something else, as well—a single bright thought. Adam had always been her particular kind of boy. And she knew that, she had settled for that. But now there was something new. For if Adam was able to love her mother, then he could love her, as well.

Harold as a Kind of Choice

25.

Sometimes it caught Bea by surprise, so many years now after the fact. It seemed impossible that she had ever been so innocent. Or that she had ever felt so much. Nowadays, walking to work through the darkness or alone in the house, it would come to her all at once like a struck match—that long ago drive. That summer.

The endless miles unfolding like a shared vision until they found themselves, a pair of castaways, washed up on an empty shore. And into that widening awareness of all that might be true, the evening unfolded. Lamplight on the walls of the room, the fire banked and burning. The figures dressed like something out of the Gilded Age. And all of it Weland's idea, of course. To snap them out of their boring ways. To coax them toward a glimpse of something great. From the beginning that had always been his gift. However awful he might be, however heartless or indifferent, sometimes he could drown you in wonder.

Jonathan was uncomplaining, of course, but Teddy, Drexall, and Margery hadn't done life-drawing in twenty years and they sketched with an air of aggrievement. Weland, who had seemed old in the classroom, was a youngster here, sprightly and cajoling.

"I think," he said, "we need some added interest."

He set down his charcoal and carefully wiped his hands on a rag. Then he stepped into the bubble of light beside the naked woman. She glanced up. "Don't move," he said. "We're just adding a figure."

The sudden juxtaposition was disconcerting—the lounging elegance of the tuxedo beside all that skin. He turned to the circle of faces. "Buttoned?" he asked. "Unbuttoned? Jacket off?"

Margery was the first to recover. "Off, I think."

Weland removed his jacket and draped it over the arm of a

chair.

And perhaps thinking to put him on the spot, to get even for all this drudgery, Drexall said, "More, I think. Or do I mean less?" And glancing at the others, "Lose the shirt, do you think?"

"Keep the shirt," said Teddy, short, plump. He pursed his lips. "But lose the pants."

But Weland was unruffled. With a cool smile he unbuckled, unzipped, and stepped out of the pants, draping them over his jacket on the sofa. "And the shirt? Buttoned? Unbuttoned?" But he wasn't waiting for them. He loosened his tie, undid the shirt. His chest was smooth. He wore pale blue boxers.

"Touching?" he asked.

"No. But look at her. Sideways glance. You had plans, but she's lost interest. Joan? Look away. Something else has caught your eye. Pretend you're not naked."

"Ah, Teddy," murmured Weland. "You should have been a writer."

They leaned over their sketchpads with a *scritch, scritch* of charcoal. Bea stood there watching—intensely aware of Ash aware of her. Their fingers reached out and brushed.

The movement caught Weland's eye. "Miss Anderson, right?"

"Yes."

He nodded at the empty easel. "Take a pew."

A moment's hesitation, her heart pounding, then she hurried over and turned the sketch pad to a fresh page. But she had no idea where to begin.

"It's awfully pedestrian," Drexall was saying. "A little too Motel Six."

And Margery with a thoughtful air, "I wonder if we need the boxers, Weland?"

Without a word he bent and skinned them down, taking an ostentatious moment to lay them neatly aside. He was slim and muscled, though running a little to softness around the waist. His heavy penis hung negligently amid its copse of hair. He turned to smile at the naked woman. "Lovely weather we're having."

And that was Weland, as well. She had to give him that. He never asked you to do something he wouldn't do himself.

So when he asked Ash to pose, what was there to do?

"Buttoned or unbuttoned?" Margery asked.

"I think we'll leave that to Miss Anderson."

Weland dressed, Joan slipped on a robe, and Ash stepped into the lamplight: t-shirt, shorts, wide-eyed from the road. It was only later she learned how terrified he was. In that first moment she was too anxious to notice.

She started to draw, but it was terrible. She tried to erase, but of course it just smudged. Impatiently she turned the page. Every five minutes, at a word from Weland, Ash changed position, but it didn't help. It was like falling down a well.

"That's enough."

Weland stepped up beside her—like class but worse—and started leafing through the pages.

"That's nothing. That's nothing. That…." He traced a long finger over the paper. "That's not right. The weight's all wrong. And that's just boring." He turned to her. "Why bother sketching if you care so little about him?"

She couldn't feel the withering in the boy's chest, but her face burned.

Weland leaned close, dropped his voice to a whisper. "What is it you want from this model? What's the focus of your exploration?"

She swallowed. "I don't know."

He turned to Ash. "Are you prepared to help us with this?"

And now she could see he was nothing but one entire pounding heart. "I don't know what to do," he said.

"Then you've come to the right place. Because we do."

And she heard that we and she wanted nothing more in her life

                                    D. K. Smith

than to be part of that. Weland turned back, "What are you doing here this summer?"

"I want to learn."

"What do you want to learn?"

And she was suddenly breathless at the truth of it: "Everything."

26.

"Do you know what the main ingredient is? In art? In any art?" Weland demanded. "It's love. All that wild energy stored up between two points. That moment just before it sparks. That's it. That's all of it right there. And it's our job to find that spark. To breathe it into life. Everything great in a work of art is there in the moment before you begin. If it's not, it never will be." He stands at her shoulder and together they consider Ash. "What do you want him to do?"

"I… I'm not sure."

Weland frowns impatiently. "You're here to learn? Here's the first lesson. A painter should never be too comfortable. How can the inspiration find its way if you're too closed off?" And abruptly he began to unbutton her flannel shirt.

How could that be real? Who would do such a thing? Perhaps she's made this part up. But it's how she remembers it. There was a kind of frowning impatience about him that quieted her. A disinterested attention. And on some level she was simply relieved not to be sketching.

He drew off her shirt, tossed it aside. Under the overalls she still wore the t-shirt. The room was cold. "Do you have something under that?"

"A bra."

"Take it off."

A moment's hesitation, then she reached down and untucked the shirt, started to pull it up.

"No. Just the bra."

She stood uncertainly. Then crooking her arms behind, she reached up under the t-shirt and unclasped the bra. She drew her arms into the sleeves, straining against the fabric, working beneath the bib of the overalls, slipping one shoulder free then the next. It was with a kind of triumph that she drew out the crumpled bra and held it out.

"I'm not going to wear it," he said, and she dropped it blushing.

But now the t-shirt hung on her, stretched out and thin. She was conscious of the fabric rough against her cold nipples.

"Good," said Weland. "How do you feel?"

Her smile was tense. "Lighter."

He turned to Ash. "She can't see you. How can she fall in love with you if you're all covered up?"

The boy stood very still. His stomach roiled. Everyone's eyes were on him. And to their number now was added Bea, breasts heavy against the thin fabric, a look of pleading on her face. *How can she fall in love with you if she can't see you?*

"Would you take off your shirt for me?" said Bea.

"Don't ask," said Weland. "Tell him."

But he was already drawing it over his head. She could see his skin shrinking against the cold.

"Left leg forward, please. Shoulder back. Arm up. Not so much. Good," she said. "Hold it."

She began to sketch, and even Ash, who knew nothing, could see the strokes of the charcoal were looser, more confident. But under Weland's gaze it didn't last. After the first start, she grew hesitant, self-conscious. Ash could see he was somehow letting her down.

"What is it? What's wrong?" he whispered.

"Nothing."

"What am I doing?"

"Nothing."

But she was leaving every drawing too early, yanking back each sheet with a jerk.

Weland bent to her ear. "How can he love you if you're hiding from him?"

Her throat tightened, but there was no room for hesitation. She set the charcoal down and reached up to the right strap of the overalls. She left a graphite smudge on the t-shirt as she unbuckled and let it fall.

She was reaching for the other when Weland stopped her. "Just the one," he whispered. "Find the spark."

The overalls sagged, half-open, hanging on her hips. The t-shirt clung like a tissue to her skin.

Weland turned to the boy. "Modesty is the death of art. Take them off."

There was nothing else to do. Unbuckling his shorts he let them fall.

"Underwear, too."

Bea watched him. She could almost feel the cold air and embarrassment tighten his flesh. His eyes were on her. Could she, couldn't she? Another moment. Reaching down under the overalls she skinned the t-shirt up over her head. The cold air was just part of the shock. She felt the weight of her unconfined breasts like something brand new.

"What do you want me to do?" he whispered.

"You watch me, and I'll watch you."

27.

The bedrooms were all spoken for, so they put him in the tool shed with a sleeping bag and a box of matches. Bea was alert to every movement as she crept through the darkened cabin and out. The sound of the shed door was like the scrape of a boat against the rocks. The darkness was perfect. With a click and slither of straps she shed the overalls and slipped inside the sleeping bag, hands and feet like ice.

"Are you happy to see me?" she whispered.

"I can't see you."

"Are you happy to feel me?"

She was encased from neck to ankles in thermal underwear, nubbly and snug. But in the darkness there was a kind of shared vision: remembered firelight, the memory of nakedness like a taut wire between them. They whispered though there was no need.

"Did you see the drawings?"

"I saw them."

"It's like the charcoal was alive in my hand."

He, too, was dressed against the cold, but her fingers found their way over him as if drawing him again. "This little bit of shading here. I'd never noticed it before. Stretching down like a shadow at sunset. And the way the muscle here, the *latissimus dorsi*, widened like a river into the side of your ribs." His face was close, the warmth of his breath. Her lips pressed lightly against his throat, the corner of his mouth.

And she lowered her voice even more. "We can't do anything. Not now. Is that okay?"

"What?" He was almost drunk with it all. "What do you mean?"

She hesitated.

"Just not now," she said. "I had a sort of a nervous breakdown in high school."

And in a way it was true. She'd had a series of increasingly intimate friendships with girls growing up and into high school—intense and emotional, but unsurprising. Then junior year had brought something new in the form of Mr. Devins, the art club adviser, and it was nothing she was prepared for. He told her he admired her painting; he admired her passion and feeling. But what she needed, he said, was experience. When he ended it, everything, even her art, turned pallid and uncompelling. She tried repeatedly to recapture that sense, to transform experience into art. She went to extremes. But she couldn't hold onto it. Every boy was less than he seemed, and the feeling seemed to flow out of her, leaving her weaker and weaker each time. Until now. Weland's instructions made a new kind of sense to her—the charcoal in her hand, the desire building and building, just short of a spark. It was something brand new.

"Is it all right if we go slow?" she whispered.

And Ash, who had never in his life gone anything but slow, could only nod.

"You can touch me."

He tried to slip his hand under the taut hem of her shirt, but the fabric was too tight.

"Can we take this off?"

"Don't do anything," she whispered. "Just look."

She hunched up on her elbow, helping him drag the shirt up. She felt her breasts escape, slipping lushly into the unencumbered cold.

He strained for the sight of her. Then he remembered the matches. The first one broke. The second flared and settled, licking and painting her skin.

But with the light Bea grew uncertain, as if even this might be too much. When the match burned out she took his hand before he could reach for another and pressed it against her breast. "Do you remember the electricity?"

She lifted his hand away—"Wait," he whispered—but it was only to lead him down the slope of her belly until he was snugly pressed between her thighs, the nubbly fabric growing warm and humid beneath his hand.

"Do you feel it?" she whispers. "Do you feel it building? I'm going to paint like this for the rest of my life."

She woke in her bed in the wash of early light. Seeing the mist on the water, the morning light in the trees, she had never felt more like a painter. But early as it was, Ash was awake before her. There was a boat resting, snugged against the cleats of the dock. He had found a rag and a bait bucket beneath the bow and he was washing it, wiping down the old aluminum, preparing it for the day. And it felt like a perfect moment, the two of them on the verge of everything.

"I've got the boat all ready," Ash was saying. "And I noticed those steps could use a little repair. I'd be happy to take care of that."

But as if she'd been waiting for just that moment Margery said, "Your aunt will be wondering where you've gone."

He fought to hold onto his smile. "I'm sure she wouldn't mind. I could stay, for a little while. I could cook. I could drive the boat."

"There's no need. We'll take you over on our way."

And Bea could see the shock on the boy's face, the dawning realization that the whole crucial summer ahead—the firelight, the sketching, all of it more real than anything he had ever felt—would be taking place without him.

She felt a pang. But the truth was, when she watched Ash leave, ferried across to his car and away, she wasn't really sorry. Not then. There was a part of her that was pleased. She was alive to the rush of discovery—the charcoal coming to life in her hand—and even then she knew that every discovery came with a price.

Besides, this was *her* adventure after all. It was *her* life that was starting. And so, indeed, it did. Though now all she felt was regret.

28.

Bea and Jonathan married two months before Isabel was born. It was a mixed blessing. At nineteen, in the first throes of what she took for real life, she was determined to be independent; to get back on her feet again. She wanted to put that whole first summer behind her. And she didn't want a man marrying her just because he had to. Her emotions were all over the place in the last months of pregnancy—lonely, sad, elevated, triumphant. It was the hormones, she knew. But she was determined not to be merely a creature of her body, a victim of circumstance. That was something, at least, she tried to learn from her mother. A marathoner and a tri-athlete, she had shaken off Bea's father like a weight from her ankle. *Make yourself into something you'll be proud of,* she said. Though this was probably not what she had meant.

But Jonathan was kind and even-tempered and gentle; and of course he was a wonderful painter. She was learning so much. It was like the opposite of her old life—with all its impulsive hurrying, its wild choices and mistakes—to sit for hours in his studio as he painted an arrangement of bowls or teacups and crockery, all in shades of white and cream. Resting in the quiet of the afternoon, feeling larger and heavier than she ever could have imagined, she marveled at the peace of it all. And, really, the house was too large for one person. He deserved a family. It would be a way to re-set the balance of things, not just for her, but for all of them. To live among all that quiet concentration, bringing her ripeness and promise to it all.

And so they married on the steps of the Civil War Monument on the town green, beneath the image of an angel in black stone that was probably drooping in sorrow over the loss of so much life, but which seemed to her—with the spring sun unexpectedly warm through the trees and the whole town looking like the college brochure that had first lured her from Indianapolis to this tiny emblem of artistic retreat—to be sheltering them both beneath those perfect wings.

And, to be fair, the next few years were the happiest of her life. Isabel was born, beautiful and cheerful and ready to be pleased. And if the deafness was a shock—a whispered premonition that Bea had made just one mistake too many—Jonathan's calm acceptance of it all had made things right. The testing, the sign language, the endless drawing out of words, he made it just another part of life together, as if they were, all of them, a little cluster of his perfect teacups.

It was like giving birth to her own life. Just like that, she was included in the art community. Theirs was the departmental party house since the days of Jonathan's parents, and Bea took on with surprising ease the role of hostess, carrying little Izzie on her hip as a kind of badge of her new substance and authority. Refilling wine glasses, setting out *hors d'oeuvres,* joining conversations with the older, established figures, accepting the glances and smiles with the pride of marriage and motherhood and the confidence of youth among the middle-aged.

She began to set the alarm each morning in time to make breakfast for her family. She didn't need to. Jonathan ate fruit and yoghurt, and Izzie would have been pleased with oatmeal every day. But Bea, amazed by this new organism of which she was the heart, created elaborate feasts for the three of them—eggs and French toast and pancakes, fresh bread. Breakfast became the anchor of each day.

And after a few years she felt so much like the solid, stable center of it all, that she had been able to suggest to Jonathan they invite Joan and Adam to come and live with them. Adam was three, the same age as Izzie, and the house was so big. Joan was living in a tiny apartment, without light or quiet, and she wanted Bea to teach her to paint. It would be an artist's commune. She would extend this bounty of food and love to them. She would teach her what she knew, and they would be painters together—an extended family. And Jonathan, of course, said yes.

But then came *The Wide Bed*, and there was no time for an anchor. And then there was no need. It all fell apart. Acrimony. Divorce. All the years of upheaval. But even then there was something enduringly true about that earliest sense of their family. So that even after she divorced Jonathan and—turning her back yet again on men—married Joan, the family continued in a new version of itself.

Jonathan moved out to the carriage house, so that Izzie and her father could stay close and so that, as the years passed and everything tumbled around her and that whole early sense of her strong and authoritative self became, in retrospect, unimaginable and foolish, Jonathan was still there, reminding her of what she had almost been. Until, as if to make the point that even Jonathan could not hold together everything Bea seemed determined to ruin, the studio had burned to the ground and Jonathan had finally left.

She made a point of never asking Weland what he thought of it all—back when Jonathan first moved out and Joan moved in. She hadn't wanted to know. But one evening he had smiled sadly and nodded and said he completely understood. And it was clear, once again, that he took the whole awful reorganization as just another homage to his own force of personality.

But say what you will about Weland. He gave you what you asked for. Or worse, he gave you what he knew you wanted.

29.

In the years after *The Wide Bed* sleep became her chief reward. Early to bed, dozing late, she simply could not get enough. While Joan, who had nothing but energy, woke up early and worked all day in her studio, painting until seven or eight at night.

Bea had thought there could be a kind of love that was cool and undemanding. She was done with being overshadowed. She was done with being undone. They would be there for each other; they would care for each other; they would support each other in their work. What was that if not a kind of love? But then Joan discovered painting, and it was as if the god of ego had tracked Bea down again, and she was reduced once more to a looker-on.

Joan wasn't a good painter, but that didn't matter. She only painted nudes, and for the longest time she had only painted Bea. To paint and be painted was as near to love as made no difference. Reclining naked in an easy chair, one leg crooked up over the arm, her head leaning back, Joan painting—it was like a return to her best self. That was the magical thing about Joan: she could see that charge of eroticism that Bea herself couldn't always find. And it was a pleasure to see all that Joan was seeing.

Long days in Joan's studio became the erotic center of their lives. She would give Bea instructions: move the hand, shift your weight, tilt your head. But after a while she didn't even have to explain—Bea could read what she needed in the way Joan turned or leaned or frowned. And all she had to say was cooler, or hotter. Show me disdain, desire, disappointment.

Bea learned to give her what she needed. And afterwards, when Bea herself needed something more, Joan would hover over her, naked and murmuring, shadowing her body with her fingertips or the light sable touch of a paintbrush or her tongue, drawing out sensations like a conductor coaxing from an orchestra all that she herself could feel.

But then Joan's attention shifted and she began to paint herself.
Don't you want me anymore? Bea had asked.
But really, what was there to say? *This is art, babe. It's not love.*
When of course, by that time, there was no telling them apart.

Joan began lifting weights; sculpting her body and then painting it. She started shaving again, as if even the shadow of body hair interfered with her vision. She would stand or squat or bend in front of a full length mirror, twisting around to see the shapes imposed on her muscles and flesh. Her paintings grew larger, her focus smaller and smaller. Her breasts, the slope of her belly, the parted lips of her vulva like a Georgia O'Keefe without the floral deniability. She moved beyond flesh and blood. Her surface grew shiny and smooth as plastic. And she began to find an audience. Lesbian art collectors who saw strength and allure in the deliberate renunciation of warmth; internet billionaires who liked the way the body took on a technological gleam.

And all the while Bea was in slow retreat. She had nothing to compare to Joan's endless confidence. She tried one last time in the fall—tried to recapture what she had once felt—and it was a disaster. And then, as if in keeping with her deepest fears, her eyes began to go.

On the scale of terrible things, it wasn't so bad. When the cataracts got bad enough she could have the surgery—insurance would pay for it then. And really, it seemed somehow fitting. What did she need her eyes for? She had already wasted all her chances. So she bought a wind-up timer shaped like an apple and she parsed her day into half-hour units—breakfast, exercise, shopping, cooking. She waited for each ding of the bell, and at the end of the day she could sleep.

She began listening for the sounds of Joan quitting for the day—the scrape of her chair, the particular pattern of footsteps that carried her on a last circuit of the studio. Then Bea would hurry to get ready for bed, and the two of them would pass in the hallway outside the bathroom, Joan headed down to dinner, Bea heading to the respite of sleep. "We're sure on different schedules," Joan had once said, and Bea had shrugged and smiled. Though after she took the bakery job, she didn't even have to do that.

Now she was living her life in reverse. She woke up in the evening and ate breakfast. She worked through the darkness, slept through the day—or tried to. But sitting in the kitchen, waiting to grow tired enough for bed, even sleep had turned against her.

A painter was all she had ever wanted to be. But she had somehow mistaken desire for ability. Over the years her expectations retreated: early fame, eventual fame, some limited critical acclaim. She clung to a sense of unappreciated excellence. *So-and-so was good, of course, but her line was shaky. She was trite where Bea would have been singingly original.* With every year she had to work harder to see herself as still full of potential—someone merely undiscovered.

But with the disintegration of her family, she stood revealed. She would never be what she had hoped, what she had counted on. And it startled her to see it so clearly. It wasn't that her time might never come; it had never even been likely.

For so long she had been terrified of giving up painting—if she wasn't a painter, what was she? Well. Now she knew. She was an artist of insomnia.

She would drift off like the tail-end of an idea and wake to find herself sitting in a chair or lying on the sofa with the feather duster in her hand and her cleaning supplies arranged on the table. It was like a series of spells she would fall under. She never fainted or felt light-headed. It was more gentle than passing out. More like a sudden, engulfing resolve to sleep. When she woke she rose seamlessly into the ongoing, indifferent day.

At first she was embarrassed. But her family accepted it with surprising calm. She would open her eyes to find them busy and unconcerned or gone away about their business. And if at first she would apologize and hurry to catch up with her tasks, gradually a little thread of anger strengthened her resolve, and she would simply wake and check her watch, and join in whatever was happening around her.

Today it was a knocking on the door.

11:30. The windows bright with day. The sound was so hesitant she thought it might be the old Izzie, sweet and uncertain, come back to check on her. But she opened the door on a blur of black suit and beard, the stance of a nervous deer.

"Is it too early or too late?" he said.

"Late for what?"

"Weland said something about a meeting. Apparently we're on a search for beauty, and I'm his eyes and ears. Of course, I might have gotten the time wrong. I've been a little distracted lately."

She found herself smiling. "I don't think it's today."

"He seemed pretty definite. He made me promise."

"Weland's promises are the most appealing things about him. Come in. I'm just about to make dinner."

And oddly enough, it was true. The sudden appearance of an audience pushed her gently into action. "Would you like coffee? Or there's wine."

He set the shoebox on the table. "Which are you having?"

"Wine it is. Would you mind getting it? I was just in the middle of cleaning up."

She turned to the crowded sink. It never bothered Joan to see the place a wreck, but Bea could only hold out for so long.

As if reading her mind he said, "Where's your wife?"

"She left this morning. She has a show in San Francisco. We loaded up the rental van, and she's on her way."

"Driving to California? Alone?"

"Far as I know."

And he shook his head. "Where does she get the energy?"

And that comforted her as well.

"Why don't I do those?" he said. "You're making dinner."

"You don't have to."

He slipped off his jacket and rolled up his sleeves. "Idle hands are the devil's playthings."

"Joan thinks it's bourgeois to sweep or clean. She thinks her energy should only be spent making art."

Harold soaped and rinsed a plate. "And what do we think about that?"

Bea shrugged. "You can't live in a pig stye." And as he started to set the plate in the drying rack, "You have to rinse them again. I usually just run them under the faucet one last time and then stack them front to back."

Silently she cursed herself, but Harold seemed not to mind. He rinsed the plate and set it to dry. "Are you limping?" she asked

"Just a little accident. Weland fell on me."

"I hadn't realized we had so much in common."

He smiled. "Tell me about *The Wide Bed*."

"You're not really going to do this for Weland?"

"I seem to have a little time on my hands. And I was beginning to wonder what it would be like to be filled with light."

"You can't believe everything Weland says."

"So why don't you tell me about it. Give me someone else's perspective."

And why would she want to? Rake through all that again. When she'd finally put it behind her. But there was something about him—so dragged down by life. So obviously at the end of his rope.

And, really. It was a comfort to talk to someone who looked as broken as she felt.

"*The Wide Bed* is like Weland," she said. "It's the worst thing that ever happened to me, disguised as the best."

Harold and *The Wide Bed*

30.

Weland brought the book to the Gang of Four. He passed it around—he'd bought copies for everyone—and told them all to paint what they felt. He even gave Bea a copy. When Weland was looking for inspiration, he didn't discount anyone.

The book made her impatient.

"You didn't like it?" Harold asked.

"I just didn't believe it."

She painted Joan, and it was terrible. No voluptuousness, no sense of languor or ease. She just couldn't get a handle on it. But that was all right. None of them could. They all brought in their work and hung it along the wall in the big studio, and Weland wandered around, searching for a hit among all the obvious misses.

"A book is a book," Drexel complained. "And a painting is a painting. Let's just do nudes, then, if that's what you want."

But that wasn't it. Weland had a vision—or at least the makings of a vision. He just needed the details. "This book is the answer. We just haven't found the right question. Change partners everyone. New models, new scenes. Get drunk or stoned or sleep-deprived or laid. Do whatever you have to, but give me something new."

That night at dinner Jonathan asked, "What do you think of the book?"

"Honestly?" They had begun drinking wine with dinner, though Jonathan never had more than a glass. "I think it's ridiculous. Two people so in love they can't think of anything else. They do nothing but talk, and eat, and have sex. Then they break up."

"You don't think it's erotic?" he asked.

She flushed. "Of course it's erotic. It's supposed to be erotic. It's porn. What do you think of it?"

"I don't know. You're probably right." But he said it with a wistfulness that, like the drinking, was something new in him. "I'm beginning to agree with Weland. I think there's something there. Do you think you could be that woman?"

She felt herself blushing. "I'm nothing like her. I think that's obvious. And I'm not going to suddenly turn myself into a model."

"Just for me. Just to help me get at whatever this is."

And after all he had done for her, what could she possibly say?

"Just promise me you won't make me look foolish."

Because there *was* something in it—she knew. She could feel it. But nothing for her. She had already experienced her share of love, and it was nothing like this. And yet. The wistfulness in her husband's voice made her wonder. If she could help him paint his way to whatever it was he thought he saw—some new feeling; some new idea—maybe he could show her what he'd found.

Jonathan was tall and thin, a pair of shoulders from which to hang a baggy shirt, and a narrow waist cinched in so tight he seemed to be held together by that thin brown belt. He was bald and closely cropped, as if everything extraneous had been stripped away. He had the reputation of a painter's painter—which is what you say about someone who's been doing it forever and still doesn't sell very well.

His grandfather had been a butcher and had urged him into the family shop too young. The boy didn't care for the smell of blood, though his eye was caught by the gleam of the fascia and the bright knobs of bone protruding unexpectedly out into the world. At the age of eight he cut his hand trying to filet a standing rib roast. His grandfather, across the table, stared in disbelief, waiting for the cry of pain. But the boy just stood there, clutching the hand against the bright spill of blood.

His grandfather stuffed a towel into his fist and rushed him to the emergency room, and still he never uttered a sound. The old man blamed himself, and Jonathan supposed he did, too. Who puts a boning knife in the hands of an eight-year-old?

"That pretty much took care of sports," he said one afternoon standing over a naked Bea, catching the first of the afternoon light on the warm field of her skin. "And the violin. But I could hold a paintbrush. I think my grandfather was relieved I didn't hate him. Though I suspect he was a little concerned at how much red I used those first few years."

She would watch him after that, the way he carried his hand when it didn't have a brush in it: curled against his side or pressed flat against his sternum with a mournful air, as if every pain was a remembered one.

At first it wasn't a success. She was nervous, ill at ease—her naked body somehow strange, her breasts heavy and awkward. Feeding Izzie she had grown accustomed to them, just another part of having her daughter in her arms. But now, lying alone, she could not seem to arrange herself.

It was Jonathan's idea that she hold her. "It's the *Pièta*," he said, sketching easily with a thinned wash of pigment as the infant lay smiling in her arms.

"I don't think this is what Weland had in mind." But she leaned back in the chair wrapped in the infant's cheerful murmuring.

"I think that should do it for today," he said at the end of an afternoon.

"Can we look?"

"Of course."

She wasn't sure what to expect. Something like the Gang of Four—all that ravaging paint and heavy color. But what she saw was miraculous. Since Izzie's birth she had felt tired and puffy, as if her body had somehow stretched in the wash. But on the canvas, in a glow of diffused sunshine, she looked rounded and light as rising dough. Her brown hair shiny on her shoulders. Her breasts graceful and her own again.

"How did you do that?"

He smiled. "You cannot turn a silk purse into a sow's ear."

She started to read the book in earnest, and they would sit in his studio and talk. This was when their marriage really began, and like every beginning, it held the shape of their end. They moved the narrow bed in from the guest room. They had thought about their own bed, an enormous California king. "It needs to be full of possibility," said Bea. But when she posed alone, it looked vast and empty.

She bought white sheets—Jonathan preferred to sleep in broad washes of color—and a new down comforter, because that's what the book said. They assembled it like a honeymoon couple planning their nights together.

But reading the book had been a mistake. All that passion. Even when it glowed inside her head—a voyeuristic warmth—she couldn't live up to it. She had nothing to offer. She tried to call up the summer on the island. She tried to remember the moments with Ash, or Weland as he had first been. But that summer had withered her, and two years and a lifetime later, the memory gave her nothing she could use.

"It just a book," said Jonathan. "Pretend you're her. Drained by an afternoon of love-making."

But that just made her sad. So they began to coax her into the role. She lay down on her side, turned away with Izzie in her arms, as her husband drew up the covers to help her relax. Lying there she felt the warmth of the sun. She felt the infant chest rise and fall, the heart beat against her hand. After a moment Jonathan slowly drew down the covers, measuring the effect: shoulder, breast, waist, hip.

"Good," he said. "Don't move. Think erotic thoughts."

"Coffee and croissants on a Saturday morning."

"Close enough."

Harold stirred. "So that was the first great painting of *The Wide Bed.*"

"Not even close," said Bea. "But it was the first great Jonathan. I wish you could have seen it. He kept it in his studio. He said it was his inspiration. The texture, the skin…."

"Your skin."

"Nothing to do with me. But he found something. So, when the Gang of Four came back again with their new responses to the book…"

"To my book," said Harold wryly.

She smiled. "Exactly."

"I suppose Jonathan's was carried by acclamation?"

"Strangely, no. Everybody liked their own. But Weland liked Jonathan's. So while everyone kept painting the way they always had, Weland started painting like Jonathan."

Harold considered that for a moment. "So *The Wide Bed* is all about motherhood?"

"No," she said. "Not quite."

31.

Weland stopped by to see how Jonathan was doing—he was more used to the house than Bea would ever be, and he never knocked. Hurriedly she drew on her robe and sat with Izzie in her lap for moral support.

"*Beatricé,*" he said with a smile and a nod. "Little Izzie."

His expression didn't change as he gazed at the paintings; what he was seeing she couldn't guess, though he hesitated over the brushwork and the shadings of light. In the end he said, "The new texture is tremendous, of course. That light is Vermeer. But in the end it's just a still life. It could be a sack of flour with beautiful skin."

When he left, Jonathan stood gazing at the pictures while Bea huddled in her chair. Then she walked to his side. "Vermeer," she said encouragingly, but he just shook his head. She took his arm. "It's not your fault. I *am* a sack of flour."

That night she set up candles all around the bed. She opened a bottle of wine. She put Coleman Hawkins on the stereo, and when Jonathan stepped into the room she said, "Dance with me."

He was an excellent dancer. Light on his feet. "Kiss me," she whispered.

He kissed her lightly on the lips. "I don't think this is going to work," he said gently.

"We'll see about that."

She slipped down onto her knees and drew down his pajamas.

"Bea."

"Don't talk," she said.

She breathed on him, kissed him. She took him in her mouth.

After a moment she felt his hand lightly on her head. "Beatrice."

"Who do you want me to be?" she whispered.

"I don't think it works that way."

The next morning in the bathroom mirror she cut her hair, grasping handfuls and snipping it off at the top of her neck. She let him choose the color: a pale bright blonde. It looked like sunshine on the box, but it turned her hair to metal—though in the painting he brought it back to sunshine again. The color tamed the curl a little, but not enough, so she moussed it back, binding it into a helmet that turned her face round-cheeked and startled, but on the canvas made the line of her neck and shoulder delicate and fine.

She set Izzie up in her playpen with a *Little Mermaid* video on mute. Then she lit candles in the studio and took out the bottle of wine. She took a piece of sketching charcoal and darkened her jawline to the faint shade of stubble. And, looking up at Jonathan, she said, "You're going to have to work with me on this."

She handed him the wine glass. He drained it like medicine. She unbuttoned his shirt. "Close your eyes," she whispered.

"Izzie?"

"She's fine."

She ran her fingers over his pale chest. Her breath followed her fingers down as she unbuckled and unzipped. His penis was sunk in its own mysterious thoughts, but she grasped it firmly, felt it twitch in her grip. She took him in her mouth. He began to stir. After a while she drew back, catching her breath. "Now you can open your eyes."

And he looked down at her, short-haired, dark-chinned, her beard smearing like mascara. And laying his hand much less gently on the top of her head, he came with a groan of something between determination and surprise.

Bea washed her face and brushed her teeth. Then she stepped back into the studio.

He arranged her on the bed, facing away, perched on one elbow. The other arm folded down over her breast as if she were half-rising from sleep. He adjusted her legs, demure but teasing, narrowing the line of her hips. "Look back," he said. "Just a little. That's it."

She felt awkward at first, like a twisted statue. But she grew accustomed to the pose, and over the next few weeks she would slip back into it as if it were a mold her body had made. They worked easily together, talking about household matters, grocery lists, favorite recipes. He told her about his parents and grandparents, snared by this little town as if in amber. She told him what it was like to have a slim and elegant mother when you were neither of those things. Izzie trundled around the room, touching everything they hadn't moved and stirring the air before her as if conducting her own murmuring music.

At the end of each day they stood before the painting, and gradually Bea learned how to think about it. She didn't look like this woman, didn't feel like her. The woman was slim and graceful and beautiful—the sleek hair, the slender hips. And the expression, peering back over her shoulder with a faint seductive smile, was somebody else's entirely.

"I'm not that thin," she said.

And he hovered a finger and drew the line from her now-graceful neck to the slender waist. "That is your back exactly."

As the days passed the background filled in. The window, the bed, the rumpled covers looking soft and beckoning as anything she had ever seen. On the chair in the corner of the painting she saw her white robe, draped like a shed skin and painted now in that breathtaking blue, so that, worn and familiar as it was, it became brand new.

When the Gang of Four assembled again with their paintings Drexel had five, Margery six, Teddy had a dozen—"I was on a roll," he said. Jonathan had just the one. Weland, of course, came empty-handed. "Think of me as the master of ceremonies."

They all walked slowly around as if circling an idea, but really they were just waiting for Weland. He stood before each one, taking it in.

"Clearly you all know how to paint," he said. But then he started around again, moving more quickly. "I wouldn't fuck her. I wouldn't fuck her. I wouldn't fuck either of them. I wouldn't fuck her."

He ended up in front of Jonathan's painting, standing with his back to it, facing the stony expressions of his colleagues. "This is going to be big," he said, "if we don't fuck it up. Go back. Do it again. Do it like this. But from now on, I want you to paint with your brush in one hand and the other down the front of your pants. If you're not getting hard or wet, then you're doing it wrong."

"This is a collective," Teddy said angrily. "We don't take orders from you."

"This is not me giving you orders, Teddy. This is the Zeitgeist speaking through my lips. This is the muse giving you the straight shit. This is me asking if you want to be famous. If you want to jump on top of this thing and ride it all the way to the cover of *Art Forum*."

When they all filed out Jonathan stayed behind. Weland turned back to the picture. "This is new," he said.

"Mm."

"What's that texture? Makes me want to rub my dick against it."

"Just something I've been working on."

"Is that Bea?"

"She's got something, doesn't she."

Weland shook his head. "That light. That skin. I didn't know you had it in you."

"Neither did I."

"What's the trick?"

Jonathan smiled drily. "I imagine you'll figure it out."

They stared for a moment longer. "Still," said Weland. "It's not quite right."

"No?"

"It's beautiful, elegant, graceful beyond words."

"And?"

"This woman hasn't been fucking for an hour-and-a-half in the hot summer afternoon. She isn't exhausted by love, lying on damp sheets, sore and tingling, with her pussy raw and the smell of her cunt in the air."

"What makes you think so?" Jonathan said coolly.

"This woman isn't startled by all she's been through. And she's definitely not lying there just beginning to smile at the thought of doing it all again."

Jonathan frowned. "You don't want much, do you?"

"Of course I do."

Back in his studio Jonathan said, "Weland wants to paint you."

"No."

"It might be worth doing."

"Absolutely not." She hesitated. "Didn't he like your painting?"

"Oh, yes."

"He's never painted anything so good."

"Don't worry. He will."

That made her mad. "I don't want to pose for him."

"Then don't."

"I like what we're doing here."

"So do I."

She stared at the picture, at the woman in the picture. "What did he say about it?"

"He said it wasn't hot enough."

"Is that what he said?"

A moment's hesitation. "He said it didn't make him want to

fuck her."

And that made her angry as well.

So when the next round of paintings was unveiled, every member of the Gang of Four would have fucked her. Did, in fact. Anything for art. And from then on, for almost two-and-a-half years, everyone painted something different, but all of them painted her.

32

Bea's voice faded. She peered through the blur of her wasted eyes and tried to read his expression. How could he not be appalled?

"A penny for your thoughts," she said.

"You're almost out of dish soap."

She offered up a weak smile. "I feel like Scheherazade. As long as I keep talking, you won't realize what a terrible person I am."

"I don't think you're a terrible person."

"It hasn't even begun to get bad. Have you heard a lot of confessions in your life?"

"We don't really have confession in the Anglican church. But I ate a lot of cookies and drank a lot of tea, and I listened to anybody who needed to talk."

We only see ourselves clearly twice: once when we discover all that we're capable of doing, and once when we tell someone. All these years she had resolved to be silent. To leave the past alone. She had almost forgotten the kind of person she had been.

She'd been ready for Weland when he stopped by her studio. He knocked and came in like a gentleman caller, and she seated herself, impervious as a stone, ready to say no.

He talked to her about her vision of the book. Where did she think the heart of the story lay? He cited individual scenes and descriptions from memory, as if it were a story he himself had lived. He needed her advice. He wanted to prove, with her, the emotional terrain—the hardships and depth of feeling. Was it love? Lust? Did they understand each other? Was their coming together an act of creation or just an act of desire?

Bea was familiar with sex and beds and men. But Weland's engagement with the story—it was almost a myth of love, he said— left her feeling shallow and uncertain. Did she have her favorite moments? he asked. Wasn't it the most amazing blend of passion and earthy humanity since *Lady Chatterley's Lover*?

She had never read *Lady Chatterley*, though she went out that evening and bought it. These were, she said, all good questions. She'd have to think about them all. And she walked him to the door. Though she agreed, as he left, that there was no real reason not to try a few poses. A few of the calmer moments. Just to get a sense of it. Try to see the passion through the ordinary moments of peace and calm. She said she'd think about it. And when he left she carried her copy of *The Wide Bed* to the Taft Bar and started to read again from the beginning.

"You look gloomy for such a sunny day. Of course, it could be this bar. Doesn't anyone else think windows might be nice?"

A man was standing before her, dark-haired and smiling in jeans and a corduroy jacket. It would be untrue to say she didn't recognize him, though it took a long moment for her thoughts to catch up. "Ash," she said.

And he smiled. "You do remember."

Now Bea fell silent, and after a moment Harold reached for the wine. Slowly he refilled their glasses, as if to give her thoughts a chance to settle. She felt his eyes on her face. "And so the plot thickens," he murmured gently. "Some stab from the past?"

"I guess you could say that."

They had been through a lot together, good and bad. The bad had been bad; but the good had saved her. Now the sight of him carried her back.

"You look different," she said.

"Not me. I'm exactly the same. And you? Are you different?"

"Way different." She was smiling now; she didn't know why. "Are you here to save me again?"

"Of course. Why else would I have come?"

She invited him home for dinner. "You can meet my husband and daughter." She gave him a sideways glance, but he seemed unsurprised. "How long are you staying?"

"A few days. A week. It's pretty open-ended. Did you ever move out of that terrible apartment? Whenever I think of you, I picture you there."

She laughed. "What an awful place. Do you remember?"

"I do."

"I've come up in the world. Wait till you see."

She led him into the kitchen, smiling at the thought of how it must look after all these years. Jonathan and Izzie sat before Janson's *History of Art,* propped open on a Constable landscape. They each had a set of watercolors, and they were painting as fast as they could. Every so often Izzie would jam the brush between her lips and, hands quick as butterflies, sign something brief but obviously heartfelt.

"I am not," he said patiently. "And use your words."

She snatched out the brush. "Chidder!" she cried.

"Good. Much better."

"Yo' hwa' chidda!"

"Good. Very good. But now you're way behind."

She tapped him smartly on the wrist. He set down his brush and signed, a little ponderously, as he spoke. "You are way behind."

"Shi'" she said angrily.

"Sound every letter," he said. "Tuh. Tuh."

"Shi-tuh!" the little girl said.

"Good. Much better. But don't say that. People can hear."

"Cheater!" she said.

"Very good. Excellent. Ten seconds."

The two painted rapidly until a light started flashing on top of the timer. The girl put down her brush and raised her hands like a calf-roper at the end of her round. "Ta da!"

"Bravo," said Bea applauding lightly. "Brava."

Smiling, the man bowed in his chair, and the girl, following his eyes, looked delighted. "Hi, mo'. Daddy's cheati'g agai.'"

"I'm sure he would never do that," said Bea. And then, "This is Ash. He's an old friend of mine from college. You remember Ash, don't you, J?"

"I believe I do."

"He was at the island that first year."

"Of course. And I think I saw you at one of Weland's parties. Some time ago."

"Ah," said Ash. "That might have been me."

Jonathan turned to his daughter. "The great thing about making a fool of yourself at one of Uncle Weland's parties is that nobody remembers it afterwards."

The girl was staring at his lips, but still she tapped him impatiently on the wrist. When he signed, even Ash could see what looked like a lot of yelling and maybe some falling down. The girl was delighted. She regarded him with renewed interest, as if he were going to do it all again.

"If it's any excuse," he said, "I was very young. And it was long before you were born."

"Not so long," said Bea.

Izzie started to sign, but Jonathan tapped her on the wrist. "Words."

"Everythin' in'erest'g happn' befo' I was bo'n."

"I know how you feel," said Ash.

Jonathan was idly sketching on a small pad beside his place, using the watercolor brush in light, easy strokes. There seemed no concentration involved, but gradually the image of Izzie appeared, hunched and attentive.

"Is my hea' tha' big?" she asked.

"It's just perspective."

"It's fa.'"

"Fat-uh. And, no. It's brainy. It's crowded with thoughts and creativity."

"I don' lik' my head."

"I do," said her father. And he dipped his brush and decorated the painted upper lip with a quick, blue mustache. "How's that?"

"Betta.'"

Bea had moved to the stove. "I thought we'd put Ash in the guestroom," she said casually.

"Of course. The more the merrier."

Later, when dinner was over and Jonathan had taken Izzie up to bed, Ash said, "She's adorable."

"Thanks. She's a handful."

"And Jonathan's very nice."

Bea smiled a little shyly. "It's all a bit surprising, isn't it?"

"A bit."

"He's a wonderful painter. And he's so good with Izzie."

"I can see that."

She picked up the empty wine bottle. "What do you say? Shall we open another?"

They settled on the sofa, its cushions curving like loaves of bread. Bea turned and, lifting the wineglass out of his hand, kissed him.

Surprise lasted only an instant. They clutched each other, their hands frantic, mouths demanding, with the faint creak of floorboards overhead and the sound of running water distant in the pipes. Only slowly did they draw apart. Bea sat back, a searching look on her face. But Ash said nothing. He was an older, wiser man now, and when Bea made no further move, he reached down and picked up his wine glass with remarkable *sangfroid*. He was proud of that. The old Ash could never have managed it.

"So, how are things?" he said.

"Let me turn on some music."

They listened to Oscar Peterson as they sipped their wine. "Weland wants to paint me. He's asked me to model."

"Are you going to?" he asked.

"I told him no."

"Because you know where that leads?"

"Don't be a jerk. Please?"

"Sorry."

She frowned down at the glass in her hands. "It's not really me he wants. It's some woman from a book he found. *The Wide Bed.* Can you imagine? What a title. Why didn't they just call it *Fucking*?"

And they both sat unmoving as the echoes of the word faded. Bea swallowed some wine. She had forgotten the scent of him, something warm and unnamable and instantly familiar. She said, "He thinks it's going to put them all on the map."

"Have you read it?"

She glanced over, teasingly. "Have you?"

"Of course. Didn't you like it?"

"Sure," she said. "I like sex. I'm not a weirdo."

"Well, good."

"It just doesn't seem real to me. I mean, it's not much like life, is it?"

The music came to an end. Twisting around to reach the controls, the cant of her hip, her breasts crowded negligently against the back of the sofa, she glanced up. "I mean, what do I have in common with some sexpot from some hot book?"

"Now you're just being modest."

"Be serious."

He shrugged. "I suppose you could embrace whatever part of it applies."

"It doesn't."

"Then pretend it could."

She settled back as the music resumed. "Do you know how long I've wanted to be a painter?"

"Eight years old," he said.

She smiled. "I could never tell if you were listening."

"I'm always listening."

"So I thought I'd be there by now."

"You're only twenty-two."

"It happens young or it doesn't happen."

"That's not true."

"You either have it or you don't. I tried to paint a scene from this book. I couldn't do it. That's me in a nutshell. I can't even make pornography sexy."

"Here's a thought," said Ash. "Just pretend. Tell yourself this woman is you. Imagine it's your story."

She shook her head wearily. "Jonathan and I are good together. And we're good for Izzie. But that's not one of the things we're good at."

"But you could be. I know you could."

She gave him a grateful smile. "No, you don't. You don't know anything. I'm just a woman talking dirty to an old boyfriend."

33.

Weland believed in public spectacle. He was a man ahead of his time—but only a few minutes—and he wanted to be sure of his direction before he went sprinting ahead. So he threw a party. And he arranged on the high white walls of his living room a series of sketches in various states of completion. And from each of the Gang of Four he selected a single painting.

Jonathan didn't like looking at art in crowds, and Izzie seemed to find the whole party boring, but Bea was caught between embarrassment and pride. As she moved through the crowd she felt the tug and current of her passing. People studiously avoided her gaze and then looked askance, comparing her to the woman on the wall.

"See?" whispered Ash in her ear. "Nothing to worry about. You are clearly the best looking woman here. Let's stroll around and make fun of the other paintings under our breath."

They gazed at one of Teddy's. He was a master of the seascape, and he had somehow given his bedroom scene a rocky and tumultuous air. Every detail was heavy and fixed so the figures looked mired in the moment. Bea started to relax. She may not understand the passion of *The Wide Bed*, but she understood it better than this. She stepped back to get a wider view, and collided.

A hand went to her shoulder as if to steady her, and Weland's voice was in her ear. "You're causing quite a stir."

"Am I?"

He gave Ash half a nod and then glanced at the knot of people clustered before Jonathan's painting. "I happened to mention that you were the model. I hope you don't mind."

"I wish you hadn't done that."

"I thought they had a right to know. To allow them to

appreciate the work."

"Are all the models here?"

"Of course. It's just a little experiment. Let's go look at the others."

He led them like a tour guide around the crowded room. As people stopped to exchange a few words with Weland they would nod and smile at Bea. "It's a beautiful painting." As if trying to decide how best to give her credit. A surprising number of them—university donors, administrators, strangers—had read the book, and they confided in her that, although they didn't remember much of the story, she seemed to capture it perfectly.

"And what have we learned tonight?" said Weland at the end of the evening. Jonathan and Izzie had long since left.

"That Jonathan is a wonderful painter?"

"Yes, yes." He smiled patiently. "But that's not why they liked it."

They liked it, he said, because it reminded them of themselves. Of something they thought only they truly understood. Some hidden, treasured moment of passion and pleasure—of youth—remembered or imagined in all its sharpest yearning. They read a book that had nothing to do with them, and they stored it away. Memories of beautiful people making love on a summer afternoon and then driven into heartache and loss.

"That was a genius move," said Weland. "All that heartache."

It made something vital out of dime store pornography. It made something lasting. Because even when they finished it, when they closed the covers and put it down, they cared about those two. They envied them their passion, and they were grateful for their unhappiness. They could pity them and they could let all those urgent moments of passion and loss settle into the uneventful landscape of their own lives. They could let it sink into the background.

"Until now," said Weland. "Until they looked at this. At you. You returned them to the brightest moments of their youth. Even if they were only imagined. They look at you and they see themselves as they would love to have been."

They walked home, she and Ash, through the dark and silent town, lost in their separate thoughts. And as they drew to a stop before the back door they heard a thin and frantic mewing rising from the sprawled yew bushes along the side of the house.

"What's that?" said Bea, her hand light on his arm. "Can you see it?"

He had his phone out, the flashlight insubstantial in the swallowing darkness. But he searched among the prickly branches and found, at the hollow base of the bush, a tiny kitten calling out into the night as if she had strength for nothing else. He scooped her up, far less substantial than her cries. In the warm cradle of his hands the kitten began to purr.

"Oh, the poor thing," said Bea. "Where did she come from? Come on. Bring her inside."

In the bright kitchen the insubstantial weight became a thin, orange tabby, skinny and frail, with wide, peering eyes vaguely searching for the source of so much light.

Isabel came scampering down the stairs and Jonathan followed more sedately. "How di' you lik' the show?" she demanded. "Daddy sai' it was good."

"Daddy's work was the best. Even Weland agreed."

Jonathan gazed at them mildly. "And this is our prize?"

"It was outside in the bushes."

He walked over and with a fingertip stroked the top if its tiny head. "Sounds hungry."

"Ca' we feed 'er?" asked Izzie eagerly.

The kitten seemed to fasten onto the girl's voice, as if reaching out from one tiny thing to another, and turned its face like a flower.

"Is it blind?" whispered Ash.

Jonathan dangled his fingers in front of the little face and it moved as if vaguely following them. "Not blind, but something. What would she like, do you suppose?"

The saucer of milk was as big as a dinner plate beside the mewing creature. It seemed not to know what to do, so Bea got an eye dropper. Izzie dripped milk onto her lapping tongue until the dish was empty, then she stroked the little head. "Goo' girl." And the kitten sat wide-eyed and wondering, as if at the mystery of it all.

34.

"I'm going to model for Weland," she said at breakfast the next day. She had made omelets, and they'd turned out beautifully, except for one that she kept for herself.

Ash looked up wearily. "Really? And you think that's a good idea?"

"You never know," said Jonathan slowly. "He might be onto something. Weland is uncanny about this sort of thing."

"I'd like you to come along," she said to Ash.

"Where?"

"To Weland's studio."

"To do what, exactly?"

She set a piece of buttered toast on his plate with a proprietary air. "To keep me safe. Like you always do."

Weland seemed unsurprised to find them both at his door. He was dressed in white coveralls so clean and unspotted he might have been merely a painting of a painter. On the walls were all his Old Masters, and in pride of place, on an easel directly behind the sofa, was Jonathan's painting of Bea.

"Good," he said. "I'm glad you're here. Are you hungry? Do you want something to eat? Something to drink?"

"Not for us," she said.

"Excellent. Please be seated." He waved her with a touch of formality toward the sofa. And to Ash, "Don't go away."

Bea had braced herself against this whole afternoon, trying out in her mind the various poses she had seen in the paintings at the party. Trying to incorporate them into some understanding of who she would have to be. But when she settled herself Weland lifted the book from the table and handed it to her. "Why don't we start by reading. Just that first section. I've marked it. It's their first afternoon together. They've only just met."

And it didn't help that she knew what Weland was doing. He could feel how stiff she was; he was trying to warm her up. But it wasn't working. The book just made her more bashful. She stumbled over the sentences, catching on a word or phrase as if it had been lying in ambush. Even glancing back at the painting didn't help. She heard Jonathan's voice: *He said he wouldn't fuck her.* And it made her angry all over again.

After a few minutes Weland said, "Ash? Why don't you read."

It was a relief to hand him the book. He had a nice voice; she'd forgotten that. He had read to her again and again that terrible summer. But never anything like this. She blushed at first, fought to keep all expression from her face.

"Why don't you close your eyes," said Weland.

Sitting stiffly upright, she did. She tried to make herself relax. And gradually the words warmed in her mind. Weland had begun to paint, she heard the hurried rasp of pages turning as he went from sketch to sketch.

And then, "Thank you. That's enough," he said. Ash stopped reading.

"You can get up and stretch."

"I wasn't really doing anything."

He smiled. "I was painting your aura."

She got up and walked to the easel. Weland was leafing through the pages. Bright and sun-filled, like glimpses of Jonathan's picture—that same sense of light and ease—but in all the different poses the Gang of Four had tried with their various models and colors and styles. There wasn't much detail but they were beautifully imagined, and she was nude in every one. Pale and unconfined. The loveseat had been transformed into an elaborate divan, an overstuffed chair, a wide and rumpled bed. She looked easy and relaxed, even mischievous.

"How did you do that?" she said.

"It's my superpower."

She felt a dawning disappointment. They were undeniably beautiful. And sexy, oh yes. The imagined sunlight draped her hip and spilled over her breasts—impossibly firm and rounded. The remembered breasts of a nineteen-year-old. And the face. He had simply made up the expression. A tensed, half-wincing look of longing that cast the whole reclining figure into a dream of passion.

"That isn't me," she said dully.

"Yes. It is." Ash's voice was suddenly at her shoulder.

She glanced up shyly. "Really?"

"Oh, yes."

"You read beautifully," she murmured.

"It must be *my* superpower."

"Lucky for us," said Weland.

And if Ash was feeling awkward and out of place, an unnecessary addition to the moment, the painter gave no hint that he noticed.

"I have some fruit," said Weland. "A bottle of wine in the fridge."

"Are you going to have some?" Bea asked.

"Not when I'm working."

"Then I don't need anything."

He glanced at Ash. "Maestro?"

"No, thanks."

"Then let's move on to phase two."

He arranged Bea on the sofa, fully dressed but reclining. "*La maja vestida*," he said with a smile. "Our own clothed maja. Remember the pose?"

And with a tentative look she raised both arms and linked her hands behind her head.

"Brava," he said. And to Ash, "In Spanish a *maja* is a woman of the lower classes, brightly dressed, though not exactly respectable. Which must have made everyone smile at the time. The model was Josefa de Tudó, Countess of Castillo Fiel. She was the mistress of Goya's patron, the prime minister of Spain. And to cap it off, the painting of her—reclining in a colorful but very risqué outfit—was the second of two. First he did an identical painting of her nude. *La maja desnuda.* Perhaps he thought she was brightly enough dressed on her own."

He stepped behind his easel and, with one last approving glance, drew from his pocket a joint: pristine, white, and delicate as new idea. "I'm going to suggest you both have a little of this."

"Not for me thanks," said Ash.

"Really, I have to insist. Just to get started. You're crucial to our endeavor. And there's no limit to what we must do for art."

Weland handed him the joint and with the grace of a *maitre d'* held a lighter to the tip. "*Beatricé?* You'll have some? For the good of our art."

She started to get up. "No. Don't move. Not a muscle." And to Ash, "Take it over, would you?"

She was smiling as he approached. "I'm afraid I'm not allowed to move." And she raised her lips, pursed and waiting.

He held the joint; she drew in the smoke, breathing it out as if forming the cloud on which she reclined. Without a word Ash bent and kissed her. Her eyes widened, but her startled lips, soft as a rose petal, bloomed under his mouth.

"And now," said Weland drily, "let's see what we've got. Maestro. Take us to the second bookmark."

And Ash began to read.

Their first meeting had been all supple surprise. The warmth of the summer tuning their bodies to every response. But the second was pure anticipation. He climbed the stairs and saw her, in a dress of cotton gauze against the heat, and didn't stop until he had crossed the wide room and held her pressed against the wall, kissing her as if it were all he had ever wanted.

Bea listened, grateful for the smoke. She was aware of Weland painting, aware of how he had posed her, the way he had instructed her with that teasing smile. But it was Ash's voice she was tuned to, and with every movement she felt herself wrapped more closely in the dream of the book.

The dress was light as a veil, its thinness a provocation. His hands slipped beneath it over her throat and breasts. And her senses seemed always just ahead of his touch, anticipating, waiting with a kind of stealthy pressure building in her heart. He drew her to the sofa and sank onto his knees.

Bound in her pose, as if straining against her own muscles, Bea could almost feel the hands, the mouth, the breath hot on her skin. She lay back with the familiar voice in her ears, and tried to imagine what it would be like to be wanted like that. She tried to feel what the woman felt, as her lover bent to kiss her throat, as he drew the dress up over her head. His lips, his hands, the skin of his body sliding against hers—as if the whole world had grown nerve-endings and was leaning into his touch.

And when they were done for the day and walking home they kept bumping together as if by accident. She would draw him into every shadow, every hidden place, and they would kiss and kiss, as if it were the only thing in the world they could never stop doing.

35

"How was it?" Jonathan asked at dinner.

"It was okay. I'm not used to modeling for anyone but you."

And later, in the spilling light of the hall lamp, they lay on the sofa frantically kissing, their mouths demanding, their hands hurrying past clothing to the reservoir of lush sensation beneath the cool, ordered surface of her life.

"You feel good," she whispered. "You feel so good." And it must have been the scent of him, the sudden rush of feeling, but there rose to her mind the long ago echo of her own voice in the darkness of the shed on the island a lifetime ago. *You know we can't do anything.* It made her smile.

He must have heard it as well. His breath was warm against her ear. "You're not wearing your overalls."

"I could put them on."

"No. That's all right. What we really need is a cow bell."

And she laughed, a little gasp of breath.

And their moment had come, she thought, just like that. And all that had happened over the last three years—how can it only have been three years?—seemed in that instant to reshape itself. Not a series of losses and mistakes but a slow path designed to draw them out, to tease them, to bring them finally to this. And it filled her in that instant with the new shape of their lives, tangled but sweet. All their mistakes finally transformed into a kind of triumph.

Above them, in the depths of the house, there was a rush of water in the pipes. For Bea it was the most natural of sounds; it was an old house and sometime every night Izzie would make her sleepy way to the bathroom and back to bed. And in that moment she felt happy—that she had somehow earned this, that her life was now bending to its proper course. All the settled fullness of it reaching back to pick up this one missed thread and weave it in.

But she could feel him hesitate.

"What?" she murmured. "No. It's okay."

"Someone's awake."

"It's just Izzie. She's going back to sleep." And she pressed in closer. "It's okay, Ash. It's okay. I want this."

And she pressed him close, her lips to his ear. "I need you, Ash," she whispered. "This is our moment. Please."

But she could feel him drawing back.

"No," she whispered. "Kiss me. Do you feel this? Do you feel it?"

But she could sense his thoughts drifting—out of the sheltering moment into the hovering world.

"No," she pleaded. "Tell me. Tell me you want me. Tell me you want to fuck me."

"I do. God, I do."

"Can you feel how wet I am?" She clutched him against her. "Can you? Can you feel everything I'm feeling?"

But it was a mistake to speak the words. To say them out loud. She could feel them turning against them both.

"Oh, Bea," he whispered. "I love you. I've always loved you."

"It's our moment, Ash. Don't you feel it? This is ours. We get to have this."

"How can we?"

Because there's a difference between knowing something from afar and meeting it face to face. "You have a husband. You have a daughter. What would they think? What would it do to them?"

"They'll understand. They will. They want us to be happy."

But she could see it was too late. The weight of it settling onto him—Ash who was always so kind, so nice. Too nice. And she felt a kind of fury rising. Was that it? Was that her life? All those missed choices and chances—the whole tumbling disorder—and no way to make it up? She had bound herself tighter and tighter, from one misjudgment to the next. And now what? Nothing? No hope? The anger boiled up, spilling over. Onto Ash, onto Jonathan, to Weland. Fucking Weland! The carelessness of him. The ease. How willing he was simply to seize what he wanted. The world put everything within his grasp and all he needed was to take it. And she could have nothing?

And she remembered the expression on the face in Weland's sketch. *Her* face. It had embarrassed her at the time: so tender and charged with feeling. It was nothing she recognized. But there it was, captured in paint. *That* woman had looked like someone who felt intensely. Who could take what she needed from her life.

The next morning at breakfast she said, "I think I'll try it on my own today."

Ash sat still for a moment. "I'd be happy to go."

"No. I have to learn to stand on my own two feet." And she dropped a kiss on the top of his head. He would always remember that kiss and her parting words. "You've sent me on my way."

In that moment could she have foreseen all that would happen? Would she even have cared? She was angry and desperate to have somebody see her as she wanted to be. Someone to free her from herself.

And surely Ash must have felt that, as well. In the years after she had imagined his day. He must have walked all over town that afternoon, tying and re-tying the knots of his life. He had known she was married—but to an old man. He had imagined her unhappy. And so she was. He must have thought of himself as her rescuer. But in the end it was more than he could do. Faced with the fact of the family she had made, the life that seemed so firmly in place, he could not make the leap. He could not help destroy all that. How would she not regret it? He thought of it as a moral choice. An act of unrequited love.

But for Bea in that moment it wasn't about regret. She knew regret. This was just cowardice. And Weland, whatever else he might be, was not a coward.

So Ash must have crossed the green slowly, taking his time. Imagining her stepping out into the sunshine, stiff from not moving, blinking in the bright light, and turning to find him there. He must have thought she'd be pleased to see him. But when he got to the house there was no sign of her. So he sidled up to the big bow window. Not spying. Just glancing in. And, of course, there they were.

In the glow of the studio, the book he'd been reading aloud had somehow come to life. The couple slowly writhing on the sofa might as well have been stirred into motion by the sound of his own voice. And standing in the sunlight, as far outside the moment as could be, it must have seemed less like something Weland had done, than his own terrible fault. It was the cow bell again. All over again. Nothing high-minded. Not a moral choice. Just a simple loss of nerve. Nothing more. With no chance of ever being undone. For it's not just our actions that lock us into our lives but the sum of all we cannot do.

36.

Bea fell silent. Reluctantly she raised her eyes, afraid of all that she had given away. Harold had seemed so broken, so undone by life, that nothing could shock him. But now. A stranger, a priest, a man lost in his own despair—how could he not be appalled? He sat there without a word, as if letting all her shame and regret wash over him.

"I'm a terrible person," she whispered.

"I don't believe that."

"I deserve my life."

"Oh." His touched the lid of the shoebox. "It can't be about deserving. Where would any of us be?"

"But what am I supposed to do now?"

After a moment, he stirred. "You tell me. What comes next?"

"I've been trying to figure that out for years."

"No. I mean, what's the next thing you do on a normal day?"

She smiled weakly. "I don't really have normal days anymore."

"Well, what would it look like if you did?"

They lifted the sofa out of the way and vacuumed up a year's worth of dust. They brought the stepladder up from the basement and while Harold steadied it Bea climbed into the corners with an old t-shirt wrapped around a broom and swept the ancient crown molding.

"This is a nice house."

"It isn't mine. I'm just the one ruining it."

They walked around with matching dust cloths, performing a kind of synchronized dance, moving through each room as if it were a scattered story they were summing up. They cleaned the mirrors till they squeaked, and the banisters till they shone. Stains, scuff marks, fingerprints, everything lifted up under their efforts. By the time they were done Bea was sorry to see it coming to an end. Standing there she reached out for any additional task. "How do you feel about painting?"

"I'm not really artistic," he said.

"The mud room?"

"Of course you have a mud room."

Tucked in behind the kitchen, it was where the washer and drier lived amid racks and shelves of overcoats and muddy boots. It was where the tools were kept and the Christmas decorations stored and the stray bits and remnants with no other place to go. It was the room that allowed the rest of the house to be tidy, and it was always her abiding shame.

Terrible green walls, cracking plaster. A wide patch of damp that had gradually spread down from the ceiling and curled around the window frame. And over all, a faint smell of mildew that seemed to anchor the room in its own air of dreary abandonment.

"I keep meaning to paint it," Bea said hesitantly.

"Oh. That's not even the start."

She turned. "It's not that bad."

"Oh, yes."

"I'm sure you've seen worse."

"I'd like to say I have…." But his voice trailed off. He pointed up toward the corner where the tar-water stain, leaking down from the roof, had spread like a bad idea. "You've got to fix that leak before you do anything. Then all the plaster will have to be pulled and patched. You might have some issues with the wall there. Though it might," he conceded generously, "just be more of the roof. And the window will have to be seen to. Then, maybe, you could start to paint."

"I thought you were a priest," she said.

"What is a priest but a handyman of the soul?"

"There's got to be a quick fix."

     D. K. Smith

"Dynamite."

"Oh, come on," she said. "We're starving artists, remember?"

His expression softened, as if the sight of so much damage, reduced to a solid and mendable shape, offered its own kind of hope. "I could maybe do the work for you. My schedule has unexpectedly opened up."

"We could pay you," she said. "Well. Not much. Meals, maybe. We could pay you with food. That doesn't sound ridiculous, does it?"

"Hasn't anyone ever told you not to invite a stranger into your house?"

"My ex-husband left town. My daughter hates me. My wife has run away. I can't sleep, I can't paint. Being murdered in my bed actually sounds pretty good to me. Come on," she said. "Why not? I'm a terrible cook. How can you resist?"

"It is a little old-fashioned," he conceded.

"That's the spirit." And Bea found she was smiling.

Harold at Home

"First we have to get all this stuff cleared away."

She looked around wearily. "Never do today what you can put off till tomorrow."

But there was no stopping him, and once he set to work all she could do was help.

"Where can we put it? Do you have a basement?"

"I wouldn't go down there."

"An attic?"

"Too many stairs."

"Where then?"

"We could bury it in the back yard."

But she bent and hoisted up an armful of coats and led the way through the kitchen, past the foot of the stairs, to the narrow white door of her studio. It had been a den back in the beginning—a perfect, cozy room of soft furniture and light. But Jonathan had decided she needed a nice studio, and so all the furniture was redistributed through the house, and the room—large and square, with a beautiful pair of windows—was turned over to her. If she never really settled in, it was partly because she couldn't shake the feeling that it was all just too nice for her.

Harold followed with an armload of boots. "Where would you like them?"

"It doesn't matter."

"I don't want to clutter up your space."

"Believe me, clutter is not the problem."

They started in a corner—building a pile of shoes, boxes, ancient board games, like an avalanche in reverse—until the mudroom was empty. Looking around at the bare floor he said, "That wasn't so bad."

Though for Bea the emptiness only made the room more appalling. This is what she had done to this beautiful old house. The paint was drab, and the damp looked like a map of Asia seeping across the ceiling and vanishing past the inside wall.

"What's beyond that?" Harold asked.

"It's a storage closet."

He gave her a patient look. "I don't suppose it's empty."

She had almost forgotten all that was there. The broken lawn furniture and boxes of Christmas ornaments, the garbage bags stuffed with old children's clothes, scrapbooks of photographs and newspaper articles and all the household memorabilia about which she had been so proud early on. They stolidly transferred it, piece by piece, as if picking through the whole massed accumulation of her failures. And in the end they came to the farthest corner—she remembered going to so much trouble to bury them deep. Not her oldest mistakes but her biggest. A stack of paintings leaning against the wall.

"Are these your husband's?"

"No. They're mine."

They carried them into the studio, and she turned them over one by one, as if she had forgotten what they looked like and was hoping to be surprised. Some of them were very old: portraits of Joan and Izzie and Adam, painted over time as if to highlight how little progress she had made.

"This are nice."

"You're supposed to paint what you love. This is what I loved."

Five old paintings, done over the course of eight years. The children seemed to grow quickly, her technique much more slowly. The bodies gradually developed their proper mass, the shading grew more convincing. And if they were never more than amateurish, there was something intent in them all—some seriousness behind the plain, flat surface. There was Joan, reclining on a sofa like a traditional Renaissance nude, with Adam and Izzie like attending cherubs. And then one based on Michelangelo's *Pièta*, in which Joan sat in the overstuffed chair and Adam, as a young and skinny Christ, lay drooping across her lap.

"They're good," said Harold.

"They're not."

"I like them. What happened to Izzie?"

"Puberty," said Bea. "She just got too embarrassed."

"It doesn't seem to have bothered Adam."

Indeed, his crucified Christ was remarkable for its relaxed self-consciousness, never looking quite dead, as if always ready to sit up and smile for the painter.

She had thought they were her best work. She'd invited Weland in to see them.

He had looked for a long moment and then just shrugged. There was nothing really there, he said. She wasn't using the nudity for anything. Really, the picture was just about itself.

"Weland is a monster," said Harold.

"No, he's not."

"He's an egotistical horror."

"That doesn't mean he's not right."

"Do you know he actually told me that selfishness might be the purest thing we could do?"

But that just made it worse. Bea stared at the back of the final painting, unable even to reach out.

Harold turned it over.

"This is good."

And it was. It startled her; it had been such a disaster. But now, gazing down at the painting, to remember even a little was to remember everything.

The picture was unfinished: Adam and Eve before the fall.

Izzie in an elaborate outfit of silk fig leaves, and Adam scantily draped in a plain white sheet. It should have been comic; there was something so overwrought in the mismatched pair. Izzie hunched and disapproving, every inch of skin obscured. And Adam, skinny, upright, resolutely dramatic. But there was something serious about it, something sharp and vibrant. Eve was vague and unfinished, as if the girl's reluctance extended even to the paint itself, but Adam was all vividness. The musculature, the shading and mass of his skinny torso, it was lapidary and fine. It seemed to coalesce all the peripheral vagueness into a bright core of concentration and tenderness.

"It's wonderful."

And it was. Far and away the best of her work. The texture, the colors welcomed the eye and drew the viewer in, despite the ragged X carved into the center of the canvas, collapsing the surface and leaving the edges raw and curling.

"So why did you slash it?"

"I didn't," she said. "I think Izzie did."

38.

You have to paint what you love. That's how she remembered it—the first thing Weland taught her. Though what he'd actually said was: You have to love what you paint. A small difference that only gradually became clear to her.

The first thing she'd ever painted was a dead bird, a blue jay, that had flown into their picture window and snapped its neck. It was so sad, and it lay there so intricately beautiful and still, that for a moment she thought she could rescue it.

"Save the colors, save the bird?" he asked. "How old were you?"

"Eight."

Her mother had been shocked by how calmly she focused on the face of death, and more than a little impressed. She sent her to summer classes at the local Art Museum.

"You know how it is when you're young and fearless. You make nothing but progress. I was the best painter in my grade school, and one of the best in junior high. By high school I was just one of a group, but I was determined. That was my advantage. I might not be the best, but I was the most serious."

"Serious is good."

"I was plump as a girl; I had started to develop early. And it was all just a big embarrassment. I wanted nothing to do with it. Art was a way to ignore all that. I was a nun for art." She smiled ruefully. "I remember telling my friends that. Some were even impressed. It put me safely on the outskirts of things. Even my mother left me alone. All I wanted was to paint. But you know that thing about putting all your eggs in one basket?"

"No," he said drily. "I've never heard of that thing."

She smiled. "I was raised Catholic. I used to love confession. As a little girl I'd pour my heart out to the priest."

"How many sins does a little girl have?"

"I've made up for it since."

"Well," he said gently. "Tell Father Harold."

She had come to Ashdown because it was small and not too famous and not in the City. She thought all the best painters would be drawn to more famous schools. There was a girl in her high school who went to Parsons, another to RISD. But this was where her art teacher had gone, a long time ago, and he thought it might be a good fit. "I told myself I needed a program that would fit my style. But really I just wanted a small pond where I could be a big fish again."

It didn't turn out to be that, of course. But for a while it was something better.

Weland was a good teacher. You wouldn't think it now. But when he focused his attention, you really felt it. For a girl who was looking for someone to take her as seriously as she took herself, he seemed like the perfect choice.

"There was an internship," she said. "Years ago. When I first came. One painter was chosen each summer to go up to Studio Island." She saw something in his expression. "I know. Ridiculous name. I'm not sure who came up with it. Weland, probably."

"I wouldn't be surprised."

"An outhouse. No electricity. A handpump in the kitchen sink. But beautiful. And thrilling to be chosen. It was the beginning of my life as a real artist."

"I can imagine. Was it far away?"

"A long, long drive. I got a ride with a boy. He was going up there. He had an aunt in exactly that spot." She smiled. "I thought he was making it up, but it turns out he did. I thought he just wanted to drive me. And that was nice, too."

"It sounds nice."

"It's hard to remember now, but it was all so exciting. I cooked and cleaned—that was the deal—and I painted."

It was the evenings that she lived for. Painting by candlelight in that long hour and a half before dinner. They would set up their easels in a circle in the big living room beside a huge fire and they would paint Joan.

"Your Joan?"

"Not then. But yes. Each summer they chose one painter and one model."

"Sounds like fate," said Harold.

But that was later. The part she remembered most vividly, even now after all these years, was that first evening. The night she arrived. "Weland had a cruel streak, I think. But who knows? It was a great idea. So maybe cruelty isn't the issue."

He suggested a different model—the boy who had driven her up. He had hesitated at first. But then Weland told him: Ignore the rest of us. Just pose for her. And he did. Fully dressed at first, though not for long. He stood, awkward and embarrassed, but with his eyes locked on hers.

"And that was something, too" she murmured. "To have him focused only on me. To have him waiting for my response."

Weland had up behind her. He laid his hands on her shoulders. *Loosen up*, he said. *Loosen your wrist. Loosen your mind. Art is about love.* And he asked if the boy would take off his shirt if Bea took off hers.

"You're kidding," said Harold.

"It's that kind of a story," she said simply.

Bea had removed her flannel shirt, the boy had removed his. And then, *How about the pants?* said Weland. So Bea undressed slowly until she was covered only by the bib of her overalls. All gooseflesh and chills, and a little knot of something like fear or excitement or love—a tight thread running between Bea and the boy.

It's not embarrassment, Weland had whispered in her ear. *It's art.*

And it was. The best work she'd ever done. The figure seemed so real. Roughly drawn, but alive with desire. Hers, his. It seemed to raise itself off the page. And that was the beginning for her.

"That moment. It was like my hand was wired directly into my brain, my heart. I felt it, and it would appear directly on the paper. It was thrilling."

And if her wires got crossed? If painting and life and desire got so inextricably mixed that her whole life came undone? Well, as Weland would say, that's the price of art. You take the good with the bad. But here's the thing he didn't say. You can't always tell them apart.

And here's the other thing. Just because there's a beginning, doesn't mean there will be a middle and an end. Or rather, the middle may have nothing to do with the beginning. But the end is always the end.

So after the summer, there was Izzie, and she married Jonathan. And then Joan and Adam moved in. A family built around art, when everything seemed arranged for their happiness. She painted Jonathan when he had time to pose, and Izzie when he didn't. And then Joan and Adam. Painting and painting, practicing and practicing.

Then Joan began to take it up, as well. It didn't matter that she had no training; she simply decided to try.

At first Bea encouraged her. She offered her guidance and suggestions. It made her feel generous to pass on part of what she had learned. Joan's paintings weren't good. Even then she had that hard, untouchable surface, and a stubborn two-dimensionality to her work. No one would mistake them for real people. But she was untroubled by that, and Bea was always complimentary. Then a strange thing happened. The more Joan believed in her own painting, the less Bea could believe in hers.

She forced herself to work. Eight hours a day. That was the goal. Just a regular working day. But it began to weigh on her—the looming prospect of so much time. Each day became a burden that kept her from beginning, while Joan would just paint and paint. She reduced it to six, then four, then two hours. Then one. She would force herself to paint for an hour. Though by that time she didn't really believe in it anymore. Like someone on the outside looking in, she had lost her faith.

Then along came *The Wide Bed*, and a reprieve.

It had its good moments. All that attention. The satisfaction of being at the center of so much beauty and success. It carried her along. She didn't have time to paint.

"But I sometimes wonder what it would have been like if I'd never even heard of that book."

Because after the roller coaster of fame, with everything altered, she could never quite find her way back to her own painting. Nothing was as good. She couldn't begin. Whereas Joan, who had never held a brush before they met, simply could not stop.

And then Bea thought, paint what you love.

39.

So at the end of last summer she brought out her earliest work again. Adam and Izzie. A pair of tiny cherubs bathing in their little wading pool. She thought maybe it wasn't as bad as she remembered. So she began.

At first she wanted to do the same portrait twelve years later. Nudes in a swimming pool. But thirteen and a half is not one and a half. And while Adam was unembarrassed at the idea, Izzie was adamant. So Bea settled on an allegorical painting. Venus and Mars. It seemed sufficiently old-fashioned to give her some breathing room. A bit of ironical fun, if anyone should ask. A little deniability. And she brought out her overalls again, for good luck.

They spent hours, the three of them, trying on different costumes, draping and arranging and searching for some pose that would speak to her. All the allegory seemed foolish even to her, but it was a short leap from Venus and Mars, to Adam and Eve. And then shorter still to her daughter and step-son, grown so much older and yet still the same. She thought of herself, her art, grown so withered and cold, and she wondered if the one might allow her access to the other. Adam and Eve, posed on either side of her very first sketch from the island. So she set it on an easel, the sketch of that naked young man. Tensed with embarrassment and aching desire. It was a touchstone for her, and she set it between the two points of her life.

For the first time in a long time the thought of painting filled her with hope. And when she started to sketch, in a pale wash of diluted color, she could not misstep. It was like a gift.

But from the beginning Izzie was shy and restive, determined not to wear anything less than a lot. But standing beside Adam, who was pleased to wear almost nothing, she seemed to be from a different painting. Bea tried to reach out to her, but she just grew more stubborn and withholding, while Adam was a dream. He seemed to feel that same connection to the work, to the emotion of the painting. He was like a modern incarnation of that first, long-ago figure. He seemed to hold that out to her again, that spark of inspiration. And he would pose for hours.

And so.

Once she had blocked out the two figures, Bea started to have them pose separately. It allowed her to concentrate, to work no faster than she wanted, to draw out for herself the excitement of painting again. And if the picture of Eve seemed to lose its way—if Izzie seemed faint-hearted and irritable and disgruntled until finally she just quit altogether—Adam blossomed.

Skinny and intense, eyes locked on her, he was a vivid model, and they seemed to draw a cloak of concentration around themselves. They seemed to feed each other as she moved slowly and certainly toward some veiled completeness that was holding itself out to her.

"I can't really explain what I was feeling," she said. "I try to re-member, but now it all seems so far away."

Every brushstroke was a revelation. She wanted only to draw it all tight. To feel the painting grow from that connection between them. It carried her back to the memory of the island, to the intensity of that first night. She felt in touch with her own creativity in a way she hadn't since then. And she felt, as she painted, that she was giving her full attention to her children for the first time since they were infants. For the first time in such a long time, she felt like a good mother.

"It sounds ridiculous now," she said.

"No. It doesn't."

But there must have been something in her manner, something too cold, too self-absorbed. She must have been too wrapped up in herself, because she could feel, one day, that Adam wasn't quite with her anymore. His attention seemed elsewhere. The energy and awareness seemed somehow defused. And Bea realized how much she had come to count on the sharp engaged attention of her son.

Her eye was drawn again to the charcoal sketch. The figure of that long-ago boy who had been so aware of her, had given her so much of his longing and attention that it seemed to invest his whole awkward, hesitant stance. And she remembered that distant moment, the air on her naked skin, the charcoal knowing exactly what to do. And she thought of all those group portraits that Joan had done in their early years: the three of them, naked in that big armchair. Izzie and Adam laughing at the idea of it, cuddling and striking poses.

"Somehow," she said, "it all got tied together in my mind."

She put down the brush. With a little breath of hope she drew the t-shirt up over her head and let it drop. Her body was no longer what it had been, not so sleek and untried. But she felt the touch of the air and the long-ago familiar brush of the overalls against her breasts. It was tied now to so many things: posing for Joan, for Jonathan. Cuddling together with her children. The memory of Izzie at her breast at the start of everything—unwrapping herself like an afternoon snack. It made her smile to think this was something she could still call on. This feeling that embedded her now in the full breadth of her life. And she saw the answering look on Adam's face. A new quickening of concentration.

And as if teasing her, knowing he was altering the picture, he let the toga slip from his shoulder. He was always like that as a child, brazen, playful, wanting to be chased or attended to or comforted.

When they were all posing on that big armchair, often he would stand, just out of the picture, wanting to be cajoled, waiting to be drawn back in. It was like a game of tag. You're it. No, you are.

She had picked up her brush and loaded it, and gazed up at Adam, wired into the moment, the thread taut between them. And she saw the line of tension running through his muscles, and she knew she could capture it. Just that moment. Just there.

And the boy, the young, skinny, dear little child, all elbows and shoulder-bones and ribs—who had been just the other day a plump and laughing cherub at her side—threw off the long-wrapped fabric, let it fall from his hips, and stood with a bright, transfigured face, straining and taut. And he cried, "Oh, Bea! I love you, Bea!"

God help her! Oh, the poor poor boy! And what could she do? She couldn't think. She could barely breathe—her chest hollow and aghast. What had she been thinking? Stupid, stupid! What kind of a monster was she? She tried to speak. She tried to think of what to say. But in the end she could only turn and flee.

"How awful," said Harold.

And it was, of course it was. But it was worse than that. Much worse. Worse even than Adam's terrible embarrassment, standing there so brave and undone. She was shocked, of course. And horrified. She berated herself over and over.

But afterwards, as she cast her mind back, it grew increasingly clear to her that Weland would never have run away. If anything he would have relished the moment—drawn from it the last drop of feeling, made from it something great.

And it settled on her, in the days and weeks after. It dawned on her slowly and weighed down her heart. It wasn't simply that she was blind and unthinking—a thoughtless woman, a terrible mother. It wasn't only that she was selfish. No. In the end it was something far worse. Something irrefutable. She would never be a great painter—she saw that now, clear as clear could be—because she would never be selfish enough.

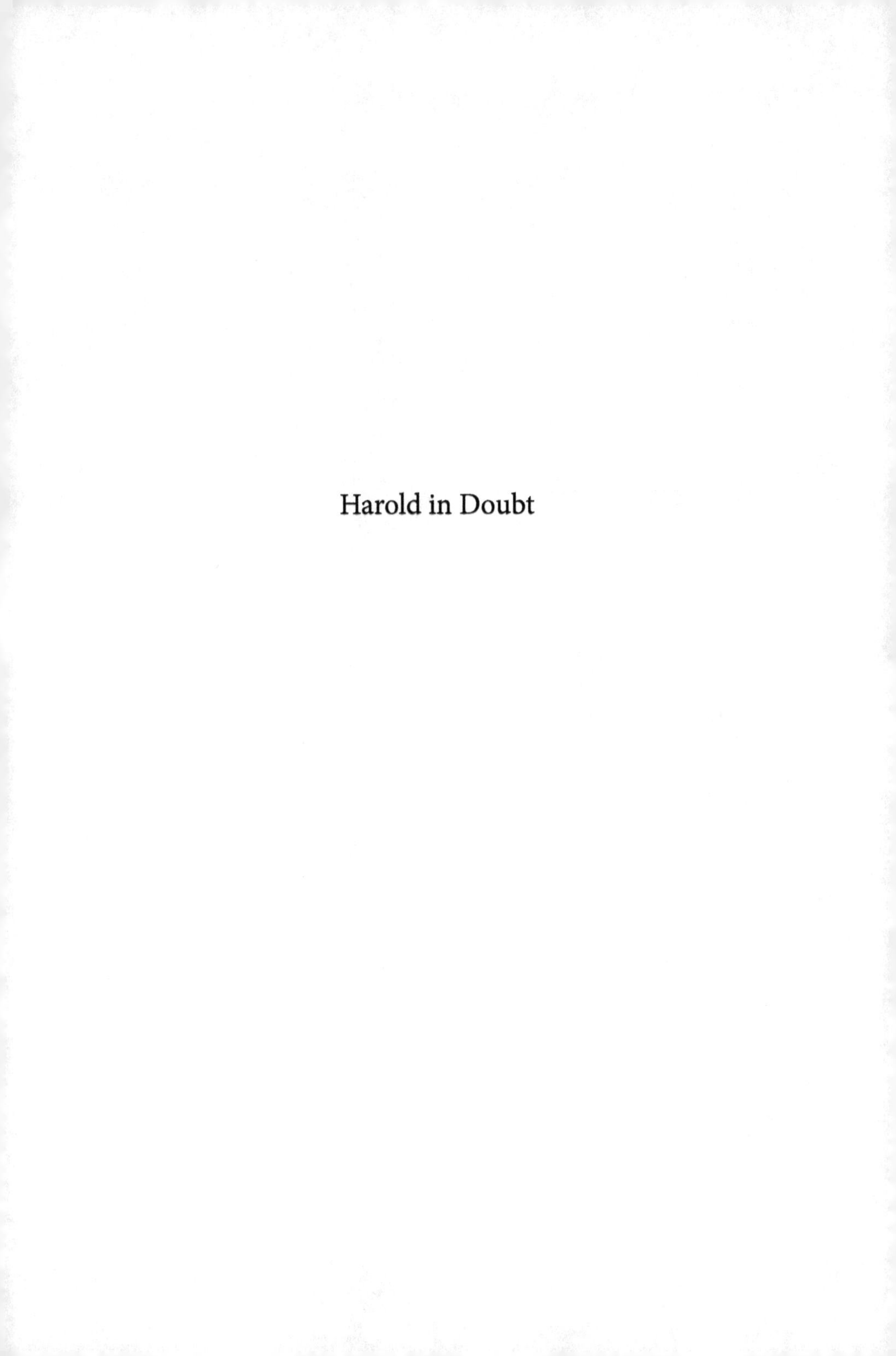

Harold in Doubt

40.

In his dreams he hears her crying. Quietly sobbing from her room down the hall. Of course the room is gone; the whole Rectory is gone. But the sobbing continues, achingly sad. When his daughter cried it was as if all the sorrows of the world had slipped into her heart, as if no one had ever been so desolate. And he would give anything to comfort her. But lately he has forgotten her. He realizes that now. He has let his mind wander, and somehow he has left off in the middle of a game.

They would play hide and seek. It was her favorite, but always rife with anxiety—she was a nervous child, tiny and young, without any real faith in the stability of things. They would play in his study. She would say, I'm going to hide under the chair, or in the closet, or behind the curtains—the basic tenets of the game were still foreign to her, but the essence was there. She would hold his attention, making certain he was watching, as she squeezed herself into the smallest of spaces, peering up at him to be sure he had not forgotten. And then she would tell him to close his eyes and count to ten. And when he opened them he would have to find her.

He couldn't move from his desk, but he would hunt in all the places she couldn't possibly be by calling them out, naming them, describing particular corners of the room in increasingly elaborate ways: up in the middle of the ceiling behind the lampshade on the electric sconce, behind the row of books at the top of the bookcase, beneath the huge and ancient armoire where his vestments were stored like angels in the off season. Are you in my top drawer? Are you under the carpet? Are you in the pocket of my work pants? And she would find each guess unbearably funny, and her laughter, unconfinable, would spill out into the room.

Then she would tease him by suggesting places, as if she could draw him away from her true location. And when he would describe himself tiptoeing across to remove, with a flourish, a pillow from the chesterfield or the elegant covering from the parakeet's cage, she would chortle in perfect triumph. No, she would say. He'd never find her.

But one day he had been distracted. Miss Pru was ill. He'd had to make arrangements for home visits and medicine. He had to talk to the doctor and arrange for the next gloomy step in her progress. Sara was at work, and she had warned him not to forget…something. His absent-mindedness was becoming a luxury he fully embraced in those dark days. Unimaginable now, when he couldn't forget anything at all. But at the time, his daughter, silent and huddled in the corner beneath the old Bishop's throne, had momentarily slipped his mind.

He had stepped out of the study to fetch some papers, and then made himself a cup of tea, and tidied the kitchen—a gesture to Miss Pru, who had never in her life allowed dishes to lie unwashed for so much as a morning. But in washing the dishes and putting them away he had slipped further from his game with Bea. And when he stepped back into the study, he heard her crying.

That was bad. Heartbreaking. But this was worse—her sobs coming to him from the depths of his dreams, from no place he could find. And though in the past he'd been able to hurry over to the Bishop's Chair, to scoop her up and tell her he had found her, of course he had—that she was right there, and he had known it all along—now he was trapped in the darkness. And all he could do was listen. I found you, he tried to say. But she was beyond his finding. Then the darkness seemed to clear a little. A vague sense of sight, almost cinematic in its dawning, revealed the spider, plump and furry, huddled in its shoebox, weeping in a quiet voice that only he could hear.

And he woke up.

41.

His daughter had loved to shop: clothes, jewelry, anything delicate and brightly colored. She would fondle the fabrics—stretching them, rubbing her cheek against them with a painstaking attention that would not be led astray. Returning home with a bag clutched in her hands she wore the grimly satisfied air of a miner returning from the rock face with her pockets full of ore.

He had bought her a bracelet once, an inexpensive bangle from a rack at the children's counter. They had passed through jewelry on their way to socks and underwear, and he had seen her eyes drawn to the jingling wrists of the cashier. She paused before a display of the most pedestrian tights to glance, haunted and surreptitious, at the click and glitter of them.

With great casualness he had strolled over to the wall of bracelets as if toward a flock of birds that had landed unexpectedly, and almost reluctantly Bea followed. *These are pretty,* he signed.

She shrugged. *They're okay.*

He chose one at random. *This is my favorite.*

It's okay, she agreed.

But she was reaching out, touching with a single fingertip one after another in a little pattern of her own devising: costume pearls, sapphires, rubies, sequins. A little nosing fingertip sniffing out the beauties of each. Then she brushed once, twice at a ruby band, then rubbed it gently as if erasing any sign of interest.

Do you want those tights? he asked, all innocent inquiry.

She glanced down, frowning—annoyed to discover she was still holding them. She went and hung them back up.

When she returned he was at the register. She regarded him without a word, a small forest creature watching the last of the acorns disappear—her face drawn into a look like the edge of despair but which he would now hold in his heart forever as an expression of the deepest hope.

He presented it formally, pinching two corners of the bag so that the pink-printed ribbons and bows of the paper unfurled beneath her gaze, and she took it without a word.

Sara had always made a point of telling her to say thank you for the slightest thing. "Thank Mr. Bancroft, Beatrice. Say thank you to Mrs. Swenson." She was determined that she be well trained. But in this moment—when she took the bag without the slightest sound, pinching the corners as he had done, holding it tightly in front of her as they walked out to the car—each moment of silence was another pearl added to the string. And when she finally spoke it was to whisper, "I like this bag."

A month ago, hollow and unreal, he had wandered through the children's department in Denning's. Racks of clothing like so many tiny children floated in the air, as if Bea and all her companions had gathered in the dim and festive elegance to remember, however briefly, what it had been like to wear the cares and pleasures of the world.

Today—stepping into *Iguana Gardens*—was nothing like that, but it brought the memory whispering back. No racks of clothing, no tiny children. But a whole store devoted to the small and colorful. Plastic fronds, bright feathers, brightly colored fur. Recorded noises of a tropical forest pattered and screeched off the walls so that, standing in the doorway, Harold felt buoyed aloft on the busy updraft of sound.

There was no sign of a human being, as if the whole store had been turned over to its mild and thoughtful denizens. But after a moment he made out the bright figure of Garden authority moving resolutely among the aisles. She wore a skirt and vest of orange and green, a bright yellow blouse, and a pert little cap like an air force cadet's. Her eyelids were peacock shaded; her lips the same bright blue. And her hair—bound up in pigtails beneath the jaunty cap—

jostled like a dashboard hula dancer.

"You look like a stewardess on the Mars to Neptune run."

Izzie offered him a dismissive frown, but he could see her trying on the image. She carried an enormous guinea pig in her arms, its fur all twisted cowlicks as if it had been groomed to within an inch of its life.

"Was he trying to escape?"

"He jus' gets lonely. His littermates have all found homes and he's beginning to wonde' if it's him."

"I hope you told him he looks very handsome."

"I think he's afraid tha's not enough."

Harold nodded sympathetically. "I can see that would be a worry."

"Would you lik' to hold him?"

"Better not. I'm not sure I have anything to offer, in the circumstances. But I did have a question. You mentioned a witch the other night. When we were out."

"Madame Reeve."

"You said you were studying with her."

"I'm her apprentice. I'm really lucky she took me on."

"The things is," said Harold reluctantly, "I was wondering if she did any sort of consultations? I've been having some bad dreams lately. And I have a few questions I'd like to ask her."

The girl looked doubtful. "I'm no' sure she does dreams."

"Well, it might be more than dreams. That's the thing. I might need a little help with the occult."

"Well," said Izzie. "She's very nice. And she's a powerfu' witch. I'm sure she could help in some way.

"So, how does it work? It's been a while since I've had any dealings with a witch. Do I make an appointment? Do I need a referral?"

"I have a lesson with her Thursday. You could come along, if you want."

"That would be great. Thanks. I'll count on you to protect me. In the meantime," he raised the shoebox in his hands, "I worry that I've been shirking my responsibilities. I was thinking we might be ready for an upgrade. And I thought I'd better consult an expert."

Izzie frowned over that for a moment. "Let me put Hercules back, and we can head to *The Land of Enchantment*."

42.

The desert section was in a back corner of the store: shelves of glass cages with fine white sand and an array of broken twigs like scattered coral—as if the ancient seas had only just withdrawn and left the world a drier, crueler place. Here and there, testing out the inhospitable landscape, tiny apocalyptic creatures moved. Scorpions carried the burden of their claws with a delicate, balletic ease. Orange and black lizards contemplated the ground before them, as if they had put down something precious long ago and now couldn't remember where. Tarantulas stood stock still—little hunched figures of threat and surprise—or picked their way slowly over the ground.

Harold's hold on the shoebox grew more cautious, as if only now remembering what he carried. He said, "How big a cage do you think it needs?"

"It's bad luck to call her 'It.'"

"Her."

"See? What kind of a monster would keep a 'her' locked away? Are you going to let her out?"

"I don't think so. She's frightening enough as it is."

"You'll want to keep some kind of a screen on top, so nobody gets in. You don't have a dog or a cat?"

"No."

"Weasel, ferret, hamster?"

"No."

"Chinchilla? Iguana? Monkey, parrot, macaw, turtle, snake?"

"Gosh," he said weakly. "How boring am I?"

But Izzie gave him a kindly look. "Don't worry. She's going to fix all that."

On a nearby counter, as if in the face of so much that was

sinister, someone had arranged an elaborate landscape. From *Oceans of the World* there were little plastic treasure chests, bright fans of kelp, and a sunken pirate ship that seemed to have embedded itself in the smooth Formica seabed. A little row of palm trees had been transplanted from *Turtle Island*. And an array of plush and feathered shapes, still smelling of catnip, were arranged in a short parade.

"Clearly you have a gift," said Harold.

"It's Adam. He's very talented."

"Did he work here with you?"

"Not exactly work. He said his role was to bring charisma to the place."

"Well, that's important, too."

Izzie reached under the counter and set before them a shallow plastic tray.

Harold examined it for a moment. "She's not a turtle."

"We won't tell her it's for turtles."

"It looks a little bleak"

"We've got a tiny TV you can put in there."

"Color?"

"No. Just black-and-white."

"What else?"

"Sand, usually. They're desert animals. A rock or two. It's like living in Tahiti. Do you think she'd like a palm tree?"

"She hasn't said no."

"Sometimes Adam and I used to heat the rocks with a hair dryer when it got chilly. They like to sit on them. Soak up the warmth."

"You and Adam sound like quite a team."

"He's very smart. And brave. Well. He's afraid of mice. But I think he feels sorry for them. He feels sorry for everybody except people."

"Do you feel sorry for them?"

She shrugged. "Nobody wants to be locked away in a room the size of a closet. But most people let them out, whatever they are. And you don't buy an animal unless you like it."

"I didn't actually buy this."

"Present?"

"No."

"Well," she considered. "Maybe the universe just wanted you to have a spider."

"That's what I'm afraid of," he said. "What do you suppose the universe wants me to buy her?"

Izzie considered for a moment. "Adam had this one customer. She kept buying cat beds. And her cat used to keep clawing them to bits."

The first time the woman had asked if she could return it. She said it was defective. But it looked like a knife fight. Great handfuls of stuffing hanging out.

"Adam said it probably wasn't the bed that was defective."

So he tried to explain to her, after the third time, that maybe the cat didn't want a bed. Oh, no, she said. He doesn't like to sleep on the floor. He needs someplace soft.

"So Adam said, Why don't you let him come in and pick it out himself?"

"Smart."

"He thinks of everything," Izzie agreed.

So she brought the cat in. A huge white Persian with a flat, angry face like he'd just bitten down on a garlic clove. She set him down in the middle of the cat aisle and stepped back.

"What happened?"

"He sits there looking around for a long time. Then abruptly he turns and stalks away."

They found him lying sprawled on the largest German Shepherd bachelor pad in the store. Genuine faux-sheepskin, leopard backing. Tulip lay in the center like a fallen paratrooper in the middle of a football field.

"Tulip?"

"Names are magical," Izzie agreed.

"So you're saying we should let the spider decide?"

Harold drew the lid from the shoebox. The spider was huddled in one corner. He prepared to tip her out onto the counter.

"Careful. Spiders are very delicate. You need to hold them gently. And be careful not to drop them."

"Want do you mean 'hold them'? People pick them up?"

"Sure."

"They don't bite?"

"They don't want to. Too much trouble. If you're not dinner, they won't waste the venom."

"Venom?"

"The world's not a picnic. Do you want a little leash?"

He looked up. Her pale and painted face was impassive. "Do you have one?"

"No."

"Does anyone?"

"I doubt it. But it's a cool idea, isn't it?"

Gently she reached down thumb and forefinger and picked up the spider. The legs started churning frantically, but Izzie was unperturbed. She set her down in the chaotic landscape of Adam's imagining, and for a moment the spider sat transfixed, as if all her spidery thoughts had never compounded anything so remarkable.

"She looks interested."

In fact she looked overwhelmed. The feathered toys, the deep-sea treasure, the small sunken ship—it all seemed too much for her. Standing there in that crazy setting she looked so different from the other creatures. So plump and uncertain beside those scarecrow shapes.

Now she gathered up her courage and approached the row of plastic palm tress, tiptoeing up as if they might, like a restive herd, go galloping away. Reaching out a pair of tentative legs, she nudged the stiff fronds, uncertain what to make of them. Then, when nothing startled her, she drew closer, peering around as if to take in every aspect of the wonders before her.

She passed the ship under quick review, as if disdaining anything so obvious and dull, and then glanced at the little stand of plastic kelp, then back to the palm trees. And all the while she was moving by feint and indirection toward the coiled grandeur of a cat toy—rumpled feathers, the glint of sequins. She touched it, touched it again. Then reaching out she drew the purple feather delicately through the tiny combs of her claws as if marveling at the workmanship.

When she turned back to the other objects she kept a back leg on the toy for as along as she could. And when she finally ventured away Harold could see in the bright fluorescent light a tiny, gleaming filament of her own, drawing itself out between the spider and her treasure, as if even in parting she could not bear to lose touch.

They chose the widest of the plastic trays, and laid out a level plain of soft, white sand. Then two flat rocks to form a cave, and a tiny pond before it like some desert watering hole. In the end neither could resist the palm trees, and off to the side Harold set the cat toy, bright and bejeweled.

"Now all you have to do is lift her in there," said Izzie.

"Could you do that?"

"She's your spider."

Reaching out Izzie hovered a fingertip over the plump little waist. "Just there. In the middle of the legs. Be very gentle."

Harold felt queasy. His palms were damp. But cautiously he grasped and lifted. She seemed to cling to the countertop for an instant, every foot reluctant to let go. But then she came free and rose into the air. Her legs started racing, and his heart jumped—he almost dropped her. But instead he lowered her carefully into her new home and let her go. She scurried forward and stopped, as if realizing the worst was over. And Harold stood marveling at the lingering softness of the fur and the strange solidity of the little body, so appalling and yet so cunningly constructed.

That night in his room he opened the little carton of grubs that Izzie had given him. They lay in the bottom like dirty grains of rice. He remembered his earlier indiscriminate feeding: old flies and milk and bits of bread, anything he could find that might do.

The spider seemed to remember, too. She cowered beneath a palm tree. But as he brought the carton over she seemed willing to give him a second chance. Stepping out she looked up with something like eagerness, and he sprinkled the grubs around her. They pattered like a spring rain onto the fine, white sand. She stepped over and hunched delicately by one and then the next, silent and unmoving.

After a while the spider turned back, surrounded now by little dried husks. It looked up at him. *More?*

"Spiders can't talk," said Harold, though of course that didn't matter. He used to talk to Bea, at first, after she was gone, though it always made him cry.

More?

"Why not?" he said. "Grubs for all my friends."

He sprinkled in the last of them, and the spider dipped its head and went about its work.

When it was finished it settled back and looked up again. It started rocking on its legs, a little movement up and down like a steady pulse. "I can get you more," said Harold. "I can get you anything you want."

But it just sat there, gazing up and beating like a little heart.

43

The witch's house was a small grey saltbox with a front porch and a narrow driveway. It was neat and freshly painted, with the manicured grass and immaculate plantings of someone trying hard to blend in.

"I wouldn't have thought witches were so into home maintenance," said Harold.

"Reeve lives here with her brother. Bernard designs computer games. I think they've always lived here. Reeve says it's a good neighborhood because students don' really care about stuff, so nobody complains if the spells get a little strange."

Wheeling Henry in her cart Izzie led the way around the side of the house.

The garden was a wonder. From a wide stone bench it stretched away to the distant boundary. Large and small, tiny and sprawling, leaves billowed up to catch the sun and breeze, or huddled under the shadowy comfort of muslin awnings. And in the center, barely rising above the tangle of green, a stone fountain stood in a low, square pond, spilling its steady liquid rustling into the stillness.

On the bench, like a mermaid on her rock, a woman sat in flowing shades of green. She regarded him from the shadowed veranda of her wide straw hat as they approached. "And what have we here?"

"This is my friend Mr. Harold, Reeve."

"Ah," she said drily. "The author. I've heard so much about you. And what brings you to our charming little hamlet?"

"Mr. Harold used to be a priest."

"Isn't that something. Father Harold. And did you believe in God?"

He hesitated. "I believed in George Herbert. After a while it amounted to the same thing."

"And what about love, Mr. Harold? Did you believe in love? Or just pornography?"

He opened his mouth to reply, but then just closed it again.

The witch smiled. "People have funny ideas about witches. Scary old women in stylish black, turning princes into frogs and frogs into God knows what. Is that your experience, Mr. Harold, would you say?"

"Well," he conceded. "The scary part is true."

"Good. Fear is always a good beginning. But modern witchcraft—not just the arts of Wiccan but the larger understanding of the whole, steady flow of power in the natural world—all that depends on a true understanding of love. You have to recognize how powerful it is. How it connects everyone, for good or bad. You have to realize what a killer it is."

"Oh," said Harold. "That much I think I know."

He sat down on the bench. Her eyes travelled to the elaborate plastic cage on his lap. "Did you bring me a present?"

He slipped off the cover. The spider was hunched beneath a palm tree like a castaway on a wide beach. Reeve gazed down at it without expression. "What are you doing, Mr. Harold?"

"Can I ask you a question?"

"That depends. Do you really want an answer?"

"Do you believe in the spirit world?"

"You mean something like a séance? I'm a witch, father. Not a medium."

"Not like that. Not exactly. But is it something you believe? That spirits can be restless? That they can haunt the living?" He ran his tongue over dry lips. He was staring down into the box as if, having removed the cover, he could not look away. "Do you believe in the transmigration of souls?"

"Ah. If you mean reincarnation, father, I think you should say what you mean."

His voice was a whisper. "Yes."

"Souls coming back from the dead? I didn't know that was part of church doctrine."

"Is it anything you know about? From your reading and study? Is it something you've come across? Or is it just ridiculous? Tell me if it's just ridiculous."

"Everything is ridiculous, father." But her voice turned almost gentle. "What exactly are you asking me?"

"You know what I'm asking."

"No, I don't think I do."

"Nothing. It's nothing," he said abruptly. "Never mind."

"Is this a theological discussion we're having?"

"No. Forget I asked." He started to cover the box, but she laid a cool hand on his wrist.

"What is it, Harold? What are you thinking? Don't be afraid."

"It's crazy. I can't say it out loud."

"You have to, Harold. That's the rule about magic. You have to say it out loud."

"How can I? It's insane."

And she leaned toward him, almost confidingly, but with that hard smile on her lips. And he could see that, yes, indeed, witches were a cruel bunch.

She matched her whisper to his. "Do you want to ask me if it's possible? Is that it? Do you want to know if it can be true?"

"No," he said. "Don't tell me. I've changed my mind. I don't want to know."

"It's too late, Harold. Don't you see? The question has been asked."

She leaned back on the bench, taking in the wider view. "I blame it all on modern science. It's taken away our greatest comforts. But you, Harold. You're a man of faith, aren't you? Isn't that the whole point? Belief precedes the fact? That's your bread and butter. All you have to do is believe."

"I'm not sure I can."

"And you want to know if I do? Is that it? Is that what you're asking? You want to know if you can have your daughter back? If that's even possible?"

His hands curled hesitantly around the plastic cage.

"You look like a man who's afraid of spiders."

"I am."

"Fear is just a pathway, Harold. You know that."

And with a cool, deliberate hand she reached in and lifted out the delicate creature.

"Don't hurt her!"

But the spider went still in her fingers, as if transfixed by her touch. She held it up before him, and he flinched. "Hold out your hand."

"I can't."

So she set the spider down gently on the back of his wrist.

He had almost forgotten. It was another game of theirs. When his daughter's teeth were new and she was still fascinated by them. They would watch wildlife documentaries together and Bea would observe with special care the sharp, snapping fierceness or the slow, ruminating crunch of teeth through leaves or stalks of bushes. And they would play a game. She would announce the animal, and he would hold out his hand. She would take it solemnly in both of hers, and bending down a delicate, birdlike face, she would bite him gently on the wrist. I'm a shark, she would say. I'm a panda. I'm a gazelle.

Now he stared down at the spider. "Don't move," he whispered. "Please don't move."

And it might have been a dream. The spider stood there, perfectly still, as if this was all it had ever wanted. And even as the witch reached out to lift the spider back into its cage, he could feel the delicate pin-prick of the claws on his skin like little teeth.

44

Today, Izzie explained, they were working on a potion. "Reeve thought it was something I needed to learn."

"We're just beginning now," said the witch. "A good potion could take weeks or a month to make. Sometimes it's just a question of timing. Harvesting each ingredient at the right phase of the moon. And then you have to warm it for a night and a day in the blood of a murdered stag."

Harold peered over. "And that's necessary, is it?"

"Crucial. You need all that selfish masculine energy cut short by violence and bad luck."

"Reeve says we can use a heating pad," Izzie confided, "and a warm-water bath."

The witch gave a philosophical shrug. "It won't be as strong, but Izzie's still a young witch. She's got a tender heart."

"But not you," said Harold.

She gave him a cool look. "There's no room for tenderness in a love potion."

Izzie had pulled on her own green robe, and now she cheerfully knelt by Henry's cart removing her equipment; gardening gloves, pruning scissors, tweezers, and a small plastic protractor.

"Do you have your list?" called Reeve.

The girl held up a sheet of paper covered with intricate notes.

"Is that from Gardner?"

"Mostly. But I found a copy of Agrippa in the college library."

"Good girl. We'll start with the herbs. Remember to be mindful of the shadows and the state of your heart. No timidity. Wait for just that moment of fierce commitment. Your power and control are crucial in the moment of harvesting."

"Yes, Reeve."

"And set the timer. Remember, slow is better. Draw out the energy."

"Yes, Reeve."

"Wait."

She drew from the pocket of her robe two tiny boutonnieres of sharp green leaves. "We're working under the sign of *ilex aquifolium* today." Dutifully the girl raised her chin, and Reeve pinned the piece of holly onto the collar of her robe. Then she handed her the second. "For Henry. Don't let her eat it. I didn't bring one for the spider."

"That's okay. They can share."

Izzie turned and wheeled her way along the stone path into the middle of the garden and dutifully set to work.

Harold watched with an air of foreboding. "This is a beautiful spot," he said.

"It's my cornucopia. Every witch needs one."

"I've never really believed in witches."

"Oh, I'm sure that's not true."

"Well. Not for a long time."

"Well, it doesn't really matter, Harold. What matters is: we believe in you."

She had lifted onto her lap a wide wicker tray in which she was sorting a pile of harvested greens, picking through the leaves, pinching off buds, dividing them into smaller and smaller stacks around the outer edge.

"Is that lunch?" he asked.

"You're more than welcome. Simmer it lightly and it's a powerful emetic. Very gentle but effective. Boil it longer, it induces sharp pains. It's like you've swallowed broken glass. Crush it into a paste and slip it into something tasty, and it will give you some of the least pleasant hallucinations you can imagine." She reached over to a smaller pile of dirt-encrusted lumps. She picked one up and carefully began pinching off the root hairs, rubbing it clean until it shone like a slender undersized radish. "It has a nice crunch and a sour, nutty flavor."

"You think it will solve all my problems?"

"Oh yes."

And when he made no move to take it, she dropped it back on its little pile with an easy laugh.

Harold gazed out over the garden to where Izzie was kneeling amid the leaves. He thought about the love potion, simmered in the blood of a murdered stag. "Is she going to be all right?"

"Oh, probably. She'll make an excellent witch, if we can just tap into all that rage."

"Really?" he said bleakly. "Rage?"

"Oh, yes. She's a caldron of fury."

Harold digested that for a moment.

"How well do you know her?" the witch inquired.

"Not very well. She's very sweet."

"Oh. She's the sweetest girl imaginable. That's part of the problem. There's no such thing as a sweet witch. Sweetness is nice. It's very pleasant. But there's no force in sweetness. No steel. That's my job. To give the rage a little air so it can burn itself out, without destroying all the parts that make her such a lovely girl."

He hesitated. "Does her mother know that's your plan?"

"Her mother hasn't a clue. You know our Bea. Perfectly nice woman. That's where Izzie gets her sweetness. But she's a dangerous mother. She thinks she's strong. She thinks she has what she needs to protect Izzie. But she's out of her depth."

"What does she need to protect Izzie from?"

"From life, Harold. Tell me you don't know that already. From love. From anybody stronger and fiercer than she is. They'll chew her up."

"And you?" he asked. "You're not going to chew her up?"

"I'm going to teach her how things work."

She reached up and drew from her collar the little bundle of holly leaves. "Hold out your hand. Come on. Don't be a baby. What do you think I'll do?"

Reluctantly he held it out, and the witch dragged the sharp, spiny leaf over his palm. It left in its wake a thin red line and the first slow droplets of blood.

"See? That didn't hurt so much."

He was watching her carefully.

"If I were to break the leaf and rub it along that scratch, do you know what would happen? Nothing too bad. A little queasiness. A few chills. It's used to bring down fever and lower blood pressure. Though that's not always a picnic either." She raised the little bundle before him. "Do you want to try one of the berries? They look delicious, don't they?"

"Are you telling me to eat one?"

"Oh, I wouldn't if I were you. Vomiting, convulsions, even death. But such a pretty plant." She reached up and carefully re-pinned it to her collar.

He started to rub at the cut.

"Stop," she said. "May I?"

She drew from her pocket a tiny square of white bread like a large sugar cube. She dabbed it along the line of the cut, mopping up little stains of red. "Such a pity to waste it. Since we're doing without the stag." She placed the bread carefully into a small wooden box and slipped it back into her pocket.

Harold rubbed at the crusted blood. Then he reached over and helped himself to one of the plants from the middle of the wicker tray. With great concentration he started to shred it into tiny, moist flecks, scattering the pieces, feeling the different textures of leave, bud, and stem all turning into moist and scattered shreds. He said, "Izzie seems to be a little on the outs with her mother."

"So you're a family counselor now, Harold?"

He said nothing.

"She's a teenage girl. She's on the outs with everyone."

"Except you."

She shrugged. "Who doesn't love a witch?"

"And Adam, of course."

Reaching over she slapped his hand. "Don't touch your eyes. If you're going to help, you need to be more careful. Just separate those top few leaves, then the stalks, and the roots go here."

He picked up another plant and started to work more carefully. "Do you really think Adam can give her what she wants?"

"Adam has a streak of selfishness which is not uncommon in the male gender."

"And you think some potion will help?"

Reeve regarded him for a moment. "What do you know about witches?"

"Just you."

"And love potions?"

"Not a blessed thing."

"There are different kinds of love, so there are different kinds of potion. There are some that make you sick with love, others that make you giddy, and some that just leave you exhausted by it all. There are some that prick you or pinch you or keep you wound up so tight you can't sit still. There are potions that will breathe a spark into a flame, and others that are like pouring gasoline. There are some that need to be given publicly, others that need to be secret. Sometimes you want the victim to know and sometimes you don't."

"Could you maybe not call him a victim?" said Harold.

She gave him a steady look. "There's nothing easy about love."

"So what are you going to do?"

"Izzie is going to make a love potion for Adam. She's going to give his heart a little jolt. I'm going to try to make sure she doesn't stop it altogether."

"I hope you're exaggerating."

She dusted the dirt off her hands. "A love potion can kill you the same way love can: all at once, or a little at a time."

"But isn't she too young for all this?"

And she regarded him almost pityingly. "You don't think Izzie knows about love?"

"I don't want her to get hurt."

"Oh, Harold. It's much too late for that."

Out in the middle of the garden Izzie suddenly stood up. "Reeve! Reeve! It's Henry. It's happening again!"

The witch sprang to her feet. Gathering her robe about her, she hurried out to where Izzie knelt beside the little cart. The cat seemed to have been roused from some terrible dream. Her eyes were wide, she was panting slowly, drawing out from the depths of her chest a low, breathing moan.

` Izzie was wild with fear. "What can we do? It's worse than before. We have to do something."

"We should take her to the vet," said Harold. "There's got to be a vet."

"She's no good! She wouldn't do anything. Reeve can help him." And she turned, wide-eyed and frantic. "Do you have the potion?"

"It's inside. Let me get it."

The witch ran lightly in the billowing robe, criss-crossing the paths, then vanishing into the house. Izzie was groaning along with the cat, stroking her head. "It's okay, Henry. It's okay. Reeve is coming. She'll be here soon." And she looked up at Harold. "Tell her. Tell her Reeve is coming."

And the fear in her voice seemed to clutch at his heart with all his remembered grief. Hurriedly he reached out and ran a hand over the wide head. "It's okay, sweetheart," he whispered. "It's okay."

Reeve emerged from the house and rushed over. She held in her hand a small vial capped with an eye dropper. As she sank to her knees beside them Harold could see what an effort it cost her to suddenly grow calm and cool. She pressed the vial against Henry's forehead, then against the side of her panting chest, murmuring steadily under her breath, "In the name of the goddess who breathes life into us all I consecrate and charge this elixir as a tool for healing and for grace. Reach out your hand, gentle mother, and touch the troubled heart of your servant Henry, and bring her your peace." She unscrewed the cap and drew up a little clear liquid. Then pressing the tip into the corner of the cat's clenched jaw, she squeezed.

"More," said Izzie. "Please give her more."

"It takes a moment to work." But she refilled the dropper and gave her a second dose.

Harold continued to stroke the cat's head. He sensed the slow relief spreading down through the body. The panting slowed. Henry turned to peer up at Izzie with the light of relief brimming in her eyes, and she began to purr.

"That's right. That's right, Henry. That's better. It's working."

"I'll make some more of this," said Reeve. "We'll have to give it to her regularly."

"Good. That's good. That'll be fine. She's good at taking medicine. She'll take it all."

After a long moment the witch capped the bottle and climbed to her feet. "I'd better put this back in the fridge."

With a glance at Henry, settling back onto her cushion, Harold stood as well. Together they climbed the stairs and stepped into a bright and modern kitchen.

"I take back everything I thought," said Harold. "That potion is amazing."

But Reeve was standing by the closed refrigerator, if she'd forgotten the spell to open it. "It's not a potion. It's a painkiller. Buprenex. I got it from the vet. She said it was all we could do."

Harold stared. "What do you mean all? It seems to help."

"There's a tumor," she said. "There's nothing to be done."

"There's got to be something."

"Don't be ridiculous, Harold," she snapped.

He digested this for a moment. "Does Izzie know?"

"She knows. But I don't think she believes."

"She believes in you."

"She does," the witch said bleakly. "What am I supposed to do?"

And there was something in the way she stood there, drooping under the weight of it all—something sad and reminiscent that seemed to reach back to all the half-remembered moments of his life. And her life, too, it seemed. For she gazed up at him and said, "What in the world are you doing here, Harold? Why have you come back?"

PART TWO

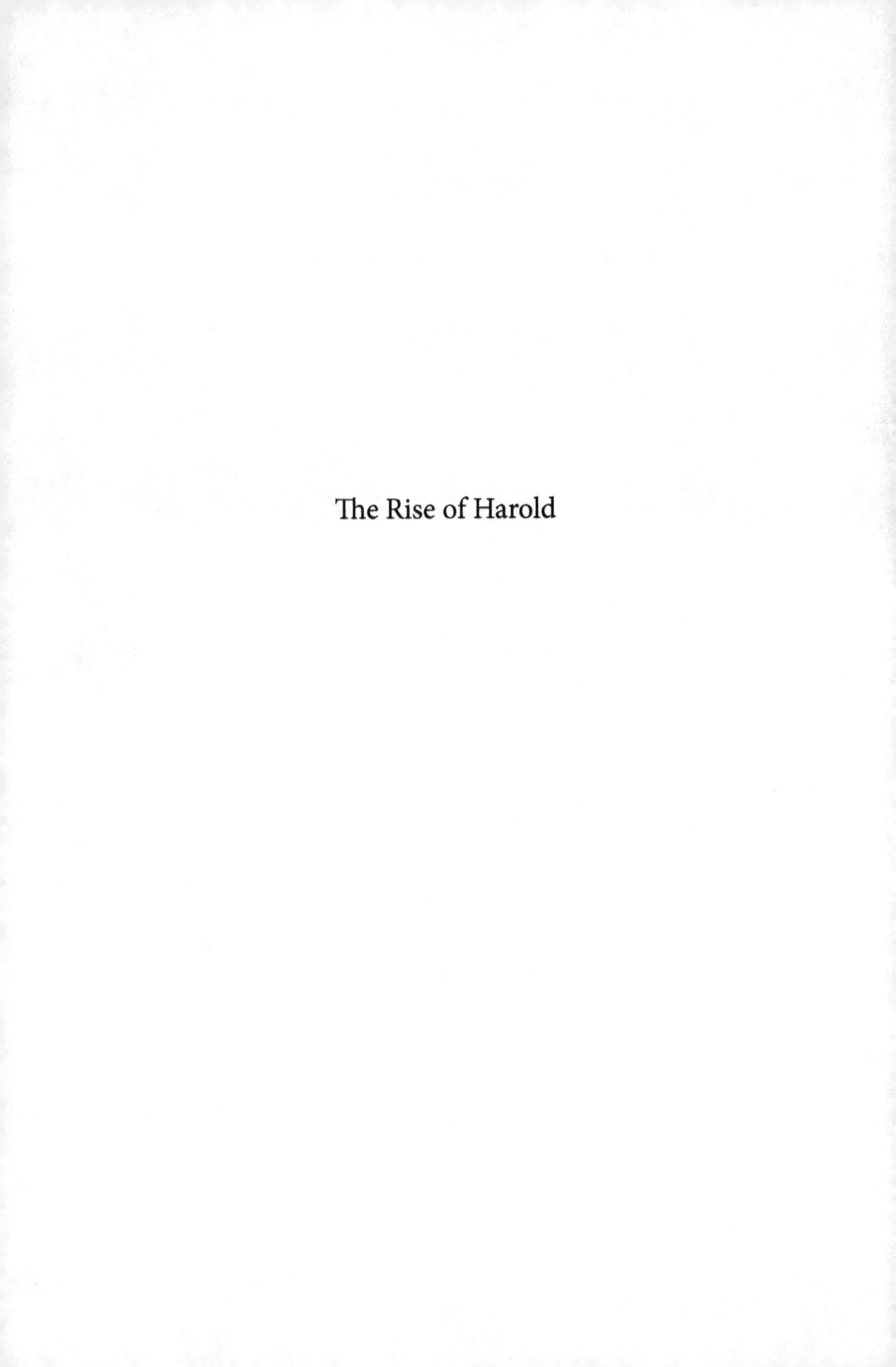

The Rise of Harold

45.

He was driving away from everything, growing more frantic with every mile as if the whole adventure, unfolding out of a single moment, was collapsing back again. The chance meeting, the long drive north, the firelight, the sketching hour—it had lifted him on a breath of wonder, then burst. He thought of the wide expanse of the college ride board. *I'm heading beyond my wildest dreams.* And it had been true. A whole new life about to start. But now with the island behind him, at the ripe old age of twenty, all the wonder and purpose were draining from his heart.

An intersection drew up before him, and a single mile marker: Pont-de-Gaillard 27 km. No other sign of life—an empty sky over empty fields as far as the eye could see. But then he remembered his own words. *I'm visiting my aunt. She lives beyond All Expectations.* And he turned.

You can only run away so long before you find yourself running towards.

The town was disappointing—three strands of wind-chipped houses strung between the unexpected grandeur of two stone churches. The downtown was a single block of stores—grocery, hardware, café—as if under the weight of all that emptiness even the townsfolk couldn't imagine more. No ATM, no hotel, and on the grocery store bulletin board, amid fliers for church suppers, prayer meetings, and a quilting club, there was not a single room for rent.

He bought a quarter-pound of cheese, a banana, and a bag of freshly-baked hotdog buns and walked slowly up one side of the street and down the other, from the prosperous sun-baked grandeur of the Presbyterian steeple to the square solidity of the Anglican nave, cool beneath the only canopy of trees on Main Street.

He came to a stop in the shade. Beyond a low stone wall a

spring welled up over a cushion of moss. There was a stone bench beside it and, hanging on a rusted chain, an ancient tin mug. He knew enough to see it as a sign. But even years later he couldn't be sure what kind—the beginning of all his good luck or the end. He sat on the bench and ate his lunch. He could sleep in his car, eat out of the grocery store. It wasn't exactly a plan. Just a way to cling to all that had happened in the last two days. He had fallen into a fairy tale and he already understood the only rule that applied: if you leave, it will vanish forever.

An elderly woman in a blue floral dress came stalking out of the stone house, drying her hands on her apron. He gazed up at her. "I don't suppose you're going to grant me three wishes?"

"Are you going to eat that banana?"

He hesitated. "I was. Would you like it?"

"Just don't leave the peel behind."

"No. I won't." And then, "This is a beautiful spot."

"Yes, it is. Have you been to the Presbyterians? It's a great showy place, but not a decent tree to be had. Nothing but elms there fifty years ago. They couldn't stop talking about them—their crown of elms. But then God smote them in their pride. Not a one survived. And the roots are so rotten, even now, that nothing will grow." She gave him a look of flinty satisfaction. "I like a story with a moral, don't you?"

"I guess it depends on the moral."

She turned back to the rectory. "I wouldn't drink from the spring. With all the run-off, it's a little chancy."

He rested and then walked for a while. The town was sun-bleached and dry. Houses and yards, out-buildings, the occasional yelp of a dog within its fence. He bought more bread and cheese and a bottle of water, and with the first grey of twilight he drove back the way he had come.

For a moment, following the featureless road, he couldn't remember the turn-off. He was certain he had come too far. But as he rounded a long curve the arrangement of spruce trees seemed suddenly to make a new kind of sense, and he turned in among them. He didn't have the darkness to make it familiar; he had to fight against the feeling that it was all too ordinary. But the gravel road extended its own familiar promise, and when he came at last to the clearing by the water with the three parked cars he turned off the engine.

Water lapped against the stones of the shore. The breeze carried a distant sound of voices. As the sky turned dark, the cabin lights came on. He wasn't sure what he'd expected. The familiar voices unnerved him; he felt so far outside it all. He ate his dinner sitting by the water's edge, then drove back through the darkness and parked beneath the whisper of the maple trees beside the church. And curling up in the back seat, with his overnight bag as a pillow, he sank into a lake of sleep.

A sharp tapping on his window woke him—the old woman frowning darkly. She seemed to grow even more disapproving as he rolled it down. "Are you running away from home?" she demanded.

"In a manner of speaking."

"You can't sleep here."

"Sorry."

"There's no parking in front of the church."

"I'm just passing through," he said. "But I'd like to do it as slowly as possible."

She weighed him in a stony gaze—and in all the years that followed he often wondered what it was she saw. Because after a moment she said, "I suppose you're hungry."

"I am a little tired of bread and cheese."

He was less needy than she would have liked—she had an

unexpectedly generous heart, and it had been a year and a half since Father Ben had died. She cooked him an enormous breakfast, a working man's breakfast she called it. Eggs, sausage, potatoes, toast, a heavy pot of tea. She sat beside him at the kitchen table watching him eat, posing questions in a prim schoolmarmish voice. How old was he? Where was he from? How long had he been on the road? She wanted him to be a runaway at the edge of his endurance, someone abandoned by his life, and he had smiled at the thought. Though by the end of the summer, of course, it was all perfectly true.

She refilled his cup, and her conversation turned to the drip in the gutters and the sponginess of the back steps, the way the shutters banged terrifically in every high wind. And he wondered how long she'd been living alone—she seemed ready to talk about anything. But then he realized her tone was not so much aggrieved as expectant. Part and parcel of the fortifying breakfast.

He wasn't a tea drinker. He'd had coffee since the age of fourteen, when he and his mother were left alone. He hadn't particularly liked the taste, but it seemed a small enough thing to do for her: share the French Press she used to share with his father. And now, as the old woman poured the bitter, tannic tea, cutting it with milk and a level teaspoon of sugar, he caught the same familiar tenor of heartbreak.

So when his plate was empty and the woman poured out the last trickle of tea, he said, "Well, I guess I'd better get to it."

46.

When they were young, he and Marshall were always left on their own during the cocktail hour. From six to eight each day his parents withdrew into their lamp-lit study for drinks and cheese and crackers. It was their moment together at the end of the day, and whenever he wandered past the door he would step into a rustle of pages and a murmur of voices that seemed all but unanchored in the world of things.

There was no one his age in the neighborhood. All the young parents had moved in at the same time, and all their children had arrived on schedule. His appearance had taken everyone by surprise. And it was not the least of Marshall's kindnesses that he allowed a shy and awkward brother nine years younger a role in the complex, recondite games that tended to evolve among the children of academics. It was early on, when he was celebrating his fourth birthday and a crowd of twelve- and thirteen-year old boys had cheerfully hijacked his party, that Marshall gave him his name.

"Alan's a dorky name," he said. "You need a new one. That'll be my birthday present." And he raised his fork. "I hereby dub you, Butt Wipe."

"No, no," said Leslie, the son of an astrophysicist. "People will make fun. How about Dick Wad?"

"Toad Spittle?"

"Crap for Brains?"

"Ass Hat?"

He had been caught between pleasure in the attention and a vague disquiet that this might cause some problems down the line. But it was Marshall, after all. "Whatever you like," he said.

"Ass Hat, it is." And he kissed him on the forehead. "Now you can't wipe it off."

His parents weren't pleased, but he was attached to his brother, who generously shortened it to Ash. The name came and went and came again over the next ten years, but with the death of Marshall and his father on their way to Georgetown Law School's first-year orientation, it became the least of his problems and one of the few things he had to hold onto.

For the first month after the accident his mother slowly came apart. She taught her classes, she cooked their meals, she sat across the kitchen table and pushed her dinner around on its plate. But then she went to bed early, and Ash could hear her sobbing through the wall.

Then one day it occurred to him. And when she came home from work at six o'clock he was waiting with the cocktail tray and the shaker and a fresh piece of cheddar cheese and a box of Wheat Thins. He had set them up on the table in the study across from the double desk, with the lamp on and Shubert on the stereo. He had put on a suit and tie and shined his shoes, and he was standing like a head waiter by the two big armchairs.

He half-expected laughter. But she sank into the chair, and he poured her drink. She waited, as if for her life—so damaged and bent—to reshape itself around her. Ash caught her hesitation; he poured himself a drink. Then he sat down in his father's chair and asked her about her day. She took a hesitant sip and told him, slowly at first, about the faculty meeting. About her afternoon in the library. About the particular difficulty of Donne's holy sonnets—the looming Calvinism like a terrible dread, and the desperate mixture of hope and despair that seemed to turn every poem into a struggle. Fearing that she might run down, Ash took a small encouraging sip of the bitter gin every time she slowed.

The cocktail hour expanded to fill their lives—she seemed to have no strength for anything else. They would sit in the study from six until bed time. Shubert on the stereo, or Mendelsohn, or finally

Beethoven. That was a measure of their grief, as well. Listening to his father's favorites, they would drink whiskey or gin, depending on the season, and talk about her day. They discussed her work, her graduate courses, the progress of her research, and Ash would sip his cocktail—extra soda and bitters being the only adjustment to his tender years that either of them would allow.

He wept alone in his room; his mother didn't allow reminiscence. But in the evenings they sat together, and as the years passed and the sharpness of their grief dulled, it remained the most comforting part of each day, when even the most ordinary conversation was recast into shadowy alignment with all that had vanished.

Into this space the metaphysical poets extended themselves, since they, at least, had not altered. They were the subject of his mother's current book. She would read long stretches of verse aloud, working out her argument, making her case. And as he got older he would take his turn. Ash didn't read very well. The words shifted under his eyes, and he stumbled over the uneven lines. So he would study for their conversations. His mother focused on a narrow number of poets each term, so during the free portions of his day he could work his way through the texts that were her mainstay and support. Herbert, Donne, Marvell, Milton, Spenser, Sidney, Shakespeare. The lyric Shakespeare, his mother would say, as if distinguishing her own interests from anything that might be perceived as popular. And so Ash read, and memorized, and welcomed himself into the array of poems that preserved, like a roof over their heads, the sturdy structure of their lives.

He didn't go away to college. There were many good reasons not to. The local university was excellent. His mother's job gave him free tuition. And he could tell that she preferred him to stay. She didn't say so—she never would—but she was steady now, settled into their routine, and he couldn't be the one to disturb it. He lived at home and spent his days at the university, and he felt that somehow he had succeeded against all odds in keeping the whole teetering ship of their lives afloat.

He wasn't sure when his mother started seeing Clement Bishop. Or why. Perhaps it was the name, so steeped in connotations of medieval learning. Or his trim appearance. Or his voice, deep and perfectly suited to hushed library tones. Perhaps it was the complementarity of a new and related field. Or maybe just the obvious: that nothing, not grief, not even comfort, lasts forever.

Ash began seeing them together around the university, in the shaded corners of the courtyard, at his mother's office. Then one day he stepped into the house and heard their voices rising from the study. A conversation so low and even-toned, so unexcitably interesting, that his heart sank.

He was startled by his anger the way you can be startled by a companion you have too long taken for granted. He tried to fight back, he tried pulling away. He spent more time at the library, more time at his campus job. He started drinking with a co-worker, a plump, intense girl with issues of her own. But he got no reaction at all. He decided to do a junior year abroad. Study in France. At the *Centre d'Études Médiéval* in Rouen. His mother barely noticed. He was preparing to go, had made the arrangements, when everything changed.

With his mother's stroke, he and Clement became the same age. After visiting hours at the hospital they would return, just the two them, to his mother's study and sit at the small mahogany table and sip their scotch. He was grateful for Clement's presence. But at the same time he marveled at the fact that he and Clement—who, after all, had known his mother for such different lengths of time— should behave so exactly the same.

When she emerged from the hospital, calm, smiling, but

moving with a delicate balance that seemed almost like absent-mindedness, she allowed Ash to do nothing for her. Over the years he had transformed himself into a colleague, and now she couldn't ask a colleague for the sort of intimate and embarrassing help that she required. So she turned to Clement.

They were married the following week, and Ash saw her less and less. She would smile at him. But whether it was the stroke or the time or just the nature of things, she seemed to regard him with a slight hesitation, as if it took her a moment to fit him back into the story of her life. By this time all the programs to Europe were closed. So the junior year abroad turned into a junior year away which turned, with more abruptness than Ash could possibly have imagined, into his life.

47.

With breakfast behind them the old woman led him out to a weathered shed in the back corner of the yard and unlocked the door. "You'll need Franklin's tool box."

It wasn't so much a box as a wide wooden tray, battered and paint-licked and crowded with tools. It was very heavy. But under the woman's expectant gaze he hauled it out.

As a boy he had mowed the lawn, raked the leaves, shoveled snow in the winter. But anything more complex had always been the province of the series of handymen his mother had found through the university. Ash had watched them attentively but with a kind of dread, as if, like his father and brother, these people, too, might simply disappear and leave him with their tasks to be done. So that now, hoisting the toolbox, he moved with the reluctant assurance of one who has at least seen it done.

She led him to the back of the house and stood before a wide porch. It had been beautiful once: elegant pillars and balustrades, gingerbread buttresses under the eves. But a hundred winters had dragged it down, leaving the floorboards warped and the broken railings gapped like an untended smile.

The extent of the damage appalled him, and in that moment Ash realized he could simply leave. There was nothing requiring him to stay. But when the woman glanced over, frail and doubtful, as if even she had not realized how bad things had grown, what he said was, "Leave it to me."

When she emerged an hour-and-a-half later with a hopeful expression and his lunch on a tray—a mug of tea and a huge sandwich crowded with ham and cheese—she found him still perched on the steps, his shoulders drooping like the roofline.

"I imagine you're just trying to figure out where to start," she said. "Measure three times, cut once. That's what Franklin always said."

"What else did he say?"

"Sometimes for lunch he would bring a chair out, or eat in the shed if it was raining."

And setting the tray down on the grass she hurried away before he could draw her into his own delays.

In the end he had to do something, so he started on the window. The frame had weathered to grey, and the heavy shutters hung askew. Searching through Franklin's jars he found screws that were long enough; and using the step-ladder and a small mechanical drill like an ancient egg beater he extended the holes so the new screws had something to bite. Then, a squirt of glue into each hole and he was ready to begin.

But he found himself one hand short. He had to hold up the shutter, center the hinge, steady the ladder, and screw it in, all without toppling over. He shifted this way and that, tilting the heavy shutter and fumbling with his tools. But in the end he wedged the ladder under the sagging corner. Then scurrying up, he clamped the hinge with his left hand, leaned a shoulder to brace the shutter, and propped the bottom with his knee. Then, poised like a contortionist at the top of a flagpole, he plucked the screws one by one from his mouth and tightened them home.

His satisfaction was ridiculous. He stood for a long time admiring his work. Then he walked around the house and re-performed the trick on every window in turn. When she came out again at five Miss Pru found him in Franklin's chair—the sagging porch unaltered. It was a long, disappointed moment before she noticed the shutters standing sharply to attention.

"Put the tools away," she said gruffly. "Dinner's on the table."

He sat down before a plate piled high with meatloaf, green beans, boiled potatoes, and canned peaches for desert.

"I've had my dinner," Miss Pru said, but she sat primly across from him sipping decaf coffee. And perhaps noticing that he had mentioned so little about his own life, she told him about hers.

The rectory had been elegant for more than a century: the deliberate antithesis of every shed and farmhouse around. There were public rooms for comforting parishioners and a study meant, even then, as a space of erudition among the dusty fields. Prudence Bascomb had come to the rectory a few weeks after Father Ben's arrival—a seventeen-year-old with too much energy for such a small town and too little interest in farming. The new parson had a wife, but word had come back to the church committee that she was at a loss. She had grown up in a family of well-educated clergymen, believing in God the way a young woman who lived at the beach believed in water. She had not cleaned a house before or done her own laundry.

Prudence was a help with the cooking and cleaning, but she could do nothing about the smallness of the town or the unrelenting vastness of the fields. When his wife left, Father Ben found himself as empty as the horizon. But Prudence loved the Rectory—the cool stone, the kitchen's tiled floor, the wide soapstone sink that seemed like an entire domain just for her. Gradually she filled the vacancies in his life, tending him as best she could. She had a small house of her own, but she came daily to cook and clean, priding herself on not living in—not a servant but a caretaker in every sense.

Father Ben served his parish faithfully for forty-two years, but it was no longer a post anyone wanted. There were perhaps a dozen parishioners—elderly women and a few men—and the diocese couldn't justify the expense. They had been more or less waiting for Father Ben to die. But when he finally did they were no longer paying attention.

Miss Pru continued to sweep and dust daily, she polished the wood every week. She made sure the closets were tidy and the drawers fresh. And the congregation continued to meet for their church socials and coffee hours. And if they had to do without the weekly service, well, it was the nature of the world that you couldn't have everything exactly as you wished. And they were pleased to hold out just a little longer against the Presbyterians.

After dinner Miss Pru got up to wash the dishes.

"Can I help?" said Ash.

And as if she had only just thought of it, "You can read the paper, if you like. It's nice to hear a man's voice around the place."

At the end of the evening she gathered him up along with her coat and purse. She turned the lights off and, with one last glance at the orderly hallway, closed and locked the door. Instead of energizing him the dinner had robbed Ash of his strength, and he stood unsteadily in the cool night air. As she headed down the walk he followed. They stopped beside his car.

"You can't park here," she said.

"No. I understand."

"Just pull around the corner into the church lot. I don't suppose anyone will notice."

He sat behind the wheel as if he were already driving— the lake and island waiting, the route through the darkness securely settled in his mind. But he didn't turn the key. The dinner, the long day's work—he found himself smiling in what he thought was anticipation but which, as moment followed moment, became a kind of proleptic satisfaction. As if he were already looking back from a distant time at the surprising course his life had taken. He was living in a car in an obscure corner of another country with the whole summer opening up before him. How could he possibly have traveled any further from himself? And as the distance between his plans and his dreams slowly shrank to the space of a single breath, he fell asleep.

Miss Pru never asked him if he wanted a job, but when he was still there in the morning, with his head wedged awkwardly against the car door and a thin gleam of saliva on his cheek, she offered him a satisfied nod and told him breakfast was on the table. Ash discovered he was ravenous. Then she led him to a narrow bedroom off the kitchen where, arranged on the bed as if for a life-sized cardboard doll, were Mr. Franklin's clothes, old but perfectly clean. Gloves, shirt, t-shirt, boxers, socks, and heavy canvas trousers. Beneath them on the floor, an ancient pair of work boots.

"When did he leave?"

"He passed away four years ago."

"Was he a large man?" inquired Ash, eyeing the waistband.

"Well. He wasn't very tall and he wasn't very thin. But he was a hard worker and reliable." She glanced over at the bureau. "There might be some of Randall's things toward the back of the drawers. He was before Franklin. He was very easy on his clothes."

When she left, Ash stripped and drew on the boxers, the socks, the soft and spotless shirt, as if they were a kind of spell—every bit as strange as everything else. He buttoned and buckled himself, cinching the belt tight. The shirt bagged wide over his waist and the pants rode high. But the boots—as if already knowing everything he didn't—were a perfect fit.

He stepped into the kitchen.

"Mr. Franklin would wait until fall to clean the gutters," said Miss Pru. "But it's been a few years, and I don't think we need to stand on ceremony."

The Rectory was three stories tall, with a high slate roof and gutters twenty feet in the air. Ash had never been good with heights, though he rarely got such an opportunity to remind himself. Still, he raised the ladder, clanking like a drawbridge, and set it with a bump against the house. Then they stood for a moment together, gazing all the way up.

"Have you ever cleaned gutters before?" asked Miss Pru.

"I never have. But I think I grasp the concept."

"Franklin wasn't much of a hand on ladders those last few years. And Randall… Well."

Ash could feel a flock of second thoughts alighting all around them. But before Miss Pru could speak he set his foot on the bottom rung and started up.

He was surprised how solid the ladder felt. How easy to climb. He scooped the packed and composting leaves out of the gutter and scattered them below. Then he descended, shifted the ladder, and climbed up again, working his way steadily from left to right. The sun was warm. The town lay all around him, houses and trees and fields, as if it were something he had taken out of a box and assembled on a table top. He fell into a rhythm. And then, stretching out an arm, leaning just a little too far, he felt the whole weight of the heavy ladder shift and unbalance. It teetered. And for a long, long instant he hung on the narrow edge of disaster before finally settling back. Ash didn't move. He hunched in place, gripping the ladder, until his breathing returned to normal.

When he finally finished he climbed slowly down, collapsing the ladder raucously back to its original length. Miss Pru—who had been standing at the sink waiting for the sound, repeating under her breath a prayer for those in need of protection—now walked stiffly out and said, "All done?"

"All done."

"Church, too?"

He turned and gazed up at the high Norman tower. It rose above the canopied trees and seemed to wedge itself like a cliff against the sky. "Don't worry," she said. "The Lord watches over those who watch over him." And then a little more gently, "I'll have your tea waiting."

He could just get in the car and drive away. There was nothing holding him here. It was all as gauzy as the start of a dream, when you could wake yourself up at any time—except for the sense of all you'd be missing.

So he walked around the building, the suddenly paltry ladder under his arm, looking for the best place to start. And slowly he realized there were no gutters to be seen. The heavy slate roof ended in the high open air.

When he returned to the kitchen all Miss Pru said was, "That one's Franklin's chair." And with the thinnest of smiles she set down a large mug of tea and a sandwich thick with ham and Swiss. She tidied the kitchen around him, humming under her breath, as if the solid presence of a man resting from his labors was as welcome as the sunshine in the intricate dance of her day.

48.

There was always work to be done—he filled the day with work. And at night he drove through darkness and parked at the water's edge, haunted by the distant lamplight and waiting for his fate to find him. For the fact was, it grew less and less real each night. He couldn't bring himself to call out across the water. Couldn't make himself intrude on all that he remembered. When he thought of Bea he could no longer quite imagine their meeting. It had somehow gotten lost between the vividness of his memory and the solid recurring facts of the day-to-day. He told himself there was plenty of time; he was just getting settled. But listening to the murmured voices—so distantly self-sufficient amid the lamplight and wonder—he felt the tug of their two lives drawing apart and he was powerless to change his course.

But fate is a promise as well as a threat.

The ancient Plymouth—all jaunty fins and grill—came cruising through the sunshine, windows open, the two girls tanned and lively as a summer's day. Wordless in the shade of the maple trees, re-setting the flagstones of the front path, Ash watched as they drew up in front of Halladay's Market and sauntered carelessly in.

He found them huddled in the modest produce section, conferring over their list. Bea in her overalls and a borrowed pink t-shirt; Joan in Bea's red flannel shirt over denim cut-offs too short for their pockets. They were laughing. They could not stop handling the fruit, as if it were all as exotic as the rest.

He shadowed them for two aisles, trying to prepare his story, then suddenly came upon them. A little wildly he thought about pretending surprise, but Bea spotted him and without the slightest hesitation said, "Hi, stranger. We thought we might run into you."

"So, where's the town?" asked Joan. "Margery said it was small, but I thought at least there'd be people."

"We keep them inside for special occasions."

Bea was smiling at his clothes. "Looks like your aunt has put you to work."

"Oh, yes."

"I bet she was happy to see you. They probably don't get a lot of visitors here."

"No. She was pretty surprised. I see they've got you working, too?"

"Weland says that's why God invented interns. Groceries and laundry once a week."

"There's a laundromat?" said Ash.

"Apparently. Speaking of which." She turned to Joan. "Do you want to see about the rest of this? I'll get the clothes started."

"Suits me. The sooner we're done, the sooner we can leave."

So once again they climbed together into a car, and it was as if they had never gotten out. She was smiling. "So this is what you look like. I'd almost forgotten."

"I was thinking the same thing. I can see all this drudgery agrees with you."

"Oh, yes."

The car had a manual shift up on the steering column, and she handled it with a muscular competence that seemed newly learned. They made a slow circuit of the town.

"You're sure about this laundromat?" he asked.

"That's what Margery says."

"Let's try a block over."

"There's another block?"

She turned, and there it was: a high tin shed with hoses and a pair of huge stalls big enough for the largest farm machinery. In the room next door was the laundromat. The windows looked glazed with condensation until they drew to a stop and realized it was dust.

The 'closed' sign did not look new.

"This is not going to go over well," said Bea.

"Guess you'll end up washing your clothes in the lake."

"You think you're joking. Down on my knees in my underwear scrubbing Weland's shirts against the rocks."

"That," he said, "I would pay money to see."

She laughed and touched his arm the way she had touched the fruit, as if it were all brand new. "We'd better return to the mother ship for instructions."

But as she turned the car he said, "You know. I think my aunt has a washing machine you could use."

It was like a game they were playing, standing so close without touching. The rectory was empty, Miss Pru out on her errands. In the laundry room off the kitchen the machines looked bright and inviting, and as he kept a wary eye on the door, Bea began cheerfully to load the wash, sorting by lights and darks. "Who cares more about color than a bunch of painters?" She closed the lid, started the machine. He had almost forgotten the scent of her, the hushed clamor of their breathing.

"What are you looking at?" she said playfully.

He kissed her. His hands found her waist beneath the overalls. Hers settled lightly on his shoulders as if to keep him from floating away.

"Now I remember," she murmured, smiling against his mouth. "I don't suppose your aunt is out of town."

"No. Sorry."

Reluctantly she reached down and lifted his hands from her waist. "I wouldn't want to shock her."

"Does this mean I won't get to see you washing clothes in your underwear?"

"It's a long summer," she said. "Who knows what will happen?"

With a smile he glanced toward the kitchen. "Are you hungry? I could make us some lunch."

"That's one thing about Weland. He does feed us well. But I wouldn't say no to coffee."

"We have tea."

"Knock me out," she said.

He put the kettle on the stove and assembled Miss Pru's cups and saucers with a faint air of playing house. Bea sat down at the table and laid her sketchbook down beside her.

"Did you bring me something?" he asked.

"It's what Weland says. Always be ready. I thought I might run into you." And the sudden shyness was like a fuse between them.

"Knock me out," he said.

She made a space among the tea things and opened the wide book. Drexall in a tuxedo shirt, with the jacket hanging jauntily from one shoulder. The bow tie was undone; the shirt unbuttoned over a white undershirt. He turned the page and there was Drexall again, a heavy-breasted roué with a cigarette in one hand and her hand in her pocket.

"That's really good."

"I know, right? That Weland is amazing. I've never done anything so good. Ten minutes a sketch. That's all he gives us. Be quick; don't think." Her fingers settled lightly on his arm. "He says he wants to sharpen our sex appeal."

He sat very still. "And what does that involve exactly?"

"Weland says everything worthwhile is about desire. Everything you do or touch or taste or imagine."

A flutter like beating wings behind his ribs. "I think I would go that far."

"But you can't squander it," she said. "You have to store it up, all that feeling, like a battery in your chest. Don't waste it. Don't use it up. Just pour it into your painting. That's the secret."

He swallowed, his mouth gone dry. "That is something I'd like to see."

She laughed again, as if she simply could not contain her high spirits. "Sorry. No visitors. That's the rule. Weland says it's like a nunnery. We're all in seclusion. A convent of passion and desire, but all stored away. All for art. We're nuns for art."

And with that she turned the page, and there was Joan, casually stripped to the skin. The willowy tautness of her body, the distant expression, as if she hadn't even realized she was posing.

"Joan's amazing," said Bea. And as she turned the pages Ash tried to assume an air of distant, artistic appreciation. Joan turning this way and that, seated on a chair, straddling the back, bending over as if to tie the shoes she had neglected to put on. Bea laughed. "She doesn't care if she's wearing clothes or not."

"I can see that."

"But Weland says that's the problem. He doesn't want us drawing nudes. He says he wants us drawing naked people. He says there's got to be something transgressive about it."

"That Weland talks a lot."

"I know. Right? But look."

With the next page it wasn't so much that the pose had changed—Joan was still naked, one hip cocked, her hands on her waist. But she was peering out at the viewer now with a thin, approving smile. And there was something there, some suggestion, not in the nakedness of her breasts or the dark smudge of pubic hair, but in the solid planting of her hands on her hips, the poise of her fingers, as if she were counting off something in her mind.

"And what exactly is she looking at?" he asked.

Bea grinned. "You know the rules. It's all in the give and take. The energy between painter and model."

"And what were you wearing then?"

"Wouldn't you like to know?"

His pulse gave a little jump, but Bea had turned back to her drawings with a mixture of pride and surprise, as if, even remembering the moment, she couldn't stop marveling at what she had done.

The kitchen door opened with a bustling click, and Miss Pru strode in, her arms burdened with grocery bags, her face expressionless as she took in the scene.

Bea was unaware of the danger. She stood up cheerfully. "Hi. I'm Ash's friend." And she held out her hand.

"This is Miss Pru," said Ash. "My Aunt Pru." The woman gazed stonily back. "Aunt Pru, this is my friend Bea. She's a painter. She's spending the summer on an island nearby."

"It's an artists' colony," said Bea. "At least, it will be by the time we're through with it."

The sketchbook still lay open. Adjusting her glasses, Miss Pru regarded the drawing of Joan for a long moment before straightening up. But in the end all she said was, "Of course. Ash has told me so much about you."

"I was just showing him my recent work, but I have some drawings of him from last week, if you'd like to see them."

"Oh," he said hurriedly. "I don't think you need—."

"Thank you, dear. I'd love to. In the meantime, I think your tea is cold. Why don't we see about a fresh pot."

She set her grocery bags down on the counter and picked up the cups and saucers. "I'm so glad Ash has given you my mother's set. They're the nicest we have. I'll get some fresh ones."

She carried them carefully to the sink and rinsed and dried them. Then she lifted down the blue and white church crockery and arranged a plate of Jam Thumbprints. Bea had the sketchbook open to a new page.

He hadn't remembered there were so many. Small charcoal sketches crowded here and there on the page, gradually giving way to larger, more emphatic drawings. There he was, no shirt, no pants, awkward and embarrassed. Though he drew some comfort in the knowledge that it didn't look much like him. Until Miss Pru, gazing down with unsettling attention, said, "That's the boy to a T."

The ding of the washing machine released him. "I'll get it."

He moved the heavy armload of laundry into the dryer and set it running. And as if on cue, there was a knock on the door. Joan let herself in. She sat down without invitation and began eating from the plate of cookies and drinking from Bea's cup. "Next time you do the shopping," she said still chewing.

Miss Pru glanced at Ash. "Another close friend?"

"This is Joan," said Bea. "And this is Ash's Aunt Pru."

Joan's eye caught the sketch pad. Bea watched with a smile as she riffled through the pages to the drawings of herself. "That was a good night," said Joan around a mouthful of crumbs, and she tapped it with her finger as if she just couldn't keep her hands off.

When the clothes were dry, Bea tumbled them into the duffle bag, and the two girls turned to leave. Miss Pru was watching grimly, as if counting the forks under her breath.

"I'll clean this up in a moment," said Ash.

"No such thing. It's my kitchen. I'll clean up."

He followed them to the car. Walking Bea around to the driver's side he opened the door. She stepped close and dropped her voice. "What would you do to me now, if we were alone?"

He caught his breath, the answer lodged in his chest.

She laughed and kissed him on the lips. "Remember that feeling. We can use that. See you next week."

And he watched as they drove out of town, the laughter escaping like steam from the open windows.

When he returned to the house Miss Pru refused to meet his eyes. She was washing the dishes, banging the sturdy plates around but careful of the cups and saucers. He stood there awkwardly for a moment. "I can explain."

"What were you thinking? You can't just help yourself to my things."

"I know. I'm sorry."

"You're never to use my mother's china. It's delicate. And very precious to me."

"I'm very sorry. I didn't know. I shouldn't have invited her back."

"This isn't your house, you know. You can't just do anything you like."

"I know. I'm very sorry. I wasn't thinking clearly."

"I don't suppose you were."

She washed and rinsed and stacked. "So who is she? Your little artist? Is she your sweetheart?"

And that made him smile. "Oh, I hope so."

She gave him a measuring look. "Judging from that sketch book, I can certainly imagine."

"It wasn't like that. Not exactly. We've only just met."

"And you couldn't have just told me? Do you think I'm some heartless dragon? We could have put a nice tea together. I could have baked something. We could have entertained them properly."

Ash was startled into silence. "I didn't know they were coming."

"I won't have sneaking around in this house."

"No. I understand."

"This is a rectory. You can't disrespect it."

"I know."

And then slowly, relentingly. "She's very pretty," said Miss Pru.

"I think so, too."

"I'm not so sure about the other one."

And that gave Ash a warm feeling as well, because of course he was thinking exactly the same thing.

49.

His daily work began to expand. Mrs. Blackburn had a screen door that hadn't fit for years; Mrs. Pilgrim's back shutters were loose; Mrs. Crabtree's front steps had rotted close to disaster. Miss Pru felt very strongly that, since he was the Rectory's man, he shouldn't be spread too thin. But she was not unreasonable. She was prepared to lend him out, a little haughtily but with a genuine sympathy for the less fortunate.

She had a fierce work ethic. Unrelenting and dour, she would watch from one window or another as Ash labored through the summer heat. But whenever—drenched in sweat, face smeared with dirt or the punkie sawdust of wood left unpainted for too many seasons—he would lower his tools and sink to the ground (perhaps just a shade too dramatically, though in fact he was working harder than he ever had in his life) Miss Pru would vanish from the window as if running to report him. But a few minutes later she would emerge with a glass of lemonade or a mug of tea or a sandwich, and set it down sternly at his side, as if this were just another task in which he was going to be found wanting.

And then one night over dinner she said, "You should go visit her. Your girl. Drive out there."

He remembered the distant lamplight in the windows, the inviolable sense of the island at night. "She didn't invite me."

"Don't be silly."

"She said it's a retreat. They're nuns for art. What if she doesn't want to be disturbed?"

Miss Pru took a moment to chase a carrot down on her plate and spear it with her fork. "Take an afternoon off. Don't forget to bathe. And comb your hair. Faint heart never won fair maiden."

He drove slowly through the afternoon and down the last of

the gravel road. Then he waited in silence at the water's edge as if he'd come all this way for a signal. But there was no sign of life. He felt for the rope and pulled. The skiff came free. He reeled it in, bobbing a little on the gentle waves, bumping its nose against the answering shore. Gingerly he stepped in and drew himself over like someone crossing a bridge made entirely of his own hopes.

He had explanations ready, but they vanished with the need. The island was deserted. He let himself into the toolshed, inhaling the scent of smoke and old wood as if already knowing this is what he'd remember in years to come. He crept into the house. He thought it would seem more familiar, more remarkable. But the rooms, ordinary in their plank furniture, their gingham and floral fabric, seemed too quaint for his memories.

He helped himself to an apple from the fridge, and then to a slice of cheese. He saw the labels and butcher paper from Halladay's Grocery, and it gave him a smiling, proprietary feeling, as if he knew more of this place than they did. In Bea's room he glanced over her books, pressed his face into the carefully folded t-shirts and flannels that were her sole preparation for the exoticism of the summer. Then he carried one of her books, *The Portrait of a Lady*, down among the trees by the water's edge and read in the dappled shade until the distant whine of the outboard motor lifted on the breeze.

Hiding among the trees he watched the figures trudge up the slope toward the cabin. They had dressed for the sun in long, loose trousers and shirts, except for Joan, who wore her cut-offs and Bea her overalls. They looked weary and sun-drained, but the sight of her made his heart lurch.

He drew back further at their approach and stayed there as the darkness slowly wrapped itself around. Lanterns were lit, the windows glowed—softly at first and then more brightly. The aroma of cooking drifted out into the night air, making his stomach pinch. Creeping up to a window he hoisted himself carefully onto a woodpile, peering in cautiously past the curtains. The group had dressed for the evening once again. All the men and Drexall in black tie, Margery in a silver tea dress, Joan in something short and Bea— it took him a moment to recognize her—in another of Margery's anachronistic gowns, her hair elaborately bound into a silhouette of some older time.

They were eating and conversing, sipping their wine, utterly unconnected to the weary figures trooping up from the boat. One by one they were taking turns with their sketchbooks open on an easel, walking the group through the day's work. Abruptly Drexall stood. "I'll be right back. I'm for the little boys' room."

Ash scrambled down from the woodpile as he heard the screen door slam. He hurried back among the trees and watched as the short tuxedoed figure trudged along the path through squares of fallen lamplight into the outhouse. He heard the door latch. His heart was pounding. Surely this was his signal to leave. But he had made himself a part of this group, in spite of them. So when Drexall emerged and traced her way back to the cabin, Ash started again toward the window.

But at once the screen door banged again, and Bea appeared, lifting her unaccustomed skirts, feeling her way cautiously over uneven ground. She slipped into the outhouse. And when she stepped out it was into a wash of moonlight. He could see her hair just starting to come down in the back, the dress, a little loose, had shifted on her shoulders, and she looked just for a moment like a young girl playing dress-up.

"Don't be startled," he whispered, and she leapt with a rising squeak that might have belonged to any small night creature.

"What are you doing here?" she hissed. But already he could heard the smile in her voice.

"I came to see you."

"You're not supposed to see me. I'm on retreat. We're all on retreat. Until we get our acts together. We're incorrigible old ladies, according to Weland. And we've got to snap out of it or we're all going to die poor and unknown."

With every word he was drawing closer. "That sounds terrible."

"It is. I'm learning things that no one my age should ever know."

She flattened her hands against his chest, though whether to keep him away or draw him close he couldn't be sure. "Look at you, learning all sorts of things yourself," she said, her voice a murmur. "Sneaking around. Frightening poor defenseless girls. Tell me what you did today." The dress, cloudy silver in the moonlight, seemed insecurely draped, offering a narrow space between her body and clothes into which his thoughts could slip. "Did you paint a house?" she whispered. "Repair a car? Mow a lawn?"

"I was fixing Mrs. Crabtree's front steps."

"And how is Mrs. Crabtree?"

"She's good." All his breath seemed trapped in his chest. He could not have spoken louder if his life depended on it. His hands slipped around her waist. "Do you want to dance?"

They moved in a tiny two-step over uneven earth. "I love the way you smell." His hand hesitantly traversed the pale silk and found the weight of her breast, unconstrained beneath the fabric.

"Do you think I'm an incorrigible old lady?" she murmured.

"No."

"Did you come all this way for me?"

"I did, yes."

They kissed. "Where can we go?" he whispered.

"Nowhere." But she was smiling teasingly. "Where would we go?"

"Anywhere. The trees? Somewhere private?"

She reached up and pressed his hand to her heart. "Doesn't this feel private?"

"I want to touch you."

"You are touching me."

But she turned within his arms—as if they were dancing still—and with her back pressed against him drew his hands forward around her waist. And as if she were gathering up a waterfall of silk she reached down, dragging up the long spill of her skirts. And with a firm hold on his hand she drew it down and under to where all fabric ended and the cool of the evening gave way to mossy warmth.

"Tell me I'm an incorrigible old lady," she whispered, a little breathlessly. But he didn't have the breath to reply. "Why have we stopped dancing?" she murmured, as if she had only just noticed.

He drew her snugly against him.

"You feel very good," she said. "How do I feel?"

"Good. Very good."

"I've got to get back."

They were still for another moment, then she drew herself away. His hand was suddenly his own again, cooling in the air.

"Later tonight?" he asked.

"Not tonight. We sketch for hours."

"I can wait."

"Go away," she said and kissed him. "I have to go draw."

Harold in Paradise

50.

He woke in the small yellow bedroom to the smell of coffee and the clatter of Miss Pru moving about the kitchen—a little louder than necessary in case his alarm didn't wake him. At breakfast he was ravenous.

"And how was your day off?" she asked, laying a second piece of toast on his plate.

He wore an old man's clothes so he tried to put on an old man's weary reserve. "It was okay. Thank you."

"You went to see your friend?"

"I did. Yes." And he found himself adding, "She wasn't there at first."

"On the island?"

"Right."

"I imagine they were off painting or some such foolishness."

He glanced up suspiciously, but she was sipping her coffee with an expression of careful disinterest. "Yes," he said.

"So, I suppose you went off drinking somewhere. Franklin would spend his days off at the Duck Blind over in Braithwaite. Though it was certainly none of my business."

"Oh," he said. "No. I didn't go to the Duck Blind. But I'll certainly keep it in mind."

"Don't put yourself out. I don't think his days off did him a bit of good." She glanced at him over the rim of her cup. "Though it doesn't seem to have hurt you."

Ash sat up a little straighter. In fact, he was exhausted, but that seemed completely beside the point. "I spent the day sitting by the water reading."

"Some folks pay a lot of money for that."

"It was very peaceful." But then, in the spirit of honesty, "She eventually showed up."

Miss Pru spooned up the last of her soft boiled egg and straightened her shoulders: another task completed. "And was she happy to see you?"

And he couldn't have kept the smile from his face for all the toast in the kingdom. "I think she was, yes."

He was replacing broken shingles on the rectory this morning and even the terrible heights seemed only to add to the brightness of his memories. He extended the ladder up to the very edge of the high roof. Whatever Franklin's drinking habits, he chose his tools well. The ladder was stiff, and each step was rock-solid—though just a little higher than the last. The roof was not steeply pitched—just a long, smooth incline—and the only bad moment was stepping from the ladder across all that empty space. He spent a long time trying to gather up his nerve, then he simply stepped across, and stood there marveling at the ease of it all. He began to think he had the wrong approach to life. Clearly he should be a little more adventurous.

The shingles were rough under his boots; it was like hiking on a hillside. He consciously tried to stroll, counting the broken shingles, testing the loose or crooked ones, careful not to look down. In the end he made ten trips up and down the ladder with bundles of shingles, increasingly thinking how efficient he was, how ridiculously simple it was all turning out to be.

The day ended with Mr. Skylar's weathervane—a small repair, at the very top of the house. The Skylar place wasn't large, but Mr. Skylar's grandfather had had an eye for the dramatic, so he'd built the house as a series of high-angled gables, much taller than they needed to be. Ash had to extend the ladder as far as it would go and balance it against the sloping roof. Mr. Skylar guided him. He had done this often as a boy, scampering up like a squirrel under the proud eye of his father, though since his wife had died he hadn't been up for much—the loss seemed to affect his balance. So he stood on the ground with a steadying hand, thinking about how brave he'd been as a boy and calling instructions up the ladder.

Ash carried Franklin's tool belt slung over his shoulder, trying not to think about the height. Instead he thought of Bea, trying to recapture the feel of her, the intimate weight of her breast, the scent of her on his fingers. He thought about the way she nestled the rounded curve of her bottom against him, and the warm smoothness of her thigh as he traced his way up under the gathered skirt. The ladder was solid. It barely moved under his weight. Mr. Skylar shouted encouragement. And Ash was thinking how fat Franklin must have been, judging from his waistband, and how much easier this whole job would be if old Mr. Skylar would just stop talking, when the tool belt caught briefly—just snagged for a second, the claw of the hammer on the edge of a rung. It tugged him mid-step, twisting him off balance. He jerked it free. The ladder stayed where it was, braced against the roof, but the tool belt kept moving. It slipped from his shoulder, slid down his arm. He clutched at it, felt the ladder tip, made a hectic grab for that, and fell.

It wasn't a clean fall. He snatched at the gutter, but it bent like a drinking straw, folding itself down in a long, twisting curve. It slowed his fall. And for one frozen instant it seemed that everything would be all right. That it would all turn into some zany adventure. And he had time to think about the rose bushes below—how they would cushion his drop but he needed to shelter his head and oh those thorns would be a problem. Then everything speeded back up.

He missed the bushes, landing with a crack that echoed, white-hot, up the bones of his leg. Then he lay for a while on the grass, gazing up the long, long ladder all the way into the sky, while Mr. Skylar hurried away for help, and Miss Pru came running, no longer frowning now: her face shining with fear.

There was a long ride in Mr. Skylar's Lincoln, stretched out in the wide back seat. Then the emergency room in the Braithwaite Provincial Hospital, and a white plaster cast, surprisingly heavy—*whatever you do, don't get it wet*—stretching from his strangled toes to just below the knee.

By evening he was back, with the last of the pain-killers drifting away, lying in the grand, wood-paneled comfort of Father's Ben's room. Through the haze of drugs and pain he worried about this. His room off the kitchen would have been more convenient for Miss Pru. But she seemed so brusquely satisfied with the comfort of the larger bed that he said nothing more.

"I'm very sorry, Miss Pru."

"I knew it was too high."

"I just got a little distracted."

"It was probably that old Skylar. He could talk the nose off a donkey."

"I'm sorry for all the trouble."

"Shush," she said fiercely. "You save your strength." And she set a tray on his lap, with a bowl of soup so golden and richly fragrant he thought he must be hallucinating.

"Oxtail," she said crisply. "It's for the blood."

"The doctor said I could get up tomorrow."

"That doctor looked ten years old. You'll stay right where you are for a few days." And she fastened a pair of brisk, staccato pats onto his shoulder. "In the meantime that old fool Skylar is here. I imagine he wants to apologize."

"For what?"

"You just let him. He's gotten himself into a tizzy over this."

51.

It was as if Ash had only just arrived in this strange town; as if his life, like his ankle, had been reset. Everything was more difficult. The arrangement of the streets and houses seemed suddenly distorted, every task further away. Even the ground itself had grown more treacherous and uneven. Miss Pru found him a pair of crutches, some ancient reminder of one of Franklin's mishaps, and he levered himself up the stairs and down, out into the garden, and one afternoon in that first week when he was determined to prove he was essentially unhampered, all the way to Halladay's Grocery, where he sat beside the shelf of locally produced maple syrup with a pounding heart and the knowledge that he had ruined everything just as it had begun.

"What have you done to yourself?"

He opened his eyes. A slender figure leaning down between him and the sun—his heart lurched. But it was only Joan, looking thin and wiry in her cut-offs, with the white pockets hanging down below the hem and the flannel shirt tied above a bare margin of skin.

"I fell off a ladder," he said.

"That can't be good for you."

"I'm all right." He glanced around. "Are you alone?"

"Just me, this week. Bea's too busy being teacher's pet. It's a lot of responsibility being an artist."

"I can imagine."

"I'll bet you can." And she gave him a thin smile as if assessing him across that cool distance. "You want to give me a hand? Maiden in distress and all that." She dug into her pocket. She had to burrow in—her reaching fingers filling the pocket below the frayed hem as if to demonstrate just how short they were. She drew out the list.

Ash levered himself up. He felt clumsy beside her, but he was determined that Bea should hear he wasn't bedridden and helpless. As she strolled just a little too quickly up and down the aisles he had to work to keep up.

"So how are things?" he asked. "What's the state of the arts these days?"

"Oh, God. Don't get me started. Scratch, scratch, scratch. Drawing all the time. Painting all the time." She reached out for a can of crushed tomatoes and weighed it for a moment. "If I poured this over my head and let it run down my tits, do you think it would be art?"

Ash managed a smile. "I'll bet Weland would want to sketch you."

She laughed. "He's a slave-driver. It's nothing but work, work, work." But she smiled at the thought, or perhaps she was still considering the crushed tomatoes. She added them to the cart and then took another for good measure.

"So there's nothing fun about art?" he asked.

"You can't even guess. It's exhausting." She was looking over her list, but now she nodded her chin toward the canned soup. "Grab a few of those Minestrone, would you? Margery is steeped in nostalgia for canned soup with saltines."

As Ash leaned past, she made no move to get out of his way. "How many?" he asked.

"Three. No, four. You can't have too much soup."

The tails of the work shirt were loosely tied. The waistband of her shorts bit into her spare flesh. "So, what's it like, being a model?" he offered, as he set the cans in the cart.

"Don't ask me. You should ask your girlfriend. For such a Shy Gwendolyn, she's got a little vinegar in her blood."

He glanced up, startled. "What do you mean?"

Her look was knowing and slow. "I hear you paid us a visit."

"How do you know about that?"

"That Bea could not stop talking. She's all a-flutter."

And he couldn't help the smile. "I'm a little a-flutter, myself."

"You know our Bea has given up on sex."

"She mentioned something like that."

"Retiring from the world. Funneling all her passion into art. All of Weland's bullshit."

"She told me."

"I don't really get it, myself," said Joan.

"You're not saving yourself for art?"

"I'm not saving myself for anything." And she leaned forward conspiratorially. "And what about you? Are you a handmaiden to art?"

He found himself blushing. "I like art."

She laughed. "Of course you do. Who doesn't like art? But just a word in your ear. There's not much progress to be made with our girl Bea, if you know what I mean. Even if you hadn't broken your leg."

"It's just my ankle."

"Still. It's got to be disappointing. How long are you laid up?"

"Six weeks."

"Wow," she said. "That is some bad timing. But maybe it's just as well. There's so much work to be done. Art doesn't just make itself. Turns out I could stand there all day, naked as the morning, and it wouldn't matter a bit, if some artist didn't come strolling along with a hard-on for me. That's the thing. You've got to have a naked woman, or two or three. But it's not about that. No, sir. You're standing there twisted like a pretzel, your tits in the air. And it's all about the brush. Or the pencil. Or that long, thick piece of chalk. If you get what I mean. It's all about the loins." She laughed. "Can you imagine? They all paint with their dicks. Even the ones who don't have one. Waving it around as it if were God's finger. *I point to you. Your ass is the key to a whole new revelation.*" She shook her head. "What a trip."

They had come to the back of the store, where the little bakery was laid out in racks of bread and pastries. Joan gazed with satisfaction. "And now we come to the nub of it all. The key to unlocking our little Bea's heart. That is, if it's her heart you've got your eye on."

Ash said nothing. She picked up a little cardboard tray of brownies, thickly frosted and sealed beneath a shiny layer of cling-wrap. She drew her finger slowly over the surface, pressing a long groove into the chocolate. Her finger came up unmarked, but she rubbed it against her thumb as if savoring the texture. "She is a sweetie, our Bea."

"No argument from me."

"No argument from anyone. But she is one serious character. Working, working, working. Drexall says she's never painted so well. But you know Drexall. She'll say anything."

"What will she say? Does she talk about me?"

"Drexall?"

"Bea."

"Oh, you silly bear. We all talk about you. You know what they say? A picture's worth a thousand words? And they are making a lot of pictures."

She moved forward with the cart, past the deli case, down an aisle of paper goods where, with almost too much care she selected paper towels, tissues, and a large bundle of toilet paper—all the ordinary products that seemed so at odds with the images in his mind. But Joan was still smiling. "Really. I don't know what it is about that girl. She's just so plump and spicy. I'm standing there, naked as the day, and everyone's looking at her. Glancing over, sneaking a peak. You can see them, all those sanctimonious oldsters pursuing the highest reaches of art. And they're just trying to imagine her naked. There I am, spread-eagle across some easy-chair, and they're trying to picture her ass, or trying to guess whether she's shaved or not. It's a little dispiriting."

"So she's not naked?"

"Our Bea? Heavens no. Everybody else. We're all standing around, our pussies to the breeze. But Weland's given her a special dispensation. We finally got her bra off. Finally. But she'd rather set herself on fire than take off those overalls. Though it is amazing how far you can unbutton them and they still hang on. Can you imagine? A room full of naked people, and our Bea in the middle half-dressed like a farmhand."

The image glowed in his mind. He lowered his voice. "Can you tell her something for me? Tell her I'm coming again, as soon as I can?"

She glanced down at his cast. "That's going to be a little tricky, isn't it?"

"I'll manage. Will you tell her? That I'll meet her in our usual spot?"

"You have a usual spot? Isn't that sweet. You come whenever you like. I'm sure we'll all be delighted to see you. But you'd better bring your brush. Or better yet, leave your clothes behind." She lowered her voice and leaned forward, capturing somehow Weland's ponderous intonation. "*It's all about the loins.*"

He drew back. "You're not that nice a person, are you?"

She laughed. "Nice? I'm fantastic. You want to see? Is that what this is about? You want a hint of what you're missing?"

And almost carelessly she lifted her hands to the plackets of her shirt and popped open the snaps in one quick jerk, leaving the flannel to hang like curtains around her shallow breasts. "And suddenly it's art," she said. "Is that God's finger I see?"

"What are you doing?" Hurriedly he glanced around. The store wasn't crowded, but a few of the regulars were going about their business, mulling over the needs of the day. "You can't just do that here."

"Honestly. You are such a treat." She gazed around, a study in bland carelessness, as the cashiers began to notice and the owner in his white butcher's jacket wore an expression like a startled sunrise.

"I like this place," she said. "It's so friendly."

And stepping closer she said, "I hope it's all right if I stop by to do the laundry. Their clothes get so dirty. And it'll be fun. Maybe we can fool around." She laughed. "You want to kiss them goodbye?"

And turning, she wheeled her cart along past the butcher's case as if she were strolling in the sunshine without a care in the world.

He left, but he was unsurprised when she knocked on the rectory door. He glanced up warily, but she was all buttoned and prim. "Thank you," she said to Miss Pru. "It's so nice of you to let me do this here."

"Happy to be helpful," she replied, though the smile didn't reach her eyes. "I hope nothing's wrong with your friend."

"No. We're just taking turns. Ash, would you give me a hand with this, please?"

He was aware of the long bare legs, the taut midriff—the sudden shock of her breasts still fresh in his mind. But Joan seemed to have put their whole conversation aside. While the clothes washed and dried she sat at the kitchen table, her legs propped on a neighboring chair, paging through a copy of *Southern Living* she'd picked up in Halladay's. When everything was folded and back in the duffle bag she hoisted it up. "Thank you again," she said to Miss Pru. And to Ash, "You take care of that ankle. I'll say hi to Bea for you. If I can just get her attention."

That evening he drove out to the island and picked his way heavily down to the shore. But the rope was gone, someone had reeled it in, and the little skiff was nowhere to be seen. There was no cell service. No telephone on the island. And though for an instant he almost shouted over the water, the memory of Joan's cool smile kept him silent.

Miss Pru found him a battered oak writing chair in the rectory attic—a leftover from some ancient schoolroom. It dated from Father Ben's earliest days, when he would take it out under the maple trees to write his sermons. But it was much too awkward for Ash to carry, and much too heavy for Miss Pru. They spent a leisurely lunch conjuring up all the increasingly outrageous ways of getting it down the narrow attic stairs and out onto the lawn, but in the end Ash just strung a rope from the immense steam radiator beside the attic window, and with the help of two ancient wooden pulleys they lowered the chair with surprising stateliness three long stories down to the wide grass.

He fitted it with wheels, and it became a rolling workshop, half crutch, half carry-all. His days were spent trundling up and down the streets to his various projects, setting up a series of base camps from which he could work. In the middle of the morning Miss Pru would find him with a thermos of strong tea and freshly baked cookies, and after a few hours more he would make his way home for lunch. Then out again into the world. In the end too much of his day was devoted to preparation, to going and coming, and too little to actually doing—but the summer days were long, and the heat seemed to lend itself to a kind of slow time.

He fixed the hole in Mrs. Becket's fence, re-attached the mailbox on Mrs. Renner's front door, patched the stucco on the foundation of Mr. Lucian's chicken coop. He spent three successive afternoons on the front porch of Mrs. Reynolds' house, prying out the rotting boards, cutting and re-cutting replacements, sanding them by hand, his back knotted with the effort, the heavy cast sprawled before him. He forced himself to go further and further on his crutches, building up his endurance until the ache in his arms matched the deep red glow of his ankle, while he waited for the next laundry day.

He was replacing the light fixture on Mrs. Cummings' back porch when he saw the Plymouth trundle into town. But instead of continuing on to the grocery story, it pulled at once into the shade of the Rectory maples and seemed to hesitate for a moment before Bea climbed out and strode resolutely into the house. Hurriedly Ash reached for his crutches, but by the time he got halfway there she was already emerging with his thermos of tea and two sandwiches on a tray.

"Look at you," she said. "You're walking, just like a real human boy." She hefted the tray. "Your aunt told me to bring you this."

"On your own today?"

"Going solo."

"Good," he said, "I'm not sure I like Joan as much as I used to."

"She said you could not take your eyes off her breasts."

Ash flushed. "It wasn't like that."

Bea smiled. "Don't worry. It sounded like nobody else could, either. And Weland liked the story. He said now we were getting somewhere."

They settled onto the stone bench by the spring. She wore her overalls despite the warmth, as if it were a kind of message between them. "How's the ankle?"

"Good."

"The island's not the same without you."

"I think that's what Joan was trying to say. But it didn't sound as if you missed me."

She smiled. "Joan gets a little possessive. But it is amazing. I'm learning so much. I think we all are."

But Ash couldn't help imagining what she might be learning from Joan. He remembered her mention of intimate friendships in high school, and wondered if even a nun for art might still have time for friends.

But Bea's thoughts were elsewhere. She raised her face into the afternoon warmth. "Do you feel that? The air? The breeze? Just right across your skin? The sunshine? Of course you do; we all do. But how do you keep it? How do you hold onto it forever?" She breathed deeply. "Imagine the colors of it. The shapes. The weighted space of the canvas, the layers and fields. Imagine capturing it forever. Coming back to this feeling whenever you wanted. Whenever you looked at a painting."

And though the words didn't seem quite her own, though he could almost hear Weland's voice echoing behind, he couldn't take his eyes off her face.

"It's like everything is more powerful," she said. "Everything is more than just itself. You feel the colors, taste the sounds. You lie back on a beautiful summer day and you try store it all up. Your soul is a battery, filling with sensation. And then you pour it all out into your work, so that every time you look at it, every time anyone looks at it, you feel all the things you've ever felt."

He watched her carry the tray back to the rectory. Then they drove to the grocery store and strolled up and down the aisles. Ash half-expected a little ruffle of attention in the sparse crowd, but the shoppers went about their business with perhaps an extra glance now and then, just so they didn't miss anything. Bea stopped at the paper towels and looked around as if at the site of a famous car wreck. "Is this where I'm supposed to take off my shirt?"

He drew very still. "I don't think it's anything that's actually required."

"How does she do it? Just like that. She's so brave."

"Or psychotic."

"Did everybody look?"

"I thought the butcher would have a heart attack."

"How about you?"

"I actually did have a heart attack."

Her fingers fiddled with her shirt button. "Do you think anyone would look?"

"Oh yes."

"The butcher?"

"He would be utterly overcome."

She offered him a sidelong glance. "Do you wish I were Joan?"

"Not for a second."

"Good," she said and took his arm.

As Miss Pru washed the lunch dishes, they sorted the laundry, added the soap, as if they were just pretending to do the most ordinary things—as if there were something wild and bright about it. And it was true: he wanted to hold onto it all. Every sensation. The scent of detergent, the domestic slosh of the washing machine in the stillness of the afternoon.

Miss Pru dried her hands, and with a glance at them both, she gathered up her errand bag. "I'll be a little while," she said needlessly and left.

Ash was sitting on a chair, resting his cast, when Bea stood up and walked slowly over. She pressed his knees together and stood over him, straddling his lap. Bending low she kissed him, and he drew her down.

"Am I too heavy?" she murmured.

"No. Just right."

She leaned back and, one and then the other, unclipped the straps of her overalls. "Just imagine I'm painting you," she murmured.

"Be sure to get my good side."

She took his chin lightly in her hand and turned him this way and that. "I think either one will do." She reached up to the buttons of her shirt.

"What if she comes back?" he said.

"Do you think she will?"

Her fingers moved from button to button. The shirt parted slowly over pale skin and the widening slope of her unconfined breasts. *We finally got her bra off.*

His throat was tight. "We could go upstairs."

"Feel the moment," she whispered. "Store up every second of this. Touch me."

His hands slipped into the open shirt and curved hungrily around the weight of her flesh.

"How do I feel?"

"Good," was all he could manage.

"How do you feel?"

A little breath of laughter bubbled out; he bent his head and kissed her, nosing aside the warm flannel, drawing gently on the crinkling flesh of her nipple.

"Oh my," she murmured, her head leaning back. "Just imagine the picture I'm going to paint."

He walked her out to her car and stood balanced on the crutches as she rolled the duffle bag into the back seat and swung behind the wheel.

"I could come out to the island tonight," he said.

She smiled. "I'm not going to have your drowning on my conscience."

"I'll risk it."

But her smile grew more serious. "This is nice, isn't it? This?" She seemed to take in the whole afternoon. "I'm working on something now. Something good. Better than I've ever done. I don't want to jinx it."

"I understand," he said, though he didn't. Though he would.

She saw his disappointment. "It's my work, Ash. My art. I'm on the verge of something good, I can feel it. I've got to give it my best."

"I know. I want you to."

She leaned in close and dropped her voice. "It'll be something. You'll see."

But he couldn't help himself. "Aren't I something?"

And she laughed and put the car in gear. "Of course you are. You're my muse, buster. How cool is that?"

53.

Whatever you do, don't get it wet.

That night he heard the distant murmur of thunder drawing near. He sat on the edge of his bed, testing the weight of his cast, feeling the delicate weave and grate of the bones in his ankle. The night was thick beyond the glass. A deeper rumble echoed. Then a shattering brightness shook the window, and the sky upended itself in a torrent of sound.

He was frozen between excitement and dread. He didn't have to go. She wasn't expecting him. But perhaps, even then, he felt the first premonition of the limits of love. Anything that fills can empty; anything bright can fade. Love's fierceness has to be defended against all that would make it less. If he had the chance and didn't…. what would that say? Everything is a test. Every moment of love is founded on what you cannot help but do.

So he dressed. And he found in the back of Franklin's closet, a heavy yellow raincoat with a wide hat like a sagging parasol. And hoisting himself on his crutches he crept out over the newly-leveled flagstones and drove through the storm, rain sluicing across his windshield as if he were already underwater.

Lightning turned the surface of the lake convulsive, like another part of the sky. Every flash seemed to catch him in the open. The crutches were aluminum; he left them in the car. The pain in his ankle was a kind of comfort in the midst of all that fury. He stripped down to his underwear, unveiling his skin to the pounding rain. He had brought a plastic bag to keep his clothes dry, though they were already damp going in. He carefully wrapped and taped a garbage bag around the cast so that he stood at the water's edge like a nearly naked Christmas toy escaping its package.

The first step was almost impossible, levering himself down to the shore over shifting, rain-slick rocks. But when he eased into the water he felt his confidence buoyed up. Almost at once the lake found its way into the garbage bag—a chill trickle as it slowly filled. He tried not to think about the plaster. He bobbed along over the uneven bottom until he reached deep water, then pushed off. The sudden drag of the cast was terrifying, a grip on his ankle pulling him down. He fought to keep afloat. But the water was warmer than he'd expected, and with only his head exposed the tumult of rain made the muffled comfort of his body more real.

At the opposite shore he balanced on his good leg, hauling himself upright with the long drooping branch of a cedar tree. Hand over hand he climbed out into the downpour, from water into water. The garbage bag dragged at his ankle, the bundle of clothes was sodden. He dropped them by the shore.

The cabin was sealed in darkness, every lamp extinguished. His body felt extinguished too, cold and weary—his ankle like a bag of sand. But he hobbled forward until he stood beneath her window. It was high overhead; there was no climbing up this time. So he found a fallen branch and tapped against the screen.

And it struck him in that moment—balanced on one leg, feeling the weight of the plaster softening around his ankle, wearing nothing but his sodden underpants and chilled to the bone—how ridiculous he looked. How unutterably foolish. It was that thought that saved him. It dissolved him into giddiness.

So when Bea's face hovered at the screen, she looked out on a pale, gleaming, naked, laughing man like a wood sprite in a plaster cast. A broken, resilient Pan, alive to the ever-startling pleasures of youth and waving the sodden white banner of his underpants in greeting.

"I'll be right down," she whispered.

The creak of the screen door was lost in the rain. Her voice was a sudden whisper. "Ash? Ash!"

She stood on the porch beneath the overhanging roof, hesitating before the downpour. Gone were the overalls. She was dressed from neck to ankles in a pale flannel nightshirt, so modest and demure she might have come straight from her own separate dream. "Do you have an umbrella," she whispered.

He laughed. "Do I look like I do?"

"You can't come in."

"Then I guess you'll have to come out."

He felt her balance for an instant between the sheltered calm and the rush and tumble of the storm. But it was already decided. How could it go any other way?

Hunching her shoulders she stepped out into the sudden shock of the rain. The nightshirt, breezy as moonlight, flattened at once against her skin, glued to her body as she ran so that, arriving in his arms, she was wrapped and pleated in a heavy, sodden cocoon—her body muffled, her hair plastered to the sides of her cheeks. "Sweet Jesus, Ash. What have you done to me?"

They kissed and clung, the heat of their mouths the only warm moment in the night, until she drew back. "They can see us."

"Come with me."

He had almost forgotten the pain in his ankle.

"Lean on me," she yelled.

Together they hobbled toward the trees where an ancient cedar drooped its boughs into a series of hand holds as if waiting for them. He steadied himself against a branch. She stepped into his arms. She felt solid beneath the matted flannel, but somehow disguised. All the separate parts of her—ribs, waist, breasts— indistinguishable under his hands.

"Your skin is so cold," she whispered. But it wasn't. It was glowing in the air.

He wrestled the heavy fabric, looking for some way in. "Remember," she said earnestly. "We can't do anything."

"I just want to touch you."

"Here."

There was a long row of buttons running down from the collar, looking oddly prim amid the unruly storm. She carefully undid the middle five.

When he reached up to help she said, "No. You said touch." Smiling through the downpour, "Once sense at a time. Close your eyes."

The darkness became perfect; the lightning an intermittent orange glow. He felt the rain sluicing down his chest. She took his fingers and guided them through the narrow gap in the placket. He felt the wet flannel cling to his hand, and then he was through into tented warmth, molding himself to the swell of her breast. "Tell me how I feel," she whispered.

"Secret," he said.

"Kissing is touching," she whispered, and he felt her lips blossom against his.

Her hands were on his chest, smoothing their way over skin and muscle. Her voice was low, a smiling incantation: "Clavicle, deltoid, pectoralis major, rectus abdominis, abdominal oblique. Weland says we need to include every sense. A painting isn't just something seen. It's felt and tasted and smelled. It's got to reach down inside you." And she reached down.

How could his mouth be so dry when the whole world was awash? "That Weland is very smart," he whispered.

"Oh, yes." Her fingers were light, and then firm around him. "Open your eyes."

Her eyes were bright, her lips parted. "No more touching," she said and stepped back.

He was about to protest when he saw her hands moving up to the remaining buttons, undoing them from collar to sternum. The nightshirt gapped open. She reached her arms up, crossing them over her breasts as if to shield them. But then, grasping the two sides of her collar she drew them down, parting a flannel cocoon. Her throat, her shoulders, the delicate hollow of her clavicles, the rising slope of her breasts. But she had miscalculated, the opening was too small. She was bound in fabric.

She started laughing. "You'll have to help me."

He reached out and took hold, gathering the hem, dragging it up, taking her hands, her arms with it. Hauling all that heavy fabric toward the clamorous sky. Her body appeared by degrees: knees, thighs, belly, breasts upraised by the tug of fabric, then sinking free into their own pale state of dark-tipped composure. Her head was caught, her arms entangled. As Ash dragged upwards she turned the sleeves inside out, drawing her hands from the last grip of the cuffs as if swimming free. Her face rose to the surface, eyes closed, dark hair springing slightly despite the rain.

A flash of lightning lit her up. So pale and streaming, so solid and smooth.

"Don't do anything," she shouted above the rain.

"I won't."

"You promise?"

"I promise."

"The eyes are the windows of the soul," she cried.

"Do you see my soul?"

"I do! Now tell me what you see."

Some memories are like a treasure buried so deep you can only catch a glimpse now and then. You have to draw your comfort from the knowledge that they are are still there, protected somehow by all that obscures them. In the years when Ash will think back to this moment—and at first he can think of little else—he will wonder what was going through her mind. Surely it was love. Of course it was. But having said that, what have we said?

"We should swim," she cried.

"We're swimming now."

He pressed close and they came to rest against the sloping trunk of the tree. He pinned her gently along its length, his hands smoothing the long map of her body as she leaned back, arms overhead, grasping the branches for support. The sky lit them up. Her body gleamed. The rain ran down the slope of her skin.

The night stood still. They drew out the time as if there could never be an end. Until the storm, having met its match, began to drift away. And afraid of being left in a moment more ordinary, Ash drew himself free and, gathering up his belongings, slipped into the water and away.

54.

In the morning he drove to the hospital and had the sodden, shifting plaster replaced with bright fiberglass and a steel stirrup under the instep. "We have these for little children," said the nurse, "who don't have the sense to take care of things."

And it was true, he had become a child again. But this time brand new. Not his own childhood but the one he had always imagined, unfettered by grief and responsibility, as if the world had been saving this for him. As if he had shaken off the burden of his own life. All through June and into July he worked in the bright sunlight, a series of tasks he had never done before—plumbing, carpentry, window repair. Everything turned itself to his hand. And at eleven he would break for a mug of strong tea mellowed with milk and a plate of cookies still warm from the oven. Then work until lunch. Then dinner at five. There seemed barely time between meals. And then asleep by seven-thirty. Seven-thirty. In later years, when nothing else made him smile, that did.

And what is more, Miss Pru clearly approved his early hours. She sent him off to bed with a satisfied glance and went about the last of her chores. And in his bedroom Ash would set the alarm for the middle of the night so that, buzzing with excitement, he would rise in the darkness, tearing himself from the soft confinement of his dreams, and dress as if for a new morning—fashioning out of the twenty-four hours two entirely separate days.

Cast and all, he waded into the chilly water, cautious on the slick stones, drawing himself out, naked and dripping by the low drooping branches of the cedar tree. And she would see him from her window, a darker silhouette against the grey water. And she would come out to him in the flannel nightgown, so prim, so ghostly, as if fleeing some cozy story for the darker pleasures of the night. She greeted him with low-voiced desire like a winding spring that tightened over the course of the summer. Tighter and tighter. For they never made love.

Perhaps it was a matter of experience—Bea with too much and Ash too little. Perhaps he was afraid of spoiling it. Perhaps he felt tied to this vision of art, a crucial part of some larger excitement. Or maybe he was just being Ash. Having learned a life of such slow accommodation, he could act in no other way. So each night he moved from one dream to another: his body weary and his heart ringing with wonder.

Then one morning he woke up shivering, with an ache in his muscles and a pounding in his head. He forced himself out of bed, dressed, and sat at his usual place, but Miss Pru took one look at him and pressed the back of her fingers against his cheek.

"You're burning up."

She ordered him to bed. And the next day, when the fever was undiminished, she sent for the doctor. He was a thin, amused man with sparse hair and the soft impress of fifteen extra pounds straining the buttons of his shirt. He examined him and, with an indulgent smile, said, "Mononucleosis. The kissing disease. I guess we don't have to wonder what you've been up to."

At first Ash was frantic. There was no phone service on the island, no way to get word. He imagined Bea, sitting ready by her window, growing jaded and impatient. It invaded his dreams. But then the ancient Plymouth appeared in town, and Miss Pru invited the girls to do their laundry again. She served them tea while Ash, storm-tossed and feverish in his narrow bed, listened to the clink of china drifting through the wall. When they left Miss Pru appeared in the doorway. "I told them you were contagious. Your girl said to get well soon."

Instead, he slept.

Three weeks he spent in bed with the fever's lazy lassitude wrapped about him like a quilt. Miss Pru moved him up to the paneled elegance of Father Ben's room because, she said, the air was better. And she found for him, in the spaciousness of the ancient bureau, a voluminous red nightshirt, which he drew on, ducking under the flannel hem and swimming up through the comforting folds, his mind alive with remembering. She brought him meals under silver dish covers that had for almost a hundred years been used to serve visiting dignitaries and, more recently, Father Ben himself during his long last illness.

She cooked medicinal recipes from her grandmother's family, out of ingredients so clearly suspect that she declined to give them any but their Polish names. *Rosòl. Zurek. Flaczki wolowe.* From the depths of the kitchen she brought up soups and stews and tender fragments of meat— tripe and sweetbreads and delicately sautéed chicken livers—in a fragrant golden broth of garlic and turmeric.

It was, in a way, the most luxurious time of his life. Drifting through those hot afternoons, weary and becalmed, he let his mind float back over images of Bea, returning to them again and again, until there wasn't a hope in heaven of separating memory from dream.

55.

It was late in July when he finally climbed out of bed, suddenly aware of all the days that had passed. With a panicky heart he forced himself back to work, but just standing at the door of the toolshed exhausted him.

"You're still too warm."

"I can work."

But it wasn't work he thought about. He tried to tell himself it didn't matter—three weeks out of a summer. He had his whole life ahead. And he'd been sick; he couldn't have moved. But at heart he knew he was somehow to blame. Like some character in a fairy tale he had fallen into a reverie, and that never ended well.

He waited for Bea to arrive; surely she must have heard about his recovery. But when the Plymouth trundled back into town, it was only Joan.

"Why didn't she come?" he demanded, and he could see her smiling at his pettish tone.

"She's gotten really busy. That Weland is a slave-driver. Art doesn't make itself."

"Doesn't she miss me?"

"Of course she does. How could she not?"

He pushed himself, trying to make his muscles stronger, but by the end of each day he was thin as smoke. He started going to bed at seven-thirty again, but when he opened his eyes, half-drifting in the darkness, the prospect of swimming to the island appalled him and he sank back into sleep.

But one afternoon Miss Pru led him out to the garage. He followed obediently, one leg light and weak, the other an anchor. She stopped before a peg on the wall where a dark shape dangled unsettlingly.

"Franklin called them his duck pants."

They were clearly homemade, based on a design from a hunting catalogue. A pair of heavy waders carefully glued around the waistband to a rubber inner tube. They looked cumbersome, awkward— something between a ballet tutu and a giant frog.

"They've held up pretty well," said Miss Pru doubtfully. "I don't think we want to deflate them, though. That might just be asking for trouble."

"This doesn't strike you as a terrible idea?"

She took a moment to decide. "The course of true love never did run smooth."

He drove slowly through the darkness and parked as close to the shore as he could. The inner tube flopped from the backseat onto the ground, and he hauled it to the water's edge. The evening was graceful and serene—soft sounds of the water, the whispering breeze. The duck pants lay jumbled at his feet like a practical joke just waiting its turn.

He leaned against a tree and tried to drag them on, one leg then the next, but his balance was uncertain, and he felt himself growing more ridiculous by the moment. In the end he hauled them to the water's edge, with the innertube springily balanced on the shore and the waders stretched out into the lake. He got down on the ground and squirmed into them, then slipped the suspenders into place. When he hauled himself upright the inner tube shifted and bobbed, as if casting aside the hope of romance to go for the big laugh instead.

Clumsily he edged out over the rocks, but slipping into deep water the pants came suddenly into their own. The ribbed rubber soles gripped the rocks, and the inner tube went from duckling to swan in one swift instant, launching him almost inadvertently out onto the dappled surface.

There was, he realized, no way to steer. He kicked his legs and found himself spinning slowly under the wide night sky. And somehow, in the softness of the breeze, with the faint lapping of the waves allaying his heart, his worry gave way to a kind of wonder. He was silent as driftwood, light as a twig, his cast now as weightless as the rest of him.

But gradually he became aware of a low sound, like a squirrel gnawing an acorn. A scritch-scritch-scritch that seemed to rustle its way insistently through the silence. He turned toward the island and saw the faint glow of lamplight spilling indistinctly beyond the screen of trees. His heart leapt. The image came to him in a single instant—Bea somehow keeping vigil there all this time, caught in her own answering dream, resting in the golden light, half-waiting, half-remembering.

He paddled himself into motion, keeping to the center of the water. And as he drifted closer the glow came slowly into sight through the thick branches, painting the curving boughs of the cedar tree. He slowed his motion, once again aware of his cumbersome shape. He didn't want to appear like this, awkward and foolish after all this time. So he scanned the shore, looking for some place he could land and disentangle himself before stepping out into the lamplight. But he was drifting faster than he thought and before he could stop he had cleared the overhanging trees and eased around into view. And all his plans vanished with the vision before him—as dreamlike as anything he had imagined, but of course much worse.

A circle of kerosene lamps had been set on the ground, marking out like tent stakes the dome of light. It painted the earth, the bark of the tree, the drooping branches, and the figures coaxed into perfect stillness. Joan leaned back against the trunk, her arms up over her head, hands laced among the branches. Her naked body followed the curve of the tree, half-reclining, half-supported—the arch of her back, the shallow exclamation of her breasts, the smooth line of her thighs, parted and braced as if by someone only she could see.

And within the brightest circle of light stood Bea before her easel, naked as the figure she drew, naked as she, herself, had been on that night in the storm against that tree. And the others were there, of course. Sketching, sketching. Not naked, but all in stages of disrobing, as if to stay connected to the wordless passion that Joan, under Bea's frowning guidance, was reimagining so vividly.

He didn't cry out. How could he reveal himself, so clumsy and foolish? He floated there in the shadows as the water drew all the warmth from his body. Joan shifted under careful hands as Bea molded her into each new shape and posture, leading her through every remembered sensation of that long ago night.

"Slower," whispered Weland. "Show us everything you're feeling."

And Bea would carefully arrange the arms, the legs, as if the glowing woman were a figure of pure sensation to be shaped like clay.

And that was, perhaps, the final reason Ash was unable to move. Not simply that he would be ashamed to be seen, a graceless amphibian in a world of such sleekness. And not because he could not, for all the life of him, have known that he would say. But because he knew, without thought, that this would be the very last time he'd have this moment, this fantasy of passion and beauty, to call his own.

56

His life became a shadow-version of itself. He tried to put it out of his mind, tried to harden himself to the realization. But as with any nightmare: as much as you want to escape it, some part of it always calls you back. At night he rose from his bed and trundled the duck pants into the car. And he floated for hours within sight of all that had seemed most magical. He heard the rustle of water on the rocks, the distant murmur of voices. But the group never returned to the cedar tree, and every night he waited, on the verge of something that had always already passed.

Then one night, floating in the darkness, a great cry rose up from the bank. A woman's voice. Bea. He recognized it at once. He thought she was frightened at first and he started to splash toward the shore. But after a moment he realized it wasn't fear but fury. So he settled like a frog on its lily pad and waited with something like satisfaction.

The shouting, the noise was outrageous. A smash of crockery. And again. One dish after another. And now other voices, lower, more reasonable. Urging, arguing, trying to be calm. It was an anthill of voices swarming up and over, and Ash floated, calm and exultant.

Then, with the unmistakable slam of a door, a figure appeared on the porch, shadowed against the windows. He recognized her, even in the distance. She turned and ran into the woods.

He didn't know what it meant, but he was grimly pleased by the wreckage. A fight. A lover's quarrel? He waited for Joan to burst out and follow, but the cabin just settled into silence. He thought of Bea, alone among the trees, angry and hurt, and he was turning to follow her when he heard the scuff and clunk of the skiff being launched. He craned around. Beyond the curve of the shore he saw the unmistakable image of Bea, hunched in the bow, drawing herself across the channel. He called softly, but she was lost in her rage. Climbing out onto the shore she vanished among the trees, and a moment later the sound of an engine startled into life. The bright flash of headlights turned and scattered away through the trees.

But now another figure separated itself from the darkness of the cabin. Joan? No. It headed slowly down to the lake. And floating there a stone's throw off the dock, Ash watched the man, a little unsteady on his feet, as if after all the uproar he hadn't yet found his balance.

Weland halted at the water's edge and, patting his pockets, he drew out a pack of cigarettes. A little blossom of flame and a thin cloud of smoke. He looked like a man whose plans had gone awry, as if he had set up a whole complex vision of beauty, only to see it hijacked by love.

Ash thought he would simply dislike the man—for drawing Bea's attention away, for changing her, for throwing Bea and Joan so closely together and then just standing by. But this was a different Weland, thinner than he remembered and more rumpled. More absorbed by the turn of events. He finished the cigarette and was about to flick it out over the water when his eyes settled on Ash with an air of unstartled weariness.

"Hello," he called. "Beautiful night."

And only then did Ash realize how thoroughly drunk he was. "Beautiful," he agreed.

"How's the fishing?"

"A little quiet right now."

Weland nodded. With the introduction of an audience he seemed to collect himself. "What are you using for bait?"

Ash hesitated. He remembered the hand-lettered sign in Halladay's. Worms $3.00 a ½ doz. But then he thought of his father at his desk long ago, peering through the gooseneck magnifying lens as he made his little loops of silk and feathers. "Dry fly," he said.

"Good for you. What type?"

"Yellow mayfly."

"Little late for that, isn't it?"

"I guess we'll see."

"I thought everyone used worms around here." He raised one foot and tamped out the cigarette against the sole. Then he slipped it into his pocket and when his hand reappeared it held a silver flask. "Looks awfully peaceful out there."

"It is."

"Bit raucous here, I'm afraid. I hope we didn't disturb you."

"I don't think the fish heard."

"Then they're the only ones who didn't." He tilted up the flask for a sip, then seemed to recall his manners. "Care for one?"

Ash could feel the cold of the lake seeping into his legs. "I wouldn't say no."

Weland capped the flask and, without hesitation, threw. Ash almost cried out. He couldn't believe the man. Too drunk to aim; too drunk to care. But it flew in a glinting, graceful arc, and he clutched it frantically, hugging it to his chest within a slowly expanding circle of relief and surprise.

Weland waited as if he had expected no less. Ash took a sip and then another. And hurrying now, not to be left behind by the moment, he drew back the flask and threw. Awkwardly, a wobbling duck of a throw, but close enough. Weland, stepping left and low, gathered it out of the air. He weighed it in his hand. "You from around here?" he called.

"Over in Galliard. This your island?"

"No, thank God. Just visiting. There's something about islands—they're never what you think they'll be. Perfect place for concentration, but not much room for a quick getaway." He took another sip and offered the flask again. "What's your name?"

"Franklin. No, thanks."

"Not a drinking man, Franklin?"

"Not a catching man. I'd like to retire with my streak intact."

"That's no way to be. Risk, Franklin. Every day a little further than the day before." And without warning he threw. To be fair, Ash almost caught it. The flask bounced against his fingers in the darkness and vanished with a hollow plop.

Gazing for a moment, Weland laughed quietly under his breath.

"I'm sorry," said Ash.

"Never mind. It's the little failures that prepare us for our big success. It was almost empty anyway. Do you know anything about women, Franklin?"

"I do not."

"That is the only honest answer."

He lit another cigarette and blew a faint cloud in the moonlight. "Art, I understand. Passion, sex, desire, need. Those are my materials."

"You're an artist?"

"And then some. I am an impresario of passion. But of all the various raw materials an artist needs to draw upon, it's always people that disrupt the mix. It's like alchemy."

Ash smiled. "*Whatever dies was not mixed equally; If our two loves be one, or, thou and I love so alike, that none do slacken, none can die.*"

It seemed to stymie Weland for a moment. "Exactly," he said. "Is that yours, Franklin?"

"John Donne. Something my mother used to read."

"It's a beautiful thought." He finished his cigarette and this time flicked it out over the water, a glittering speck that went out with a hiss. "But I tell you this much, Franklin. Beauty is beauty. But women are women. And there is only so much you can do."

And without another word he turned and walked back up to the cabin.

Ash lay in bed that night, weary and uplifted—the sight of Bea in the boat, straining to escape. He had half-expected her to be waiting for him at the rectory, and he had parked and approached through the shadows not quite daring to whisper but waiting for the slightest sound. And such is the force of our own desire, at every step as he crept into the house and through the laundry room and into the kitchen, he was ready to come upon her—waiting and grateful, apologetic and newly conscious of all that was between them. But the house was empty.

The next day he kept glancing up the street, waiting for the Plymouth to appear. And after a while, it did, driving coolly along and parking in front of the Rectory. Joan climbed out.

She strolled over to him, as if deliberately taking her time, but when she got close he could see her expression was uneasy.

"Is she all right?" he demanded.

"Oh. She's fine. Just being a drama queen." And then, against every likelihood, her voice softened. "I just thought you might want to know. She's left."

"I know. I saw her leave."

"No. I mean really left. Drove away. Headed back to school. She's pretty upset."

"What? Why?"

She considered that for a moment. "No one said love was easy. And maybe art isn't quite what she thought it would be. Anyway, I thought you might be enough of a drip to want to help her."

"Why should I? This is your fault!"

"Not just mine."

"You broke her heart."

"It's just a little bruised."

"What can I do?"

"Golly, Galahad," she said sarcastically. "I don't know. Maybe

go after her."
So he did.

Harold In Purgatory

57

He pulled into the gravel driveway in the ancient borrowed Saab. He barely remembered the house, the apartment, he been gone so long. Not the day or two he had promised but more like a lifetime. He was sitting there, letting the road-rush die away—it wasn't as if he had a plan—when the sudden rap on the window made him jump. For an instant he marveled at the way moments of his life kept repeating: not Miss Pru now knocking at the glass, but Reeve, standing, frowning down at him. She gestured impatiently to unroll the window.

"You're late," she said.

But before he could reply she ducked her head into the car and kissed him. "What's the first thing that occurs to you?" she demanded.

"I've been on the road for seventeen hours."

"I guess you'd better get out of the car, then."

She had called him every week, every few days at first—checking on him, reminding him of his obligations, making sure he didn't run off with their car. Though of course that was exactly what he'd done. And if at first she threatened to call the police or a bounty hunter or come right up and repossess it, she had revised her plans when he described how far he was from anything resembling public transport. So instead she resolved to call him regularly to make sure the car was all right. They were brief calls, often insulting, her tone as acerbic as Miss Pru's expression. She would ask him how the car was doing—whether he was checking the oil, keeping the tires inflated—and then, brisk as an afterthought, what he was doing this week to waste his time. And he would tell her about the town, about work, about his made-up aunt—never what was most on his mind. Cool and distant and disapproving, she and Miss Pru together were the perfect opposite of all that he was feeling. And it amused him at first to have two such cold women in his life when the secret motor of his heart was running so hot.

He pulled from the car the same overnight bag he'd started with. That seemed strange, as well—that everything he'd been through could fit so easily into such a small space. Nearly two months. He felt battered by the time. Transformed. The cast on his ankle was the only solid thing about him. And as he limped slowly through the dusty rooms of his apartment with Reeve trailing behind, all he could do was murmur weakly, "Home, sweet home."

She regarded him: rumpled clothes, bleary eyes, the frantic glint of too much rest-stop coffee. "You should come upstairs," she said, not tenderly. "You need a shower."

"I have a shower."

"Do you have a towel?"

With a dismissive scowl she went to get one.

In the bathroom he moved slowly, his body groggy from the road, his mind a nest of bees. He undressed, stepped under the shower. He was startled when she joined him. Hadn't he closed he door? *Tell me you don't want me here,* she said.

"I'm a little out of it," he murmured, and she seemed to accept that. She dried his back, helped him into bed. "Isn't it nice to be home?"

It felt like a dream—how could it be anything else? But Ash had forgotten the nature of their conversations: work, Miss Pru, the emptiness of the town. They had been a comfort at first. *Isn't it nice that I keep calling?* We forget that every conversation has two sides. And though they meet in the middle, they do not always align.

He woke up alone in the darkness in a room that smelled of dust. He got up and dressed. Finding his way into town, he bought a pizza, then walked until he found the house: tall, yellow, with a four-square roof. He wasn't sure he'd recognize it, but there it was. The windows were dark from the ground to the roofline, but there was a single weak light in the attic. He walked up the driveway, past a shiny, out-of-place Mercedes, and found a narrow door. When he tried the knob it turned. A single narrow flight of stairs went all the way up to a distant door.

He climbed, he knocked. There was a faint brush of slippered footsteps and the door opened on a solid, wild-haired woman in heavy tortoiseshell glasses and a haggard expression. Despite the heat she wore a yellow velour bathrobe, belted and zipped, and on her feet thick grey socks. She regarded him for a moment, not as if she didn't recognize him, but as if she didn't see the point. "Hi, Ash."

"I brought you dinner."

She started to cry.

The attic was one enormous room. No walls. Just a steep, high ceiling of ancient particle board, yellowed and bleak. There were four large windows dormered into the roof, but they had long since been painted closed, and the room smelled like a sealed trunk: ancient cigarette smoke, unwashed clothes, and an almost forgotten hint of turpentine.

The kitchen was a stove, a refrigerator, and a huddle of cabinets all standing in the open just off to the side. There was a Formica table and chairs, a sofa, a mattress, not so much arranged as abandoned in the wide inhospitable space. In the corner a bathtub and toilet sat, bleakly unprotected by walls, while across the dusty floor were scattered a flannel shirt, overalls, a pair of underpants and socks, all plucked like feathers and discarded.

He drew her into his arms as she sobbed.

"Don't cry," he murmured. "Don't cry. Look at all the room you've got."

He asked her if she had eaten.

"I'm not hungry."

"I brought pizza. What's your favorite kind?"

"Anchovies and roasted garlic."

"It's not that," he said.

Her voice was muffled and damp. "I have to lie down."

He walked her over to the rumpled mattress, and she sank down. Her breathing was heavy and uneven.

He said, "I'm just going to use your bathroom."

He was self-conscious, but the distance and her own obliviousness offered some privacy. He unzipped and lifted the seat, and then he saw, lined up on the back of the toilet, a row of amber pill bottles, all empty.

"Jesus, Bea! What did you take? What have you done?" He shook her roughly, but she didn't care.

He managed to roll her onto her side and, God knows how, got a finger down her throat. Then, sweat-soaked and wrung out with vomiting, she lay heavily in his arms until the EMTs arrived.

She stayed the night in the emergency room, and he half-slept in a bedside chair. Then he drove her home in the morning. "Do you want to change out of that robe?"

But she just sank down onto the terrible mattress.

"Where are your clothes?" he asked. She had lost all desire for language. She just waved toward the door.

The car keys were in her overalls. He was already accustomed to the long, narrow stairs, but the cool of the evening surprised him. The back seat of the Mercedes overflowed with dirty laundry. He scooped up an armful, and carried it upstairs, then went down for another and another. Beneath the waning pile he found the crumpled duffle bag and a hard, archeological layer of stretched canvases. He drew the first one out and turned it to the light. A nude. Joan, of course.

He carried them up, half a dozen of them, turning them just enough to see that they were all the same. "Don't look at them," Bea said feverishly. "Did you look?"

"No."

"Put them against the wall. Turn them around. I don't want to see them."

He sat down on the sofa, a knot of weariness. "I love what you've done with the place."

"You don't have to stay."

But when it was clear he would, she said, "It's a legacy. A famous apartment. It gets passed down from painter to painter. I was really lucky to get it."

"And the furniture?"

"It all came with. The pots and pans, the furniture, the light."

"And the light's good?"

"They say it will break your heart."

Though even Ash could tell it was too late for that.

He bought soup for her, because that was all she would eat, and crackers and ginger ale. He treated her as if she were sick, as if that were the problem, and listlessly she accepted his care. He slept on the sofa that night because she didn't want him to leave.

"Tell me when I should turn off the light," she said.

"Just give me a minute."

He used her toothpaste on his finger. He washed his face with a thin crescent of Ivory soap. "Okay."

He lay beneath a single unwashed sheet—it was too warm for anything else—and an ancient pillow, part of the legacy no doubt. He thought of the endless sky in Gaillard, of the breezes over the lake.

"Good night, Ash."

"I saw you that night."

"Which night?

"Out by the tree. You and Joan. All of you."

She grew still. "We were working."

"Stop it." And he was proud of himself for that. It could so easily have come out angry or pleading.

"We were painting."

"I saw what you were doing."

"Then you know it's true."

"That was our tree," he said.

"Of course it was our tree. That's why we were there." And now she was the one pleading. "Don't you understand? That's all that art can be. The most precious thing you have. The most intense thing. It's nothing without that."

"Is that what Weland says?"

"It's the truth. Not just because Weland said it."

"But that was ours."

"Ash. I need to paint what I feel. Otherwise none of it matters. None of it's real. It needs to be real." And she sounded so wistful now.

"But why not other people? Paint what's real to them. Why do you have to take what we had?" He dropped his voice to a whisper. "That night. It was everything to me."

"That's what I'm saying. I have to paint what's most important. And that was it, Ash. That was the realest thing in my life."

And lying there he wished she had said *you. You're the realest thing in my life.* And he wished she hadn't said *was.*

58

Bea gave herself up to fatigue like a trout to the butter in a pan. She wouldn't tell him what happened. But one day, returning from the store, he met Joan coming down the stairs. She gave him a cold look but said nothing, and when he asked Bea about it she just dissolved into weeping.

He could do nothing to move her. And like castaways in the tropics the long hot days of listlessness drew the energy from their muscles, leaving them languid and drained. Finally, under the weight of all that inactivity, he began to clean. He started scrubbing the sink with the ancient remnant of a scouring pad and then worked his way out from there hauling the extra burden of the cast. He found a ragged broom in the corner and a mop the color of dirt. He spent the afternoon sweeping the apartment, mopping the floor, cleaning the cupboards, as if those months as a handyman had prepared him for exactly this. And like a good handyman, he saw salvation in all the long list of things that needed to be done.

"I think we'd better wash these clothes."

"There's no washing machine," she said dully.

"We'll go to a laundromat. Come on. It'll be fun. Do it for old time's sake."

But the most she would do was move to a kitchen chair while he stripped the bed.

That evening he carried the duffel bag of laundry around the block to his apartment and emptied it onto the kitchen floor. Overhead the muffled sounds of music and voices drifted down. As he bent to the pile, loading armfuls into the front of the washer, he heard a brisk knock on the door and then the sound of it opening.

"I don't think you're supposed to just walk in like that," he said.

"I saw your light on. I thought it might be an emergency."

Reeve was dressed in jeans and a soft silk shirt the pale cinnamon color of her hair. She carried a bottle of wine and two glasses. "I thought you'd been murdered," she said, "or kidnapped."

With a glance at the pale glint of bra and panties running like a vein of satin through the tumbled pile of laundry, she said, "I admire a man who's not afraid to show his feminine side."

"I'm doing this for a friend."

"And those are his?"

"She's sick. I'm just taking care of her."

"What a nice guy you are. And here I thought you were new in town. I'm going to open this bottle now," she said. "You're not going to run away again, are you? If I accidentally pour you a glass?"

When he got back to the attic Bea had moved the paintings, and now they were lined up along the wall beside the bed: a row of nudes, but not—he noticed now—all nudes.

There were five paintings of Joan: standing, striding, one with her arms half-wrapped across her breasts as if against prying eyes. The paint was thick, as if Bea had struggled over the naked body layer by layer and just couldn't bring herself to stop. The final picture was of Weland, standing in an unbuttoned shirt with the bowtie undone—slightly foolish in boxer shorts, black socks, and shoes. There wasn't much detail, as if the painter hadn't been looking very closely. A little comma of paint for the crook of the mouth, an air of sheepishness captured in the slight hunch of the shoulders. It almost made Ash smile, perhaps because it wasn't Joan.

"Weland says a painter has to see herself in her work. Every portrait is a self-portrait. But I don't recognize anything."

"I recognize her," said Ash, but Bea just shook her head.

59.

"We should paint this place," said Ash.

The high sloping ceilings had darkened with the years to the color of tea-stained paper, and the ancient windows made even the sunlight look dusty and reluctant. Bea said, "How about black?"

"How about white?"

She peered around like a moth under a jar.

"Come on," he said. "It'll be stupid."

They bought three gallons. It would eventually take twenty. They accumulated equipment as needed: wide foam applicators that crumbled against the wooden studs, sheepskin rollers that frayed and snagged, and finally heavy brushes, wide as they could manage, ponderous with paint and dripping like an ancient engine block. He bought a step ladder, but when he set it up, the sky was not more out of reach than the peak of the ceiling. He replaced it with an aluminum extension ladder that ratcheted up, but when they leaned it against the highest point, the legs slid out like a giraffe on a skating rink, so they had to nail two-by-fours to brace the feet. And when Ash climbed to the top, hauling his cast like an extra reminder of all the empty space beneath, he felt like a bird on the end of a too-slender twig.

He thought it might take four days. It took them the rest of the summer. At first Bea watched from the sofa, but after a while the hopelessness of it drew her in. They spent all their money on paint and supplies. Food came from whatever was leftover—ramen, broth, the occasional perfect apple. Ash bought a large jar of honey, and they each took a spoonful at every meal, living like hummingbirds on a diet of sugar and effort.

They started at the bottom, working in opposite directions: edging around the floor on hands and knees. Bea lost herself in the delicate, repetitive motion of the brush, and when they finally met up at the end of their circuit Ash had painted three-quarters of the room, but Bea's face was intent with a kind of remembered pleasure.

The work was hard on the arms and shoulders. After the first week everything was over their heads. They painted in the mornings, before the sun rose enough to bake the room. In the afternoon Ash went out to exercise or shop or to live whatever amounted to the rest of his life. But when he climbed back up the stairs he always found her in bed, peering around at the rising tide of white as if waiting for it to crest.

The heat was terrific. Ash stripped off his t-shirt and wrapped it like a turban around his head against the drips and sweat. But Bea seemed determined not to notice. She wrapped herself in her grief, wearing every layer she could: baggy shorts, t-shirt, a loose sweatshirt. She said she was cold-blooded, but he could see the sweat running down her face.

The bathtub provided the only relief and the only source of privacy. An ancient claw-footed monster, it was speckled with rust and mounted with a circular curtain. Bea used it as a changing room, stepping high over the rim and drawing the curtain snugly behind her. At the end of the day they filled the tub with cool water and took their turns. Bea started with the curtains tightly closed until she realized Ash could simply turn his chair away. So they sat back-to-back inspecting the slowly-accruing evidence of their labors.

The fumes made them light-headed.

"I think we should probably get some air in here."

The windows were enormous—eight feet tall and four feet wide, double-sashed and mullioned—but too high to look out of except at the sky. When Ash climbed to examine one, he found layers of paint thick as leather binding the joints. Trying to move it was like moving a cliff.

"You could just smash the glass."

"Let's make that plan B."

Like any castaway, his strategies developed from the tools at hand—a dusty collection from the back of a cupboard. A wood chisel, streaked with rust, finally sank into the space between boards. A jagged utility knife cut a fine line along the tough, painted seam. And on the off chance that this would be enough—that the universe was merely waiting for the opportunity to help—he braced his hands against the lower sash and strained.

"I told you it was hopeless," called Bea

"You didn't say hopeless."

"I thought it was understood." But there was a glint of humor in her voice.

"I have not yet begun to fight."

Their planning sessions grew more giddy as the fumes grew stronger. Pacing back and forth in front of the sofa he walked her through every possible solution, like a mime running through his routine: Loosen the sides with the chisel. Pound up with the hammer. Buy a car jack and force the whole thing open. Hire a gorilla from the zoo and put a banana just out of reach on top of the sash.

In the end he took the whole window frame apart, prying out the long vertical moldings that held the sash in place and disassembling every piece. The more he removed, the more aware he became of how huge the window was—how heavy and delicately balanced. He moved like a safe-cracker, slowly disarranging the whole complex mechanism. In the middle of his work he glanced out and recognized, as if for the first time, the four-story drop to the sidewalk below. And the vision of two hundred pounds of glass and wood pitching gracefully through the air settled heavily into the pit of his stomach.

"Are you sure you know what you're doing?" called Bea.

But in the end it was almost flawless.

With the bracing strips off, the huge window became docile as a plow horse. Arms caked with dust, Ash dragged the bottom out of its frame. It was abruptly entangled in the ancient sash cords that rose up into the walls where the lead counter-weights hung. He struggled for a moment to lift it free, then propped it awkwardly on the sill as the sudden breeze bathed him.

He drew out the knife and started sawing at the rope. It parted, and like a magic trick the frayed end snaked up over a hidden pulley and vanished into the wall. The thump and clatter of the sash-weight echoed like a distant disaster as it fell, while in the same instant the whole window lurched in his hands. Suddenly, impossibly heavy, wildly unbalanced, it carried him this way and that. The wide canyon of empty air yawned open from his knees to his shoulders as the window dipped and nosed toward the gap like a button trying to slip through its hole. He braced himself against the jouncing ladder; and with a wild grunt of effort managed to wedge the window back into place.

Bea was on her feet, clutching the back of a chair as if preparing to throw it out after him if he fell. "Was that supposed to happen?"

He didn't have the breath to reply.

When he cut the second sash-rope he was braced and ready. And with the window free in his hands, he stepped the whole enormous weight of it down the ladder to the floor.

Together they sanded the edges, shaved off all the ancient paint. They rubbed furniture wax to make the bare wood smooth as glass, and then a mixture of vinegar and water to polish the glass into air. When he finally walked it back up the ladder and slid it into place he felt dizzy with relief. He hurried the bracing strips back where they belonged, and the window was just a window again. It slid open, smooth as could be.

He went out and bought a six-pack of beer. When he returned Bea was in the tub. He sat down in the chair admiring his handiwork, feeling the breeze against his arms and face as if it were something he, himself, had made.

In later years he could never really reconstruct the state of his feelings. Never quite remember what it had been like. Looking back it was impossible to understand how he could have behaved the way he did. But he was full of hope even then. He hadn't seen Joan for weeks; he'd had Bea all to himself. They were growing closer and closer. How could she not choose him?

But it's no good trying to make sense of love. Our feelings are always shaded, even if our actions are black and white. Sitting there quietly Ash noticed, with oblique awareness, a slight, uncertain movement in the monumental solidity of the scene. A tiny shift, just out of the corner of his eye. And he was just beginning to wonder what it might mean when the window—almost frictionless with all that polishing—slammed shut with the sound of a gunshot exploding in the room. He was half-warned, half-wondering, and still he jumped. Bea screamed.

Lurching up from the bath in a cascade of suds, she flung her arms around him, sobbing and clutching as if everything she had ever feared was here in the room with her. He was aware of her body, slippery and solid in his arms.

"What was that?" she moaned.

"Just the window."

"Jesus. *Just* the window."

And she grew still, only then remembering how naked she was. Ash was smiling as he loosened his arms and let her sink modestly into the water. He didn't notice at first. It wasn't that obvious. It's not as if she showed. It was just the sudden self-consciousness when she eased herself down, as if she had become an unexpected burden to herself, that revealed the smooth rounding of her belly so at odds with the haggard thinness of her face.

"Don't leave me," she whispered.

But at that point, even for Ash, there was nothing else to do.

60.

The comfort of his apartment surprised him—the plain walls, the cool empty rooms. That night, when he heard the music and the laughter, he climbed the stairs and knocked on the door.

Reeve opened it and stood regarding him. "So," she said. "Not kidnapped."

"No."

Then, stepping back, she said, "You're going to want to see this." And she ushered him into a room full of smoke and low purple light.

Bernard was standing there in a white bed sheet, twisting a wreath of oak leaves into his sparsely bushy hair, the remains of a joint held negligently in his off hand. "Hail to thee, blithe spirit. Bird thou never were. You may enter the inner sanctum of the coven of Maude."

"What are you wearing?" asked Ash.

"Nature is the only mother of us all." And leaning forward to extend the joint he whispered, "They're a poly-cotton blend. Don't tell Maude."

It was unclear whether the group was a cluster of practicing witches who liked to play music or an abbreviated chamber orchestra in need of a little mystery in their lives. But they made room for him without a murmur. Some nights they worked on a version of Beethoven's final string quartet expanded for oboe and base clarinet. Other nights they didn't. Tonight they were playing something Russell had written that changed key every eight bars in a pattern he wanted them to guess.

"The thing is," Bernard explained as he led Ash to the linen closet, "everything is strange if you look closely enough."

All the white sheets were in use so Ash chose a Marimekko

print in greens and browns. He kept his underwear on. "It's not a big deal tonight," Bernard conceded, "but don't let Maude find out."

He sat on the carpet wrapped in his sheet and thought of Bea in her high, lonely attic. The bong went around with every key change; nobody guessed the pattern. At some point Maude told him he had a very primitive soul, and Ash thought maybe she was right. Later in the evening they tried to levitate Reeve, but ended up only raising the lower part of her sheet to reveal that, unlike Ash, she had committed herself unabashedly to the whole evening's endeavor.

Then Maude decided they needed to try prognostication through animal entrails—she was taking Vertebrate Physiology and produced a white rat, stiff with formaldehyde. But Reeve had an allergic reaction to the chemicals, which, she said, smelled like the inside of a stomach, and had to excuse herself. Out in the garden Ash held her long hair as she vomited pitiably into the flowerbed. And as she knelt, pulling herself together, he noticed over the shoulder of the house a distant shift in the leaves of a broad oak tree as Bea's attic lights came on.

Three months after first arriving in town he finally unpacked. All the suitcases that had come with him at the beginning of the summer went into the closet. And he tried to imagine what a college student would do in a brand new town before classes began. He went out walking during the day, forcing himself to explore, stopping in bookstores, pizza shops, coffee houses. And in the evening, when he heard the music, he wandered up the stairs and sat in the thin cloud of smoke, trying to levitate someone or cast a spell or bring some wild magic into the world.

Every day he waited for Bea to knock on his door. But when she finally did, it caught him by surprise.

"Can I come in?"

It was almost unbearably ordinary to see her standing in the afternoon sunlight on his front porch. Gone was every exotic thing. He felt like an altered vision of himself as they sat down "in the kitchen. In the end the worst of his anger had lasted little more than two weeks, but it left him with a kind of distant curiosity—as if the fact of having lived the events of his life only made them more difficult to comprehend. He was making a tuna sandwich for himself, so he made one for her. He poured them lemonade.

"I miss you, Ash."

"Who's the father?"

But really, why even ask? He thought of the painting of Weland—how wry and sheepish and jaunty he looked. You have to love what you paint. And he could see now it was the best thing she'd done.

"What am I going to do?" she asked.

And he couldn't help himself. Despite the simmering anger, the image caught him like a sudden spark in the mind. The two of them and the child. Not an idea; certainly not a plan. Perhaps just a spasm of foreclosure—the last glimpse of a room before the door shuts. "No idea," he said.

"I'm not going to keep it."

"What about Weland?"

"He doesn't get a vote," she said. "Will you come with me?"

In the morning they went to the free clinic. It was almost like a date. He knocked on her door, and she greeted him in a dress he had never seen before: hair washed and brushed, face smooth. The clinic was in the basement of a brick office building on the outskirts of the downtown. The walls were painted pale blue. It smelled like a vet's office: rubbing alcohol and animal anxiety—an impression that wasn't helped by the copies of *Cat Fancy* magazine scattered in the waiting room. She didn't let go of his hand, even when her name was called.

"We'll need to see you alone for now," said the nurse, "but he can come in later."

After twenty minutes the nurse reappeared. "We're ready for you."

It was much less than expected. The doctor handed her a pair of amber vials. "They're marked," she said. "Take this one first, then up to twenty-four hours later, this one. You should have someone with you."

"I'll be there," said Ash.

"No driving. No operating heavy machinery. There will be some spotting. Some cramps, usually, though that varies. Anything more than that, come back and see us."

Bea took the first pill in the car with a bottle of water. "Okay," she said. He never saw her take the second.

It was on their return that Ash noticed the shiny Mercedes was gone from the driveway. In its place was an empty patch of gravel and crabgrass, as if the whole point of Weland's car was to demonstrate how shabby everything looked without it. They climbed the stairs wearily.

"This place is a shithole," Bea announced.

And it was true. He had carried away the image of high white walls, bright and fresh. But now the paint looked mottled, and the old wood had leached away any brightness.

She pressed her hand fleetingly against her stomach, but her expression was determinedly brisk. "I think maybe I'll sit down." There was a faint sheen of perspiration on her forehead.

"How are you feeling?"

"Just a little queasy."

They sat on the sofa. Along with excellent light the apartment came equipped with a collection of board games, piled on a shelf in the corner. Monopoly, Candyland, Risk.

"We could play Monopoly," he suggested.

"I hate Monopoly."

"Candyland?"

"Would you read to me?"

And so he read to her from *Cat Fancy,* which he had somehow neglected to return when they had left the clinic.

"I think maybe I'll just lie down." So he helped her onto the mattress, and from the muffled comfort of her pillows a small voice murmured, "Thank you, Ash."

And with that, they had somehow come full circle. He stayed with her until she fell asleep.

In the morning he called, and she said she was fine. The next day, as well. On the third day she called to ask if he felt like a drink.

And so they went out. *Freddy's* was dark and shabby, throbbing with a backbeat and smelling, unexpectedly, of peppermint schnapps. They drank beer, and then beer and tequila, and then just tequila, and danced like crazy people—fiberglass cast and all—until their shirts were drenched and their ears would not stop ringing. They walked home through the cool night. Bea moved determinedly around the attic lighting candles. The glow rose up, shining off the high white ceiling and filling the space like a bubble of hope. "Dance with me," she said and locked her lips against his. "You like me, Ash. Don't you? You like kissing me? You like the way I feel?"

"Yes. Yes, I do."

But they were two strangers trying to impersonate that lovesick pair from the summer. He marveled at all that had happened to that first feeling of wonder. And even in the moment his mind kept slipping ahead to how it would all seem afterwards. They kissed. They drew off their clothes, heavy and damp, and dropped them where they stood. Bea glanced at the cast.

"Don't give it a thought," he said.

They made love on the sofa, then again on the mattress, and finally against the kitchen counter holding on for balance and panting hoarsely as if it were a race they were determined to finish.

Afterwards, lying together under the high canopy of candlelight, it all seemed to have happened without him.

They started taking evening walks after making love, strolling along the storybook streets. And though the route might change, the final stretch was always the same, past the town green and the distant sight of the narrow Federalist house. Ash didn't object; it was, he hoped, a way for Bea to disentangle herself from all the old feelings.

But one night the sounds of a party filtered out from the lighted windows. The beginning-of-term Open House; a tradition in the department. Ash had never heard of it, but Bea seemed unsurprised. People were coming and going; there was no difficulty slipping in.

Weland looked elegant in a pale suit and bow tie, refreshed from the summer and at ease with the crowd. His smile was untroubled at the sight of Bea. And the scene at the end of the evening—the smashing of glasses, the shouting in the kitchen that spilled out into the house—it was almost unsurprising to those who had attended so many of Weland's parties. But it made an impression on Ash. He took Bea home with a sense of protecting her, with a determination to be on her side. But when the semester began and he discovered she had signed up for Weland's life-drawing class again, even he had to face the facts. He left town the next morning.

Harold in Limbo

61.

Miss Pru made no comment on his return, as she had made no comment when he'd left, merely standing aside now to let him in as the bus drove away. If she seemed older than he remembered, he was feeling older himself. But he added his sudden departure to the growing list of his regrets, and he determined to make it up to her. The next day she took him to Braithwaite to have the cast removed, but he carried the phantom weight of it for weeks.

He chose Mrs. Bleeker's front porch. He needed something so broken there was no way even to begin. The foundation had rotted slowly at first and then all at once, dragging the roof down like the sagging corner of a mouth. She had taken to using the back door.

"It looks bad," she said hesitantly.

"Yes, ma'am."

"Can you just patch it there? Just lift it and patch it? Maybe put another post under it?"

"Maybe."

"Mr. Franklin would always say, I think there's a perfect solution hiding in there somewhere."

Ash nodded. "Thank you, Mrs. Bleeker. If you'd like me to try to get in touch with Mr. Franklin, I will."

"I'm going to go put in a pan of brownies."

He knocked the broken columns out with a sledge hammer, and the corner sagged even more. He climbed a ladder and stepped onto the unsupported roof. It gently collapsed, and he rode it to the ground. It gave him an odd satisfaction to see something as solid as a house coming to pieces in his hands. Rounding the front corner with the brownies Mrs. Bleeker stood, wide-eyed and pale.

"You might not want to see this," he said as he lifted the plate gently from her hands.

"I have coffee."

"That sounds wonderful."

He spent three days just pulling it apart—breaking up the rotted roof, hauling away the rubble. In the end it looked as if some ravenous giant had taken a single large bite out of the ancient house. Then he ordered the lumber.

"Are you planning to move into Mrs. Bleeker's?" asked Miss Pru one night, as she set his plate before him.

"It's going to be a thing of beauty."

"I think she was just looking for a few quick patches and some paint."

"There's no room in this world for bad workmanship."

He supported the remaining section of roof on a forest of two-by-fours while he rebuilt the floor. Then he started at the broken edge of shingles and built out over the gap. He ended each day hunched and exhausted, arranging his tools in the crowded shed. That was the last of the day's discipline: remembering all the edges, keeping them sharp. And then the evening began.

He had started driving to the liquor store a few times a week, so there would be a bottle of rye waiting for him on the table. At first Miss Pru watched without a word. Then, without a word, she lifted the bottle from his hand and poured it down the sink. "Your dinner's getting cold."

"You said Franklin was a drinker."

"Franklin fell off a ladder and broke his neck."

"That doesn't sound so bad to me."

She slapped him. Just like that, out of the blue. It startled them both. But Ash was the first to recover. He gazed down at the bright foods arrayed on his plate—orange squash, pale mashed potatoes, a vivid slice of fried ham—as if it were the colors themselves that had set his ears ringing. "I've always hated squash."

"It's good for you."

"It tastes like dirt."

She seated herself grimly and lifted her knife and fork. "I've gone to all the trouble to cook it. The least you can do is eat."

So he started to keep the bottle in his bedroom and drank under cover of night. But after a while he found that, where he used to be afraid to remember, now he was beginning to forget. The pale slope of a breast, the long complex curve of her thighs. He would wake in the morning with nothing certain about her.

It was Miss Pru who brought the bottle out and put it in the cupboard beside the cooking sherry. She had a glass waiting for him when he came in, and another after that, and another. Then she put the bottle away. But he didn't mind. They listened to the radio at night—Father Ben had hated the television and wouldn't have one in the rectory—and Miss Pru would ask him to read aloud from Dickens or Trollope or the day's paper. He was shy at first—the words still tended to dance and shift under his eyes—but the whiskey helped. It was his childhood all over again. He read slowly, picking his way through the story. And gradually he found a perch in the unwavering routine of his life.

62

On Saturdays Miss Pru cleaned the church, though since Father Ben's death it never really had a chance to get more than a little dusty. The nave was narrow but imposing, with high stone walls and mullioned windows. The mid-afternoon sunlight warmed itself on the oak pews and the modest grandeur of the pulpit. She used to spend hours over it, dusting and polishing, arranging the flowers, draping the unused altar. It was like a present she wrapped again each week—less like cleaning than remembering. She started to bring Ash along.

The first time they went he brought his glass. The quiet was soft as dust. "You don't suppose He minds the drinking?" said Ash.

"She," said Miss Pru. "Almost certainly a she. And no, I don't suppose She does."

He'd half-expected her to genuflect upon entering the nave but she just frowned over her work.

"I used to come here sometimes when Father Ben was preparing for the service. It was my favorite time. I would sit in the back, and he would practice his sermon. He was so young back then. It's hard to believe how young we both were."

One day she had asked him how he did it. How he could get up in front of all those people. She had been so shy when she first started at the Rectory. But he had smiled. Would you like to try? He had offered her a steadying hand as she climbed up into the pulpit. That was the first time they had touched.

Now she moved the dusting cloth smoothly over the back of a pew. "I don't suppose I can tell you how it felt."

To be standing there, looking out at the empty church, so grand and echoing. Father Ben had been pleased with her nervousness. Try it, he said. Say something. But she had been tongue-tied with him standing so close.

So he had gone out past the low railing, pausing to genuflect before the altar. That had seemed such an important a part of the moment—he was so graceful and serious in his long white surplice—and she had watched him settle in the front pew smiling.

Her mouth had gone dry as dust, but that didn't matter. In all her months at the Rectory she had only memorized a single thing.

> *How do I love thee? Let me count the ways.*
> *I love thee to the depth and breadth and height*
> *My soul can reach, when feeling out of sight*
> *For the ends of being and ideal grace.*

She hadn't even learned the whole poem. And when she drew to a stop the last words lingered—the thinness of her voice merely tying the moment more securely to all that she had felt. And it had been a thrill knowing that her words, small as they were in that enormous space, could travel all that way to the first pew intact.

So when she saw how sad Ash was, how pressed into the smallest corner of his life by all that he had lost, she said, "You should go up front."

He smiled uncomprehendingly, and she had been afraid, at first, that he would treat it as a joke.

"Give me the glass," she said.

"It's where I keep my memory."

But he set it down in her open hand.

She seated herself in the front row. She had a bad moment as he climbed the three steps into the pulpit; he looked so dull and spiritless. She said, "Is there something you'd like to say? Something you'd like to read or recite to someone."

"Who?"

"Anyone."

"I don't think I believe in God."

"It doesn't have to be God."

So he stood for a moment. The last time he had been in church was almost ten years before—the small but crowded university chapel. He had recited a poem by George Herbert, one of his father's favorites, because he had wanted to participate but had no words of his own. Now he cleared his throat.

> *I cannot ope mine eyes,*
> *But thou art ready there to catch*
> *My morning-soul and sacrifice:*
> *Then we must needs for that day make a match.*

He stopped and gazed out in faint surprise at the clear, subsiding echo. Miss Pru sat very still.

"See?" she said. "God believes in you."

63.

It became part of their routine. When they had finished the cleaning he would climb into the pulpit and read from his father's copy of George Herbert—two or three poems from *The Temple* all but memorized years ago. And Miss Pru would sit in the front pew and listen and fit herself into the sound of it. With the years she had lost the precise timbre of Father Ben's voice, but she'd held onto the feeling. And with the unfamiliar words hanging on the air—a different young voice but the same ache of longing and loss—she would listen with an air of prim patience that was the only form of heartache she could allow herself after all these years.

Then one Saturday evening, over dinner, she asked if he would mind reading something else. Hesitantly she laid it before him, softly leather-bound: *The Book of Common Prayer*. The volume felt oddly heavy and supple—the thin pages seemed to turn themselves, so accustomed to the motion. He wouldn't need to read much. They had long ago moved to the shorter service. Father Ben had grown so accustomed to it in his later years that anything longer seemed to startle him a little. And, of course, Ash could wear whatever he liked. Though she wondered—he and Father Ben were almost of a size.

By that time he had been a handyman long enough to realize all the different forms repair could take. He protested that he didn't believe; it would be disrespectful. But she told him there was more to faith than belief. Miss Pru, herself, was unmoved by God. But she had faith in companionship, in the comfort of remembered words. It didn't have to be more than that. Father Ben had believed in many things in addition to the word of God.

The next morning she woke him at seven o'clock with a knock

on the door and a breakfast tray in her hands. It was an old man's breakfast. Dry toast with a little butter on the side, half a grapefruit carefully sectioned. A single hard-boiled egg lying peeled and clammy on a folded napkin.

"I've laid out the clothes," she said. "The service is at ten. You'll want to be in the sacristy by nine-fifty."

She slipped the prayerbook onto a corner of the tray. "Page thirty-nine this morning. Read slowly. Remember, you're a comfort."

He read the service over and over with breakfast, and then again after, trying to set the words firmly in his mind. He dressed. The clothes were neatly pressed, the white shirt freshly laundered, the black vest and suit coat smelling faintly of Old Spice.

Miss Pru wore a festive frock with a small floral print and a matching bag. She surveyed him with a critical eye. "I think perhaps just a touch of this." A tube of Brylcreem, crumpled but surprisingly untroubled by the passage of time. "Just a dab on Sundays, Father Ben used to say."

Ash took a dab. "A little bit more," she said. "Your hair looks in need of restraint." He accepted the comb she held out and drew all the wild hair straight back.

"That's a little severe, I think, dear. Perhaps a nice part. On your strong side."

That left him to wonder for a moment until she touched his right temple as if removing a fleck of dust.

She sat in the first pew, upright and poised as if to offer help at a moment's notice.

The quiet of the church, the cautious expectations of the prim, kind woman in her Sunday best. Just for a moment it was more than he could do. The silence seemed overcrowded with memories. Too full of ghosts even to begin. But he told himself it was just reading aloud. That was all. His mother's study again. A small enough thing to offer in the face of so many dashed hopes.

But as he stepped behind the altar, the door of the church opened, and Mrs. Bleeker entered, dressed for spring. And then Mrs. Blackburn. And Mrs. Pilgrim. And Mrs. Crabtree. With damp palms he reached for the prayer book, then noticed the larger, more official volume on a low brass lectern. There was a small red arrow at the point he was to begin.

He started shakily enough until the moment of the first response, set in italics as if, down through the ages, clergymen had needed a reminder to leave room for their congregation. The scattered voices joined in without a pause. He read and then they read. He spoke and they responded.

When he completed the service with *the peace that passes all understanding,* he bowed—because there needed to be a bow somewhere and he needed a moment to clear the tears from his eyes Then he walked back into the sacristy and sank down onto the hard wooden chair. He might have hidden there for the rest of the day if Miss Pru hadn't come to fetch him.

"Come along now," she said. "Everyone is dying to meet you."

And it didn't matter that he had, just the week before, mended their steps or their porch swing or the lintel over their door. He was handed a cup of coffee and offered one of a plate of brightly frosted cookies, and he listened to a series of conversations about the state of the gardens, the rectory, the town, the quilting club, the weather, as if all these gathered women were determined not to concede a single jot of the moment's unexpectedness.

64

And so began for Ash the long high-wire chapter of his life, when each step grew increasingly solid and a whole new vista of satisfactions opened around him as long as he didn't consider too carefully. His life was an obvious fiction, the falseness of it apparent to everyone. But somehow it all continued, step by step, day by day, as long as he didn't look down.

He worked during the week, conducting an unending series of interventions in the slow dissolution of the town—propping up outbuildings, resurrecting fences, repairing windows and gates and mailboxes. And when one of his customers brought him a mug of coffee or a piece of zucchini bread out in the back corner of her garden where the porcupines had nibbled away at the base of her fence, he accepted it in the spirit in which it was given: a determinedly unconsidered embrace of the world as it seemed.

And on Saturdays he would put on Father Ben's clerical black, and with Miss Pru as a kind of prim translator, he would visit the townsfolk again in a different guise. The ill, the lonely and unhappy. They would greet him as if they hadn't seen him for a week. And they would talk in low earnest tones; he would hold their hands as they wept. And together they joined in a kind of willed obliviousness, facing down again and again the small nagging pressures of common sense.

He was terrified at first. He had no idea what to say to people, no wisdom to offer. Though soon it became clear that none was needed. A chance to talk about a husband who had passed away. Or a dear pet lost. Or a moment of great emotion from thirty years before that, faded though it was, had grown vivid again in recent years. It wasn't wisdom but comfort that was needed—consolation in the face of the worst that life could do. And after a while he ceased to worry that it was all a lie. The kindness of it flowed from day to day: the satisfactions of his work, the comfort of his weekly visits, the growing sense of being somehow woven into the whole complex web of things.

His childhood was no help to him at first. His mother's years of work on John Donne's poetry were less than useless. She and Donne were too alike. Too inextricably bound to themselves. All that love and pride and despair, the whole self-defeating puzzle of the heart, dressed up in such faultless erudition. It gave him nothing to hold onto. But like a castaway who had managed to save only a single book, he turned to his father's battered volume of The Temple.

Where Donne had pushed and wrangled his ambition all the way to the Deanship of St. Paul's Cathedral, George Herbert seemed to recede into his own private devotions. He had begun as a child of privilege, a bright and diligent student, a scholar at Cambridge. He was perfectly aligned for a life of accomplishment. But even in his twenties his health was failing. And as if to re-inscribe this sign on the larger shape of the world, his patrons, one by one, died or fell from favor. His life collapsed around him. He became, at thirty-seven, the parson of a tiny church in rural England; he died at thirty-nine. And somehow in the process he turned a life of illness and disappointment into art. Into love.

Ash pored over the poems because they were his father's, and eventually they became his own.

> *Lord, how can man preach thy eternal word?*
> *He is a brittle crazy glass;*
> *Yet in thy temple thou dost him afford*
> *This glorious and transcendent place,*
> *To be a window, through thy grace.*

Faith is different from belief.

Ash never quite believed in God, but he had faith in George

Herbert. Faith in the power of disappointment and grief. Faith in Herbert's abiding sweetness and love, if not quite in his own. Always and forever we build our lives on the remnants of our lives. Amen.

And every Sunday he would take his place at the altar. And under the eyes of his scattered congregation he would fit himself into the graceful shape of the liturgy—the firm, indomitable expectation of it all: one part leading to the next to the next. Under their joint attention the service was transformed into a single flowing moment, carrying its listeners along on the whole winding journey of possibility, loss, and comfort.

Sitting in the old familiar church—as they had for forty, fifty years—they would find themselves again among their memories of youth, standing, sitting, kneeling back in the full flood of their lives. So that when the current of prayers returned them once again to the familiar and expected end—*Let the peace of the lord that passes all understanding keep your hearts and minds in the knowledge and love of God*—they rose as if from a dream of childhood, lighter and refreshed.

And they would greet him in the narthex with a kind of grace: tight-lipped or smiling, hunched or standing straight. And then coffee and sandwiches, cookies from someone's kitchen, and the murmur of old familiar conversations, strengthened now by the pleasure of remembered times.

And then one evening after dinner Miss Pru fell into a little moment of silence. "There's something I wanted to talk to you about."

It was about the church. The diocese had remembered them at last. Word had gotten back to them about the new pastor, and they were going to send a Diocesan Inspector to get to the bottom of whatever it was.

Ash just stared.

"They're going to close the church if we don't have a proper pastor," she said.

"I'm not a proper pastor."

"You just need to convince one man."

But he had barely convinced himself.

"It would mean a great deal to us," said Miss Pru.

So of course he had agreed. The man wasn't coming until November, and a lot could happen in the meantime.

65

It wasn't that his life began to mend. He simply grew accustomed to being someone else. So when the battered red Saab trundled into town again and Reeve unfolded herself—so slender and surprising in a pale silk shirt and slacks—she could not have looked more out of place. But under the spell of this new life Ash wondered if even this might be true.

It was a hot day, and he was rebuilding part of the low stone wall around the spring. He straightened up, smeared with dirt and sweat, and walking up to her without a word of greeting, kissed her, feeling the thin startled lips blossom under his own. Would she like some lunch? he asked. Or a cup of coffee? She wasn't hungry, she said. So he suggested they go for a ride. He drove her down a narrow country lane—with nothing but fields and trees in view. She seemed determinedly unconcerned, glancing around at the passing scene, until they stopped by the side of the road. And in a wordless turmoil they spilled from the front seat to the doorway to the soft cushioned grass, freeing themselves from their clothing in a hurried, feverish struggle that left them sprawled and panting beneath the indifferent sky.

"So," she said breathlessly. "Are you glad I'm here?"

He drove them back to the Rectory and with an air of formality introduced her to Miss Pru. He was determinedly unconcerned about her response—he was an adult after all—but she welcomed Reeve with the same brusque politeness with which she had first welcomed Ash.

They felt themselves oddly buoyed by her formality, bound together in the face of such a cool and elderly demeanor. Miss Pru showed her primly to the guest room at the back of the Rectory, and Reeve followed demurely, carrying her bag down the long hallway and setting it on the bed. But really it was just a gesture. When Miss Pru went home at night they had the whole wide house to themselves.

"Put me down," she panted. "On the bed."

In her slacks and blouse she was nothing but angles: elbows, knees, and jutting hips. But out of her clothes she turned elongate and smooth. When he reached down to cup her ass and lift her she was all muscle and bone, squirming against him for a tighter fit. He would clutch her, rocking on his feet until he found his way in, and then all that spareness gave way to a lush demanding warmth.

Now he turned, straining, trying to ease her down, but her hips were slick with sweat and at the last moment she slipped away, bouncing on the wobbly springs.

"Wait," she whispered and, shifting backwards, reached up to grip the brass bars of the headboard. "Okay."

The mattress was narrow, a former maid's bed, in a room so prim and unassuming they couldn't pass it up. With her skin glowing amber in the light of half a dozen candles, she stretched out like an image of grace. Her parted legs enclosed him. Her ribs were startling beneath the pale skin, her breasts the shyest thing about her—shallow and rose-tipped, they seemed to hold themselves aloof from all that the lips and hands and hips were doing. Even the terrible squeak of the bed, rising like a rusty plea in the silence, became just another source of wild encouragement.

Word spread immediately that the girl had taken up residence. And one by one all the elderly women in their tidy homes contrived to run into Miss Pru or invited her to tea or simply knocked on the door, impatient with the roundabout maneuvers of their younger selves. They couldn't keep from disapproving. But remembering all the things in their lives that they hadn't dared do, their disapproval took on a pensive air.

Ash was concerned. But Reeve smiled at the interest of the town. When they walked to Halladay's or went strolling down the main street she moved with a languid air like a fish in an ocean of wistful attention. And when they wandered out into the wide evening behind Mr. Skylar's corn crib while the owner, on his tractor, roamed his fields in the distance, Reeve would draw his attention to the nearness of the houses or the distant voices coming to them on the breeze as they hurried out of their clothes. And at the center of that oblivious world they spun a narrow cocoon of scented warmth and urgency.

Guerilla fucking, she called it. Slipping out at night to grapple frantically beside the little spring in the front garden, or in the alley behind the grocery store, or down at the crossroads in the shelter of a long abandoned cabin as the occasional late-night grain truck thundered past. Anything was possible. She seemed intent on finding something he would balk at, but in this new life, with so much already behind him, there was nothing he wouldn't do. And if in later years he would sometimes stand stock still at the distant wonder of it all, in the moment their fierceness lent a kind of ongoing conviction, as if they were striving to prove something solid and permanent about themselves.

Even the house seemed a willing accomplice. In the parlor he bent her over the elderly armchair that Miss Pru favored for its air of distinction. Perched on tiptoe, draping herself forward, her pale ass and legs in bright counterpoint to the dull brocade, she pressed her cheek to the cushion, arms limply extended as if already exhausted by all that was about to happen.

Once in the night, she drew him tight against her, her whisper warm in his ear. "You like me, don't you, Ash?"

"I do. I do."

"Tell me you like me."

"I like you."

"Let me get on top."

And changing places as if in a crowded booth, they shifted, squirmed around, and she settled herself firmly. He peered up at her—breasts suddenly much less shy, eyes tightly closed, face set in a look of distant concentration—all their tense eagerness reduced to the small rocking precision of her hips. They balanced together on that drawn-out moment. Then she was gasping, gritting her teeth, catching the pleasure in her throat as if determined not to let it escape—though in the end she offered up a low breath of laughter, chagrined at having revealed too much.

Afterwards they would bathe together in the rectory's gleaming bathroom, dazed with pleasure and steam. And if there came to him in those moments, abrupt and unbidden, the memory of an old claw-footed tub, curtained and bleak—or if, sitting out in a neighbor's yard with a disassembled doorframe in his hands, a cool breeze brushed his skin and carried him back without warning to the just-opened window in that too-warm attic room—well, nothing in life is unlayered.

66.

She had brought her laptop, and that was apparently all she needed to continue to promote and organize Bernard's video games. They were going to form a company. She was thinking of law school. She set herself up in the kitchen, and while Miss Pru went about her chores Reeve typed away beneath the overhanging shelter of a baseball cap, constructing complex charts and business models.

Ash assumed that Miss Pru disapproved. She carried a distracted frown with her throughout the day. But when it came time for the morning break, she set out the over-strong tea and fresh-baked cookies without a word at Reeve's side, and then went out looking for him. It was only afterwards he realized that, in Reeve, she was gathering together all the remaining hopes she held for his happiness.

And really, it should have been perfect. How could it not be? Every desire in his life coming true except one. And surely love comes in different forms. After all that had happened, didn't he deserve someone who loved him? An adventure of his own? Not everything needs to be a tragedy. You can't be disappointed with someone just because she doesn't quite fill your thoughts. But it came to him in moments alone, when the past crowded out the present, that few things are as heart-breaking as something almost right.

"It always takes me a moment to remember who I am," she murmured confidingly one night as she nestled in his arms. And he had agreed, though in truth he was always himself.

The enticement of her skin, the shifting impatience of her movements, her eager hands on his hips urging him into motion. He tried to lose himself in her. But he would suddenly be reduced to an onlooker, frowning down at the slow insistent movement of their flesh. He was a safe-cracker feeling his way to the proper combination, a bomb maker offering ongoing adjustments all the way to the moment of combustion. He would turn her, arrange her in the moonlight with a new leisure and deliberation—against a fence post, on a hillside, in the shadow of an overarching barn—and gazing down at the narrow pathway of her spine, the splayed curve of her, rounded and pale as the moon, he would catch himself observing as if from another time. Having come once she was never close to coming again, but he would listen to her breathing in time to his own, and when he came with a groan she would smile and stretch like a cat who has earned a nap.

She would do anything he asked. And in the bright familiar daylight he thought back to the night with a sense of wonder bordering on disbelief. But he was unable to hold onto the shape of their passion. As he moved through his day, from Mrs. Baker's sagging deck to Mrs. Carmody's well to the long reclamation of the Bertrams' fence line, he was aware of the rawness of overworked flesh or a lingering ache, like a bruise, on the until-then-unnoticed ridge of his pubic bone. But try as he might he could not fit all that wild sensation into the shape of his heart.

It was only later, in the quiet of Father Ben's study as he prepared for the Sunday service, leafing through old sermons and allowing his mind to wander into the past, that the nights would come to him in a form he could keep. The low light of the study leant itself to reverie, and the vivid excitement—always a little distant and self-conscious—was transmuted into something softer and more evocative, as if all they did at night—so frantic and fantastic—only grew real in memory.

67

Reeve was half-amused, half-intrigued when she learned he was writing a book. Trying to capture all that was most crucial in his life, he said. Trying to get at the ache that came to him in the quiet moments, though he didn't tell her that. He showed her the early pages, and she cast him a sideways glance. "So that's what you were thinking," and handed them back, not ungratified.

He tried to capture what was most vivid, drawing on the fierceness, the heady frantic excitement. He worked to fix it on the page, to turn it into his life. He wanted nothing more than for this to mean everything. But even as he sought to pin it down, the heart of it kept slipping away. And though it was, by far, the most impassioned thing he had ever added to the steady stream of his days, he couldn't seem to make it real.

Then the title came to him—from the confining narrowness of the beds in the rectory, the inventive and varied effort of the night time sorties, and from the memory, growing softer and more luxurious in his mind, of the wide mattress in that high attic room. And if from time to time the events of the summer came back to him with too much clarity, that only freed him from the constraints of fact. And he learned what so many others have learned to their comfort and distress: if memory becomes less accurate with time, it also becomes more true.

He would write in a notebook at the desk in the study on Sunday afternoons, the time when Father Ben used to compose his sermons. He would dress in his clerical suit and collar, as an anchor against the pull of the past, and he would try to turn his passion and heartbreak into strength. Miss Pru was pleased. She saw it as a choice he was making, choosing her and Father Ben over the new distraction. For she had been watching with some anxiety the variety of goings-on—none really hidden or unnoticed—and it seemed a good sign, a favorable bending of events, that he was settling even further into his role.

So, every Sunday he conjured up the mattress at the center of a wide, white space, windows open to the breeze of the summer afternoon. And in those sheltered hours he gathered all the unraveled threads of his heart and wove them together in the bright, flat light of the Canadian prairie until they became brand new.

And Reeve? What could she think but that all her efforts to make him hers alone were paying off? She let him write, provided he would read selected passages at night, his voice murmuring in her ear as they lay damp and tangled in the candlelight. So that, too, became part of the remembering for Ash—binding the strands of imagination and memory beyond recovery.

Father Ben had always written his sermons on a small, green Olivetti, and Ash took to bringing it out and typing up his pages. He was startled by how long the story grew. The flow of handwriting had the shape of an ongoing dream, but the mounting pages seemed so stern and fixed that he knew they would someday have to come to an end.

And then one Saturday afternoon, while he and Miss Pru were out visiting Mrs. Blackburn, who had sprained her ankle and was bedridden, Reeve began to read from the beginning. And perhaps it was the typeface, so much cooler and more distant than the warm sound of his voice; perhaps it was that she had never heard the story at any length. Or perhaps she had just not been listening carefully enough.

She confronted him that night, furious and hurt. "You've been fucking someone else," she said, "all this time."

"No! Of course not." But he didn't seem surprised.

"God damn it! God damn it!" she cried. "She doesn't love you. You know that! She doesn't care about you! Why can't you love me?"

And he wanted to, more than anything.

She tried to coax him one more time, to prove this story was theirs. "Fuck me," she whispered. "Show me you mean it."

But that had never been the problem. And even as they moved so furiously together, trying to lock the moment into place, part of her wondered if he was already making of this night, too, some completely different story.

She left the next morning, taking the manuscript with her. She told him she was going to burn it. But instead she read it again and again, until the story had nothing to do with her. Until she found herself wondering, with a kind of bitter, vengeful, satisfaction, what it really had to do with him. Though when she showed the pages to Bernard, he thought they might make a good video game, or at the very least, a book.

68.

This is the other thing about beginnings. The first is hard; the second even harder. But after that they get easier and easier.

When Reeve left, Ash waited to see what would collapse, but really his whole life just became more the same. He moved in his work from yard to yard, and every new prospect showed him the same sight: a town he was, in his own small way, bringing back from the edge of collapse. And each day at noon Miss Pru brought his sandwich and mug of tea, and they would sit together, talking about the task at hand, or the dinner that night, or the last sermon or the next.

It used to be that Miss Pru was careful to keep the two parts of his life separate. To talk about church things only with the parson on Saturday and Sunday, and to talk about the tractable problems of replacement and repair with the handyman during the week. His whole identity had divided on his arrival, and Miss Pru had been careful to keep it separate. But now the church inspector was coming, and they had to prepare.

His heart was broken, but not the way he expected. At night he felt queasy with the loss; he missed Reeve beyond measure. But the ache went deeper still. He was grateful to her. Because after she left there was no question whose fault it was, or what it proved. She had given him a second chance, and he had wasted it. Every version of his life had ended badly, and he could no longer hide from the blame. More than that. He could no longer look back on the summer and think that some central part of it had been out of his hands. It wasn't that he had missed his chance at love, or that with just a little more luck he could salvage some remaining portion. The fact was he had ruined every part. It was no longer his life now. It had simply become a story. But now, at least, he had the ending.

He mailed it to Reeve with a long apology. Even a witch needed a sense of closure, and he thought she might be pleased with how unhappily it ended. But she didn't respond. It was Bernard who wrote back to say there'd been some interest from the father of a friend of his, who specialized in late-Victorian erotica and who thought Ash had a fresh new voice.

And what else could he do? Because that was the other thing about a story: it wasn't anything if it didn't have to be told.

69.

In November the Deacon Inspector arrived from Toronto and put everything Ash had done to the test. He was a sharp-eyed, grey-haired man, upright and slender in a pale grey suit with a grey shirt and white clerical collar. Ash thought he looked shy at first—as shy as anyone could in such an elegant suit—but he was merely patient. Miss Pru greeted him with deference. She put him in the Bishop's Room, and for a week he stayed like the most urbane of house-guests—ready to be pleased by everything and waiting patiently for Sunday's service.

Franklin's clothes went into the closet, and Father Ash moved full-time into the master bedroom. His day rearranged itself. Every meal featured a meandering conversation about church doctrine, ecclesiastical history, the structure of a good sermon, the pastoral role of a parson in a small country town, the proper understanding of the Eucharist in an age of science and technology, and the competing roles of faith and kindness in a fallen world.

Ash had been preparing for weeks. He read and re-read *The Book of Common Prayer* and Herbert's *Country Parson*, that handbook the poet had composed in the last years of his life. He spent hours poring ever more intently over Father's Ben's file of sermons, practicing the pacing and flow of the service like a young boy with a piano recital. And like that young boy, when he sat down to lunch on Father Timothy's first day, his palms were slick with sweat.

He thought how foolish he had been to believe he could get away with this. How ridiculous even to pretend. Within ten minutes he would have given anything for a drink. And it was its own sort of miracle that Miss Pru, having cast an appraising eye over the elegant table, had stepped into the pantry and returned with a bottle of Saint-Émilion, a glance at whose label left the deacon wreathed in smiles.

Perhaps it was the forgiving warmth of the wine, perhaps the elegant room, but as they drank and talked Ash found himself carried back to his mother's study, to those earliest years of worry and striving, so that, like the deacon, he too was calling upon a lifetime of preparation. Where Father Timothy quoted Saint Paul, Ash quoted Donne and Herbert. And it was clear even to the Deacon that he was speaking out of a long tradition within which he had found, through considerable effort and suffering, his own place. He was speaking as a man who had looked into the souls of strangers, who had, in fact, created himself around the empty heart of another, not once or twice but over and over. A man whose tone and sadness and pleasure in a text must have looked from the outside like its own kind of faith.

The week fell into its familiar rhythm. Father Timothy rose early and strolled around the town. For a man with such an expensive suit, he was very easy to talk to, and Ash watched uneasily as people gathered in little knots and eddies to share the momentary pleasure of his company. Then lunch was long and leisurely, drawn out over a bottle of Bordeaux. And then a nap and tea. And then they walked together around the narrow streets—two elegantly dressed men in a world of denim and plaid—talking, always talking. And then the decanter of whiskey in the comfort of Father Ben's study, and dinner in the dining room, and the last of the wine out in the garden under the splendid canopy of maples. And it was under the maples, beneath the wide roof of heaven, that Father Timothy moved from doctrine to faith, and from faith to love.

"Do you remember First Timothy, Chapter Three. The role of a priest?" he asked. "Timothy tells us the sort of man we must expect to be if we're going to embrace the church. *Not a novice, lest being lifted up with pride he fall into the condemnation of the devil.*

Moreover he must have a good report of them which are without; lest he fall into reproach and the snare of the devil."

"I'm not lifted up with pride," said Ash. "Anything but."

"And do you have a good report?" He wasn't smiling. But there was something gentle in his voice.

And Ash thought of those little groups of townspeople gathered in the wake of a morning's stroll. "I hope so. I hope I do."

The deacon cradled the last of the wine in his hands. Beneath the maples the grey suit was dappled by moonlight. "What drew you to the priesthood, Father Ash?"

And was there a faint glint of irony running through his voice? The set-up of some elaborate shaming trick? It was the kind of catechism he had been accustomed to as a boy, though never about himself. His mother would ask a whole series of pointed questions about the speaker in a poem or an angel in Paradise or the unfallen figures of Adam and Eve. And though it was haunting to realize she knew more about the speaker of Donne's Holy Sonnets than she would ever know about him, he was grateful now to have lived a childhood so completely out of his depth.

Ash set down his own wine glass and recited,

> *"Immortal Love, author of this great frame,*
> *Sprung from that beauty which can never fade,*
> *How hath man parcel'd out Thy glorious name,*
> *And thrown it on that dust which Thou hast made,*
> *While mortal love doth all the title gain!"*

Father Timothy looked thoughtful and raised his glass to his lips. Then, after a moment, "I've heard about your *mortal love.* And your broken hearts."

"Just the one heart," said Ash.

"That's not what I heard. I heard she drove away crying."

"Oh. Yes. Two hearts."

"You won't be the first man to flee from love into the arms of the church," said the deacon.

And Ash looked up in surprise. "I'm not sure it was exactly that." But his voice faded off as he considered.

Father Timothy crossed his legs and smoothed the line of the pale grey pants. "Father Ben was a very dear friend of mine. We were at seminary together. We have loved each other all these years. If never quite as I might have wished."

The breeze sighed through the branches overhead. The whole great dome of the sky seemed to hold them at its center. "I'm sorry," said Ash.

"We are made in the image of our Creator," Timothy said. "But God is everything. So how can we be surprised that there are so many different images of Him. We can spend our whole lives wanting something without getting it. But we must be careful not to do *only* that. Sometimes we want it so much we can feel it drawing us, bending our whole soul toward it. And we take that ache as a kind of strength. We live for love. Even hopeless love. But we must be careful not to live *only* for that. We strive to live in our hearts; but even then we must live in the world. As it is, not as we wish it."

Ash made no reply.

"And do you remember the rest of Timothy?" the deacon asked. "*Likewise must the deacons be grave, not double-tongued, not given to much wine, not greedy of filthy lucre. Let them be the husbands of one wife, ruling their children and their own houses well.*"

He smiled sadly down at the wineglass in his hand, and after a moment took a sip. "It's a hard task not to be double-tongued. Not to seek comfort where you can. I never married, though Father Ben did. I tried not to be glad that he wasn't happy. And then I strove to be happy when he was. Love can be a source of strength, Father Ash. A force for striving and betterment. It can. We must make a life for ourselves, even if it's not all that we might choose."

"I'm not sure I can do that," said Ash.

"Perhaps you already have."

After a moment Timothy lifted his face as if to weigh his

thoughts in the cool night air. "We are none of us blameless. But still. *For God so loved the world, He gave His only begotten Son, that whosoever believeth in Him should not perish, but have everlasting life.* Where is there a man whose love can match that? But we must take from it what we can. Love, whatever kind of love, is key."

Ash prepared for Sunday's service in full regalia: the white alb, with it's rope cincture, the narrow green stole, and hanging from his shoulders the heavy chasuble stiff with embroidery. It leant him weight, anchored him to his role, until he walked into the sacristy and found Father Timothy, not sitting in the congregation but splendid in his deacon's Dalmatic, ready to help lead the service.

Ash's courage turned to water under the deacon's clear gaze. He stumbled as he stepped behind the altar, his foot catching in his robes. But Timothy latched onto his arm to steady him. And standing together, looking out over the sparse congregation—a dozen familiar faces in their Sunday best—he laid a guiding finger on the beginning of the text. "Why don't you begin, Father Ash," he said, "and I'll fit myself in."

His cheeks were burning, his throat dry. But he began to read. And the first prayer led to the next and the next. And occasionally Father Timothy would lay a restraining hand on his arm, and he would step forward to take his part, gently directing their way through the choreography of the service. And it went so smoothly that Ash began to think he had pulled it off. Even the sermon, selected from Father Ben's file cabinet by Miss Pru, went off without a hitch. The deacon listened with what looked like admiration but was, Ash realized afterward, merely a lifetime's mixture of memory and love.

Divesting themselves after the service Ash waited for some comment on his performance. But the deacon said nothing except that he remembered that sermon—it was one of his favorites—and didn't the church get a little chilly in the autumn?

In the morning after breakfast Father Timothy departed. Miss Pru said goodbye in the kitchen, and Ash walked him out to his car. The deacon had withdrawn behind the elegance of a black suit, and Ash wondered what the color might mean. He wanted to tell the man everything. To explain to him that it had not felt like an impersonation. That over these months he had grown to fill his role. That under the older man's gaze he had felt like a real part of the spell they were weaving together. But he was afraid that might not be enough.

The deacon stood for a moment, looking around at the town. "*The eyes of the Lord are in every place, beholding the evil and the good.*" And he gave Ash a clear look. "You're not to give the Eucharist. The service is fine, but you're not to turn the sacrament into a joke."

"It's not a joke," said Ash.

Father Timothy nodded. "*So shall my word be, that goes out from my mouth; it shall not return to me empty.* We all do things for many reasons, even in the church. I am doing this for Prudence. And for Ben. I want you to look after her. I want you to be your best self. *When that which is perfect is come, then that which is in part shall be done away. When I was a child, I spake as a child, I understood as a child, I thought as a child: but when I became a man, I put away childish things.*" He gave him a long, last, clear look. "You take care, Father Ash," and he drove away.

Turning back to the Rectory, he saw Miss Pru standing in the doorway. He had not, until that moment, seen how frail she was, how thin and grey against the wide stone porch.

He continued on year after year, beginning again and then again. When the book came out he drove down one last time to try to win Bea back with his token of love, but that didn't turn out as he hoped. So he returned to Miss Pru, and to her niece, who had come home from a bad break-up in Vancouver hoping that small-town life would help nurse her bruised heart. He and Sara had that much in common. And of course they had Miss Pru. And then little Bea. And really, they did pretty well, all things considered.

But finally, after all the different kinds of heartbreak, Bea died, and then Miss Pru. And there came the end. The church closed, and Sara left, and the Rectory burned, and finally he left, too. As if, in the end, it hadn't been his life at all. It was all just part of Miss Pru's dream, and when she died it ended.

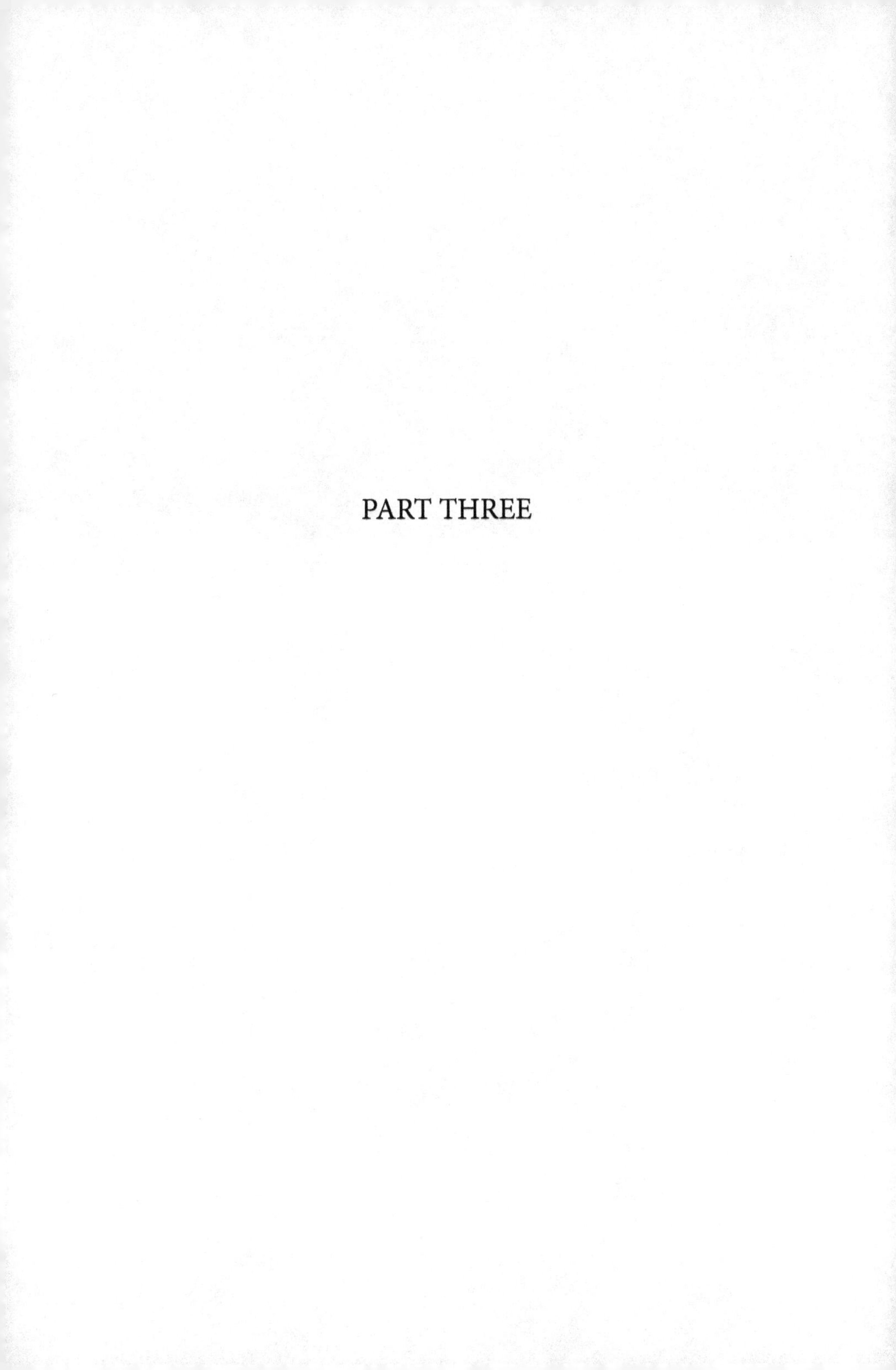

PART THREE

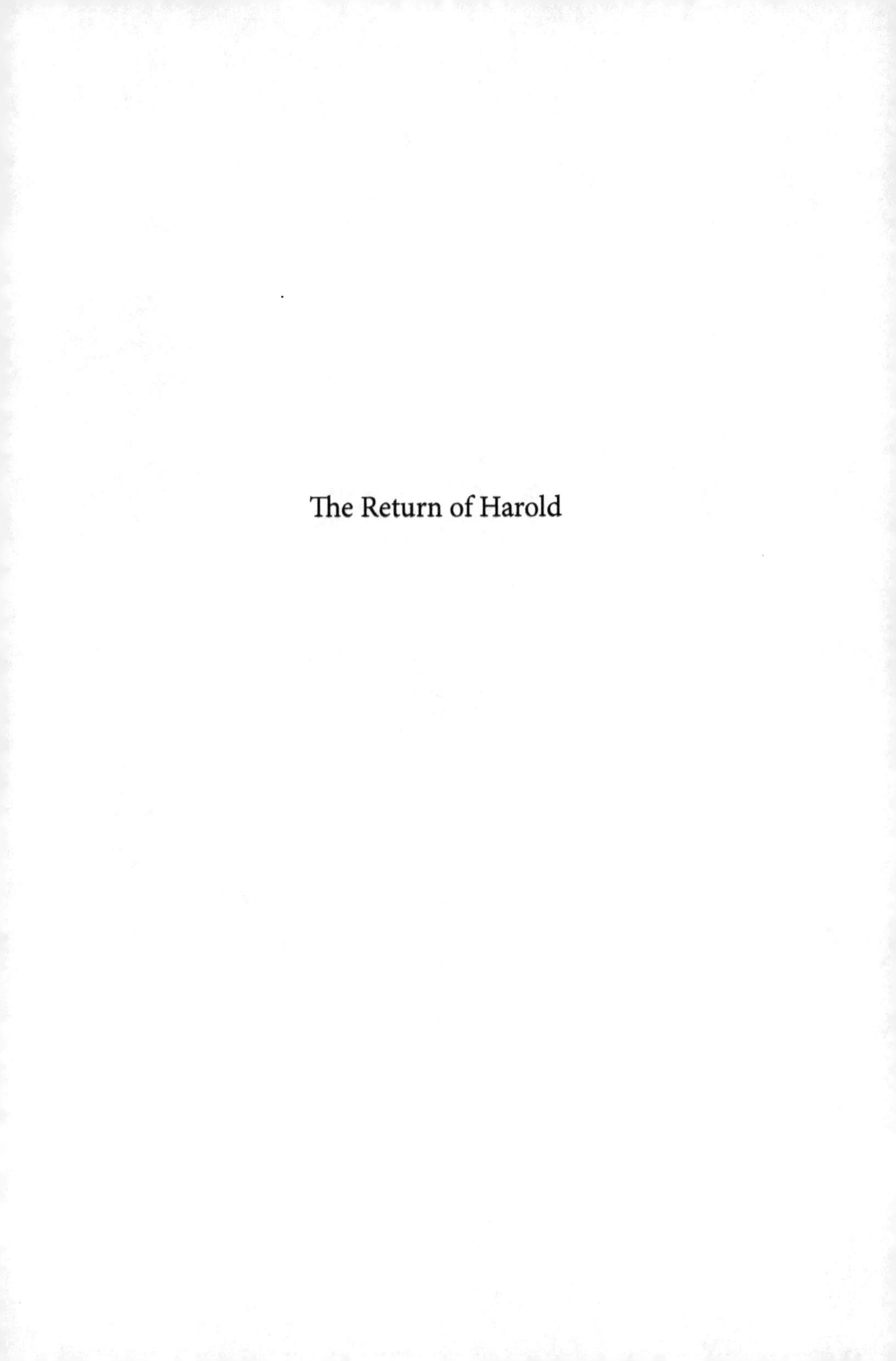# The Return of Harold

70.

Walking home from the bakery at the end of a long night, strung out on coffee and an endless vista of rising dough, Bea felt a kind of dread. As if after the reprieve of the night her whole life was tightening around her again—every bad decision waiting there in that most familiar of places. Today she carried a sack of over-baked rolls and a sourdough loaf that had rested against the side of the oven. Joan didn't eat bread, of course. And Izzie made it a point to cook her own meals. But Bea couldn't bear to throw them away, so she ate her mistakes, the dark charred flavor adding itself to the last moments of her day.

But this morning, turning into the driveway, she saw the blurred figure by the back door and slowed. She switched glasses, switched again. It seemed to say something about her life that here was yet another stranger looking vaguely familiar. Then he turned and she saw it was Harold. Though dressed now as someone else altogether—work pants and a pale blue shirt cinched at the waist. He looked oddly attentive as she approached—an indistinct blend of posture and purpose—and she realized she had never seen him sober before.

"What are you doing here?" she asked.

"I thought I'd get to work. The mudroom? Tell me you remember. Because you mentioned meals, and it is breakfast time."

"I did say they weren't good meals, didn't I?" But she was already unlocking the door with an unexpected lightness of heart. "Those are your handyman's clothes?"

"Mine as much as anyone's. I inherited them. I think they're good luck."

"You think?"

"Well, I seem to have survived all my worst mistakes."

She turned on the kitchen lights and looked around at the empty room—cold and still, like an engine you knew wasn't going to start.

"Should we be quiet?" he asked.

"No need. We're the only ones here. My wife is on the road."

"You mentioned that. And Izzie?"

"She stops by after work, but I'm never sure when that will be. I used to make her breakfast, but now she makes her own. And we just ignore each other like two ships passing on the ocean."

"That sounds a little lonely."

"Doesn't it?"

She turned wearily to the stove. "So what would you like for breakfast?"

But even the thought exhausted her. She sank into a chair. He had set something down on the table, a shallow plastic cage like a little desert island. And she must have been tired indeed to be so untroubled by the sight of the spider gazing companionably out from under a palm tree.

"Why don't I put something together," he suggested.

"That wasn't the deal."

But he turned unresentfully to the fridge, browsing through the shelves. And some part of her marveled at how easily even such a complete stranger could accept how disappointing she had become.

"So, what would you like?" he asked.

She hesitated. "I usually start with a glass of wine."

No murmur of disapproval. It felt like a gift to end her day with someone who had absolutely no claim on her. Who, at eight-thirty in the morning, without comment or reproach, could take down a bottle of Zinfandel and set a glass before her.

She almost asked, "Does this seem awful?" but shut her jaw against it. "Help yourself if you'd like one."

"I might make some coffee. First day on the job. I want to

make a good impression." And as he loaded the coffee machine and set it brewing, he asked, "How was your night?"

"Long," she said. "Simple. It's only when I return to my life that things get complicated."

She had meant it as a joke, but he seemed to be giving it more thought than it deserved. *Great, she thought. Pity. He's known me less than a week.* But it was like a little blossom of relief that here was one person, at least, who didn't despise her for all that she had done.

Her glass stood empty, but Harold was there like a kindly bartender. "More?"

"I usually drink alone. It's less embarrassing."

"Nobody here but us."

She looked up at him, not even a priest anymore in his bunched and faded work clothes. "Did you used to hear confession in your last job?"

"The Anglican church doesn't really have confession. That was actually something that worried me early on. I didn't know what to tell them." He poured himself a mug of coffee, and even that had a faintly clerical air, as if he were meditating upon her sins. "Turns out you don't really need to say much. You just have to listen. I'd stop at people's houses for coffee and baked goods, and they would tell me whatever was on their minds."

She offered up a bleak smile. "I forgot to mention. I've got some bread here. It's fresh but a little burned."

He spread his hands in benediction. "So tell me whatever is on your mind."

"How did you become a priest? Was it a calling? Did you feel the universe reaching out a guiding hand?" Her voice was wry but nothing else about her.

"I used to wonder," he said, "what it all might mean. I thought every moment was building toward something. That it was all coming together. But in the end it's hard not to see it as accidental.

One thing after another. Turning left instead of right. Showing up at one place instead of another. You'd like it to mean something bigger, but I don't know. It's hard to see."

She nodded. "I think I'd be happy if I could be sure it was all just a series of accidents. I think it would be a relief. But I've been thinking about Jonathan. And Izzie. And other people. Thinking about how many different ways I could ruin someone's life. I used to think I was moving forward; I had such faith in it. There was something I was meant to do, someone I was meant to be. And I thought I could put everything else on hold—just for a little while. *Wait right there. Just hold on till I finish this. Just don't move, and everything will be wonderful.* But it's like I could never quite get back to that moment. Things get started, one thing leads to another. Never quite what you expect. Never what you meant to do. And then, all of a sudden, it's too late. You look around and think, How in the world did I get here?"

Her glass was empty again. She looked up at Harold. "Izzie thinks I drink too much."

"What do you think?"

She smiled bleakly. "I think I'm a pretty pathetic character, Harold. Aren't you sorry you came?"

"Well," he said and refilled her glass. "At least there's breakfast."

"My wife has been having an affair," said Bea. "Though I don't think she sees it that way."

"How does she see it?"

She just shook her head. "She's been months setting up this gallery show. A lot of correspondence. A lot of details to work out. Sometimes I'd walk by her studio door and hear them talking on their computers. It was always about the art. That's the thing. Always about the paintings. The feel of the paint, the focus, the point of view. They'd be talking about how she achieved her effects. How did she get that particular perspective? How did she get that texture?"

Bea glanced up. "Have you seen my wife's art? She has half a dozen paintings of her own vagina, each the size of a billboard. This gallerist could not stop talking about them—which was her favorite and why? I peeked in once. I don't know what I expected. They were two thousand miles apart, each in front of their screen. Joan had just interrupted her work to take a call. She hadn't bothered to put on a robe. I used to think she was genuinely oblivious. But that was just me being ridiculous again. *How did you get that curve right there? Just there. Here? This one right along here?"*

"Sounds like art to me," said Harold.

She glanced up wryly. "You have no idea."

"Oh," he said. "Some idea maybe. Have you heard from her lately?"

"Not lately. The show's a big success. Did I tell you that? She thinks she'll need to stay a little longer, just to see where it leads. And here's the bad part. It doesn't even make me mad anymore. It just makes me tired. And who am I to complain? If you knew all the things I've done, Harold, you'd be on a bus out of town, too."

"Not everything is your fault."

She sighed. "You haven't met Jonathan. He is such a genuinely nice man. Kind. Generous. He was a wonderful father to Izzie. A wonderful husband. We made a great family. I owed him a lot. And I ruined it."

"So why did you split up?"

What could she say? No reason seemed sufficient. How to explain that she had left him because he was too gentle? Too kind? Too uncomplaining? On top of everything else. "I slept with Weland. Again. Years after I swore I never would. I started posing for him. And then one thing led to another. I guess that did the trick. And not just for Jonathan. For just about everything, I think."

She kept her eyes on her wineglass, it sounded so bad. She couldn't explain it to herself—how could she make him understand?

"Did he mind so much? Your husband?"

"He didn't seem to mind at all, as far as I could tell."

"You don't think maybe just a little? Loving you the way he did? You don't think he might have wondered how you could do such a thing?"

"Oh, I think so. I've been wondering that myself. But at the time it was all jumbled together—everything I was feeling. All the ideas about art and love. And fame. Let's not forget that. *Strength is the willingness to do what you know is best for you.*"

"I'll go out on a limb and say that's not Confucius."

She laughed wearily. "Jonathan used to say: you are who you listen to. I thought that was silly at the time. I thought he just didn't have a clue about what I was feeling. What I wanted from love, from art. From myself."

"From Weland?"

"Do you see how ridiculous I am? I thought I was breaking free of my constraints. Can you imagine? I remember one time, Weland was talking—I would go to him to talk about my marriage. Can you imagine? If you knew the whole story you'd realize how truly messed up that was. But I had no one else. I had driven everyone away. So I'd pour my heart out to Weland, and he would listen solemnly and offer guidance. *You have to follow your art,* he said. And just for a moment I misheard. I thought he said follow your heart. And I burst into tears."

"You don't believe in following your heart?" asked Harold gently.

"I think that was the moment I knew how completely that ship had sailed. How many chances I'd wasted. When you're young you think they'll come to you over and over. You just have to wait for the next chance to arrive. But they don't. I climbed into a car once with a perfect stranger and thought my whole life had begun."

"Maybe it had."

"Maybe. You think you're at the beginning of something so wonderful it can't help but turn out. But that's the thing about

Weland—he's a hijacker. Art and heart. They've always been my problem, mistaking one for the other. But just for a moment he could make them seem exactly the same."

After a moment he turned back to the fridge. "You're still out of eggs, but there's some hamburger here. Maybe some fried potatoes. Oh, look. I think this used to be an onion." He found a knife in a drawer and set to work. "It's like making a sculpture of an elephant. You start with a big block of stone, and then you cut away everything that doesn't look like breakfast."

A moment later the diced onion hit the olive oil, and an aroma of enormous comfort filled the kitchen. "Oh, my," she murmured.

"Exactly. There is nothing in this world," he said, "that cannot be improved by breakfast. Do you have paprika?"

"No idea."

"Thyme."

"You'd have to ask Izzie."

"How old are these olives?"

"What olives?"

"Nothing ventured, nothing gained."

Into the pan they went. He seemed to hover in a blur of easy activity. Where did he get his energy? He turned back to the cupboard, and after a moment's search held up a can of something red. "Did Izzie have plans for these tomatoes?"

"I'm going to say no."

"And suddenly: it's goulash."

As she sat there Harold leaned down and set her plate before her, and the perfume of onions and olives and simmering meat rose like a blessing. And Bea, who hadn't really cared about food for such a long time, lifted her nose to the aroma. She was suddenly close to tears. But that's the thing about the world: heartbreaking and foolish and ridiculous as it is, comfort comes in all its shapes. And abruptly without thinking she turned and kissed him, just like that. Pressed her lips against his motionless lips.

He didn't move.

She drew back, eyes wide, heart suddenly awake. Like one of those moments when, falling asleep in the middle of a task, she would wake to find her life ongoing.

"Ash?" she said. "Is that you? Have you come to save me again?"

71

Harold was alone in the mudroom when Izzie appeared, wheeling Henry along like a midway performer abandoned when the circus left town. She looked exhausted—her grey housekeeper's smock limp and dispirited, her eyes haunted. It took all he had not to wrap his arms around her.

"You're just in time," he said gently. "Your mother's gone up to bed. I made her breakfast. I thought you might not feel up to it this morning." And he saw her shoulders droop at the thought of one more thing slipping out of her control. "How's Henry?"

"She's good." And with a worried glance at the cat, lying mounded uneasily in sleep, "She's taking her potion. I think she's all better."

"And how about you? You look a little tired."

"I'm okay."

"Do you want some breakfast? Are you hungry? I could make you something. Mac and cheese? There are hot dogs in the fridge."

But she looked like someone who had lost faith in anything so ordinary. "Henry's not very hungry, and I don't want to eat without her. You left Bea all alone in the kitchen."

"I know. I'm sorry. I thought she'd be more comfortable there. And I wanted to talk to you. I wanted to tell you something."

Izzie looked up wearily, as if she'd already gotten all the bad news she could bear. "I don't feel like talking now."

"I know. I understand." And really, he thought, where was he supposed to begin? "The thing is, I just wanted to tell you. We've met before. You and me. I'm a friend of your mom's. An old friend. I just wanted you to know. Remember when Henry came to you? Remember that night? I was there. With you and your mom. And your dad."

"I know," she said. "When we were out walking the other

night." And more reluctantly, "I'm not sure that was real."

"No. I mean years ago. When you and Henry first met. I was there. I brought her in."

"What do you mean?"

"Your mom and I. We found her in the bushes. I brought her in and set her down in front of you, and you gave her milk."

"That was you?"

"I just wanted you to know that Henry means a lot to me, too. You and Henry. You both do. That night meant a lot. I just wanted to tell you."

She nodded. Though what she was thinking he could not guess.

But with that, Izzie seemed to notice his outfit for the first time—the battered work clothes, the heavy boots. "What are you doing?"

"Your mom's hired me. She wants me to demolish this room."

Her eyes widened. "What do you mean demolish?"

"Well. Technically I think I'm supposed to save it. But it's not clear how that's going to work." He drew her attention to the ceiling. "There's a leak up there. It's rotted the plaster all the way back to the corner. And the plaster has rotted the lath—all the little boards underneath. It's got to come out."

He could see the idea taking shape in her mind as she followed the familiar line of the walls. "How much of it?" she breathed.

"Everything. I've got to tear it out until I come to something solid. This wall, that corner. Part of the ceiling. Probably that corner of the roof. Then I re-build from there. If there's anything still standing."

Izzie was moved beyond words. *Won't the roof just fall down?* she signed.

He weighed his two hands up and down. *Maybe. Do you want to leave before I start?*

He got her a chair from the kitchen. And since he was up, he heated a can of soup and made her a bologna sandwich. Then, setting the tray on her lap, he picked up the sledgehammer and weighed it in his hands.

She hunched like the audience at an uncertain dinner theater. "Have you done this before?"

"I took down Mrs. Bleecker's entire front porch once. The whole thing. I knocked out the pillars and rode the corner of the roof all the way down to the ground."

"Didn't she mind?"

"You know. Now that you mention it, I think maybe she did. Turns out she was just expecting a little patch and paint. I told her that was unworthy of her; there are no half-measures in life. But I'm not sure he understood."

"What did she say?"

"She made me coffee and brownies. At the time I thought it was really sweet. But afterwards I wondered if she was just trying to talk me out of it." He raised the hammer.

"Wait! Did it all work out? With Mrs. Bleecker? Was she happy in the end?"

"She'd been using her back door for twenty years. The first time she walked out onto her new font porch she said she felt like a new woman."

"Really?"

"Well. She burst into tears. But I think that's more or less the same thing."

Izzie's voice grew hushed. "This is going to be bad, isn't it?"

"I wouldn't be at all surprised."

And with a crash he buried the hammer like a cannonball in the plaster.

He thought about that long ago time—returning to Gaillard after the summer with nothing left of all that he had hoped to keep.

He remembered the drinking and the wreckage: Mrs. Bleecker's porch, Mr. Lucian's chicken coop, the whole sagging fence line of Mrs. Becket's back yard. He marveled at the fierceness of it. The utter disregard for all the mounting devastation. He had lost everything. Then lost it again. All he felt was despair.

But now.

Slowly chewing her sandwich Izzie gazed with round-eyed satisfaction as he smashed the wall again and again, and then piled the broken pieces on a heavy sheet of plastic. When he broke through to the lath things began to look really bad. The wall buckled like a ship on the rocks; the rubble skittered across the floor. But Izzie seemed to draw comfort from each escalation of the damage, leaning into it as he worked. And after a while he asked with feigned casualness if she'd like to take a swing.

She breathed for a moment like a mouse anchored to the ground by the tremendous weight of the hammer. Then she turned with a cry and like an avenging fury swung with all her might. The first blow bounced off, but the second landed with a hollow crunch. And then for a space of time she could not stop. She smashed the wall again and again, pounding away at the plaster with her chest heaving and all that destruction shining in her face.

Finally she stepped back, sagging onto the hammer at rest.

"You are definitely getting the hang of this," he said mildly.

She looked up at him, panting and fierce. "Can I be your friend, Harold?"

And he stood very still. "Of course," he said. "I'd like that."

"We could be partners."

"That would be good."

"I hate my family. They say they love you, but they don't. My mom. My dad. Even Adam. They all lie to you. And Wheedle. They go behind your back. But partners, they tell each other the truth, don't they?"

"Yes," he said after a moment. "I guess they do."

"You won't ever lie to me, will you?"

"No."

"Have you ever had a partner?"

"No. I've always worked alone. You'll be my first."

The girl nodded with satisfaction. "I like your outfit," she said.

"Thanks. I like yours."

But she cast a frowning glance down at the housekeeper's smock as if even that had let her down.

Peace comes, when it comes, in unconsidered ways. Harold arrived at the house each morning in time to welcome Bea home from work. He'd sit by the back door in the warm charcoal scent of the ruined garage, and find himself floating between present and past—carried back to the burning Rectory, back to his daughter, all the way back to the smokey, kerosene light of the island. He could feel not just the morning but his whole life gathered around him.

When she arrived he would follow her inside without a word, and while she went upstairs to change into pajamas and a robe, he put on the coffee and opened a bottle of wine. Then he started dinner. Always something fresh, no leftovers; simple but fragrant. And when she came downstairs he was ready with a small plate of cheese and crackers or artichoke dip or cheese shortbread—any of the host of snacks his mother had made for their long cocktail hour each day—all of it freshly arrayed in a small, domestic pageant of flavor and comfort.

They would sit and talk about her night at work, his progress on the mudroom, all the smallest things they had seen or thought since last they met. Nothing of the past was allowed to intrude—all that history, all that blood under the bridge. Instead they drew all worry from the world, and Bea found herself against all expectations growing gradually more heavy-eyed.

And as she headed up the stairs Harold would already be slipping into the mudroom. It was crucial that he not appear to be expecting anyone. The world was arrayed in chance. But Izzie, who had pugnaciously maintained an erratic schedule for most of a year, arrived every morning at eleven. Gone was the grumpy housekeeper's grey. She had made a new outfit, modeled on his own. She couldn't match Franklin's time-weathered pants, but she had found a pair of Carhart overalls and sewed onto them a series of wildly colored patches and seams so they looked as if they'd been dismembered by years of hard service and drawn back together by a firm if exuberant hand. She chose an eye shadow the color of blood-stained khaki and a lipstick as brown as the ancient lath.

She would step into the mudroom just as Harold was ready for lunch, and it was his turn to be waited on. After the first day he tried to help, but she was fierce in defending her tasks. She made a mug of strong tea, smoothed with milk, and a substantial sandwich of meat and cheese with lettuce and a scattering of the mild peppers he had once admitted he enjoyed. She laid out a few cookies; she was still prospecting for which kind he particularly liked, but she enjoyed them all, so nothing was wasted. She brought it all in on a tray—the flavors of his past—and each time when he protested that it was much too large, she would take, as her own portion, part of his, and together they sat as if in a vacant field contemplating the day's work.

And all this time Henry lay curled asleep in her basket at a safe distance, and Bea the spider—who had bonded with the cat the way a climber bonds with a mountain—perched intently on her recumbent shoulder, like a tiny construction foreman overseeing the work, while upstairs in bed, Bea listened for the back door and the sounds of Izzie's arrival, and when the pounding rose through the fabric of the house, it came to her like a distant comfort and eased her into sleep.

72

Sleepless and unshaven in white coveralls Weland answered the door like an appliance repairman on the verge of a nervous breakdown. "Oh, for God's sake! Where have you been? What are you two dressed as?"

And perhaps, just for a moment, it did look too much like a morality play: white on one side, black on the other. For Izzie had done her best to match Harold's clerical air. She'd found a dark suit in the thrift store but had rebelled against its plainness. So she'd added lapels and a pocket square of bright cerulean blue, and adjusted her eye shadow and lips to match. You look like a disco vampire, he had said, and she'd frowned in satisfaction.

"It's Saturday," Izzie explained. "This is pastoral care."

"That's right. We go from door to door bringing comfort to all the cranky, obnoxious, and irritable shut-ins heavily laden with the cares of the world."

"Well, Christ!" snapped Weland. "What took you so long?"

He stepped back as Izzie wheeled the cart past. She had wedged the plastic cage onto the back, and Bea rode just above Henry's shoulder gazing around like eagle-eyed Cortes on a peak in Darien.

"For pity's sake! Can't you leave that thing at home?"

"She likes to get out in the world," said Izzie.

"Well at least keep it covered."

"How would you like to walk around with a cover on your head?"

"I might as well," he muttered, "for all the good it's doing. Come on. You know your way. Coffee's there. Scotch is up there. I think Mindy left some pound cake somewhere."

And really, Harold almost felt sorry for him. It was like

nudging a sore tooth. Though in this case, of course, it was someone else's tooth. "Is everything okay, Weland?"

"Of course it's not okay!"

"Been drinking enough coffee?"

"Get in here! Hurry up! I need your eyes. And your hands. Bring me another cup; not too much coffee. This is a nightmare!"

The studio was unchanged since the last visit: wide bay window, walls crowded with paintings. But now, arranged across the elegant curve of the sofa, the sketches of a naked woman had been replaced by the woman herself. And Weland stood glaring down at her as if he would gladly change her back into sketches if only he could.

She was solidly built and carelessly nude, with long pre-Raphaelite hair like an explosion over her shoulders. She was darkly tanned around the pale silhouette of a missing bikini, and with arms curving up over her head she lay back, eyes closed, ankles demurely crossed. Harold hesitated at the sight, glancing down at his companion, but a lifetime in the shadow of art had left Izzie unsurprised.

Weland was at his easel, painting quickly and angrily as if the colors were laid out and numbered and he was already disappointed.

"I don't want to interrupt," said Harold.

"Don't talk. Don't stand there. Sit."

"Won't your friend find it distracting?"

"She's in her own world."

And he could hear it now, the wisps of an intricate piano solo escaping into the air. The thin white cord of her earbuds snaked down to the phone on the cushion beside her, and occasionally the woman's hands twitched at a particularly difficult passage.

"So, do you paint the earbuds?"

"Don't talk!"

"It just seemed like an interesting point."

"Will you sit down!"

"Don't you want your coffee?"

"Jesus! Is there scotch in this?"

"Oh, yes."

And he took a long sip. The tightness around his eyes began to ease. "You haven't been talking to the press, have you?"

"About what?"

"Anything. We were going to keep it all under our hats, don't you remember?"

"Is this about your festival?"

"It's not my festival. It's our festival. *Your* festival, if it comes to that."

"Not going well?"

"Of course not! It's gotten completely out of hand. The Rochester paper called. And a stringer for *The Times*. They want to know what we're doing."

"Well, what are we doing?"

"I told them we're still refining our ideas. What else could I say? It's turning into a nightmare. I've got the Town Clerk calling. He tells me I need a license if I want a parade. A parade! I said where did you get that idea? And he just laughed. The mayor's office called. They heard something about naked models posing all over town and what did I think I was doing?"

Harold glanced over at Izzie. She had wheeled the cart over to the little patio table and was arranging pound cake with more than necessary care.

Weland scowled. "And Herman Volker at the President's Office wanted to make sure I cleared it with him before we committed any University resources. The budget's tight, he said, but they could always make room for something good. He asked me what I had up my sleeve. Jesus Christ! Up my sleeve? This is a fucking disaster!"

"Language, Weland."

"Don't fucking *Weland* me. We've got to do something! We're running out of time. I need your help on this, Harold. Christ! It was your idea in the first place."

"Was it?"

"I wish I'd never listened to you."

"It does sound bad," he agreed. "So what do you want to do?"

"Ideas! For God's sake, we need ideas."

Izzie took a bite of her poundcake. "What about the parade?" she asked.

"You missed that," said Harold. "Parade's been canceled. We're giving up on it."

Weland frowned. "Not giving up. Just undecided."

"And the museum show?" asked Izzie.

"We've already got a museum show."

"Interpretive dancers all over town? That seemed like a good idea. And what about Childe Harold Days? You don't mean you're giving up on that?"

"I told you," he said impatiently. "We're not giving up. But we've got to figure out what we're doing. We need a planning session."

"I thought this was the planning session," said Harold.

"Sweet Christ! I'm going to be a laughing stock."

73

Weland turned bleakly back to the canvas and took a long pull on his scotch. The painting was nearly complete. The light, the sense of mass and solidity were beautiful, the texture complex and compelling.

"Okay," said Harold wearily. "It's beautiful. So what's wrong with it?"

"I really need you to stop asking that."

But he was frowning, leaning forward, shaping the curving mass of a thigh, working at it over and over until he caught the faint pucker of too much flesh squeezed together. Then he straightened up with a muttered groan. "Christ! Describe Winona to me."

"Who?"

He nodded at the woman. "Tell me what you see."

Harold turned. "I see a naked woman. You're the painter. What do you see?"

But it was clear what Weland saw, even after all these years. He kept reaching out, touching up the paint as if he couldn't quite leave it alone—toning down the darker skin, obscuring the tan lines, lightening the hair. Every brushstroke drawing him back to that long ago summer light as if he were helpless against the pull. And with every change he grew increasingly impatient until, scowling, he tore off the page and threw it aside.

"Winona!"

Reluctantly the woman opened her eyes.

"What are you doing? What's wrong with you? This isn't working!" But she knew enough not to answer.

"Jesus Christ," he muttered and, striding over with the brush still in hand, he began peevishly to arrange her. "Arm down. Spread your legs! No, no! This isn't Playboy. For God's sake!" And lifting one knee, shifting it, he tried to find a seductive pose.

But when he returned to the easel he looked almost puzzled. "You'd think a naked woman would be enough, wouldn't you? I don't know how this girl does it."

"Maybe she can hear you."

But Weland just shook his head. Staring for a moment he seemed to find the thread again and leaned in to the canvas. But this time it was only a moment before he tore it off and flung it away. "Jesus wept!" And he stood there before the new blank sheet, breathing raggedly.

"How about a little more coffee?" Harold suggested.

"Please shut up."

"Maybe just some scotch?"

"I need quiet!"

"I can get you a sandwich."

"It's very important that you not speak."

Weland held his brush like a stick now, like a very thin club, as if he had used up all its lightness and wanted only to bludgeon someone. "I can hear your fucking music!"

Without a word she reached up and adjusted the volume.

"God damn it, Winona! Come on! What else have you got? You're letting me down!"

She lay there for a moment as if still entangled in the melody, then she began to shift. Turning she arranged herself as if praying against the back of the sofa, but any air of spirituality vanished as she arched her back, making an open gateway of her thighs, and peered over one shoulder at him with an air of mild curiosity.

Harold glanced at Izzie, but even this was nothing she hadn't seen before. She was lifting Bea out of her island retreat and setting her companionably on Henry's back.

Meanwhile Weland had already dipped his brush in ap ale peach mixture cut with slate blue and he was laying in the long, curving landscape.

"Is that it?" he muttered. "Is that what you've got?"

He grew more confident as he worked—small eddies of shadow and muscle took shape and drew together. And just for a moment even Harold could see that he had caught something—the suggestion of flirty challenge, a blend of something distant and taunting in the angled thrust of the buttocks.

But then he seemed to lose his grasp. The painting dwindled and dulled as the layers of color slowly shifted toward something more classical. The twist of the torso grew elegant, the expression on the face more passive. By the time he stopped and stepped back he was in a rage.

He tore off the sheet and, gulping at his mug, snarled, "What else? That was nothing! New pose! God damn it! What else have you got?"

Winona didn't move. "Are we drinking now?" she asked. And Izzie glanced up with interest.

"Don't talk! New pose."

But she only shifted stubbornly on the sofa, raising her buttocks, spreading her legs wider as if offering another point in her argument.

"We're out of coffee, I'm afraid," said Harold. "Do you want me to make some more?"

"For the love of God! Just pour!"

Harold reached for the bottle and half-filled the mug.

"Not me! Take it to her!" And he glared at the model. "Don't move."

Harold approached the naked woman with the mug in hand. She was peering up at him, her expression too distant to be a smile. "And how was your day?" he asked.

"Never mind her day!" cried Weland.

"So, what do you like in your coffee?"

"Oh, for God's sake! Don't talk! Don't move! Give me something I can use!"

She tilted up her face, and he held the mug to her lips. She took a long sip like a shipwrecked sailor who has to piece out her limited supplies. He heard a delicate cascade of notes spilling out from the earbuds. "You're a musician?"

"Pianist."

"Stop talking, God damn it! Concentrate, Winona! You're just playing games now."

"One more," she whispered and took a last sip.

As Harold stepped away, she straightened on her knees, reaching her arms up mightily toward the celling to stretch the kinks out of her shoulders. Then turning and sitting back on the sofa she stared directly into Weland's eyes and, with a moment's teasing hesitation, drew her knees up and apart. "Is this what you want, Weland?"

"Hah! You think that's something?"

"How about this?"

Her hands slipped around, taking hold of her thighs. She drew her legs back further, pressing herself into the cushions. And, caught like that, beneath some unseen weight, she walked her fingers down the backs of her thighs as if negotiating a particularly complex bit of fingering. They came together at the juncture of dark hair and flesh, her fingers dabbling, teasing the pink seashell lips into wakefulness.

"Pornography," said Weland dismissively, though his gaze was intent. He seemed to be working something out, as if the entirety of the image had not yet resolved itself in his mind.

"You're the painter," murmured Winona. "Can you see how wet I am?"

"Don't talk. This isn't a fucking movie."

Her expression was grave; her voice matter-of-fact. Her fingers traced the gleaming lips. "Do you hear that? How wet my pussy is? Isn't she pretty? Don't you want to fuck her, Weland?"

"Don't move."

"Don't you want to put your hard cock right in here?"

"I don't suppose you could cover your ears," Harold whispered, but Izzie's cheeks were already bright pink.

Furiously Weland began to work, as if trying to anchor the complex shape of it all against the page. "It's too clumsy," he muttered, but his brush worked with startling speed, fastening down a line, a shadow. He was all hunched rigor—drawing out the moment—until suddenly he wasn't. All the tension drained away.

"God damn it! No! It's just too obvious! *Look. I have a cunt.* It's fucking Courbet. It's old fucking news. Give me something new, I'm begging you!" And turning wildly to Harold, "For God's sake! Don't just sit there."

"What am I supposed to do?"

"Look at it." He wave his brush at the page. "It's pat. It's ordinary. You're a priest. And a pornographer."

"Alleged pornographer."

"Find some grace here, God damn it! Find something new. Give me a story."

"What kind of a story?"

"What other kind? Passion. Heartbreak. Give me some fucking heartbreak!"

74.

Harold stood up hesitantly. He glanced at Winona. "Any suggestions?" But her gaze was noncommittal.

Then Weland's eye fell on the spider, sitting snugly on Henry's shoulder. "Jesus! I forgot about that thing. Pick it up!"

"She's not bothering anyone," said Izzie hotly.

"No. Just pick it up! Bring it over here."

"Why?"

"Let me see it."

"Forget it, Weland," Harold said.

"No. I'm serious! I need this. Just pick it up."

Reluctantly Izzie reached down and lifted Bea gently into the air.

"Oh, my God!" muttered Weland. "That's horrible."

Izzie drew back

"Wait. Bring it over."

"No."

"Please! God damn it!"

"It's okay," said Winona. "Bring her over here."

Reluctantly Izzie carried the spider over, cradled in her palm. The woman gazed down with the same level, distant interest she had shown for everything else. "Does she have a name?"

"Bea. Bea the spider."

"My brother has a snake. He's been trying to frighten me since I was a kid. But they're actually pretty. Does she bite?"

"No. I don't think so." And in fact the spider wore an air of cheerful expectation.

Winona nodded at her arm where it curved around her raised knee. "Just put her there."

"She's very delicate."

"So am I."

Gently Izzie lowered her hand, and the spider, somehow mirroring the woman's distant curiosity, sauntered out onto her arm.

Weland was almost frantic, his fist clenched around the brush, his eyes glued to the little creature. "That's disgusting!" he said. "It's appalling. Do you see that, Winona? Do you see? Oh, my God. You've got a huge, hairy spider on your arm! It's going to crawl onto your leg. It's going crawl all the way to your big hairy cunt. What do you say to that?" He started to paint. "Oh, my God! It's going to bite you, Winona. I can see its fangs. Put it near your cunt."

"No, Weland," she said calmly.

"On your thigh, then. I need it on your thigh."

Harold glanced at her, and she just shrugged. Bea was already taking direction. She had tip-toed cheerfully onto Winona's knee and was gazing around. "Now take your arms away. Oh, my God!"

Weland painted in a rage, trying to galvanize himself with fear and revulsion. His brush hurried from paper to paint, catching at the details, drawing out the moment, while Winona, the faint thread of music drifting out of her earbuds, gazed calmly at the spider resting like a sunbather on the tanned beachscape of her thigh.

Finally, exhausted, he stepped back from the easel. The scotch was beginning to tell, the sleepless nights. He dropped his brush onto his palette and stared haggardly down at the painting without a glimmer of hope.

After a moment Winona stirred and looked up at Izzie. "Would you mind?"

The girl reached down and tenderly lifted the spider. As she carried her back to the cart Winona slowly unbent. Still without any embarrassment—with, in fact, a quick glance at Harold, as if weighing the effect on him of all her practiced stillness—she began to climb into her clothes, pulling up her underpants with a little snap, tugging her jeans snugly over her hips as if covering a birdcage for the night.

All the while Weland stood peering around like an elderly host who has long since forgotten his duties. Stepping up to him, brisk and unfazed, Winona held out a hand and met halfway the slender envelope he drew from his pocket. And as if bumping by accident, she pressed her lips lightly against his. Then she turned and strolled away.

Weland swallowed. "I usually have a drink about now." But he stood like a castaway gazing around at the crumpled and scattered paintings. "Fuck it," he muttered. "Just fuck it. God damn fucking art."

75

Izzie went off to her next job with Henry and Bea in tow, folding the whole strange afternoon into the usual shape of her day. And Harold, startled into sympathy, followed Weland reluctantly out into the sunshine. They walked about the town, pausing at café tables, benches, on the steps of the War Memorial to pass a small flask back and forth. Notebook in hand, Weland gazed helplessly around. What do you see? he demanded. What catches your eye? Is that building strange? How about that woman there? Is she beautiful? Is she hot?

He could no longer distinguish what was ordinary or surprising—no longer tell something from nothing.

"Look at all these people. They shop for this or that. They run their errands. And the hours just tick away. Look at those two."

A couple in their late twenties stood at a crosswalk waiting for the light, their eyes on their phones.

"What are they feeling now? Anything? Anything at all? If someone said, Give me your strongest sensation, what would they say? Boredom? Would they even know what you meant? If they suddenly found themselves with an extra load of bad luck, would they even notice?"

Harold glanced over, but Weland was watching intently as the light changed and the pair started across the street. The woman caught her foot on the curb and stumbled. A car lurched forward; Harold almost cried out. But Weland leaned into it as if willing the scene to unfold. The man snatched at her arm. Caught her. They clung together for a moment and then, as the car drove past, they moved ahead, slipping back into a companionable distance, eyes returning to their phones.

"See? It makes no difference to them. A little more bad luck. They don't even notice."

But Harold had. In the instant the woman stumbled, as the car approached, he had seen her balanced on the edge of grief. Wide-eyed and alert, she had felt disaster looming—felt the whole world contract. And as she clutched at her companion's hand and found her footing once again he saw the shock of it bloom on her face, the sudden comprehension of all that might have been lost. And just for a moment the whole world burned brighter around her.

Weland led them along the edge of the pretty campus—made so much more prosperous in the fifteen years since he'd arrived that, looking around, he could be excused for thinking this, too, was his. They came to the art department—a former factory that had long ago left its best behind. The entrance was unimposing, the hallways narrow and crooked with the years. And despite the bright white paint it had a ramshackle air. Weland turned into one of the undergraduate studios—a wide room not so much divided as cluttered by a forest of easels. On the walls a patchwork of sketches and paintings looked like an overdecorated refrigerator.

"It's a terrible room," he said. "At the end of term it's just one huge cloud of anxiety. All the students rushing to finish, muscling ahead without any hint of inspiration. Trying to fool themselves into thinking they're just too tired to appreciate all they've accomplished. We tell them that. It doesn't have to be perfect; it just has to be done. But it's a lie, of course. So much of teaching is a lie. What's the point of finishing something you never should have started? You dangle before them all that they should aspire to, knowing from the first moment who will be disappointed and who won't."

"Maybe you shouldn't be teaching," said Harold.

"Don't be ridiculous. They need someone like me. You either teach to the lowest common denominator or you teach to the highest. Do you want to encourage everyone, or do you want to produce a few good artists?"

"What about the students that surprise you?"

"No one surprises me. Art is a mountain, it's a cliff. You teach them what they need to know to climb it. Technique, discipline, the hard work to carry them forward. And all the while the secret is: if it isn't easy it isn't good. If it isn't good, it's never going to be. If you don't see it right away—from the first moment you begin—you'll never find your way. We're condemning them to years of effort—decades of struggle and disappointment—just to find a crumbling foothold for themselves."

"Jesus, Weland."

He glanced over, genuinely surprised. "You don't think it's true?"

"I hope to God it isn't."

"Have you ever tried to make something beautiful, Harold?"

"You mean aside from my alleged book."

Weland waved that away. "In real life, most people don't. All that turmoil and distraction. They don't even try."

"So at least these kids are trying."

"And you think that's better?" He shook his head. "When I was a boy I'd look around a room like this and I just couldn't understand them—the other students. Their terrible little ideas. Their awful technique. It was like they didn't want to succeed. And then I realized they just couldn't see what I could. They couldn't see what it needed to be. They'd start with something and then just move it around like food on their plate. But *I* could see, even from across the room."

"How nice for you," said Harold drily.

"It wasn't nice. It was essential. It was life. I couldn't imagine not being that way. Who would want to? And then *Blue Spruce. The Wide Bed.* I thought it was all just the way it was going to be. How could it not? How could I not be that man?"

He stared around at the cluttered, unpromising space. "And now I understand them. All of them. These students. These little shits. Wanting so much to be painters and never realizing how far short they're bound to fall. I understand that now. It's terrible. I look around, and there's nothing I can do. There's nothing here. No one is doing anything that will give me what I need. I'm helpless. Look at it. It's like the whole world is broken."

76.

He led the way over to his desk in the corner, elevated above the others, facing out over the expanse of the room. It was piled with student work—mismatched, half-finished—and at the back, leaning forlornly against the wall, a small painting, no different, at first glance. A simple scene, crudely painted.

Weland handed it to him. "Tell me what you see."

It was set by a pond with willow trees and a white building—a mill or a boathouse. There were nude men bathing and standing on the shore, toweling off or lying on the grass in the sun. There was no action, no drama. It looked like one static moment in a world of moments. But the more Harold looked, the less simple it became. The figures, though small, were beautifully drawn, and the light was remarkable. Not quite natural, it seemed to flow through the scene like a comfort.

"Did you do this?"

"Of course not," snapped Weland. "Look at it. It's the work of a simpleton. The arrangement of characters. The complete lack of interest. And those flat colors. It's like a postcard."

"So who?"

"Jonathan. This is what Jonathan's doing now. He's churning these out up on that ridiculous canal boat, out in the middle of nowhere."

Weland took back the painting. He started to toss it onto the desk, but instead he turned it again as if he couldn't let it pass through his hands without another glimpse. "It's like his mind is broken. You've seen what he can do. It's like he's deliberately turning his back on all that talent."

"Well. He has been through a lot."

"We've all been through a lot. But this. There's no excuse for this. This is what happens when a great artist gives up."

Harold glanced up. "A *great* artist?"

And Weland sat for a moment like a chess player who wished he'd kept his finger on that last piece. "A good artist," he amended. "Very good. A wonderful painter. But he didn't have what he needed to be great. Once, long ago, I asked him if he wouldn't like to be famous. This was before Venice. Just before. He'd created that beautiful blue, and then he squandered it on an ordinary landscape. And I said, if you play your cards right you could be famous. And he said he wouldn't mind, as long as it didn't interfere with his painting."

He gave a snort of laughter. "*Interfere.* What can you do with that? When it comes right down to it, he's always had an amateur's feeling for art. He thought it was the picture that mattered. The color, the technique. As if that was the point. As if it wasn't about all the rest of it. The excitement, the clamor that a work might make out in the world. It's as if he spent all his time choosing a stone to throw into a pond and never paid attention to the splash. As if he just couldn't see beyond the stone. I tried to explain it to him. And believe me, this was entirely unlike me. I told him what he needed to do. I'd seen it right away. I explained to him exactly what was missing. But I don't think he wanted to understand."

"Maybe he liked it the way it was," said Harold.

"Don't be ridiculous. Say you go to a museum—the Louvre. What's it like?"

"Never been."

"Then I'll tell you, and save you the trip. You feel *battered* by the art. Again and again. By all the talent of all the painters of all the centuries. Every picture is extraordinary. Each one a triumph of talent and luck and opportunity. Each one could knock you right over—just make you want to give up. But do you know what happens when you walk through all those endless corridors? Your eyes get numb. Your heart goes numb. Here you are at the Louvre. Some of the greatest art in the whole history of art. And all you feel is a kind of pale appreciation."

Weland raised an instructive finger. "But then you come to the *Mona Lisa.* And all of a sudden your senses are sharp again. Suddenly you feel brand new. You look at the painting with all your attention and you notice every detail. Every line and shadow. That is greatness. It doesn't mean the Mona Lisa is a better painting. It's not more remarkable than all the other art in all the other rooms. But it is greater. And you know why? Because before you've even seen it, you know it's greater. It's waiting there for you at the center of all that fame."

He paused for a moment. He was still holding Jonathan's painting—he seemed surprised to find it in his hand. "Greatness is what happens when you lift a good painting up into the light, and all that beauty and technique transforms itself into something simpler—a kind of wonder. It's that moment that lodges a painting in the hearts of its audience. Jonathan never understood that. He thought a painting with an audience of five people, or five hundred, could be as great as one that all the world admires. He thought a painting could be great in itself. But a painting is only great *outside* of itself. It's only great if, when you lift it up, there's a gleam of light waiting to shine on it. And a host of people ready to see that gleam. *That* is greatness."

He tilted the little painting this way and that.

"I miss Jonathan. He was always the one who could help me. Lift me out of this feeling. Give me that spark I needed. I used to count on him. I always did. *Blue Spruce. The Blue Robe.* He's given me some of my best ideas."

"*Your* ideas?"

Weland looked offended. "What do you mean?"

"You steal his color, you still his painting. You steal his wife, for God's sake. And you call it a good idea?"

"I didn't *steal* anything."

"Tell me you just borrowed them."

"Don't be ridiculous! I invented them. I took something that wasn't going anywhere, and I made it great. None of them, not his blue, not his nudes, not even his wife, if it came to that—none of them would have gone anywhere without me. It was magic. Symbiosis. I transformed them all. I lifted then up and lit them for the world to see." He sighed. "But that's all gone now. He's let his talent down; he's let me down."

"To be fair," said Harold drily, "his studio *did* burn to the ground."

"That wasn't it. I mean, it's bad. Don't get me wrong. But it was that business in the park. That's what took it out of him. I don't think he ever got over it. It was all just too much for him. He's just too shy—too private a person—to be a great artist. You're supposed to show the world everything you are. Every flaw is just another kind of talent. But Jonathan didn't have the steel he needed."

The thought seemed to weigh him down. After a moment he peered up at Harold.

"How was I to know? That he'd be so weak. It's not as though I did it on purpose. I panicked, that's all. In the park that night. I gave them Jonathan's name. I couldn't give them mine. How could I? Just think what that would have done."

77

But Harold was just staring at him now. "You went cruising in the park?"

"It was just a whim."

"And you gave them Jonathan?"

"I couldn't think of what else to do."

"You're a monster, Weland."

"You think I don't know? You think it hasn't been eating away at me? It has! But I have a responsibility. Of course I do. *The Wide Bed*? All the paintings people love? They'd never look at them the same way. It would have ruined it for them. I couldn't do that. I couldn't just destroy all that. Oh," he said impatiently, "don't give me that look. You know it's true. People are counting on me. They always have. For God's sake! This whole stupid business you started. *Childe Harold Days*. It's all landed on my shoulders. The papers, the president's office, the people of this town. They're all looking to me for something tremendous. And I don't have it. I'm fucked. I'm going to be a laughing stock. Don't you think I could do without that?"

He lapsed into silence, gazing down. And there was the little painting again, still in his hand. "You never met Jonathan. But there were times I envied him. His eye, of course. His genius for color. There, I said it. Genius. But other things, as well. His generosity. His calm. I tell you, there were moments I even envied his family. Can you imagine? Me? It sounds horrifying, I know—all that uproar and effort. But I admit it. He made it look satisfying. He made it look graceful—at first, I mean, before it all went bad. I would tease him. I'd say, look at you. Who'd have thought you'd become such a family man? And do you know what he said? He said, a man's greatest strength is his children. Can you imagine?"

And for a moment Harold thought of Izzie, bleak and staring

at the blackened ruins of the studio. *A man's greatest strength.*

Weland seemed to follow his thought, as if the little trail of smoke still hung on the air. "And look what he's done to those kids. He's made them as weak as he is. The boy swallows a handful of pills. Not even the right pills. Aspirin, for God's sake. Then he throws up and just lies there, covered in puke, waiting for Izzie to find him. Then off he goes to Briarcliff to hide."

"He must have been in pain," said Harold.

"Of course he was in pain. We're all in pain. It's what you do with the pain that counts. And Izzie? I thought that girl had a spark. But now? Dressing up and wasting herself in all these petty jobs. She's become ordinary."

"Don't be ridiculous. She's anything but ordinary. She's just upset. About her father, about Adam."

"Weakness. That's all it is. Pure and simple. You can't let yourself be drawn into other people's problems."

"How can you help it? Not if you love them."

But Weland seemed to fasten on that. "Let me tell you about love. What was your childhood like?"

"Mine? Strange."

"Mine was perfect. Fucking Normal Rockwell. I barely made it out alive. I think back to it: I was nothing. It was like I didn't exist. I was an only child; my parents had me late. My mother called me her miracle baby. It was like Abraham and Sarah. They would do anything for me. When I started to paint I was too young for art classes so they hired a portrait painter to give me private lessons. Private fucking lessons! My father was a mailman. My mother cleaned houses. Where did they find the money? Then once I was old enough, more lessons. Art school. They were bleeding money for me. They were thrilled."

"That doesn't sound so bad."

"They named me Wayne." And he looked momentarily undone, as if even after all this time it still took him by surprise.

"Wayne Thomas. Can you imagine? Do I look like a fucking Wayne Thomas?"

"I could see it."

But Weland seemed not to hear. "I changed my name, of course. When I was ten. Do you know the story of Weland the Smith? It's an old Germanic myth."

"I think it's pronounced Wayland," said Harold.

"Is it? Well, not anymore. Weland was an artificer. He could make anything. Beautiful, beautiful work. He was kidnapped by a powerful king and ordered to create golden treasures."

"Did he send him to art school?"

"Shut up and listen. This is important. In order to make sure he couldn't escape, the king hamstrung him. Cut the muscles in his legs. Crippled him. But Weland was stronger than that. He created a pair of beautiful silver wings. In secret. Where no one could see them. And after killing the king and impregnating his wife and daughter, our hero flew away and lived a life of art and mischief for the rest of his days."

"Ah," said Harold. "So much for Wayne Thomas."

"Love is no better than any other prison. It's just one more thing designed to keep you from being yourself. Look at Jonathan. He chose to marry Bea. No one made him. I told him he didn't have to. But he didn't listen. And then this whole business with his studio. It didn't have to ruin him. It's as if he wanted it to. That's what I told him. In the end: no one can save you from your own mistakes."

"Oh," said Harold. "I hope that's not true."

Weland grew very still. "What do you mean?"

"Nothing. I was just thinking about mistakes."

"Whose mistakes? What are you saying? Is this about the park? I told you about that. There was nothing else I could do." His glance sharpened. "Is this about the studio?"

Harold froze. He cursed himself. How could they have gotten here? He should have been more careful. Weland's mind was twisty as a snake. He thought of Izzie. *I wish we had burned down Weland's house instead of my father's.*

"What is it?" demanded Weland. "What do you know?"

"Nothing."

"You know something."

"No, I don't."

"What have you heard?"

Harold fought to keep his expression blank. "I haven't heard a thing."

But he had forgotten what a shark Weland could be. "I can see what you're thinking. You think it wasn't an accident, aren't you? Is that what you're saying? The studio burning down?"

"No."

He was peering closely now, his mind turning like a clock. "You think someone broke in? Set fire to the place?"

"Of course not."

"Did you hear something? Did someone tell you something?"

"There's nothing to tell."

But Weland had turned thoughtful. "I wonder. I was there that night—the night of the fire. No reason. Just walking by. Looking for inspiration. I thought Jonathan might be up, but all the lights were out. Then I smelled the smoke."

"You-- what? What did you do?"

Weland hesitated. "Nothing. What could I have done?"

Harold stood staring. "Did you see the fire?"

"I just smelled the smoke. How was I to know? It might have been nothing."

"Jesus, Weland. You could have put it out."

But really, it wasn't as if he'd planned anything. He was just walking along, thinking of Jonathan and his art. And at the first scent of smoke his mind went to the paintings on the wall. Just like that, in a flash. And he thought of all the works in progress, what a pity it would be. And there among them that one painting, long finished. That first nude of Jonathan's that had launched them all on their way. Hidden away as a favor. Just a bit too much like *The Blue Robe* for Weland's comfort.

And he thought—not even thought, *felt*—all that it would mean to have it gone. Just vanish. The relief. And after all, it was out of his hands. It was fate. What if he hadn't come by? Nothing would be different. What if he weren't even here?

"I thought it was an accident," said Weland. "Fate. Not even my fate. Jonathan's. And really, the further away I got, the more I thought I'd just imagined it. It wasn't until the next morning I knew for sure."

He was still peering into Harold's face. "But you know. Now that I think of it, maybe it wasn't my fault at all. That door was ajar. I barely noticed at the time, but I remember it now. Someone was there."

"You don't know that!"

"Relax," he said. "It's just a game we're playing. We're just thinking out loud. But someone had gone in there, hadn't they? Not just by accident."

Harold felt his stomach knot. "Now you're just making things up."

"It's Izzie, isn't it? Did she tell you something?"

"Of course not! Why would you say that?"

"I know you, Harold. Hell, I invented you. I'm not blind. I've seen you with her. And she has ears everywhere."

"Absolutely not."

"She was so upset about it."

"Of course she was upset. It was her father's studio. Izzie would never..."

"Oh, you don't need to tell me. She's too kind. Much too ordinary. But I wonder." And he was musing now. "What about Adam? He doesn't cross the street without Izzie. And all that drama. The pills, the getaway. I'd forgotten about it, but it does make a kind

 D. K. Smith

of sense, don't you think?"

"Absolutely not."

"Poor Jonathan. Imagine that. His own children. Whatever you think of me, at least I'm not his family."

"Stop it!" said Harold. "This is terrible. You can't say anything!"

"Of course not. I won't." But he was smiling now, relaxed and smiling. "Isn't it something, though? Adam. I didn't think he had it in him. I mean, what kind of a person would burn up someone's entire life?"

"Nobody. Nobody would. It was an accident."

"Of course it was. Still. It's interesting, don't you think?"

And he seemed to lose himself in thought for a moment. Then he straightened up. "By the way. My car's in the shop. Can you give me a lift?"

78.

It wasn't until they were on the road that Izzie realized how drunk Weland was. He sat in the front seat of Miss Pru's ancient Volkswagen sipping from a cardboard cup and gazing around. "That Adam is a real scamp, isn't he? He's gotten himself into some hot water."

"He's been having a hard time," she conceded.

"Oh, sure. But I was thinking about poor Jonathan. Losing his studio like that—all that work. What a terrible thing."

Izzie grew still.

"Don't worry. Harold didn't say anything. Some things are just obvious. And I'm not pointing fingers at anyone. Accidents happen, after all. And really, it's a kind of life lesson, isn't it? Wouldn't you say it was a life lesson, padre? No putting your faith in the things of this world?"

What's he doing? she demanded.

No idea.

But Weland was smiling to himself now. "Your brother has hidden depths, no question about it."

"He's not really my brother. We're more like best friends."

"Of course you are." And he took another sip. "Do you know what art is, little Izzie?"

"Yes."

"Art is that touch of the divine in the ordinary world. It's that brief and difficult bridge from our own isolation to a larger understanding that transcends mere words."

"The school is just up there," she said to Harold.

"The world divides, young Izzie. There are two kinds of people.

Those who sit and watch—and those who *do.* You can't teach someone that. It's something you're born with. It sparks out of you like an explosion." He seemed to relish the thought. "And no one enjoys a good explosion like another stick of dynamite."

"This is the turn," she said to Harold. "Take a left at the stop light, just past the Dairy Queen."

"Maybe we'll get ice cream later," Weland said. "How would you like that?"

It was chilly despite the sunshine, but Weland wanted to be outside so they chose a picnic table looking out over the wide lawn. Adam came out to them, bundled up against the breeze, as Izzie unpacked the picnic lunch. Fortified with scotch Weland sat sleek and gleaming in his pale grey suit, gazing around as if the whole sunny day were his idea.

How are you doing? she signed.

Okay. What's with Wheedle?

Who knows? He's always got something on his mind.

Weland helped himself to a sandwich. "So, how are they treating you here?"

Adam shrugged. "It's not bad."

"Your mother says you're doing well."

"The guards tell me I'm the most courteous sociopath they know."

"Surely they're not guards."

"Teachers."

"Do you know what the biggest breakthrough of my career was?" He took a bite, then frowned and peeled back the top of the bread. "Is this bologna?"

"Venice," said Adam. "*Blue Spruce.*" He tried to sound bored. Wheedle was always annoying, but Adam had taken to studying him. He wore nice shoes and beautiful suits, and there was something about him that made you pay attention.

"Before that. Even before that." He closed the sandwich and took another experimental bite. "Do you know what the secret of art is? What the one defining characteristic of all great art has to be?"

Adam shrugged. "Genius?"

"Balls."

It startled a smile out of the boy. "What?"

"Language, Weland," murmured Harold.

"It's balls," he repeated. "I'm speaking metaphorically, of course. It doesn't matter if you're a man or a woman or anything in between. You've got to have balls. Not just genius. Or inspiration or hard work or talent. Without balls, you've got nothing."

"I think we get the picture," said Harold.

"I'm not sure you do." He eyed the sandwich again and set it aside. "People want to be shocked. They want to be outraged or startled. They want to be faced with more nerve than they've ever had in their entire lives. They may laugh at your work, or roll their eyes, or curse, or complain. But what they're not going to do is ignore it. Because you can't ignore balls." He glanced over at Izzie. "What else have we got?"

She was glaring at him. "Cheese and mustard."

"Hm. I'll try one."

Adam was listening closely. He saw that Harold was tense and Izzie glowering, but he realized he alone was the focus of Weland's rant and he sat up a little straighter. "You're saying it takes nerve."

"No. Not exactly. Nerve is part of it. Courage, sure. Concentration. But balls is more than that. It's a double-helping of all those things—talent and work and concentration—all put into a blender with a dash of sex and a generous pinch of ruthlessness."

"And that's enough coffee for you," said Harold, moving the cup away.

But Weland barely noticed. "People want to be pushed around. That's the thing you've got to remember. They want to be browbeaten. They may not like it in the moment, but they remember it.

And being remembered, young Adam, is much more important than being liked. The thing is, you could be the finest painter on earth. In fact, I know the finest painter on earth. And no one cares. He doesn't make anyone's heart beat faster. People don't want to punch him in the nose or throw a drink in his face or fuck him."

"Weland."

He waved it away. "It's just an expression. You know what I'm saying. You look at his work and you think: that's beautiful. But that's it. That's all. When people buy art, it's not the art they're buying. It's what art does to them. It's what it makes them feel. They want to see something in the painting that makes them squirm. They want to feel it churning around inside them, making them sweat. That's art. And I know you know this, my boy."

"I'm not a painter, Wheedle." But something had happened to the boy's scorn.

"Have you ever tried?"

"He's tried," said Izzie.

"Not very hard."

Weland waved that away, as well. "Doesn't matter. I can see it in you. I see that ballsy light in your eyes. I see the need for something other people don't need. You're an artist because you're not bound by all the usual things. You've got a hunger in you. All that business with the fire, the studio. I see it as clearly as I see you sitting there. That wild desire to do something. The frustration with the man you thought of as your father."

"He's not my father," said Adam.

Weland nodded wisely. "You are perceptive beyond your years."

"What are you doing?" asked Harold.

But Adam spoke as if it were startled out of him, "He didn't deserve Bea. And he let her go. I would never have done that."

"It's *Mama* Bea!" said Izzie, stung into anger.

"She's not my mother. And I love her. I'm in love with her."

Weland regarded him approvingly. "That's right. Passion. That's the key. You feel what you have to feel, and who cares what other people say. You've got balls, boy. I didn't realize it before, but I see it now. The apple doesn't fall far from the tree. I wasn't sure at first. I wasn't sure I should tell you. I didn't know how ordinary you might end up being."

"Jesus, Weland…."

"But I can see you now. You're a spitfire. You're a chip off the old block. Someone makes you mad, you do something about it. You want something, you take it. I'm proud of you, son. I'm proud to be your father."

Izzie sat there aghast, her eyes fastened on Adam. Trying to think of what she could say, trying to comfort him. Tell him this was nothing. A joke. Wheedle being Wheedle. It didn't mean anything.

But at the same time something else began to thread its way into her heart. Because this was suddenly perfect. This solved everything. Because if Weland was his father, then Adam wasn't just a sperm baby, and he wasn't Jonathan's son any more—not in any way. And if they had different fathers and different mothers, different families altogether, then there was no reason why they couldn't love each other any way there was. The feeling was like a bubble in her chest. She almost laughed.

"And now," said Weland, "I've got to go use the facilities." And he climbed to his feet. But before strolling away, in a spirit of fairness—because she had made such a nice lunch and he didn't want her to feel left out and because a man couldn't choose his children, after all—he turned to Izzie and told her she was a good girl as well and he was proud to be her father too.

79

They sat very still, the three of them. And while Harold looked at Izzie, Izzie kept her eyes on Adam's face.

He didn't mean it, she signed. *He's drunk. He's really drunk. You should have seen him on the drive over.*

He's been drunk before.

But he's just joking. He's teasing. You know that. He'll forget all about it.

She was so afraid for him. Afraid he'd be as angry as she was. As startled and confused. But instead she could see him trying on the idea.

Maybe I don't want him to forget.

And when Wheedle returned to lead him back to Registration, Adam followed dutifully along as Izzie stood motionless in the sunshine, still afraid but for a different reason.

Hesitantly Harold touched her shoulder. "I don't want you to worry."

But when she turned, her eyes were fierce. "Can I have your keys?"

"What?"

"Your car keys. Hurry! I forgot something."

He fumbled the keys out of his pocket, and she raced off around the building.

Harold sat alone at the picnic table. There was no sign of Izzie. But when Weland came strolling out, as relaxed and pleased as anyone could be, Harold stood up. "You're full of surprises."

"Aren't I? I think that went well. Do you think they were pleased?"

"It might be too early to tell," he said drily.

Izzie was waiting by the car, haunted and unsettled. She held out the keys.

"Did you find what you needed?"

"I forgot it. I'll bring it next time."

They were silent on the drive home: Izzie wordlessly stroking Henry's wide head, Weland floating in a little cloud of satisfaction.

"So," said Harold. "Are you going to have Adam released?"

"Of course. Eventually. There's plenty of time. We'll give him a chance to settle down a little. Get used to things. For now he's probably better off where he is. I told him not to tell anyone. Not right away. Izzie? What do you say? Let's just keep this under our hats for a while. Save it for just the right moment."

They drew to a stop in front of Weland's house, and he climbed out. "Ah. What a beautiful day. Thanks, padre. See you later, Isabel." And with a cheerful wave he strolled inside.

Harold turned in his seat. "Are you okay?"

But she had turned her ears down. He reached back and touched her knee. *Where do you want to go? Home? The hardware store? Are you working this afternoon?*

The Inn, please.

But when he pulled up at the curb, she hesitated. "Don't go yet."

"I won't." Uncertainly he turned off the car.

She gathered her knapsack and climbed out. Setting Bea in her plastic tray on the seat beside him, she hoisted Henry comfortably into her little cart. "Would you open the trunk?"

He reached into the glove compartment and tripped the lever. Beyond the windshield the nose of the car popped up. Izzie hurried around like a stranded motorist and reaching in she hauled Adam, stiff and uncurling, into the afternoon air. Then with Henry in tow she hurried her little group toward the door of the Inn and vanished inside.

Harold at Night

When he knocked on the door of the bakery after midnight a woman opened it, massive in her baker's whites, with a baseball bat in her hand. "Queer Bread," she announced, as if it were the phone and not the door she was answering.

"Is Bea Holliman here?"

"We're closed."

He held up a bulky paper bag. "I bring treats."

"You do know we're a bakery, right?"

"Please tell her it's her handyman."

For a moment he thought she was going to slug him anyway, but she called back over her shoulder, "Bea! Do you have a handyman?"

She appeared beside her, glasses dusted with flour, a round paper hat like an unfrosted cake on her head. She considered him gravely. "Never seen him before. Beat him senseless, Roo."

The building had been a firehouse for a hundred years and then empty for ten when the LGBTQ Alliance took over, renting it for a dollar a year because even haters like bread and it offered the possibility of making a little coin while still getting in their faces. At first it was awash in volunteers. Isn't there something appealing in the idea of baking bread? That yeasty aroma? All that rising possibility? It's like a career in the library—so easy to mistake it for a life of reading.

But a baker's life is hard. Like your bread you rise early. You're awake when others sleep; you sleep through what used to be your life. It's back-breaking work. Hundreds of pounds of flour lifted and stirred and then hours of rising. All that hard work, all those preparations, and in the end you're reduced to an onlooker. It's hard not to see it as an allegory. So there you are sweeping up, doing dishes, washing, sanitizing, and after a while you realize most of what you're doing is cleaning someone else's kitchen for minimum wage.

Most people quit. But Bea wanted something that took her away from her life. At the end of the day, when all the bread was sold and eaten and nothing remained—how could you be disappointed when success and failure looked exactly the same?

"So what did you bring us?" she asked.

He set the bag down on the work table. "Do you know how many places are open this time of night?"

"As a matter of fact, I do." Spreading the top of the bag she breathed in the aroma of garlic and soy. "Aren't you a nice man. There's Chinese, Roo!"

"Push your heart back in." But she came over, wiping her hands on her apron.

He started lifting out the cardboard cartons and lining them up on the table. Bea smiled as the number grew. "It's like a clown car. How hungry did you think we'd be?"

"I thought it would be better to overestimate."

"Don't worry," said Roo. "You didn't."

She was already prying off the covers. "You forgot the sweet and sour. But at least you got plenty of rice. That wasn't stupid." And stepping over to an equipment rack, she brought back three shallow steel bowls and a bouquet of spoons.

From the bag Harold drew a bottle of red wine. "Since you're taking a break."

"It's against OSHA regulations to drink in the workplace," Roo said darkly. "We could be fined just for opening it here."

"Oh. Sorry. I didn't realize."

"Men just don't think." And she drew from her pocket a plump joint, white as her apron, and tucked it in the corner of her mouth.

"OSHA's not going to mind that?" he asked mildly.

"Not if they don't hear about it. You're not planning on telling them are you?" She sparked it up and blew a stream of smoke carefully toward the vents in the ceiling. "The baking life is no picnic."

But then glancing down at the food spread out before her on the wide table she seemed to reconsider. She began to help herself.

They ate at the table. Then, while the dough continued to proof, Roo moved across to an ancient Barcalounger and drew out a battered copy of *Love's Enduring Dream*. There was no privacy; it was all one big room. But she had a white-noise machine that surrounded her with low ocean sounds, and after a while the slow sound of snoring rose and blended in.

"We can't do anything," Bea murmured with a smile. And even that seemed to reach back across the years.

"I know."

"Don't you want to?"

But he wasn't smiling. "Did Weland talk to you today?"

"Weland? No. We don't talk much anymore. Usually just when he gets an idea and wants to turn my life upside down."

She had meant it as a joke, but he seemed to give it more thought than it deserved.

"Something happened today," he said, "that you should probably know about."

"I doubt it. There's less and less about Weland that I actually need to know."

"He told Izzie he was her father."

Bea sat very still. "Of course he did."

And really, she was glad she was so tired—so that this feeling came to her not as despair but as a kind of cataclysmic chagrin. Because Weland was Weland, and it could not matter less what they had agreed on all those years ago, or how other people's lives might be affected.

"From the start," she said, "he was never really interested. I know: big surprise. He told me to get an abortion." And she lifted her eyes to him wryly. "I don't suppose I have to tell you that, do I? Do you remember? Any of this?"

"It rings a distant bell."

"And here's the funny part. I thought I had. Those pills are ninety-five percent effective. Did you know that? Ninety-five percent. But there I was. Alone and pregnant. You had left."

"I do remember."

"Yes, well. Weland didn't want to be a father, but he didn't mind being an honorary uncle. I think he even liked it. And with Jonathan it seemed like a new start. Weland could be Weland, we could be a family. We *were* a family. A great family."

"And you didn't think maybe just to prepare her?"

"Oh. Everything looks clear now, doesn't it? But I owed something to Jonathan. We both did. He loved Izzie. He deserved to be her father. And really, what do you want me to say? That I'm a terrible mother? That I ruined my daughter? That I made her life as hard as it could be? Of course I did. I know it now. How many different kinds of terrible could I be? I used to wonder about her deafness—that it was somehow my fault, as well. I used to blame myself. If I'd just given her a normal life, maybe we could all have been happy."

Harold said nothing. They sat there together for a long moment, with the low sounds of some imaginary ocean murmuring around them. Then he stirred. "Let me tell you about blame."

81.

His daughter's death was an accident. That's what the doctor had said—just bad luck. Maybe she thought she was being kind, removing any suggestion of blame. It was the universe turning against them, and really, what could you do about that?

But it left him with nothing. Not himself, not Sara, not any remaining part of the indifferent world. Because in the weeks and months that followed he had nothing but blame to live on. Nothing else to call his own.

If only he had acted quickly. If only he had known what to do. In his despair he researched all the possibilities. Anything that might have helped. Electro-shock. CPR. Pounding on those fragile ribs as if he could reach past her unresponsiveness and startle her heart awake.

He began calling the doctor at different hours of the day. What about this? What if he had done that? And she would always say, No. It wouldn't have worked, that wouldn't have helped. But it didn't matter. His whole life slipped into the hypothetical.

Even Sara, who had not been the one to let her down—even Sara had begun to look for facts. The doctors told her what it wasn't. No malformation of the valves, no tiny hole in the wall of a chamber. It was, the doctor explained, a purely electrical problem. A short-circuit. That's all. The heart works unceasingly, charging and discharging, but sometimes, occasionally, it just stops.

It was a terrible explanation. So Sara looked elsewhere. And since the doctors were no help she turned to her aunts, her uncles and cousins. She turned to gossip and stories.

She could not rest from talking about it—friends, neighbors, strangers—until the therapist told her she had to stop. So Sara began writing letters. To distant relatives and friends, drifting back along the family tree. She became fixated on how people died in her family, fascinated by the randomness—the varieties of accidental death. Great Aunt Daisy, who had simply keeled over at the age of 92 like a light switched off. And what a mercy that was. And Cousin Betty, who was out hiking in the mountains at Banff when the beauty of the scene must have caused her to miss her footing, and down she fell. And Great Uncle Walter, who had apparently choked on his biscuits and gravy, though at the funeral home Mr. Raskin observed that his windpipe was clear.

Sara was not overly imaginative, but after a while even she began to wonder. And one day, when she was having her yearly physical, she had asked about her own heart, and the nurse had wired her up to an EKG. And it was there, hidden in the static—a little rhythm of its own—so occasional it seemed like an accident, except that it came back and back like a distant signal running through the rise and fall.

She began taking a little pill—it was as simple as that. Though the rage that rose in Ash's breast was like its own terrible reprieve. Not all his fault, at least. Not all.

But that's the thing about blame. It's like water, it always finds its proper level.

"My daughter was born deaf," he said.

Bea looked startled. "I didn't know."

"But there was an operation."

"Yes. We looked into that with Izzie. But there was nothing to be done."

He nodded. Sometimes it was too severe. Sometimes the separate little bones weren't separate enough. And every surgery had its risks. But this one had gone smoothly. She had recovered so quickly—the young are so resilient, the surgeon had said—and soon little Bea was talking like a Mina Bird, chattering all day long. And it really had seemed, as Sara said, that a hand had reached down and mended even this. But in the end it wasn't God. It was the anesthetic that had reached out to touch the tiny insufficiency at the center of her heart.

"I can't even imagine," said Bea, "how awful it must be. But you couldn't have known."

He hesitated.

"When I came back all those years ago. When I first met Izzie, I felt bad for her. Bad for you. But I felt something else, as well. I was glad it hadn't worked out for you. Weland and the baby. I was glad you weren't living happily ever after. Even the deafness. I was glad of that."

But then history had run its old loop again, and he had left. And he tried to put it all behind him. He made his own life. He had his own child. And when he discovered that she, too, was deaf, he had felt it was a kind of judgment on him, for the way he had behaved.

But she was safe and healthy. And he resolved to be kinder, more at peace. Perhaps the universe had a sense of humor. Or a sense of something else: bonds within bonds. It seemed only right that he name her Bea. It seemed a kind of parallel life, running along beside all that he might have had.

And then she died, and all that blame came into the world.

And it brought back something else, as well. When Sara had been searching for an explanation she looked everywhere. Up and down both family trees. And if she had finally found her fault, she had found his, as well. He had, she discovered, a great uncle who was deaf. And a distant cousin. It turned out, it ran in his father's family. So of course it ran in his.

And if his daughter hadn't been deaf, she wouldn't have needed the anesthetic.

It had always seemed like a series of separate tragedies that marked the path of his life. There was one kind with his daughter. Another kind with Bea and Weland and all the rest. Differing moments of blame. He had known the universe was speaking to him, reaching out to highlight the connections of his life. Telling him all the ways he was falling short. But it turns out it was telling him something else, as well.

Bea sat very still. Her hand had settled onto his. "What are you saying, Ash?"

"Izzie," he said. "Did you know she was mine?"

And really, thought Bea. How could that be fair?

The past was past. Wasn't that the point? All your mistakes over and done? Bad, yes. Very bad. But finished. You could put them behind you. And she had. She had taken the pills. She had made a new start. But what was she to do now? When everything she'd built her life on was suddenly wrong?

"You never thought she might be mine?" he asked.

And she peered into his face—raggedy beard, long hair, a stranger once again. And really, she wanted to slap him. Now he showed up? Out of the blue? With this?

"And what about you?" she demanded. "What did you think? Before you just ran away?"

He looked haunted, hollow-eyed. "I didn't."

"Well, how is this suddenly my fault?"

She had taken the pills. But her body's response had been so underwhelming. A little cramping, spotting. A little queasiness. For God's sake—she had been nothing but queasy then! Her whole life a train wreck. How could such a paltry discomfort mean anything at all? And by the time she was aware, once again, of being pregnant, it couldn't have seemed less like a new beginning.

And if she had imagined once or twice, in the lonely moments, some different life—well, Ash was long gone. And if Weland didn't want to be a father, he didn't mind being an honorary uncle. And afterwards, when she had pieced her life together, it was something to have Weland's child, even unacknowledged. It shaped her life— her place in the department, her sense of herself at the center of things. Even when she disdained him, it was always somehow Weland who gave her standing—who made it seem like a journey growing out of her truest self. And now?

What would Izzie think now? What *could* she think? Her own mother? Not just lying all these years—that was a crime she'd already committed—but the foolishness of it, the ridiculousness. You hear all those stories of men suddenly confronted with paternity months or years later. They may be callous or selfish or deceived. They may be angry or wrong. But they're never foolish. But to be her mother, and not even know her own daughter all these years?

"We can't tell her," Bea whispered.

"Oh," he said. He seemed to sag under the weight. "Oh, no, no, no. Don't say that."

"We can't. Not now."

"We have to. Of course we do."

"How can we?"

"She's my daughter, Bea. "

"Not now," she said. "Not yet."

"Please."

"We can't. Maybe never."

She gripped his hand. "Imagine what it would do. What would she think? How could she believe us? How could she ever trust us again?"

"That's not fair," he pleaded. "How can that be fair?"

"Oh, Ash."

"And Weland? Fucking Weland? Again and again? He gets every-thing his own way?"

"It's what's best for her," she said. "It's what she needs. It's what I need. Please."

"And what about me? What do I need?" His voice was an ache. "What do I have after all of these years?"

"This," she said. "All this. We have each other. We have Izzie. She knows you now. She loves you. You see that, don't you? You can't tell her. Promise me that. You have to promise me."

He let his head sink onto the hard pillow of their clasped hands. "I hate Weland."

"I know."

"I hate him so much."

She reached down and stroked the ragged beard, smoothed the long hair back. "Don't think about him," she whispered. "Don't think about hate. Think about Izzie. Think about love."

83.

They began to meet in the lee of their lives, surrounded by the sleeping world. He set the alarm for 1:00 am, carving out of the darkness a second stretch of day—once again making for himself two lives out of one.

The next time he brought Thai food. Roo carried her meal to the recliner like an indulgent chaperone, while Harold and Bea sat toying with their forks until the sound of snoring blended with the murmuring waves. Then he climbed to his feet, stepping behind her with a determinedly casual expression that brought a smile to her lips. She was covered from head to food—white hat, white tunic, white pants—but every nerve in her body lay along the flushed surface of her cheeks and throat. His fingers alighted. They traced the line of a tendon down to where it slipped beneath her collar. She closed her eyes.

She was married; twice married. A failed mother, a failed artist. But he seemed to find something new in the ridge of her collar bone, the little valley at the base of her neck. She leaned back to give him more skin to touch and felt his lips on her throat.

"As a painter," she whispered, "I was always taught that love is in the eyes. But do you know how long it's been since someone actually touched me?"

She felt his fingers drift up to her top button and ease it out of its constraint. Then the next, and the next. The tunic spread wide under the pressure of his touch. But the thought of her bra almost sank her. Plain, workmanlike. "I'm sorry," she whispered. And he stopped at once. She cursed herself, reaching up to press his hands. "I'm just sorry I'm not wearing something prettier."

"What could possibly be prettier?"

"Do you want to undo it?"

And it said everything about her daunted spirit after all these long years that she waited uncertainly for his answer. When his hands withdrew, her heart dipped. But then she felt his fingers slip past the back of her collar and trace their way down her spine to the clasp.

The bra relaxed like a sloughed skin, releasing her into the warmth of his hands. And in that moment the ruffled snoring gave way to a sudden grunt and the creak of the Barcalounger. Abruptly he withdrew, turning away as Bea hurriedly re-buttoned and with an air of great casualness took a swallow of red wine to ease the tightness in her throat.

Roo stood and stretched hugely. "You leaving us?"

He was gathering up the take-out containers, stuffing everything back into the paper bag with a face of solemn distraction. "Miles to go before I sleep."

He had turned strange again before her eyes after the warm familiarity of his touch.

"We're much obliged for the grub," said Roo. "You're welcome any time."

"I'll keep that in mind." And with a glance that skated lightly over Bea's flushed cheeks, he said, "Good night, ladies," and let himself out the door.

Roo came to expect him. She accepted the food gravely and unpacked it onto the table. And Bea, perhaps with a wispy cloud of smoke escaping from her lips, perhaps with a cup of coffee before her, would nod as if he were just passing through—another incidental arrival at the late-night bus station of the heart. More and more she had a sketch pad on her knee, for in the safety of a time and place so securely outside their lives she had began to draw again. She took to sketching Harold's hands as a kind of foreplay, and when she set the pad aside for the meal it lay open as a reminder of all the touching to come.

They clung to an air of playfulness as if it would protect them—from disappointment, perhaps; from using up too quickly all that they had saved from the years. She would lead him into the slender shadow of the ovens and, standing only inches apart, they would slowly undress each other as if passing the moment back and forth—unbuttoning, unzipping, coaxing some bit of fabric aside, bringing one more narrow stretch of skin into view.

His body came slowly back to her. Pale and foreign, it was like a language she had lost, and each night she would learn it again. Once she dipped her hands in flour and smoothed them over his skin, slipping beneath his shirt until he was coated in a fine white haze.

"So that's what it's like to be a loaf of bread," he murmured, his mouth as dry as the flour.

And that, too, took them back. The building force of it. Anticipation, itself, a kind of treasure, heaped in a cupboard filled to bursting.

The next afternoon in the mudroom Izzie noticed the smear of flour on his work shirt like a ectoplasmic hand over the heart. It was only a life of the most fundamental duplicity that allowed him to rub it casually away. "Must be from the plaster."

"There's more on the back."

He waited patiently as she brushed his shirt clean. But the next night when he knocked on the door Bea lent him a set of baker's whites, and drawing them on, he slipped effortlessly into this newest version of himself.

She started buying herself lingerie. She had been young enough to disdain it with Weland, and neither Jonathan nor Joan had been moved by its frivolity. She had suggested it once, but Jonathan smiled and told her she should wear whatever she liked, and Joan just thought it was silly. But now she went shopping and, with a leisurely gaze, took in all the varieties of color and style. Bras, panties, camisoles, teddies—in anything but white. So that this, too, became part of their anticipation. Walking to work she felt it against her skin, and something in her stance, the tiny glimpse of color peaking out, would spark an answering gleam in his eyes, spinning out between them another moment's delay on the way to nakedness.

The rules were the rules of that long ago summer—one sense at a time, holding themselves in check.

"Listen," she would whisper. And squeezing one hand down past her waistband she would marvel at how wet she could become. And in the silence he would catch the faint scent of sea-salt rising on the yeasty air and hear above the muffled background of ocean sounds the slick amphibian sliding of her fingers.

"Tell me how I feel," she would whisper. And then, as they grew more adventurous in the sheltered corner of the oven, "Tell me how I taste."

She would dab a teasing fingertip of sweet and sour sauce on her neck, her breast, and once—as he unbuttoned her white and flour-dusted pants—down the pale slope of her belly. And it would be her turn to assume an expression of the most distant contemplation as he traced his tongue along the trail. She slouched a little lower in her chair like a teenager in the back of a car— nothing they did made her feel so young—and her hands came to rest on his head with little caresses of encouragement.

"So tell me what it's like to be a baker?" he murmured, raising his lips from her skin.

"Oh, there's nothing easy about it. You have to be so gentle with the dough. You have to find that secret shape that every loaf is waiting to be."

And though a tight electric quiver was rising through her belly, she continued to whisper aloud as if it were a kind of test: to prove she wasn't lost in this feeling, to prove it was so playful and unimportant that the world would never bother to take it away.

When he left, Bea would walk him to the door with an air of re-newed formality, and he would slip out into the darkness as if swimming home through the night.

84.

He began to follow different routes home. In good weather and bad he left the bakery and drove through the half familiar streets of that college town as if he could bind this present happiness onto the fabric of his past. And perhaps it was an offshoot of such determined mending that, driving past the only all-night grocery store through a deluge little short of Noah's, he saw a man loading boxes into a pick-up truck and in the wash of headlights caught a glimpse of his face.

He was tented in rain gear, lurching from the sheltered entrance to the waiting truck and back, working with a focused fury amid the pounding rain. It took Harold a moment to realize just how drunk he was. When the pick-up drove north out of town, he followed.

Rain runneling down his windshield; the damp chill of Miss Pru's ancient Volkswagen. He might have been back in Gaillard on his way to the island—heart coiling with excitement, duck pants sprawled in the back. Every moment was always on the verge of another. Up ahead the pickup drove steadily, tracing its way through the wild night. At a long bank of trees it turned left and rumbled over the ancient fretwork of a bridge.

The canal below was more ditch than stream, as if someone designed a river with no memory of how water worked. Beyond the bridge it widened into a pond. Chained to the bank was the ancient hulk of a canal boat like a half-sunk boiler—its wandering days long gone—and a ramp like a rusty sidewalk reached up to the forward deck.

Slowly Harold drew up beside the truck and, leaning across to the passenger side, rolled down his window. "I didn't want to startle you."

But Jonathan was too drunk to startle. He gazed at him patiently as if memory were a bus and he'd grown accustomed to waiting. "I know you."

"Yes."

"I'm in the middle of something here."

"Maybe I can help."

The rain pattered around them as Jonathan seemed to weigh his choices. "Get that last one," he said and staggered up the gangway.

Under the sodden shelter of a canvas awning Jonathan stowed the boxes against the wall of the cabin. Then straightening up he peeled off his gear. All that furious effort should have belonged to a wild mountain of a man, but he grew smaller and smaller with each layer until he stood there in worn shirt and khakis: neat, thin, and shocked by drink. Turning he drew from among the stacked groceries a fresh bottle of vodka and—after a moment's consideration—a can of beef stew. He lit the flame on a gas hotplate and set the can on top. As the air warmed under the canvas a smell of engine oil, turpentine, and damp wool gathered in a despondent cloud.

"I'd heard you were living on a houseboat. I pictured something else."

Jonathan picked up a coffee mug that might have been there since breakfast. He emptied it over the side and refilled it from the bottle. "No one should live on a boat in the winter. The sun didn't show its face until March. I ran through all my black and most of the darker blues."

"I heard you stopped painting."

"That sounds like something Weland would say."

"I think he was worried."

"Really? Is that what you think?"

"He said he hadn't seen anything new in almost a year."

"That sounds more like it. I've been sketching. A lot of sketching. I haven't really had the heart to paint. Though lately the sun's been nice. God's excuse for Cadmium Yellow. Did he send you here? Weland?"

"No."

"You didn't tell him you were coming?"

"No."

"You might as well sit down, then."

Harold lowered himself into a deck chair as Jonathan looked around for another mug. "No. That's all right. I'm good."

Jonathan shrugged and settled into the other chair. "How's Bea?"

He felt a blush creeping up his cheeks with the memory of all they had just been doing. "I think she's all right. Joan's off in California. Sounds as though she might not come back for a while."

"And Izzie?"

"She's okay. Have you spoken to Weland lately?"

Jonathan peered down into his mug as if the answer might be there. "Not as such."

"He told Izzie he was her father. Adam, too."

"Well," he said. "You can't ask a snake not to be a snake." But then he seemed to lose heart. "Do you have children?"

For an instant the distance closed between them. "A daughter. Two daughters."

"Then you know. I keep thinking about Izzie. What I did to make her so angry."

I wish we'd burned down Weland's house instead of my father's.

"You knew?"

"Of course. I'm not foolish."

"She's crazy with guilt. It's eating her up."

"Good."

"Don't say that."

But Jonathan's gaze was bleak.

"You have to forgive her," said Harold.

"I'm not even sure what that means anymore."

"Izzie loves you."

"I know."

"For Heaven's sake! Don't hate her. Hate Weland. He's the one who deserves it."

But Jonathan seemed to be listening from a long way away. "I've known Weland for thirty years. Do you really think there's anything you can tell me about him?"

"Did you know he was there that night? Walking by? At the studio? He smelled the smoke and he just walked away."

"Weland is Weland."

"He's a monster."

"He's not a monster."

"He's selfish. Dishonest. He's a thief. He stole your painting. Your wife."

"Oh, yes."

"He's callous. Unthinking. I don't need to tell you that."

"No. You don't."

"And what about that night in the park? He gave your name to the police. Did you know that?"

Jonathan sighed. "He told me. He always tells me. He came and sobbed, and he begged. He said it was killing him. He said it was weighing on his soul."

"And what did you say?"

"What could I possibly say?"

Jonathan reached down and felt the can of stew. He turned off the flame. "It's no good hating Weland. Believe me. I've tried."

"He's horrible. He's a terrible person."

"Yes. But he's something else, as well."

"Don't say genius."

"No. Well, maybe. It's as good a word as any. He sees things other people don't. Makes them into something new."

"That doesn't give him the right to ruin people's lives."

"No. But if you had to choose between the selfishness and all the beauty he's made. What would you do?"

"I'd run him over with my car."

Jonathan nodded as if there was always that. Cautiously he picked up the hot can and peeled back the lid, but he seemed unimpressed with the contents. "Art is never easy. That's the whole point. The stakes are too high. They're supposed to be. If they're not, then you're doing it wrong. You need to be a certain kind of person to hold up under that. Self-centered, yes. Egotistical."

"A monster?"

"Maybe. By any decent definition. But so what? The world needs art."

"It needs kindness too, doesn't it? It needs compassion."

"Oh, yes. Though maybe not as much." He refilled his mug. "People need kindness. But the world? The world doesn't care. Surely we've learned that much. It turns its back on kindness. Again and again. What it needs is something larger than itself. Something to admire. Something to draw it back from the edge of ruin. If Weland didn't exist, we'd have to invent him."

"That's ridiculous."

Jonathan shrugged. "You could imagine a world without *The Blue Robe*. Of course you could. It wouldn't be that different. The painting isn't earthshaking. No single painting is. You can say, Oh we'd be lost without Leonardo or Michelangelo or Raphael. But we wouldn't. If we didn't have the *Mona Lisa* or *The School of Athens* we'd have something else instead. The world goes on. Art goes on. That's not the point. The point is: do you put up with Weland's callousness in order to have his work? It's as simple as that. Is his particular kind of beauty worth the rest of it?"

"Absolutely not."

Jonathan smiled. "That's because you know him. It's almost always a problem—separating the artist and the art. They're rarely anyone you want to meet. Michelangelo? He was a brute. Raphael? An enormous ego. But what does that matter?"

Out in the rain and darkness there was a sudden glow. Across the pond, a bubble of lamplight was moving over the grass. Three men, slender and pale—it took a moment to realize they were naked—were hurrying down to the water's edge. One of them set the lamp on the ground and, laughing, they plunged into the dark water. Harold thought of the little painting on Weland's desk, small and bright as a dream.

Jonathan peered out through the rain. "Do you know Matisse's *Dance*? It's a study—a sketch really. Five figures in a circle. There is not a single blessed thing about it that's realistic. It's just color and movement. But it makes you so happy. It makes you want to smile. It makes you want to stop thinking.

"Too often when you look at a painting you can't help yourself. It's an occupational hazard. You think about the composition, the light. You think about the brushwork. About all the effort involved. All the hard work. But it's such a distortion, all that thinking. It's such a waste of beauty. But when you let your mind go—just feel it, just for a moment—can you imagine the relief? That's the gift that art gives us. A moment free from thought. A moment when every desire is met."

He gazed wearily into Harold's face. "That first time, years ago, when he stole my painting, my blue, I was lost. I was so angry. I hated him, more than I can say. But everything is a choice. I could choose not to hate him—after a while, at least. And the truth was, he had changed it. He had taken my painting and made it better. Made it into something remarkable. So what could I do? Oh, I know. You think I'm ridiculous. You think I'm weak. Well, there's nothing you can say I haven't already said to myself. But I knew from the first—I think I knew—that I'd never have what Weland had. That insight. That talent. You might as well call it genius. And all the envy in the world doesn't change a thing."

"So, what? You just forgive him?"

"Oh," said Jonathan. "I'll never forgive him."

"But don't you want to get even? Don't you want to hurt him back?"

"Are you looking for advice?"

"I'm looking for a strategy."

"Run away. Far away. As fast as you can. There's no winning against Weland. There's no revenge. He's too indifferent, too self-absorbed. He's stronger than hate."

"So what can I do?"

"Nothing."

The young men were done with their swim now. Picking up the lantern they traced their way back toward the white building, and the bubble of light vanished as if closing a door on all that it might mean.

"Do you know what art is for?"

"Oh, don't you start."

Jonathan smiled grimly. "It's for reaching beyond what you already know. That's it's purpose. To make us struggle. To take us somewhere we've never been. But Weland has never learned to struggle. He's had it easy from the start. So now he's lost. He's trying to reach after something new. Something undiscovered. But everything he does is what he's always done. You think he doesn't know? You think it isn't tearing him apart? There's no point trying to ruin his life. He's doing that himself."

"So what do I do?"

"Save yourself. Save Izzie and Bea. Find kindness where you can. Make a life out of kindness."

"And love?"

"Oh," said Jonathan. It was more breath than word. He climbed to his feet. Moving softly to the cabin door, he drew it open. Down a short flight of stairs the crowded room was aglow. Low ceiling, bulkheads, a narrow workmanlike bed. And lying under the covers was Weland, drowned in sleep, one bare shoulder painted with lamplight.

"Ask me about art," said Jonathan wearily. "Or beauty. Ask me about work. But love. No. There's nothing I can tell you about love."

Harold Undone

85

Harold and Izzie resumed their work, reconstructing from the dust and wreckage of the mudroom their own private version of the world. Their lunches—canned soup and sandwich, fresh-baked cookie—seemed like something both nostalgic and new. And in the moments of rest they would sit and talk—Izzie tracing a fingertip along the spider's back or running her hand over Henry's wide head as if smoothing the world into a more comfortable shape. And Harold was free to take in every gesture without fear that she might notice how intently he watched.

"He's not my father. I don't believe him."

"That's right," he said. "He's a liar. Don't let it worry you."

"But how could he do that? How could he pretend all those years?"

"He's Weland. You know what he's like. Don't let him hurt your feelings."

"But why, Harold? Why doesn't he love me?"

"He does. Of course he does. How could he not?"

"All these years?"

"It doesn't matter. He doesn't matter."

"I hate him."

"Good. That's good. We can hate him together."

And Izzie would talk about all she was learning. Every spell was different; you had to fit it to the person, and the person to the moment. Weight, dosage, personality—you took them all into account. And of course you had to decide what you wanted. There was an itching spell, a sleepless spell, and one that brought on gnawing hunger; there were aches in the joints, little flashes of light, and a jumpy anxiety that made you flinch at every sound. Izzie recounted the symptoms with relish, practicing each incantation, picturing all the ways in which Weland might suffer, while Harold basked in the companionability of their smoldering rage. What was love, after all, if not choosing sides? They had never shared her growing-up. Harold had missed out on all the early years. But now they had this in common, and the slow catalogue of spells took on all the pleasures of a childhood piano recital.

When Weland arrived, haggard and drawn, he bound them closer still.

"What a mess," he said frowning at the seat of a chair where a game of tic-tac-toe had been sketched in plaster dust. He wiped it clean and then peered down at his dusty hand as if it were a homeless person about to ask him for spare change. "It amazes me that you're still here. When there's so much that needs to be done."

"Idle hands are the devil's playground," said Harold. He drew a bandana from his pocket and held it out.

Weland wiped his fingers hurriedly and let it drop. "We've got some decisions to make."

"Are you hungry, Wheedle?"

He turned to find her weighing him with her eyes like a tailor measuring for a suit.

"No. Thank you, Isabel."

"Do you want a sandwich?"

He hesitated. He had grown more uncertain around her since the announcement of his paternity. "That's very sweet of you."

"Soup and crackers? A glass of milk?"

"I'm fine, thank you."

"I made cookies. I can get you a cookie. I could make you some coffee."

Weland seemed to consider her afresh, as if he hadn't until then recognized all the benefits of having a child. "Well. That does sound nice. I could certainly use a cup of coffee."

"And a cookie?"

He was pleased to be able to give her this, as well. "Yes. Thank you. A cookie would be delightful."

She hurried out of the room as Harold watched her go.

"I thought you'd stop by before this," said Weland peevishly.

"I meant to. But something came up."

"Damn it, Harold! I need your full attention on this. Things are getting desperate."

"I thought they were desperate before."

"This is no time for jokes."

Izzie returned with a plate of cookies and a mug of coffee. Weland took a distracted sip. "I think what we need is to—"

"Is it alright? I made it strong. The way you like it."

"It's fine, dear. Thank you."

"And the cookie? I made that, too."

He refocused his attention, buoyed by her concern. He took a small bite and chewed. "It's very good. Delicious." He took another. Then he noticed her patched and mended overalls. "What are you wearing?"

"I'm a handy-girl."

"Did you make those clothes?"

"I improved them."

He weighed the sight a moment longer. "They could be more attractive, don't you think? You could be such a pretty girl."

Harold laid a hand on her shoulder, but Weland was already moving on. He took another sip. He was looking distinctly jittery, as if every moment were scraping away at his nerves. "We've got to make some progress. We're running out of time. It's going to be a disaster."

Izzie looked cheered by the thought. "At least you have the parade."

"I keep telling you! There's no parade."

"But everybody loves a parade," said Harold.

"Stop it! We need to focus. It's about the paintings. That's what's important. That's what people will focus on."

"But aren't they going to want to see something new?"

"Jesus wept! I don't *have* anything new! That's the whole problem."

"Well," said Harold philosophically. "I suppose we could just put your picture up on the hardware building. That would be new."

"You're not helping!" he snapped, though after a moment his expression grew thoughtful. "Hm."

"Your picture?"

"No. Though it's not a terrible idea. A mural. Right there in the center of town. Big as you can make it. *The Blue Robe.* That's the obvious choice. That'll give them something to look at. Something to remember me by. Everywhere they stand they'll be looking up."

"It's not exactly new."

"It's better than new. It's perfect. Now we just need someone to paint it."

"You're not going to paint it, Wheedle?" Izzie's face was the picture of concern.

He hesitated. "I could, of course."

"I mean, otherwise, people walking by. They'll see someone else do all the work."

"The work is making the painting," he said. "I already did that. The mural is just enlarging it."

But he was turning it over in his mind now, tapping the last of the cookie intently on the plate as if to hurry the ideas along. "You know, young Isabel, you may have hit on something." Turning decisively he handed her the plate and empty mug. "I've got to get some supplies. Do you have other tools? Another hammer? Nails? Maybe a saw?"

"I wouldn't be surprised," said Harold.

"We'll meet at the studio in an hour. Don't be late!" And he hurried out.

Izzie stood gazing after him with a thoughtful expression, like someone having second thoughts about dosages.

"What was that?" asked Harold.

"Nothing." She peered down at her overalls and brushed distractedly at a smear of plaster dust.

"Don't listen to him," he said gently. "I like your clothes. But really? *Can I get you coffee? Would you like a cookie?* What have you done with Isabel?"

She smiled.

"Are you casting a spell?" he demanded.

"Maybe. I don't really have enough of his essence yet."

"His essence."

"You know. Hair, finger nails, pieces of skin. You need the essence of a person to form the simulacrum."

"You're making a voodoo doll."

"Reeve says we shouldn't call it that. That's just an urban myth. This is a basic transference spell. That's all. But I have to collect his essence first."

"Then what? You stick pins in it?"

"Probably not," she said.

"And what about now? Did you put something in his coffee?"

"And his cookie. It's a luck potion."

"You're trying to give Weland luck?"

"Oh no," she said. "Nothing like that."

Harold gathered up the tools as Izzie hurried upstairs to change. She came down with barrettes in her hair and an outfit he'd never seen before. Pink eye shadow, pink pleated skirt, knee socks, and a unicorn t-shirt that looked so scathingly ironic he couldn't help smiling. "Now those are pretty clothes."

But that made her pause. "Do I look stupid?"

"No. Never. You look like a very pretty girl."

"Good," she said with a glint of steel.

He watched as she assembled a plate of cookies then carefully washed her hands.

"You're not going to offer me one, are you?"

She looked up in surprise. "Did you want one? I thought you didn't like them." She went over to the cookie tin and lifted one out. She put it in a little zip lock bag and set it on top of the others. "We'll keep this one separate."

"You know," he said after a moment. "We probably shouldn't be poisoning Weland."

But she could tell he didn't mean it.

86

Weland was ready for them long before they arrived—his white coveralls rumpled and stained, a ragged look around the eyes. He had shoved the sofa back against one wall and as they stepped in he was wrestling with a heavy bundle like a body rolled in a carpet.

"Finally! Where have you been? Give me a hand with this!"

It was a thick roll of canvas doubled on the spool, and as he dragged it free it expanded like a rubber raft inflating in a closet. The more he struggled the more furious he grew. "God damn it. God *damn* it!"

"How much have you given him?" Harold whispered.

"I know, righ'?"

She settled Bea and Henry in their cart against the wall, and then in her sweetest voice, "Can we giv' you a hand, Wheedle?"

He straightened up panting. "Those are the damned stretchers. Ten feet by twelve. They're the biggest we can get without a special order. And that canvas is a goddam mess! I usually have someone do this for me."

"Maybe now would be a good time to call them," said Harold.

"I want to keep this on the down low."

"The down low?"

"What?" he snapped. "You don't speak English now?"

In all the years that he had thought about revenge, filling his nights with dreams of getting even, he had never imagined it like this. Over time it had grown into something grandiose—some terrible disaster that would ruin Weland's perfect life and bend it into something more resembling his own. He had never thought that somehow the whole dark mechanism could slip into something so playful.

He thought of Jonathan's warning: that Weland was stronger than hate. But this was more than hate—to be reaching out from such a startling turn in his own life: wrapped in surprise and an unexpected happiness. *Don't think about hate,* Bea had said. *Think about love.* He had thought it was gone forever, but here it was. Love, family. His life returned to him, but lived askance. Preserved in the margins of the day. And all the old hatred grown somehow distant; revenge the merest technicality. As if in a kind of overdue exchange, all his most furious thoughts were subsumed into the pleasures of a father-daughter game.

The stretchers were made to slot together at the corners, but there was barely floor space to lay them out. The longer ones had warped and they kept easing out of their slots—it was like working with pudding—and Weland was a crazy man wrestling each corner in turn. Eventually Harold eased him out of the way and held the pieces together while Izzie nailed. But even then the slats transformed themselves into a wildly bending rectangle.

"Don't worry," said Weland grimly. "The canvas will tighten it." But when he turned back to the unspooled fabric, "Jesus Christ!"

"Maybe we shoul' have some lunch," suggested Izzie.

"Not now."

"How about some coffee? I brought some cookies."

And for the first time Weland noticed the unicorn t-shirt and pink skirt. "Now that's a nice outfit. See how pretty you look?" And because she had so clearly made an effort he said, "Maybe just a cookie. I'm jumpy enough as it is."

They were like a committee struggling over a pile of laundry. Weland kept yanking at the fabric until they were able to coax him away. Then Harold knelt and drew the canvas taut while Izzie, with the eye of a seamstress, guided the scissors between his hands. They worked their way across the sheet like a pair of mice trimming a circus tent, then dragged it over the wooden frame.

"Okay. Good," said Weland. "That'll work." Though he was running a hand again and again over his chin as if even his own skin was turning unruly. "Just stretch it out. That's right. Keep it smooth."

There was no room to work. Clambering over the frame Harold and Izzie fought to keep the fabric tight, tugging it this way and that as Weland hovered with the staple gun.

"Pull it there!"

"I'm pulling it there."

"It's slippin'!"

"Over this way."

"Com' on, Wheedle! Just staple already."

"It's not straight!"

"For God's sake--."

Into this moment stepped Winona like the first bystander on the scene of a traffic accident. She gazed for a moment at the tangled scene. "Have you ever stretched a canvas, Weland?"

"Of course I have! How hard can it be?"

"It's like making a bed. Have you ever done that?"

He scowled at her. "If you're here to help, help."

"Opposite corners first. Then work your way around."

"I don't know why you think you're so smart."

There was barely room to move—they had to crawl over the arm of the sofa to get to the final corner—but Izzie and Harold worked their way around with the staple gun while Weland watched. As the canvas grew the sheer scale of it seemed to oppress him. With the last staple he edged his way closer, frowning down at the vast expanse.

"Okay," he said grimly. "Now we've got to prep the son of a bitch."

"What do you mean we?"

But Weland wasn't listening.

Like a pair of weary housepainters, Izzie and Harold began to prime the canvas. "Not so thick," called Weland. "Lots of thin coats."

"Really? You're just going to stand there?"

"What am I paying you for?"

Izzie looked intrigued. "Is he paying us?"

"Don't talk!" said Weland. "And don't move so much."

He had dragged his easel back from the wall and started to paint.

"Really? You're not even going to help?" said Harold.

"This is helping."

His anxiety, fluttering like a moth around the unfinished canvas, now settled into its familiar shape. "That damned Courbet," he muttered grimly. "What the hell am I supposed to do with this?" And turning to Winona, "Bring me a scotch, would you?"

"I'm not your bartender, Weland."

"I can do it," said Izzie cheerfully. "And I could make you a sandwich?"

"Sure," he said. "Why not?"

She made sandwiches from the cold cuts in the fridge, marking Weland's with a bright line of ketchup along one edge, just so she could keep track. She arranged on each plate a rainbow of gherkins, cherry tomatoes, peppers, and the small cocktail onions that Weland used to shock his mouth into excitement, taking a moment to moisten the onions with a little splash of potion.

Returning with the tray she entered a scene transformed. In the spot beside Weland there was now a neat pile of folded clothing where Winona used to be. And across the room she stood, graceful as a caryatid, clutching a white sheet to her breasts. Harold was slowly re-priming the uppermost section—just for compositional balance—and Weland was painting with an easy rhythm.

"Finally," said Harold. "More food."

"Just put it anywhere," said Weland. But he noticed the arrange-ment on the plates and popped an onion into his mouth.

"Thank you," said Harold as she brought his sandwich over, and lowering his voice, "Is there anything I should know?"

"Don't eat the onions."

"Right."

She carried a plate to Winona, who gave her a quick smile.

"Don't move, damn it! I'm painting!"

"Are you doing my face?"

"Don't talk!"

"How about one of those onions?" she murmured.

"How abou' a tomato?" Izzie reached up and slipped it into her mouth.

"You're a doll," she said and chewed.

87

When the canvas was primed they lifted it like a pair of stage hands and leaned it against the wall over the rows of paintings. Then Harold wandered back to where Weland stood, gazing irritably down at the easel and nibbling on an onion.

He had painted a huge room, dark-walled and shadowed as if rooted in some unlit past, and he'd filled it with people—Izzie transformed into an elegantly frocked young ingenue, Harold, by turns, a workman bracing the canvas and a deliveryman poised at the door, and Winona multiplied into a trio of women on a plinth in the center of the room.

"*The Artist's Studio*. It's a staple from every period. This bit is Titian, but without all the pinks and whites. The shadows are Rembrandt. Most of the rest is Courbet."

"You know," said Harold, "it's not altogether terrible."

But Weland turned to him bleakly. "You're a figment of my imagination. How could you possibly know?"

Izzie was coming over now, and Winona, reading the familiar signs, was drawing on her clothes. She picked up her plate and carried it over, gazing at the painting without surprise. "Is my butt really that big?"

"It might not be. That might be Courbet."

Choosing the last onion from the plate she set it tenderly between his lips. "You're just hungry, Weland. Sit down and eat your sandwich."

Harold couldn't help it: a faint glimmer of sympathy. And even Izzie seemed to hesitate. But a witch's resolve had no room for pity. "That's right, Wheedle. Eat your sandwich. And have another cookie, why don't you?"

He ate slowly, delaying the moment as long as he could—all

the while glancing up at the huge canvas like an animal at bay. Finally he stood and, rolling his work table reluctantly forward, set his copy of *The Blue Robe* on the easel beside him. The painting looked suddenly small and secretive, determined to give nothing away.

He loaded his brush and turned, but he couldn't seem to orient himself. His hand seemed unanchored in the broad expanse. He started first at the shoulder, then the upward curve of the back, then down at the hip, but he broke off again and again—put down the brush for a larger one, then smaller. Nothing worked. When finally, out of a confusion of shapes, the line of the figure began to emerge it was clearly off. Even the texture of Jonathan's painting, which he had once captured so effortlessly, eluded him. He grew more enraged with every attempt—"Jesus Christ. Jesus fucking Christ!"—until Winona, stepping forward, laid a hand on his shoulder.

"Don't!" he snarled.

"It's okay. I'll pose. You paint me. You can take the proportions from life."

Though that, of course, had always been the problem.

Harold and Izzie dragged the sofa over as Winona hurried out of her clothes. Then she arranged herself as best she could, glancing over at the painting to gauge her position.

"Stop moving, for God's sake!"

But with a real woman posing, his anguish re-doubled. He tried to imagine the body into a classical version of itself so he could transform it back into the painting he himself had made, but even as the picture filled in, the distortions grew. The flow of muscles twisted and bunched; the skin turned glossy and hard.

"God damn it! God damn it!" He daubed here and there as new mistakes kept appearing. Winona leaned forward, willing him to do better, and even Izzie felt a pang. But it was Harold—who had spent so much of his life waiting for exactly this: the sight of Weland hollow-eyed in despair—who stepped forward.

"I think what we need is a drink."

They rearranged themselves once more, this time around crackers and cheese, and all the day's frustrations became indistinguishable from a series of cocktail parties. Weland sat exhausted on the sofa staring up at the terrible picture as if it had arrived while he was out and he'd been unable to cancel delivery.

"It's a mural," said Harold. "It'll be too far away to see the mistakes."

"People on the moon could see them."

"What about using a grid?" said Winona. "You lay it out, transfer it."

"Why not just fingerpaints? I could smear it on with my hands."

"Then why not just get some muralist?" Harold said. "You can hire someone."

"Who?"

He hesitated. "Joan? I bet she could do it."

"Ha! And then she could say she painted it."

"Then how about one of those billboard people?" said Winona. "Just hire her to put this up. No one's going to mistake her for an artist. We sneak her into town. She works behind a curtain, and when she leaves we unveil the mural."

Weland leaned into the story. "She'd have to sign a non-disclosure agreement."

"I'm sure she would. But we'd have to pay her."

"I could pay her. That's not a problem." But in the end it was too much even for Weland. "Oh my God. A billboard. This is a nightmare! How did this happen? How did I come to this? I wish we'd never started! I wish you'd all just kept your mouths shut! God damn it! I'd like to set the whole thing on fire!"

And because sometimes the world is just like that, the studio door burst open and Adam stood there drenched in gasoline, holding a Molotov cocktail in one hand and a cigarette lighter in the other.

88

He hadn't planned ahead. Not really. He had the main ingredients arranged in his mind. Himself, of course, and—as if returning to a familiar theme, as if his imagination didn't reach any further—the bottle and wick and lighter. He had expected to make an impact; he had wanted to be seen. But when he first peered into the room it all seemed so much less than he'd expected. Weland wasn't alone, and that was fine; Adam liked an audience. But they were all sitting around, frowning and distracted. There was nowhere for him, so crammed with dramatic purpose, to make a place for himself. He took a deep breath, then shoving open the door he half-emptied the bottle over himself and stepped forward.

"Nobody move!"

But that wasn't right. He wanted them to move. He wanted them to be appalled. "I'll burn it all down," he cried, and that was definitely better.

Winona froze. Harold and Izzie sat staring in shock. Only Weland was able to respond.

He looked up, exhausted, wide-eyed, and took in the figure—the wild blue and orange jumpsuit, the slender boy with an open flame in his hand, hair plastered to his head in a haze of combustibility. And after all the scotch, all the sleeplessness and despair, it seemed the very image of all he had ever feared.

"Wait! Don't! For God's sake!"

His entire life crowded onto the walls, irreplaceable now that his own talent had deserted him. He had thought it was inexhaustible, but he'd spoiled it, run it dry. And now, just like Jonathan, everything gone in a moment, with no nope of anything new. It was fate—he had it coming, he knew he did. But it was horrible! He couldn't bear it! And he was sobbing now. "Oh, stop! Please stop! Adam! Son! Please don't. Please!"

The boy stood appalled, unable to move. He had expected shock and anger. Admiration, even. But not tears. He was caught in a kind of call and response: one desperate self-dramatist reaching out to the other. But he was losing his grip on the situation. The wick on the bottle seemed much too close, the cold damp spreading through his clothes. And his arm wouldn't respond; it was growing tired. He could see the lighter beginning to shake, and it was all he could do to shout, "Oh my God! It's going to blow!"

But that was enough for Weland. A father's love? A child in peril? Afterwards he marveled at the strength he'd felt. He threw himself at the boy. "No, God damn it!"

Grappling for the bottle, the lighter, Adam found himself released into action. He wrestled his hands away, but Weland followed, snatching at him, fastening onto his wrists as they struggled together—stiff and clumsy perhaps, just a little less dramatic than they might have hoped, but frantically for all that. Weland shouted, "I won't let you do this! You won't destroy my life!"

Adam, too, was alive with his own fury, and gratified with the response. This man had all but ignored him his entire life, and now he was paying attention! But as he felt the implacable grip inching toward his hands, he had a sudden vision of the whole wild moment deflating before his eyes. Weland snatching the bottle, stripping it away. The entire gesture reduced to foolishness. He twisted, struggled, he tried to wrench himself away, but he couldn't get free.

He burst into tears.

And Weland stood there clutching him, the two of them swaying together. His heart was so full. The tears ran down his cheeks. The relief. Such relief! And something more. Look at the boy. Look at what he'd been willing to do. Burst in here, his own father's studio, and burn down every scrap of his life. How fierce do you have to be to do that? How much must you feel?

He grew aware out of the corner of his eye: the burning lighter still hovered in that haze of fumes. But someone was there—

Harold—reaching out and snapping it closed. Lifting it from the boy's hand, and the bottle, too. And Adam, sobbing and sobbing in his arms.

"Good boy," he murmured. "Good boy."

He kissed the boy's forehead and smiling blearily—a feeling of such satisfaction in his own leaping courage—he looked around. He could see Winona, stunned and drained. Even Harold had turned pale. They hadn't thought he had it in him. Well, he hadn't been so sure, himself. But now they all knew. They knew what kind of a man he was. What kind of a father. "That was close," he said. "But it's okay. We're okay."

Harold stood there wordlessly. It should have been nothing. A comic interlude. All just a little overdone. A little too frantic. A little too foolish. But Izzie was staring, transfixed, somehow a victim of all she had planned—the potion, the spell. Revenge Club so clearly gone awry. He peered into her face, trying to gauge her expression, trying to guess what she was thinking. But it was clear enough. He could see what had happened, see the mistake he had made. In the end even hate was unreliable in the face of Weland's self-regard. All of Adam's anger, all the careful store of Izzie's own fury, somehow transformed before his eyes.

Harold weighed the bottle in his hand. Then he pulled out the sodden wick and dropped it on the floor. And tipping up the bottle, he took a drink.

"Wait! Don't!" cried Weland. "It's gasoline."

But Harold swallowed hard and caught his breath. "Stolichnaya," he said. "From your liquor cabinet. I thought you'd notice."

Weland faltered. He sniffed at the boy's damp hair. "Vodka? Does that even burn?"

"I thought it would," said Adam.

And even that might have been enough to undercut any

chance of seriousness. But no. Weland smiled damply. "It's the thought that counts. Look at this. You came here today because you needed me. And you knew I needed you." He wiped his eyes and looked down, finally noticing how Adam was dressed. *The Pursuit of Happiness*, so sleek and bright—like the uniform of someone come to save the day. "What is that? What are you wearing?"

"It's Happiness. It's one of my outfits."

"Izzie made it," said Harold. "She sewed it for Adam."

And that pleased Weland even more. "You made this? Isn't that fine. Isn't that beautiful! Come here. Come on. Give your father a hug."

And reluctantly Izzie moved closer, pressed herself into the little scrum of emotion.

"I hate it that you see me like this," said Weland. "That this is what I'm reduced to. I wanted so much to be a success for you."

"You are," protested Adam.

"No. I'm not. It's all come undone. I've ruined everything." He turned to gaze back at the terrible mural. "Look at that. Look how awful it is. This is what I'm reduced to. I can't do it. I just can't. I can't paint a simple portrait. After all that's happened, this is what I've become. I'm a failure."

"You're not," said Adam. "You're not."

"And what am I supposed to do now? What am I supposed to become? I'm nothing but a fraud."

"Oh, Wheedle. You're not a fraud," said Izzie and she hugged him.

And Harold just stared. He had underestimated Weland once again. He thought of the potion mixed so carefully, so carefully applied. And now he could hear Reeve's voice. *Potions that make you sick or giddy or exhausted by it all. That prick you or pinch you or keep you wound up tight.* And as he watched Izzie leaning into the matched pair of father and son with sympathy melting in her eyes, he saw clearly now that hate is never only hate—there is always a blending. Every spell is always already a love spell.

Harold at Last

89.

They settled into a new routine: not all that Harold would have wished, but some. His late night visits to the bakery, breakfast in the morning, and the long afternoons of destruction and repair. Izzie struggled to maintain a ballast of scorn against Weland's new affection, but it left her quiet and subdued. She would sit for long moments smoothing her hand over Henry's head or watching Bea gamely saunter down one arm and up the other as if even so uncertain a journey could lead somewhere worth going. Peace arrives, when it arrives, in fits and starts.

But it leaves all at once.

The slam of the front door was hurried, footsteps racing across the kitchen floor. He had a moment to half-notice all that was different—the clatter of sound, something missing from the rhythm that turned out to be Henry's cart. Izzie burst in, eyes frantic, with the large, anguished weight of the cat overflowing her arms. "Harold! Harold, where are you?"

And afterwards, in the terrible silence, he would remember that the girl, in the depths of her fear, had called out to him. Perhaps she already connected him with the way things as solid as walls could be smashed to pieces. Or perhaps—and he hoped this was true—she just liked him enough to seek him out in these, the worst of moments.

"Here!" he shouted. "What is it? What's wrong?"

"It's Henry! She hurting again. She's having trouble breathing."

The fear in her voice was terrible. And the cat, always so limp, was struggling in her arms, trying to sit up as if straining against her own muscles. Her eyes were alight with fear, and even under the clamor of Izzie's cries he could hear the hurried scrape of her panting. "What do we do?"

"Get your mother! She's upstairs."

"I can't leave Henry!"

So he raced up the stairs. With a hurried knock on the bedroom door he let himself in. The room was all shadowy calm, the blinds drawn against the morning sunlight. She struggled out of sleep. "What? Ash? Is it Izzie?"

"It's Henry. She's sick. We've got to get her to the vet."

Bea hauled herself groggily out of bed. "I'll get dressed."

"There's no time."

He pushed a robe toward her, and she dragged it on as he hurried her down the stairs.

Izzie was wild-eyed and rigid, clutching Henry as if she could comfort her back to safety. "We've got to go to the vet," said Harold.

"No! Reeve! We've got to get to Reeve. She'll know what to do." She saw Bea standing in the doorway. "Mom! It's Henry! She's sick."

"I know, sweetheart. We'll take her. I'll get my keys."

Bea drove as Harold sat in the backseat with Izzie, hovering helplessly over the panting cat. "It's okay," he kept repeating. "It's okay. We're on our way. We're on our way."

"I'll call Reeve," said Bea. And it startled Harold, just for an instant, to remember that they knew each other. As if only now did he realize how desperately entangled every part of his life had grown.

They hurried around the side of the house. Reeve was in her garden, as he'd seen her last: green-draped and solemn, but at once she was pulling off the robe to make a cushion on the hard stone. "Come here! Set her down on the bench." And she helped to ease the panting cat out of Izzie's arms, settling her, comforting and restraining her.

Izzie crowded in. "Do you have the potion?"

"Yes. Right here."

But Reeve was grim-faced as she drew from her wide basket the little stoppered bottle. She measured an eyedropper full and squeezed it into the corner of Henry's gritted jaw, but even after a moment it had no effect.

"More! She needs more!" cried Izzie.

Reeve measured and squeezed again, forcing it past the clenched teeth, but there was no comfort. Henry was growing woozy, but still she stared wildly around, searching for something that would help her, moaning fretfully with every breath.

"It's not going to work," said Reeve. She was looking over Izzie's head at Harold. "She's too far gone."

His heart was pounding. "Izzie…"

"Give her more! We have to give her more!"

"It's not enough, sweetheart," Reeve said. "We need to give her something else." And even Izzie heard the tone in her voice.

"No!" she cried. "Give her more potion! Just give her more!"

Bea was bending over Izzie now, wrapping her arms around her shoulders. "She's hurting Izzie. She's not going to get better. This is all we can do."

"No!" The girl tried to shake her off. "She's strong! She just needs more."

But Reeve was already turning away, reaching into her basket. And when she brought out the syringe and the clear glass vial, they looked so starkly unforgiving, so at odds with all the green and rustling comfort of the garden, that no one could look away. "Dr. Paula gave me this. You know Dr. Paula. She loves Henry, too. She'd only wants what's best for her."

Izzie was wailing now, her face wild with grief. "No! I don't want her to die."

"She's suffering, Izzie."

"She'll get better!"

"I'm so sorry, sweetheart." Her mother's hands were uncertain on her hair, her shoulders. "She's too sick. She's not going to get better."

"We don't want her to suffer." Reeve's voice was calm and tight, but he could see the effort it took.

"No! Henry!"

But even under her frantic comfort the cat was lost in fear. Her eyes wide, her breath rasping in her chest. "Harold!" she cried. "What can we do?"

Her voice tore at him. "Oh, Izzie, sweetheart. This is all we can do." He pressed in beside Bea and laid his cheek against the girl's hair—so soft it made his throat ache. "She's just too sick. We can't put her through this. We have to stop her from hurting. She'll go to sleep. That's all. She'll just go to sleep. She won't hurt anymore. It's all we can do." He breathed in the scent of her. He had all but forgotten the scent of little Bea's hair, her skin, the smoothness of her cheek, and the deep familiar scent clutched at his heart.

Izzie was sobbing. "I told her I would protect her!"

"You did. You did."

"I told her I would keep her safe!"

"You have."

Izzie looked up at Reeve, tear-stained and fierce . "I want her on my lap."

"Of course."

And like a little girl, younger than he'd ever seen her before, Izzie reached out her arms, and Reeve lifted the heavy sprawling cat and set her gingerly on the narrow lap. Henry's eyes widened momentarily as she felt the precariousness of the perch, but Izzie circled her arms around and, leaning down, cradled the cat. And whether it was the pain meds or the sudden familiar comfort, the low rumble of her purring rose, louder than seemed possible in the quiet of the garden.

Harold leaned down, trying to stretch his arms around Bea and Izzie and Henry all together, as if gathering them all up out of this strange place. And as Reeve bent down he tried to ignore her, tried to focus on all that he held. Close by Izzie's ear he whispered, "Tell her, remind her, what a long and wonderful life she's led.

Remind her of all the adventures she's had."

And Reeve's hands were just a shadow out of the corner of his eye, steady and purposeful, then drawing back. And Izzie, whispering, pressed the words like kisses on the cat's nodding head, "Oh, Henry. Remember. Long wonde'ful life. Remember. All th' adventures…."

And he could feel the sobs wracking her chest as if they would shake her apart. And he tightened his arms around her, pressing his lips against her temple. "And always remember," he whispered. "You. The both of you. What a long, long life you've had together. What great adventures you've shared. Remember all the wonderful things you've done."

90.

In the morning he looked for her everywhere.

They had driven her back to the Inn in the late afternoon—it was the only place she would go. It was too early for sleep, but she crawled into her narrow bed—boots, work clothes, and all—and curled so determinedly away from them, with Henry's blanket clutched under her chin, that Harold could only sit helplessly, until Bea leaned close and pressed her lips to her temple. "Do you want us to stay?"

But Izzie had only shrugged further into the blanket, weary and desolate beyond her years.

"I'll be next door," said Harold.

But in the morning when he tapped lightly on the wall, there was no response. Slipping out to the hallway he knocked on her door, then knocked again; when he tried the knob it opened. The room had looked so crowded and chaotic in that long ago video, but now it was transformed. The narrow bed was neatly made, Henry's cart was parked in the corner, all the pieces of fabric that had spilled out so exuberantly were now been carefully arranged on their shelves, and the heavy mahogany sewing machine was folded closed like an abandoned altar.

He followed the path of her routine through the day, but she had abandoned it. She never showed up at the card shop, or the hardware, or the fabric store. As his worry grew he checked the bus station, the taxi companies. He called the police. He called the hospital. He asked everyone he met, but it was as if she had slipped out of their lives altogether.

When he drew to a stop before the trim and painted house he could have been anywhere in time. The familiar driveway, the porch, the narrow path leading around to the back—his whole life had wound itself around the spindle of this place, and as he climbed out of the car he might have been searching for Izzie along the whole wandering thoroughfare of his past.

In back, cushioned in silence, the green-robed figure of Reeve moved among the foliage as if wading through a shallow sea. He thought at first she hadn't heard him, but when he sank down onto the bench she straightened wearily and turned. She wore the wide straw hat against the late sun, and when she raised her head she seemed to open up like a portent.

"Another walk down memory lane?" she said, and even now there was an edge to her voice. "How is she doing?"

"Gone. I don't know where."

"She's not here."

"No. I know."

Still amid the stirring garden she gazed at him for a moment, then she moved onto the stone path and came toward the bench. She removed her hat and let it dangle from her hand, wide and awkward like something meant to fly that has somehow lost the knack. "There are some things nothing can prepare you for. More than some. So what are you going to do?"

"I don't know. Just keep driving around."

"You're not driving now."

"No." He looked out over the garden. "I used to think I'd never come back. All those years. I thought I'd put it behind me. But I kept imagining it. On some level I knew it was all going on without me. But everything you remember is frozen in place. And on some level I thought I could just come back and pick up where I'd left off."

"Pick up what?"

"My life."

She gazed at him levelly. "Is that what you thought?"

He frowned. "Not like that."

"Are you sure?" And if the edge was back in her voice there was something else, as well. "You didn't think maybe you'd see a light on in my bedroom? Maybe climb the stairs? Maybe knock on the door?"

"No."

"Never once? You didn't think about me naked? Never thought about me tossing and turning in my bed?"

"Izzie's gone," he protested. "She's disappeared."

"No. You just haven't found her yet. What makes you think you deserve to? Swooping in like this to save the day? Everybody's hero?"

"That's not what I am."

"The rest of us here, going about our lives. Nobody here gets to call a time out. Gets a do-over. Life doesn't work that way. You can't expect it to."

He was silent.

"I don't miss you, Harold," she said coldly. "It wasn't that great. It wasn't like some big heartbreak. Is that's what you've been thinking all this time? Oh, that poor Reeve. I really broke her heart?"

"No," he said. "I don't know."

"You think I've been pining, Harold?"

"No."

"I barely even remember you. A little adventure fifteen years ago. You're a distant memory. That's all. And not a particularly nice one."

"I'm sorry."

"Sorry is easy. Everybody does sorry. Do you want me to tell you what I remember?"

"No."

"Good."

He sat huddled on the bench. After a moment she sat down beside him. "I come out here at night sometimes. I tend the plants, I work on my spells. I try to attune myself to the rhythms of the goddess."

She stopped and glanced over to catch a smirk on his face, but he was listening gravely.

"There are parts of life," she said, "that are just too hard to bear. You can't think back on them and try to pick out the pieces that are loving or happy. Everything is tied together. The happy parts are always bound up in the parts that break your heart. I used to think about how that could be. How it could work out that way. If you're meant to be the way you are, how can you love someone who doesn't love you back? How could the world be so cruel? I know," she said. "It's a foolish question. But what could be more heart-breaking?"

The scent of damp earth, the faint weedy smell of the garden carried back to him the memory of the open fields under moonlight. The half-hidden places they would find. The hushed gasp of breathing in his ear. He wanted to tell her how precious those moments had been. How they had made of him someone brand new. But it seemed so long ago, and so much had come and gone. So much blood under the bridge.

Instead he asked, "Do you think every gain requires a sacrifice? That everything we win in life, we take from someone else? You hope and dream and you make your plans—"

"Stop it, Harold. Don't tell me about your plans. You don't get to do that anymore."

When she had returned home from Gaillard, Reeve had begun to plant her garden. A witch's garden defined her. The plants sent their roots down deep into the magic of the earth, and there was no shifting them then. She chose for its heart the plants that lay along the boundary of love and death. She planted nightshade and holly and milkweed and hemlock, and a series of lesser plants to shape and guide their force. She nurtured them, and watched them grow.

"You made me, Harold. You turned me into the witch I am today. I hated you. Every ache and pain you felt. Every moment of doubt. Every anguish. Every accident you had, every twisted ankle and scraped knee. That was me. I devoted myself to you."

The thought seemed to make him weary. "And my daughter?"

She went silent. She seemed to recall herself from a distant scene. "No," said Reeve finally. "Never that. But how could there not be a part of me, even then, that felt glad? I heard about Bea and I wasn't surprised. I thought you earned it. I thought you got what you deserved. Isn't that terrible? Isn't that cruel? But don't you see what you did? I was so dark, Harold. It was such a dark time. So we ended up sharing that, as well." She turned. "I want to show you something."

And bending to the basket at her feet she rose again with something shadowy gripped in her hand. It was ragged and grimy— the dirt of how many roots rubbed into the fabric, how many potions dripped or steamed or soaked into its stuffing? It was a doll, roughly made—little more than a clutch of fabric. He started to reach out a hand. "It's better if you don't touch it."

"It's not a very good likeness," he said.

But in fact there was something in the drooping head, the exhausted splay of the under-stuffed arms that seemed to capture the very heart of him.

"I made this when I got back," she said. "That first week. I spent a lot of time on it. I searched through all the sources I could find. Scholarly works, chatrooms, suburban witches out there in their designer covens. And I knew that even if the ingredients were flawed or the spell was weak, the force of feeling behind it was enough to lift it into the realm of the powerful. See this part here?" She brushed a fingertip over one ragged quadrant of the torso. "Some people count sheep at night. I collected brambles and thorns, sharp twigs, and I would press them in one by one. And for every thorn I pressed into your heart I left one turned outward. So as I squeezed and squeezed, I drove them into my hand, and the blood would seep into the fabric."

She weighed the little doll in her hand.

"After a while I stopped—after a while. I thought all that hate was probably not good for me. I buried it out in the garden, among the roots of the holly tree, so it would stay green all winter long. And sometimes I even forgot about it. I went about my life. But then I would remember, and under a moonless sky I would dig it up again, half-expecting it to be rotted away. But it was always there. Every time I remembered and dug you up, there you were. And after a while I realized I would be a little bereft if anything happened to this. You know how it is when you've invested your life in something."

"And this is what you've been teaching Izzie?"

"Not the details. Just the heart of it. A witch draws her power from the best and worst moments. Just like everyone else. I've tried to teach her not to shy away. You can't hide from the pain. In the end it's the strongest thing about you."

"And what about love?"

She gave him a level glance. "Some people are lucky. They continue as they started: driven by love. Not many. Just a few. Most of us, over the years, are just too daunted by it all. By one thing after another. We grow frightened and weak and self-protective. We hide from love, whatever we tell ourselves. But some people... Whatever else you think about Weland—however much hate or disdain you feel—it's love that drives him. Love of beauty. Love of fame. Love of himself." She shook her head. "It's a powerful position. Even as you despair you always focus on the thing that will make you stronger. You always choose what you need in spite of every other living soul. And when you find it again, you rise up with barely a memory of all that weighed you down. Can you imagine?"

"So what are you saying?" he demanded. "What do you mean? Choose love? You think that's the answer?"

"Oh, Harold. Haven't you been listening? We never choose. I buried you in the ground a hundred times. I stuck you full of nettles and pins. I dripped blood and poison into your veins. And now look at me. Even now. If I took off my clothes right now? What would you do? Sweet mistress mother! Is there anything worse than love?"

91.

It was only in her final illness that Miss Pru allowed herself to be moved into the Rectory. All their pleas were nothing against her resolve—to keep her best memories of how things had been, as if succumbing to the present would only loosen her hold on the past. But finally he and Sara prevailed and they installed her in the Bishop's Room.

It was too much for Sara, so fresh from her own grief. So he took to cooking the meals, trying to duplicate those redolent and long-ago soups with which she had nursed him that first summer. She kept her recipes in an ancient three-ring notebook, and he would leaf through them alone in the evening. It had been a month since they had lost Bea, and this slow subsidence into death seemed merely an aftereffect of all that was already gone. In the low light of the kitchen he would hover in a state of dream, half-present half-past. And the cramped, busy handwriting of the seventeen-year-old Pru—compiling her bank of recipes and knowledge for a brand new life—seemed the final remnant of some ancient optimism. When he made each dish, the familiar aroma would emerge. But sitting in that all-but-empty house, he felt every aspect of his life vanishing like steam into the air.

He would sit for long stretches by her bedside as she dozed. With the move to the rectory Hospice had come in, and though Pru refused the modern hospital bed, she welcomed the morphine drip with its beeping monitor counting down in two-minute increments each additional promise of relief. At first it seemed insane that she should have to wait, and he would grow frantic watching the numbers trickle past. But once the system was in place and the sharpest edge of her pain was dulled Miss Pru relaxed, and he became grateful for the slow passage of time.

The morphine carried them languidly on a soft cushion of

fatigue and peace. And with the momentary comfort of each dose Miss Pru would sigh, and they would talk, slowly, dreamily, circling back to the brightest moments of her life. And he marveled that it was never the dark memories that returned to her. He, who was consumed by darkness, could imagine nothing worse than to be carried back into the past. But she seemed to float above sadness.

"Life isn't the end," she murmured once.

And he sat up, leaning closer. "What was that?"

"Just the beginning."

And he couldn't help himself. "Do you really believe that?"

A moment of doubt seemed to pass over her face, and he cursed himself. But what she said was, "Yes. How could it not be true?"

"Do you think you'll see Father Ben again?"

"Yes. I don't know. Wouldn't it be lovely? I have so much to tell him."

And it was such a pooling moment of pleasure when she first moved from the distant path of girlhood and her years with Father Ben to the life she shared with him. A smile on her thin face, head wrapped in a flannel turban, she recalled as if from no real distance those long moments at the sink, praying and worrying, as he climbed the ladder to clean the gutters on his very first day. And the warm, dulcet noontime when they sat together next to Mrs. Becket's sagging fence and spoke of nothing more than what she planned for dinner and the languor of a summer afternoon. And later, toward the end, when she emerged all at once from her sleep and took his hand, her voice was as soft as the banked summer air.

"Sadness isn't the end. Remember that, my dearest boy. Sometimes our grief is all we can see. It's the only thing that's real. But remember. All this, all of it. This is real, too. Oh, I worried so. You always put your hopes in love. You thought it was the only thing that could be true. But life. Life is the truest thing we have. Don't turn your back on this. I know. You never really believed in it. But all of us here, we believed in you."

At the end of a day of searching he returned to the high white house, and when he stepped into the kitchen he found it empty and bright, as if he had returned to the most important moments of his life only to find them abandoned. Drifting through the house—mudroom, studio, living room—he wearily started up the stairs. Every door was closed. He knocked at Bea's bedroom but it was empty, the bed unused, the shutters closed. He tried every other door in turn. Izzie's bedroom had been untouched since she'd moved to the Inn last fall. It was the only part of her childhood that remained—pink walls, pink bookshelves, a few stuffed animals, all slumped and woebegone. The curtains were drawn. But in the middle of her childhood bed there she lay, curled like a mouse in a nest of covers.

She huddled on her side staring hopelessly at the door, as if waiting for something even she didn't expect. Beside her Bea sat dozing in a chair.

Harold stood unmoving, slack with relief. Izzie regarded him wordlessly.

Don't wake her, she signed.

He couldn't help himself. He bent and pressed his lips against her forehead, smoothing his hand back over her hair. She didn't move but her fingers made a little turning movement, then a quick flight of motion.

"I'm sorry," he whispered. "I don't know what that means."

She reached up and stilled his hand.

"Sorry."

But that wasn't it. She fastened onto his fingers and drew them down so that her fists, the covers, and his hand made a complex knot in the warmth under her chin. He sat down on the edge of bed and laid another kiss, soft as a whisper, on her head.

At the movement Bea stirred and opened her eyes.

"Ash," she said with a tired smile. "Here we are."

92.

There was nothing Izzie wanted to do. Nowhere she wanted to go. She ignored her jobs, her closetful of costumes. At first she seemed to adjust her make-up to fit the calamity—pale face, dark smudges under her eyes, red eye-liner smeared here and there into a ravaged, sleeplessness. It looked, if anything, a bit overdone, until Harold realized her face was scrubbed clean. She was all cried out. And against the unaccustomed pallor of her cheeks a constellation of freckles rose into view as she grew younger and younger before his eyes.

They tried to entice her with projects. They started leaving dirty dishes in the sink, a dish towel tossed negligently onto the floor. They left the vacuum propped enticingly at the edge of the living room rug. But she ignored them all. She ate a little bit of everything he prepared, trying not to hurt his feelings, so he began cooking half-a dozen meals a day, each one as if by accident.

And while he washed the dishes, she sat tracing lines aimlessly on the surface of the table until even movement became too much trouble. He began to read to her. Whatever books he found on her childhood shelves: *Winnie the Pooh, Doctor Goat, The Little Engine Who Could.* They were all too young, and he waited for her to complain, but instead she sat with her ears turned up, gazing down into her lap. He moved the plastic tray with Bea-the-spider onto her bedside table, and Izzie would watch her as she listened, reaching out a fingertip to trace her way down the spider's back. And the little creature would stand perfectly still, as if uncertain what the sensation was but determined not to scare it away.

Then one evening, climbing the stairs to bed, she found, where he had laid them out, the midnight blouse and ballet skirt from the first night he had followed her onto the fire escape. She looked up, and there was Harold in the doorway in his nightshirt and robe.

"I want to show you something," he said.

They walked into town along the dark streets, now familiar under the shadows and silver light. "This is the Kinneys' house," he said. "They have a pool in the back yard. This is the Macdonalds'. They're getting a divorce."

He tried to remember all the details of that first night, tried his best to give her own words back to her. And just as with the children's books, he half-expected her to grow impatient with the repetition. But she listened attentively. Even a young witch could recognize an incantation when she heard it.

He led them from streetlight to streetlight, then down the alley to Madame Sophie's. He waited at the fire door as she drew out her keys and then stilled the beeping alarm. Together they turned to the shadowy landscape of shelves and counter and the front door waiting beyond.

"Do you remember the spell?" asked Harold.

Wordlessly she nodded.

"Remember. You have to believe."

And eyes closed, murmuring to herself, she reached out and opened the door.

They traced their original route like a pair of migratory birds following the draw of the seasons. They walked first toward the campus and the occasional wandering spirits of collegiate nightlife and then entered Asteroid Pizza.

"What did we order?" he asked.

"Two slices of pepperoni. And you stole a Sprite."

"I'll pay for it twice today."

They ate walking along as they had before, but that first night seemed so long ago. He looked around, searching for the familiar. "Does this feel right to you?"

"I don't know where we're going."

"I'll show you."

She was doubtful at first, but Harold guided them through the stillness. They finished their pizza and he gathered up the paper plates. They were standing by the wire garbage basket, and carefully he dropped them in. Then, as Izzie watched expectantly, he reached in and drew them out again and stuffed them into his pocket.

"You'll stain your robe."

He smiled. "That's okay."

"It won't be the worst thing that ever happened," she corrected and nodded as he said it back.

They continued on. "We're going all the way back to when you were less than two. When you went out to Weland's party with your mom and dad and your mom's friend. Do you remember?"

She nodded. "That was you. You were my mom's friend."

"That's right. We have to see it properly. We have to block out anything that isn't right."

They were finding their way together now, both knowing where they were going and both half-worried about getting there. Izzie tucked her hand into his arm.

"Do you remember that night?" he asked. "Did you have fun at the party?"

"My dad and I did. My mom seemed nervous. I think you made her nervous. Or Wheedle did."

He nodded. Every moment of the past was closer now. All their losses, all their gathered sadness. Every feeling from that long ago visit was fresh in his heart—all of it right there in the darkness just beyond them. He could sympathize with his younger self, coming back so full of hope. Not realizing it was already decided. That he was already not the man he needed to be.

They reached the dark cave of the driveway under the overhanging trees and stopped to prepare themselves. He leaned in close and whispered in her ear. "Tell me again about that night."

"It was so dark. My mom was walking toward the door, and Henry was in the bushes; she was calling to her. She had such a little voice. At first my mom didn't know what it was. She thought it might be a wild animal. A skunk or a racoon. But you looked in the bush and found Henry. You lifted her out. She was so tiny." In the darkness under the trees Izzie cradled her empty hands. "When you brought her in and gave her to me she fit right into my arms. I held her. And we gave her food, and a little bowl of warm milk. And we became friends for life."

"That's exactly right," said Harold. "Friends for life."

He slipped his arm around her shoulder, and they walked down the driveway within the lingering scent of the burn-out garage. "Ignore the smoke," he whispered. "This is before that. This is back at the beginning." Though of course it wasn't the beginning. It was never the beginning. You were always already in the middle.

They faced the back door, closed and locked since they had walked out of it an hour ago. The lights they had left on in the kitchen were still burning, but now they were the lights of long ago.

"Behind that door," he said, "do you know what's happening? Right now? Henry is curled up in your hands while your mother warms a pan of milk and your father opens a can of tuna. And they're putting down two little bowls. Tiny bowls. But bigger than anything Henry has ever seen before. And you lower her down onto the floor and she stands there amazed. It smells so good. She's never smelled anything so good. And she is so hungry. But she's so tiny. She's meowing. She doesn't know what to do. She's never been in this situation before. She's never been loved like this before. So you pick her up again and this time you move her right up to the bowls. So that her nose is right next to the milk. And you smooth your finger over the top of her head until she stops meowing. She closes her eyes. She looks like she's going to fall asleep. It's such a beautiful dream. But she leans down and starts drinking the milk. And you keep stroking her head. Do you remember how you did that? You were as sweet and beautiful as she was. And she drank and drank; and you whispered to her, telling her how much you loved her and how you would always be there with her. Just behind that door, that's what you're doing right now. Remember? You'll always be doing that. As long as you live."

93.

Bea lay in bed in the warmth of the afternoon—slatted sunlight spilling through the blinds. But the old sleeplessness had returned, days and nights running together. She stayed home from the bakery to be close to her daughter, but Izzie was closed off from the world, and she found herself too much alone. Nothing to do, no way to help. She would listen for the slightest sound, but Izzie rarely left her bedroom

For so long Bea had labored to give up hope. That had been her goal: to free herself from ambition. No more disappointments. No living for what might have been. Better to reduce yourself to the easy limits of each day—the *what* of life, not the *what if*. And for a while it had worked. Never greedy, opening her arms to the smallest of pleasures, it had begun to feel like happiness. But now all their lives had run aground, beached and separate—a castaway's existence—with no real sense of what rescue might be.

She dozed and woke and dozed again. But now there came to her through the muffling walls the sound of movement. A creak and scuff. A distant thump. Edging toward the door she cracked it open. Down the hallway Izzie emerged like a mouse from her burrow— daunted but dressed now in her carefully mended overalls—and made her way down the stairs.

Bea listened to the voices, the low murmuring, the questions and replies. They formed a hushed counterpoint to the sudden crunch of the hammer, the thump and scrabble of work. She found she was smiling. They were priming a section of the new wall, and the smell of paint rose like a memory grown suddenly vivid and close. Or perhaps less a memory than a kind of vision, taking on the solid shape of the world. That long ago attic apartment, so stifling and close. The high white walls, the open window—she felt them now in the slatted sunlight, in the promise of something so old made new. Or maybe it was simply that every memory contained its own seeds of hope. You can only run away so long before you find yourself running towards.

Work ended for the day. She listened to Izzie, having changed into, say, the plain, clerical extremity of an Amish schoolgirl, slam her way out the door with a shouted, "See you, Harold."

Then she waited. The slow trudge of footsteps on the stairs. A low knock. And he opened the door. Her eyes blurred the sunlight the way they blurred everything now. The blue of his shirt, the stiff brown pants. But there was something else, something more reminiscent.

"You look different."

But really he looked suddenly the same. He had shaved. And without the grey-flecked beard he was youthful again—startled back into boyhood.

"I wondered if it was time to turn from a wolf back into a man."

"Wouldn't that be something?"

She lay naked under the sheet. The nights at the bakery had rekindled an awareness of her own skin.

"Izzie?" she asked.

"Gone off to work. She's taken Bea the spider."

"How is she?"

He seemed to weigh the answer. "Still sad. I think she feels sorry for Weland."

"And you? How are you?"

"I recently heard him described as a creature of love."

"Is that right?"

"And I thought, What about me?"

She reached out and took his hand. "You can't tell her. Please. Not yet. I don't know when."

He gazed wearily down at her. "She says we're partners."

"You are."

"She says she can trust me."

"She can."

"How can this be fair? Now? After everything? What kind of an ending is this?"

"Oh, Ash. Look at us. Look at all we've been through. This isn't the ending." And letting go of his hand she sank back onto the pillow. "Come into bed with me."

He unbuttoned Franklin's shirt, stepped out of his shoes, his socks, his pants. He stood in the lee of the afternoon like a swimmer at the water's edge. His skin, tanned in places and pale, seemed to outline for her some complex pattern of present and past.

It was with a smile that she drew the sheet aside. "Tell me I look like a painting."

"Much better than a painting."

He slipped in beside her.

She had thought it would be like remembering. But it was more like returning to a picture you've studied and learned, only to discover it was something else entirely. They kissed as if it were nothing anyone had ever done before.

"Slowly," she breathed. "I'm brand new."

Harold at Rest

94

Weland was coming undone. Day followed day. Arms around his children, he would let his gaze drift over the walls of his studio—the crowded paintings, the huge, distorted canvas not just ugly now but pointless. It was nothing of his, nothing to do with him. He spent long hours as before sketching—Adam and Izzie, Winona, even Harold—but without any urgency or purpose. There was a fretful sweetness about him now, as if he were slipping before their eyes into a kind of domestic dotage.

As he painted he would revisit all the old ideas about Childe Harold Days, unable to let them go. Human statues? Interpretive dance? A scavenger hunt? Nothing seemed too foolish. A parade? Paintings? Not that terrible mural, but still. He looked up at his wall, his other works. They were real. All those years of talent and accomplishment. They had been the answer in the past, at every moment of his life, and they could be the answer now. It would still be a series of murals, he explained. But smaller, the size of the original paintings. He could paint them all himself.

Harold said nothing. He had become a pure observer, lifted out of his own anger by the spiraling aimlessness before him. After all the strife and discord, he marveled at this new Weland—laid low by his own selfishness, reduced to a more reasonable size and shape. It seemed a kind of moral ending, reassuring somehow: a transformation through suffering. And Harold found he could no more leave than any of them. So they began strolling together around the downtown looking for sites that might be suitable for these new miniature murals. And when they stopped at a likely corner Weland would ask: What do you think? Is this too low? How's the shadow? How are the lines of sight? As if it were all just a matter of the merest practicality.

But he never seemed to settle on a spot. And each afternoon

turned into a private parade through Weland's memories, gathering up the threads, pausing here and there to recollect. And always, wherever they were in town, he would turn to gaze up at the high peeling wall of the Grainger Hardware sign like a navigator setting his faltering course by that one settled star. And he would turn to Adam and Izzie, as if it were a new idea each time, "I always thought my face would go up there someday. That would be something, wouldn't it? Walking along the sidewalk and you see your old man's face up there?"

And Winona would pat his shoulder, and Adam would look up with that same shining expression, and Izzie would think of something nice to say. And even Harold would fall silent. Who was he to judge? What was life if not a chance to correct past mistakes?

But gradually their days became nothing more than this, and in the end Weland said it once too often. Adam looked stricken. Winona sighed. And Izzie turned impatiently. "For Pete's sake, Wheedle! Enough already! If you want your face up there, do something about it. Just take a picture! You could blow it up as big as a barn, if you want!"

She immediately regretted it—he was staring at her with a look of such astonishment. She started to apologize. But slowly she realized it wasn't hurt or disappointment that suffused his face. It was the wildest kind of hope.

95.

When the photo arrived from the processing plant, rolled inside a cardboard tube taller than a man, Weland received it with a kind of dread. It had been left at his door, and by the time Harold and Izzie appeared in the mid-afternoon he had moved it from the front step to the hallway to the kitchen counter to the corner of his studio with the slow reluctant progress of another bad idea.

They all gathered round.

It had taken days to get an image that would live up to the years of anticipation. He was a terrible model, standing awkwardly, fraught with importance as Izzie, phone in hand, directed him around the studio. He only had a few expressions and he would pose, stiff and self-important, pointing his face this way or that. In a fit of impatience she led them out into the afternoon, but once there he seemed even more self-conscious: the sun always in his eyes. He spent the nights alone in his studio—not even painting anymore, just going over and over the photographs as if surely he must have missed something. At last he made his choice, sent it off to the printer, but it left him in a rage.

"I don't even know why we're doing this! It's ridiculous! What does a photograph have to do with anything? This wasn't even my idea. You've distorted the whole thing. Made it into something ordinary. I wish I'd never invented any of you!"

And how could they not agree? Weland, long-faced and fearful, sidling up to the cardboard tube as it might explode. It was like watching that first spark alight on the Hindenburg. But in the end Harold said, "It's all right, Weland. You close your eyes. If it's bad, we won't let you look."

Izzie knelt down and cut the tape, pried off one end of the

tube.

"Careful!" cried Weland. "Don't tear it."

But she was already reaching in with eager fingers, catching at the coiled layers of mylar, hauling it out. Once started it slid easily, swooping out of the tube like a dragon from its lair. She cradled it in her arms, startled by the weight, but Harold eased in beside her and together they drew it free and laid it on the floor.

It was too big to unroll. Stretched out beside the sofa, its nose wedged into a corner, its feet against the wall, it sprawled implacably. Weland stared with a haunted look. "Is it too big?"

But Izzie, whose idea it had been after all, took charge. "We need to move the furniture."

They started to drag the sofa back, but there wasn't enough room. They bumped and shifted every piece but couldn't quite steal enough space.

"How big is it going to be?" asked Harold.

Weland couldn't move his eyes. "I don't know. I told them to give me the maximum."

"So, it's what? Maybe ten feet high?"

"Maybe." He moistened his lips. "Open it."

They shoved the sofa as far as it would go, and piled on the screen and chairs and café table, until it looked like the back of a pick-up truck. Then Harold and Winona crouched against the wall, holding down the leading edge, as Adam and Izzie slowly unrolled. The mylar was feathery thin and tough as leather, with aluminum grommets along the edge. There was a plain white margin that seemed to draw out their uncertainty, then the first color began to appear. Step by step Weland backed away as if from a rising tide, until he finally took refuge up on the sofa.

The color spread, the size distorted everything. It was impossible to tell what they were seeing. A cheek? A forehead? They peered down, waiting for the greying hair, the mustache, the vast stony face. But as the image broadened it resolved itself into a naked hip, a long back, the bright aurora of golden hair. And *The Blue Robe* expanded across the floor like a spreading pool of color.

"Holy Christ," Weland muttered.

"What happened to your face?"

"I changed my mind."

Twelve feet high. Half again as wide. Crawling backward Izzie bumped against the wall and, scrambling up, balanced precariously in the narrowing gap. "Don't step on it!" cried Weland, and delicate as a tightrope walker she bent and drew the edge right up to her feet.

"Oh, my god," murmured Weland. "It's magnificent."

It had to go up right away; that was all that would satisfy Weland. The end wall, wide and high, but already crowded with paintings. He peered up at them like a wild man. They had been a storehouse of inspiration, of reassurance and pride, but now he just wanted them gone.

"Roll it up. Roll it up!" he snapped, climbing down from the sofa. "There's a ladder out in the garage. Somebody—Harold—go get that. Winona, I think it's time for the scotch."

Izzie rolled up the mylar like a carpet, frowning with concentration. Harold returned with the yellow step ladder. He climbed up and began taking down the paintings, lowering them one by one into Izzie's reaching hands. The wall seemed to expand as it emptied.

"Take out all those screws," commanded Weland. "We don't want to risk tearing it."

It was Izzie's turn on the ladder. Electric drill in hand, she drew out every screw, and Weland pressed his cheek against the wall to gaze along the surface.

"Okay. We need to measure."

"How high do you want it, Wheedle?"

"How the hell am I supposed to know? I have to see it first."

So they shifted the ladder along, trailing a faint line of penciled x's across the wide wall. Then they changed places and measured again.

"Stop wasting time!"

"Measure three times, cut once," said Harold.

"For God's sake!"

When it was time to set the screws Izzie waivered. "You do it," she whispered.

"You've got this," said Harold. "Never mind him."

Slowly and deliberately—an affront against all that coiled impatience—they moved from point to point, Izzie up the ladder, Harold steadying her, until they stood together regarding the line of screws, straight and spare across the plain white wall, as if that, alone, was a work of great beauty.

"Well, don't stop there!" cried Weland.

They lifted up the whole heavy roll and worked their way across, hooking it onto each screw in turn as Weland paced like an expectant father.

"Careful! For God's sake!"

But it worked like a charm. Together they lowered the roll to the floor, letting it slip out slowly between their hands until they were left with nothing but the curling edge, weighing little more than the air itself. And across the wall the familiar image spread wide as a sunset. The sleeping woman thrown back across the storm-tossed bed. The blue of the robe casting into golden relief the warmth of hair and skin. And the wonder of a summer afternoon—long vanished but returned to them now in a figure of perfect delight.

Weland stood staring for a long time. When he spoke his voice sounded hoarse. "It needs to be higher."

Izzie frowned. "How much higher?"

"How do I know? A foot? Make it a foot."

"A foot is this much," she said holding up her hands.

But Weland didn't even look. "Can't you just raise it? Please?"

"We're going to have to take it down, roll it up again," warned Harold. "Every time we move it, it might tear."

"Okay. Never mind. That's okay," he said. "It's fine for now."

And he gazed up as if the thought of losing sight of it, even for a moment, was more than he could bear.

96

The afternoon passed in an orgy of looking.

Having moved the sofa to where his easel used to stand, Weland sat and sipped his scotch and stared at the painting. Vast and delicate, it filled the wall.

"Look at that. You can see the whole curve of the thigh there. I'd almost forgotten how how hard that was. Look how perfectly the balance of mass and light works. You can almost run your hand over it. And the brushwork up on the jawline. You can barely see it in the original but it's crucial. All that work and care. It's like the whole world balanced on a pin point."

The others felt no need to reply. They gazed up from their own particular vantage points: Izzie, admiring how perfectly straight the top edge was; Winona contemplating the obvious care with which Weland had treated this previous model; and Harold gazing with a pang of omniscience, as if taking in the whole long panorama of his life.

And even later, when the picture had been hung on the side of the building and illuminated for all to see, he and Bea would pause in their evening stroll—taking time out from the bakery to thread their way through the vacant, forgiving darkness. And they would look up at the picture with something like amazement at how all the changing shape of things could curve so far back on itself and still retain its initial wonder.

Weland stopped painting, stopped sketching. He gave up everything. For weeks all he did was look.

He had them remove every distraction. The chairs, the screen, the discarded paintings, the sofa itself. Everything was carried out and jammed into the rooms and hallways beyond. And when the studio was finally reduced to a large white box—with a last eager glance to be sure there was nothing left to be stripped away—Weland sank down onto the floor. And with his back against the wall he stared up at the picture as if he'd been carried away beyond the farthest reaches of doing.

Winona stopped coming by, and even Adam grew bored. But Izzie and Harold continued to visit, building it into their daily routine, as if there were something tidal in the push and pull of Weland's enthrallment. For he was brought low in a way no one had expected—reduced to feeling the way everyone else had long felt. Abject. Overwhelmed by the sheer self-absorption of his own creation. He was cowed by himself.

So they would put in an hour's work on the mudroom—they were finishing up the drywall now—and then brush themselves off and arrive at Weland's studio in time for lunch. Izzie would settle Bea onto the floor in her plastic tray and then hurry out to the kitchen. Plates of sandwiches, mugs of soup, ice water and lemonade that she tried to substitute for wine or scotch but had to settle for simply augmenting.

And later, when she was gone about her various jobs, Harold would stop by again on his own—sometimes fresh from Bea's bed—and gazing up at the painting, he would find himself adrift in time as if all the elements of his life continued to shift and recombine. Even in the middle of the night, on his way home from the bakery, he would stop and peer in through the big bay window—unable to stay away. The light was always on, the painting always glowing bright, and Weland always sitting there as if pinned to the wall.

"Sometimes it just makes me so angry."

Weland's voice was weary. He looked too drained to feel anything. Cradling a glass of scotch in his lap he was becalmed in the horse latitudes of mid-afternoon. "Luck is a cunt."

"Language, Weland."

But he just waved him away. "I'm sorry, Isabel. But it's an

unavoidable truth. Do you know the source of inspiration? The etymological roots? It's an act of breathing in. Like respiration only deeper. The spirit of beauty enters your body. Back me up here, padre. This is right up your street, isn't it? It's when God—who exists in nothing else if not in this—inhabits you. Comes in through your lungs and gains access to your heart—your soul and cock and spirit."

"Weland."

"But here's what they don't tell you. It all comes down to luck. Who thought I'd ever say that? But it's true. I'm helpless without it. And there's only so much to go round. It's a resource like any other. You've got to find it; you've got to make it. But here's the thing. It's like there's a huge generator out there cranking out this endless stream of luck, but it's leaking away. It's flowing out in all these little dribs and drabs where it doesn't really matter. I look around at what passes for good luck. Finding a parking space. Dropping a glass that doesn't break. You can see the look on their faces—like a moment of wonder. As if all creation banded together to save them from themselves. But it all just peters away."

Izzie had taken Bea out of her plastic tray and was playing mountain climber on the long, upward incline of her leg. She had made a little harness out of yarn, and it trailed from the spider's plump waist up to Izzie's hand. She lifted the spider gently back onto her lap, and Bea seemed to take the measure of the room. Then, spying once again the distant peak of the bent knee, she set off gamely up the slope.

"That is horrifying," said Weland.

"She probably thinks you're horrifying."

He sighed. "See? It's a case in point. That little fright could have been stepped on any number of times. Most people would have picked up a shoe and snuffed it out. But it's managed to escape. It has fallen into the hands of the one person in the whole world who would take care of it. The chances are astronomical. I can only imagine the amount of luck that appalling bug has sucked up. And look at me. I'm dry as a desert."

Gloomily he watched as the spider reached the top of her climb and stood surveying the wide domain. Izzie drew the yarn up slightly, lifting her from the perch. Her bent legs started running through the air.

"You're frightening her," said Harold.

"I think she likes it."

She lowered Bea back down, and she sat there with a faint air of disappointment. Izzie lifted again, and this time she rose with a kind of startled delight, dangling for a moment like nothing so much as a spider from its web. Then she twisted in the air and, grasping hold of the string, started eagerly to climb.

"For God's sake! Drop it!" cried Weland. And even Harold felt that atavistic fear: the long strip of toilet paper with the spider racing up.

But Izzie cupped her hand and held it just beneath the industrious climber, following her all the way up until she took a purchase on the girl's pinched fingers and clambered up onto the back of her hand.

Weland shook his head. "And there's another jolt of luck. Gone for nothing."

He sipped his scotch. "Ask your friend Reeve. She knows. She's been talking to me about it, refining my ideas. She's not cheap. I've never hired a witch before; I always assumed they'd be more reasonable than this. But it'll be worth it, if she comes through. And frankly, I'm not sure where else to turn."

And Harold, moved in spite of himself, turned impatiently back to the painting. "For God's sake! Look at that! It's beautiful. It's amazing. And you did that. There's no luck there. You just painted it."

"No, no, no. You don't understand. I could paint a picture like that any day of the week. I could paint that picture over and over. Or one just as good. But it wouldn't be that one. It's nothing without exactly the right moment. I could paint something today, something beautiful—if only I could think of it—and it would fizzle like a damp match. I'd have a perfectly nice painting. But that's it, that's all. But if you add a little spark of luck? You get a forest fire of a painting. Instead of just another day's work."

"Do you know what most people would give to have that as a part of their day's work?"

"Of course they would. That's what I'm saying. But they can't. They don't have the eye, the talent. So the opportunity's wasted on them."

He brought up his glass, but it was empty, as if even that proved his point. And he raised his eyes to the wall. "Look at that. I could hang it up on that building tomorrow and everyone would see. And they'd like it. They might even love it. They'd stop on their way to work or lunch or shopping, and they'd be moved. Of course they would. But then they'd just put it out of their minds. Go on about their day. Forget all about it until the next time they're out walking and they catch sight of it again."

"Well," said Harold. "That doesn't sound bad."

But Weland was alive with anguish. "Don't you see? Look at it. It could be so much more. I can feel it. This could be my chance."

97

Harold got off his schedule one morning. The late nights, the long days, the occasional afternoons behind Bea's sheltering blinds, it all caught up with him one morning, and he slept late. When Izzie in her chambermaid guise opened his door with her peremptory knock, she left him undisturbed and went about her day, so that he woke a little sheepishly at eleven-fifteen and headed to the house where Bea was already asleep. He drank his coffee in the mudroom contemplating the startling transformation: having flown as far apart as they could, the separate elements of the wall had all but drawn themselves together. It was hard not to see it as a sign.

Izzie arrived in time for lunch. And it was only then they realized that neither of them had Bea the spider. The plastic cage was nowhere to be found.

Under a glowering sky Reeve sat looking out over the shifting green of her garden. In the stormy light her robes seemed an extension of the clouds. There was a narrow column of smoke rising from a small iron brazier, and as the breeze shifted it carried the scent of sage and sandalwood and the hidden edge of something bitter on the air.

Izzie hurried up to her. "Reeve! Reeve! Something bad has happened."

The witch was lost in thought, but as the girl approached, the wide straw hat tilted back and she looked up with a startled expression.

"Izzie. I didn't expect to see you today."

"Wheedle his done something terrible."

"Well. It won't be the first time."

"He's taken Bea. He's kidnapped her."

"Your mother?"

"Bea the spider."

"Maybe she just wandered off."

"No. Her home is gone. He's been acting really strange. I think he's going to do something bad."

The witch settled the child on the bench beside her with an expression of distant concern—as if even in this moment she was listening to the wider movements of the day. "We'll go look for her in a moment. I'm sure she'll be all right."

"He kept talking about bad luck. He said you were helping him."

"Weland always gets it just a little wrong. Don't worry." She looked up at Harold with a frown. "I thought you were going to look after her."

"I thought I was."

"You've been made a guardian here. You've been given a place of responsibility in the larger order of things."

"I'm doing my best."

But Reeve just shook her head, as if she had done all she could. "I'm going to make us some tea. Sit down."

She stood and offered him her seat on the bench. Then she knelt by the low brazier. A small iron teapot sent up a curl of steam. From her basket she drew a tight clump of herbs tied together with a string and dropped them into the pot, stirring with a narrow wooden spoon.

"I've been hearing about your adventures. I gather Childe Harold Days has hit a snag?"

"You're a therapist now?"

"Everyone needs a little help. Even Weland."

"I thought he'd given up on it."

"He's a force," she said. "Sometimes, when a storm is coming, you just need to sit somewhere sheltered and let it pass."

"I wouldn't want to give the storm the satisfaction."

"I understand," she said. "But it's not the storm who suffers."

And, pouring the tea into three small cups, she brought them over. "Drink it while it's warm."

Izzie drank hers obediently. Harold sniffed and then sipped. The tea was smooth and smokey, with a trace of cinnamon and something floral as if the garden breeze had dipped into the pot.

"You have to realize," Reeve was saying. "It's not easy being Weland. But it's even harder trying to be like him. He's like a fire. Where would we be without fire? But you never want to get too relaxed around it. And you never want to touch it. All you can do is to keep him from causing more harm than absolutely necessary."

"Sometimes he makes me so mad," said Izzie.

"I know. It's only because you care about him."

"I don't."

"You do. Everybody does. That's his superpower. He makes it impossible to be indifferent. Weland doesn't care whether you love him or hate him, but he does need one or the other."

"All my life I've been trying not to think about him," said Harold.

"No, you haven't. I've never met anyone who is as bad at not caring as you are."

He finished his tea. Reeve lifted the little cup from his hands. Izzie sat lost in silence. Reeve took her cup as well, and set all three of them—two empty, one still full—down beside the pot. "I'm going to need you both to sit very quietly now. I'm in the middle of something, and it needs all my attention."

"Is this a spell?" Harold started to ask with a smile, but the words came out muffled. His tongue felt heavy, and the relaxation of the tea had grown into a general heaviness of muscle and limb. "What's going on?" he murmured.

"Don't worry. It's just temporary." She drew a pair of long green scarves from around her neck.

"What are you doing?" Izzie said with a kind of distant alarm.

"I can't move."

"Yes, you can. Just not very much. Just right now."

She eased behind them like the breeze. Harold found it hard to keep track of her movements; there was a low dread building in his heart. He felt his arms drawn to his sides. The feathery pressure of the silk wrapped behind his back from elbow to elbow. Not uncomfortable. Almost reassuring. Binding him somehow to himself. Izzie, beside him, struggled very gently. Harold leaned in, pressing his shoulder against hers.

"That's right," said Reeve. "You take care of each other." And she brought their neighboring hands together and interlaced the fingers. "Here we go. We're going to cast a spell together. The three of us. Well, the four of us. Weland has got this bee in his bonnet. It's too dangerous to let him do it on his own. So we're all going to help him. This is a spell that will take all our energy."

From the vague stretches of space behind them Harold was aware of Weland emerging. He was dressed in his own version of Reeve's robes, flowing and green. He looked awkward in the costume, but his expression was simmering with excitement. He held the plastic cage in his hands.

"Don't look at me that way," he said frowningly. "You'd do the same if you were in my place." He gripped the cage tightly. "It's an established condition of the magical world. Just ask Reeve. The currents of luck have gotten out of whack, and we have to put them back. It takes a tremen-dous amount of energy. And energy has to come from somewhere. Somebody has to pay the price."

He turned and held out the spider in her cage. "I believe you'll take it from here."

But Reeve regarded him coolly. "You have to lift her out."

"Oh, no. I can't do that."

"Fear and energy, Weland. Remember. Everything costs us something. The greater the cost, the bigger the prize."

And with delicate ceremony she reached out and removed the plastic cover from the box. "Gently. You mustn't hurt her." She lifted the cage from his hands and held it up.

"Right." He gave a shaky laugh. "The greater the cost, the bigger the prize."

A ragged moan rose in Izzie's throat. Weland was bracing himself, his face hardened into a grimace, but his hand was shaking. He dipped down and lifted out the spider. She was suddenly fearful in his grip. He held her there, her stout little legs churning the air, as Reeve set the cage down and turned.

"Hurry!" he gritted.

"Gently, Weland."

She drew from her basket the unlikeliest of props. A brown paper bag, a lunch bag, neatly folded and flat. She opened it carefully and held it out. Hurriedly he extended the spider. "Don't drop her!" Reeve commanded. "Lower her gently."

Pushed to the last of his resources he lowered the spider to the bottom of the bag and snatched his hand away. Reeve closed the top, folding it shut, running her fingers with somber finality along the crease.

Harold's voice was strangled in his throat, but Izzie managed a cry. "Don't, Reeve! Please."

"There are all sorts of threads running through this, Izzie. Years and years. Isn't that right, Harold? All that you've done? All those mistakes. All that thoughtlessness and cruelty. It takes something big to gather all those moments and make an end to them."

The witch bent down and set the bag in her crowded basket. Then hoisting the basket into the air she approached the brazier.

The rising trail of smoke had thinned as the charcoal ripened into glowing coals. She set the basket down and knelt beside it. "Weland?"

"Oh. Right."

He hurried forward and clambered down onto his knees. His robes bound his legs, and he shifted to pull them loose.

"Remember," said Reeve. "We have to be loyal to something larger than ourselves. Everything is tied together—every hurt, every heart-ache. Every action brings another. Every good and bad deed turns on itself."

"Right," he murmured. "That's right."

"Think of your luck. All your bad luck. Think of all that has happened to you. All that you have lost. And project it with all the power of your mind, with all your heart, onto this." And she held up the brown paper bag, neat as a school lunch amid all that fear and ceremony.

Weland, his eyes all but straining from their sockets, stared grimly at the bag as if he really were recollecting every grievance and fault that until now had no solution.

"Don't blink," said Reeve. "Don't take your eyes from the sight. This is the connection. This is the wire along which the current of bad luck must travel."

And she began to intone, "Oh, Goddess. Draw from this man all trace of his ill fortune. Invest in this wretched creature every dark and terrible thread, every curse and bitterness, every dashed hope and stunted wish. Oh fearsome lady, let every daunted hope and sharp, malignant gleam, every wicked strife and sorrow, be gathered here and so consigned to the flames."

And she placed the bag on the glowing coals.

Izzie's cry rose on the air. Harold struggled beside her.

Just for an instant the bag sat there, shifting anxiously in the heat. Then the first tendrils of smoke curled up. The air shimmered. And in one drawn-out instant the fire burst into place, sudden and greedy, licking at the dry paper. Harold could see the bag still rocking slightly amid the flames, and then it was alight—a bubble of fire. The heat took hold. The darkening bag began to crumple and fold in on itself. It seemed to shrink and harden, a black heart at the center of the blaze. And before their eyes it withered like a leaf, turning ashy pale at the edges, as the flames flickered and slowly began to sink.

Weland stared, frozen, holding his breath, as if he could feel it—a vapor of discontent flowing away. "My God," he murmured. "My God."

He was testing his hands, his limbs, as if he'd been bound so tightly for so long that he was only now getting the feeling back. He climbed to his feet, looking around with a sense of wonder.

The rain began, surprisingly gentle, pattering down on the leaves of the garden, catching in the flimsy green of his robe. Hurriedly he drew it off, as if this were the final part of the transformation. "Thank you, Reeve! Thank you. The world will thank you. I can feel it. This is going to be tremendous."

And dropping the robe without a backward glance he hurried away, as if destiny were as impatient as he was, and he couldn't bear to keep it waiting.

In the silence they could hear the raindrops hissing on the coals. Harold felt the damp spreading dully through his body. Beside him Izzie sat, huddled and bleak. After a moment Reeve climbed reluctantly to her feet. She gazed down at the brazier, the glowing coals subsiding into a wet slurry of grey and black.

"You should be feeling better soon," she said. "The effects don't last long. I'll go make us some coffee."

"Don't bother," said Harold.

But Reeve came over and untied the scarves. Izzie didn't move. Harold slipped his arms around her, holding her close, but she was hunched and stiff. He laid his cheek against her hair. "Oh, sweetheart."

"I'm sorry," said Reeve. "He'd gotten this idea into his head. I couldn't just let it go. There's no telling what he would have done."

He peered up at her wearily. "I knew you hated me. But Izzie.

How could you do this to her?"

The witch said nothing. With a shrug she bent over the basket again, the wide straw hat dipping down, and when she rose she was holding a neatly fastened brown paper bag.

"Hold out your hands."

Izzie glanced up at the tone, and slowly reached out her cupped fingers. Reeve opened the bag and gently tipped out its contents. The spider tumbled out and lay for a moment, a small tangled knot. Then she leapt to her feet, shook herself gamely, and peered around like the lady in the trick who, having been sawn in half, is more than a little surprised to find herself made whole.

Reeve rapped her knuckles lightly on Harold's bowed head. "Don't say I've never done anything for you."

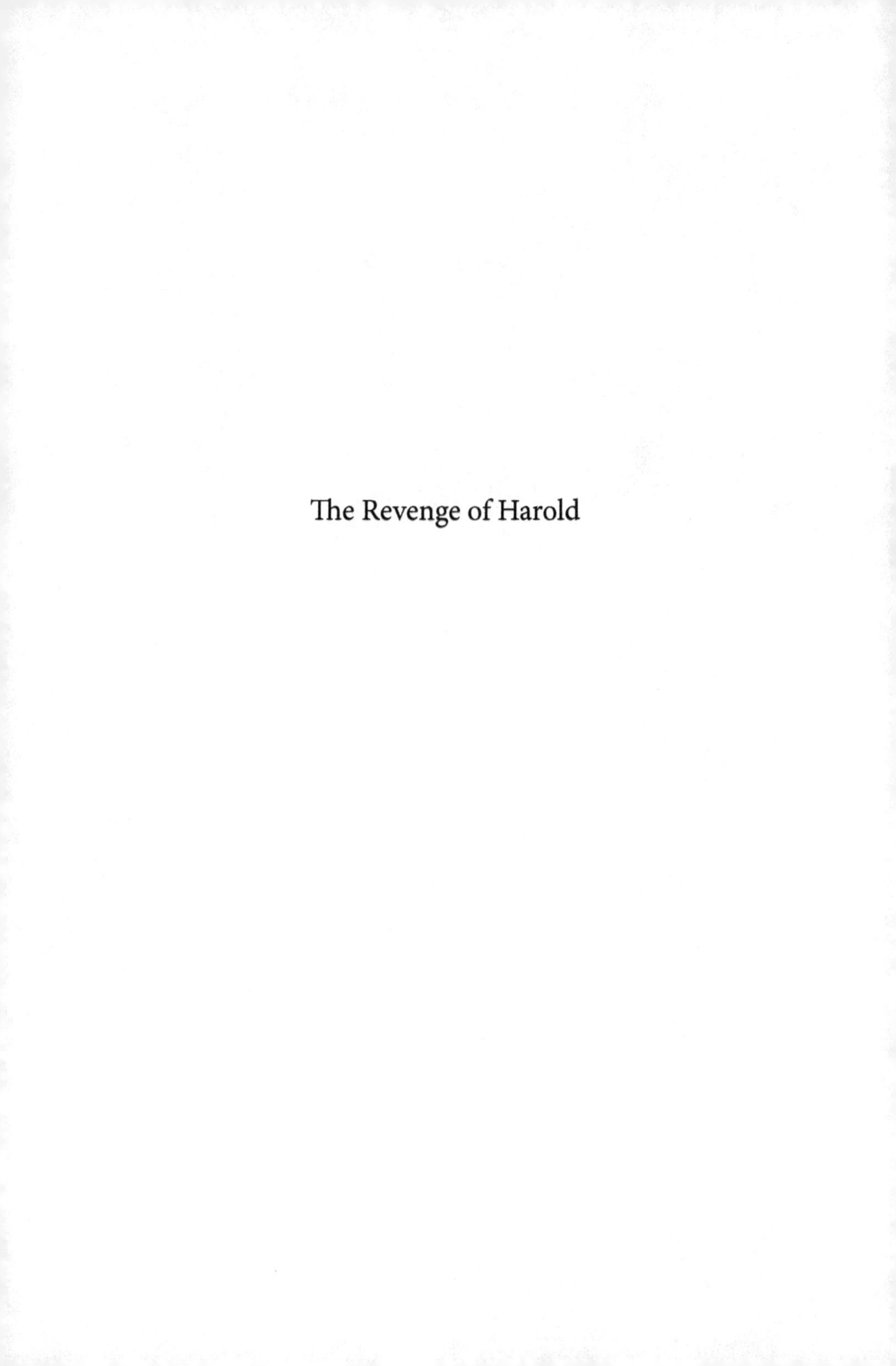

The Revenge of Harold

98.

Weland was galvanized—freed from the heavy weight of inactivity. Resolute, clear-eyed, he spent the end of June and early July reaching out and drawing together all the loose threads—workmen, public officials, newspapers, magazines, galleries and collectors. It helped that the town had been working slowly toward its Fourth of July parade for more than a month. Most of the preparations had already been made. Weland was just going to tweak them a little—find the magic and make it his own.

The response was mixed. *Art Forum* all but yawned over the phone, *The New York Times* was unimpressed. The *AP* sent a local stringer. But Weland was untroubled. He had found his faith again, and to see him moving through the day, overflowing with energy, was to be presented with such calm assurance that even the community spokeswoman for the mayor's office found herself—just on the off chance that something might come of it—working her way through the list that Weland had given her, setting up the chairs and the podium, hanging the lights, bringing out the bunting, and slowly building a stage—low, wide, and somehow brimming with purpose.

And throughout it all he bustled ardently like a magician who alone knows just what he's packed into his top hat. He checked the sight-lines, paced off the best vantage points for the mural's unveiling. And as if having trouble distinguishing himself from his painting he would climb the narrow stairway to the rooftop and stand behind the low brick parapet, looking down at the rows of chairs and the cross-work of struts and scaffolding, as if only from here could he judge the effect of sitting all the way down there.

And all the while Harold and Izzie worked grimly by his side. And if he was surprised that they would have anything to do with him—that they weren't enraged or bitter or wild with fury—he remained untroubled. This was, after all, going to be a great occasion; surely there'd be enough satisfaction to go round.

"Do you want to hear about our plans?" Harold asked one afternoon in the shadowed comfort of Bea's bedroom.

"No."

"I could tell you. We're sworn to secrecy, but I'm sure Izzie wouldn't mind."

"Please don't," she murmured.

They lay tangled in the humid sheets, his arms laced around her, his lips pressed to her temple. Lying there, he thought, they might have been a painting. They might have picked up this image and carried it back all those years and dropped it into place with barely a ripple.

"We're going to destroy him."

"I know."

"We're going to make him suffer."

"I know." Her voice was calm and muffled, drifting toward sleep. "And are you planning to devote your entire lives to that?"

"Yes. That's exactly what we're going to do."

"That's a big commitment."

"Anything worth doing is worth doing well."

"Is that what Izzie thinks?"

"Oh, yes. She's all over it."

"Okay," she murmured. "But here's a thought. You could just forget about him."

"Weland is a selfish monster."

"I know."

"He's a terrible person."

"I know."

"I've made it my role in life to destroy him."

"I can see that. But what about all he's done for us?"

A little breath of laughter blew against her cheek, and she smiled. His voice was warm in her ear. "And what has he done for us, exactly?"

"This. You and me. All these years. He brought us together."

"He did not."

She bit him lightly on the arm.

"Well," said Harold, "he didn't do it on purpose."

"No. But we'd never have met without him. Never be here, right now."

"That's a terrible thought," he murmured.

"We owe it all to Weland."

And he lay there for a long moment with that thought in his head.

"Sometimes I think back," he said. "That first moment, all those years ago. Do you remember? In that moment I thought we were destined to be together."

She smiled. "We were."

"I thought it was fate."

"It was. Of course, it was. Weland was our fate."

"Good lord."

"And here we are. You, me, Izzie. With no one but Weland to thank. Tell me you're not grateful."

"I am."

"Tell me you're not going to ruin everything."

"I won't."

"You know if you push Weland off the top of the building, they're going to throw you in the pokey, and Izzie and I would miss you."

"I'm not going to push him off the building."

"I don't want you setting him on fire. Or breaking his legs. Or running him over with your car."

"See? I like where you're going with this."

"You have to promise."

"I don't know. They're all good ideas."

She gave him a little shove.

"I promise," he murmured.

"And we don't want to get all wrapped up in him, do we? Say it."

"No, we don't."

"And we don't want Weland taking over our lives. Trust me when I say that."

"But we hate him. Izzie hates him."

"I know she does. But you know who she doesn't hate? You. That has to be worth something."

He sighed. "I liked him better when he was miserable."

"I know."

"I liked feeling sorry for him."

"You can still do that."

"I don't think so."

"Here's the thing," said Bea. "What if you had to choose? What if I held a gun to your head?" And lifting his hand she pressed it warmly against her breast. "Him or me?"

"I would choose you," he said.

"So choose. Because I choose you. And Izzie. I choose this. Just thank him for his selfishness, count your blessings, and let him go. Don't let him ruin your life. Our life. Isn't this much nicer than hating Weland?"

"I can do both."

In the early evening of July 3rd, when the stage was completed, the lights were hung, and the searchlight had been trucked in—rented for the occasion from the Chrysler dealership out on Route 21—Weland led the way up to the rooftop with Adam carrying the mural like a rolled carpet over his shoulder and Izzie and Harold bringing up the rear with the stolid expressions of workmen everywhere.

Adam had a walkie-talkie clipped to his belt—an ancient prop from the Public Works Department—and it crackled occasionally as the distant searchlight crew grumbled through their work. Stepping out under the fading sky Weland glanced around with the weary contentment of a general whose plans have been made. "Ask them if they can see me."

"Roger," squawked the radio, with a voice so laconic it was hard to distinguish professionalism from irony.

"Light me up," said Weland.

They had placed the searchlight on an adjacent rooftop, far enough away so it wouldn't blind the audience but with a clear line of sight. When they turned it on it glowed in the late sunshine—a pale, unblinking eye. Weland stood for a moment expectantly. "Anything?"

"You're there," crackled the voice.

He glanced down at his pale suit, ever so slightly paler now. "Can you make it brighter?"

On the distant rooftop they pretended to adjust the light. "That should do it."

Weland turned toward the building and saw against the brick wall a pale shadow of himself. He raised his arm in greeting and watched it respond. "Is it centered?"

"Affirmative."

"Do you remember the signal?"

"Affirmative."

"I don't want any screw ups. It has to be like clockwork."

"Affirmative."

"Okay. Let's hang her up."

Harold and Izzie moved stolidly into action. They lifted the wooden ladder and leaned it against the wall. The lower rung, newly repaired, looked bright and strong.

"Is that safe?" asked Weland.

"Should be good." Harold tapped it with his foot. "It's not as if you'd fall very far."

"I don't want to fall at all," snapped Weland. "Make a note. We should bring the ladder from my house, just to be safe."

Harold climbed as Izzie steadied it. He measured and marked the holes across the top of the wall. Then, reaching down for the drill, he set the screws. He was conscious of the height, so much more than just the ladder itself. His ankle ached—the throb of past calamities—and though well back from the parapet, his eye kept wandering over the edge. Izzie lifted the roll of mylar bound in canvas straps. Its heavy tip nodded toward him, and as he reached down, just a little too far, he felt the ladder shift. His heart lurched. His hands tightened on the rungs. And for an instant he could feel his weight hanging far out over the air.

But Izzie, gazing up at him so matter-of-factly, steadied his pulse. "You okay?"

"Peachy."

He slipped the first grommet onto its screw, felt it take the weight, then worked his way carefully along, moving the ladder, climbing again, as Weland waited impatiently. When he finally climbed down, leaving the bound roll hanging heavily in place, Weland announced, "And that's that."

But of course it wasn't.

That night Izzie and Harold returned to the scene of the crime-to-be. They had dressed for the night. The building's lobby was locked, but that was nothing to Izzie's ring of keys. They slipped along the darkened hallway. The elevators were running, of course, and they had left the door at the top of the narrow stairs ajar.

Izzie insisted on stepping out first into the open air, oblivious to the height. It was her adventure, and Harold agreed. But he remained close, one hand ready to snatch her if she stumbled. She stood for a moment at the base of the wall, looking up at the heavy roll, waiting for its moment. The new ladder was there—bright yellow fiberglass with sturdy aluminum rungs. They lifted it and locked it into place.

Izzie was the one to climb. High as it was, she swarmed up the steps as if there were nothing but anger on her mind. She worked her way along, lifting and slipping the canvas from its screws, letting it sag foot-by-foot into Harold's arms. He tumbled it onto the gravel of the rooftop, and together they worked, untying the straps.

They had discussed a variety of plans, letting their minds wander freely over the wildest possibilities. But now they knelt on the roof, gravel pressing into their knees, and gazed down at the image, so oversized and splendid. They had thought of loosening the screws so it would collapse, but their pride in their workmanship held them back. Izzie had wanted to paint *You Suck, Weland* in bright red letters across the mural. She'd brought the paint and the brush. But now, even in the pale moonlight, the beauty of the figure made it impossible. The languorous woman, captured in such a flood of feeling—a woman who, in addition to everything else, had long been the embodiment of all that was beautiful to the girl. So in the end they simply rolled it up again.

From a plastic grocery bag they scattered small mounds of dog poo they had gathered for the purpose. They scattered empty beer cans here and there and scraps of litter and a rotting piece of salmon they had been aging out of the fridge. Weland might be too strong for hate, but not for ridicule. They turned to leave—just a few more things to do. Izzie was always drawn to complicated plans.

But at the doorway she hesitated, looking back at the scene. "Maybe it's not enough."

And really, after all that had happened, how could anything be enough? But there was more to Revenge Club than just revenge. It was a club, after all. And at the end of the day a club was all about belonging. He laid a hand lightly on her shoulder. "I think it'll do the trick."

99.

The crowd began to assemble in the late morning—young children and parents for the opening parade, then progressively older teens and adults milling around the food carts among the diffident clusters of street performers and an occasional wandering mime—as a series of student orchestras began to take their turns on the low stage, one replacing another, until the evening approached with a jazz quartet brought all the way from Schenectady. Weland strolled through from time to time, alternately smiling and frowning, fussing like a *maître d'* over his tables. And if occasionally he forgot that this was the Fourth of July—that it wasn't, in fact, the sole product of his fevered imaginings—well, even Harold couldn't begrudge him that.

For with the first hint of twilight the strings of lights took on a more emphatic glow, and the texture of the day receded. Every ordinary object, painted now in silver and pearl, seemed to rediscover itself. People moved like schools of fish through the rising anticipation, and somehow, as he and Izzie strolled, the frenzied preparations of the night before—the scattered dog poo, the rotting salmon—grew more and more foolish. The rising festivities cast an air of playfulness over their plans. And even their anger now seemed part of some wider good cheer, as if their hatred had lost its edge amid the bustling hubbub of all that life could hold—everyone reduced to their gentlest selves, and all that was best and worst condensing into the cheerful day: Weland nothing more than a fussy man looking forward to showing off, and even Izzie distracted now by the low murmur of fun.

She wandered along beside him, half-scornful, half-pleased. And strolling through the wafting clouds of jazz and grilling onions she would touch his arm now and then to draw attention to something, or just walk along with a finger hooked negligently in the pocket of his coat. And as if a sparrow had unexpectedly landed on his open hand, Harold pretended not to notice.

Maybe I'll be a mime, she signed.

"You're already a mime. Besides, you just like her outfit."

White pants, tuxedo shirt, white sneakers with bright red tips like the nose on a clown.

"I do like her shoes."

"I'll buy you some."

What is it that makes a family? He glanced around at the scattered parents and children—tired, excited, bored. Surely there was room in such a wide cross-section for them to slip in unnoticed. Bea was moving about her business, oblivious to their sinister plans. Queer Bread had assembled three hundred cinnamon buns in gooey, unsteady towers in the refreshment tent, and she moved warily in her baker's whites through an obstacle course of tomato-based foods. She would smile and squeeze his hand in passing, or brush his sleeve.

It was the least of things. But for so long his life had been fastened upon its direst expectations. Disaster to disaster; dread to dread. So attuned to the chance of loss that nothing else remained— all the smallest moments reduced and overlooked, when what you needed most was just to let them run through your fingers.

He remembered all the years of longing, dreaming of his return, imagining all the ways he would become the person he had meant to be. But even in his most heroic dreams it was never this. Such incidental happiness, a summer afternoon. Voices rising around them:

"Eat this and we'll get you one later."

"It's okay, sweetie. Everyone's afraid of clowns."

"So I said, that's the thing about cotton candy. It's not a solid or a liquid; it's a state of mind."

All of it folding him into an air of such cheerfulness that everything, even revenge, was just a game they were playing.

The crowd had no idea what to expect, but they had always been untroubled by Weland, accustomed to all his fussy pride. They were ready to be pleased, and with full darkness came a new anticipation, as if there really might be something to all his plans. The tangled clutter of wires and struts receded in the darkness, and in their place pure strands of light. And even Harold, who knew how little it amounted to—a ten-year-old painting, one more speech about art—even he could feel the excitement build. And he began to chafe at what they had planned. Weland might be a ridiculous monster, but the thought of embarrassing him had faded in the gentle tumult of the day.

Bea slipped her hand into his, bumping ever so slightly against him as if even their most inconsequential steps could only bring them together. And whatever else Weland had done, he'd given him this as well.

Abruptly, as if the night had finally grown deep enough to trigger all the calamities in store, the searchlight came on with an almost audible snap—a solid bridge of light above their heads—racing through the sky and landing like an arrow five hundred feet wide of the mark. Izzie squeezed his hand in appreciation as every eye rose on a single string to find the rooftop still swaddled in darkness. A low murmur began as the men on the searchlight hurried to adjust. The shaft of light swerved here and there, and by the time the beam stood squarely pinned against the wide brick wall, the laughter was rising up.

Weland struggled to ignore it. A glowing vision in pale suit and bowtie, he stepped to the parapet, his expression set. But they could see him stepping gingerly, glancing down at the sullied rooftop, hesitating at the turn things were taking. Even from the ground they could see the expression dawning of a trapeze artist beginning to wonder about his luck—worried perhaps that he may have launched himself too soon.

"Ladies and gentleman." His voice boomed out from the bank of speakers. "Thank you all fo—" A crackle of static rose, screeching high, and then strangled itself into silence.

"Nice touch," whispered Harold. And Izzie gave an answering tug on his sleeve.

But Weland was undeterred. Stepping forward, raising his arms, he shouted, "This is a wonderful moment for all of us. The completion of a decade-long journey. A final epilogue to a crucial chapter for this town, this college, and all of us gathered here."

And despite himself Harold felt a grudging respect for the unrelenting self-importance of that voice. Maybe he didn't want to destroy Weland. But was it too much to ask that no one be beyond the little miseries of life?

"Does it make me a shallow person," whispered Bea, "that I'm actually excited?"

And Harold saw amid all the upturned faces an answering eagerness. Only Izzie had an intent and hungry look, as if she'd been thinking of this moment all along.

"It is my pleasure tonight," said Weland, "to give us all back a piece of our history. This is a familiar image to us all. We have enjoyed it, appreciated it for so long. But even the most beautiful images can be lost. For if they remain sharp in themselves, they begin to fade in our memories. And yet, like every great thing, they grow greater with each return. It is my pleasure to unveil this permanent reminder of how great art and a great town can be joined forever."

Adam stepped forward and together they turned and lifted the yellow ladder from the shadows. They set it against the wall, and Harold felt Izzie's grip tighten in his own. He smiled down at her, but he saw that her attention was entirely on the roof. She was staring up with a fierceness out of all proportion to the childish scale of their pranks.

"What is it?" he whispered. "What's wrong?" And a sudden thought. "What did you do?"

"I sawed through one of the rungs on the ladder," she whispered.

"Oh no."

He looked up at the scene unfolding. It had felt unnervingly high when they were standing on the roof, but from the ground it was appalling. They were tiny figures high in the sky, caught in the bright searchlight and suspended over an enormous wealth of darkness.

"It's okay," she said. "I just did the second rung, the way you said."

And he remembered their first night out, relishing the string of small humiliations they could commit. But now. The ladder too high, the parapet much too low. The moment was coiled for disaster. A crack, a fall. And in that instant he had a vision of Izzie, caught for the rest of her life by the events of this night. An injury, a disaster of such magnitude, and all of it laid at her door. What had he been thinking? It was as if Weland, with all his crazed immoderation, had reached out and grabbed them again. Drawn them in. Entangled them once more in that wild unconstraint.

They were straining upward now. "We've got to stop them."

"Wheedle!" yelled Izzie. "Wheedle, stop!"

But the murmur of the crowd was like a blanket of sound. Or maybe Weland heard and just took it for encouragement. He was making the last adjustments to the ladder, drawing out the moment, savoring the anticipation.

"Wheedle!" she cried.

"Weland!"

And the crowd, mistaking the tone, took up the chant.

But in the end, of course, they needn't have worried about Weland. With a little flurry of indecision the two figures bent in conversation. And with a bright flourish he stepped aside, laying a careless hand on the boy's shoulder. And Adam—offering something between an acrobat's bow and the flutter of nerves—stepped to the ladder.

"Oh, no," murmured Izzie. "No, no, no. Wait! Adam!"

But the boy was staring upward, his mind on all that lay ahead. And the crowd, taking up the cry, started to applaud. Already he was too high, towering over the low parapet, unprotected against the open air. He started to climb.

One step. Finding his balance, struggling a little with his nerves. A second. What had they been thinking? Harold held his breath. Izzie gripped his hand, twisting it as if she could guide Adam safely past the danger. He seemed so hesitant, unbalanced by his nerves. But there was a kind of spell in the air, and the boy—his weight so much less than a grown man's—passed up and over the damaged rung without a tremor while Weland, oblivious to all that protected him, stood wrapped in the concentration of the crowd.

They stared unbelieving, drawing in a reluctant breath, as Adam climbed higher and higher. Around them the mass of people tuned themselves to a single chord. They weren't about to see anything they hadn't seen before, but there were a number who remembered liking the painting when they'd first seen it. And some of the parents, thinking ahead, were growing uneasy about the appearance of a naked woman in such a visible place, while others were looking forward to that very thing. And the children were caught in the long excitement of the day and the brightness of the searchlight against such a velvety night.

Adam swarmed up the remaining steps until he stood poised near the top. From the sidewalk it looked as though there was nothing beneath him, as if he were already leaning out over the drop. He stretched out his hand, and there was a single intake of breath as he grabbed hold of the knotted straps. He tugged, and tugged again. And with a moment's hesitation the roll unwound like a waterfall of gold and blue.

And there it was. Vivid. Outsized. Bright as life.

And the fireworks, locked into the schedule, began—a *pop*, a muffled *whoomp*. But there was something wrong there, too. One rocket fizzled into view. Then nothing. And beneath the wide and anticlimactic sky hung *The Blue Robe*: beautiful, seductive, and irremediably upside down.

100.

Even then it could have been all right. Harold breathed in relief; Izzie frowned her triumph. And they had a moment to appreciate the final image of their revenge, as if the universe, after all their efforts, had reached out and given them this small final triumph.

But Adam, perched like a nuthatch on the ladder, was outraged by the sight. Forgetting his delicate balance he surged forward in a sudden fury, as if he could just grab the mural and twist it into place. And that was enough for the poor damaged rung. Weakened, half-sawn-through, it snapped. And with all the sudden torque on the ladder the legs responded, twisting apart like a too-tall man on stilts before the whole gasping crowd.

It was almost comic the way the structure seemed to soften and collapse—bending, bowing to the audience far below, with Adam a bright, slender ornament leaning out over empty darkness. And for a moment the crowd couldn't be sure this wasn't some part of the performance. There was such a weight of showmanship about it.

But the AP man had been a photographer for twenty years. He'd been in Bosnia, Beirut. He knew disaster when he saw it. And he captured Adam—afterwards people marveled at the shot—his limbs delicately arrayed like a dancer, his face a mask of wonder. A pale, slim, uncertain figure suspended on the unforgiving air.

It was this picture that would inspire the greatest of Weland's paintings. Wounded Icarus. A heart-breaking sequence that drew him far beyond anything he had ever done before. A series of nudes of such startling beauty and force that they captured the imagination of the world. The young man, battered, broken, but momentarily aloft. The terrible mixture of fear and ecstasy fastened in that instant on the boy's shining face.

But of course that would have been only part of the story, the darkest part—an artist so hungry for fame he could make use of even so terrible and despairing an image—if the grip that terror had taken on the throats of the crowd hadn't eased. If the whole gasp of anguish and horror hadn't breathed its way out.

For there was a cry, a flurry of shouts, a roar like the massed clamor of bees. And Weland—galvanized by that rising sound, by the light and the focused attention—and driven perhaps, in the deepest part of his brain, by the beauty of the complex forces shaping themselves into such a perfect image for the crowd below— leapt forward.

For those who saw—and years afterward all they had to do was glimpse one of the paintings and it would all come rushing back— they would remember it as an almost superhuman leap, an outfielder racing for that high fly ball, lifted on the force of his own intemperate need. He seemed to throw himself at the low parapet— waist-high, no more; not designed to stop him but to catapult him over the top. And reaching up as if to drag himself aloft against the downward force of all that was about to occur—and here the pale suit was an inspiration, catching and defining against the colors of the mural that sense not just of motion but of bright, inextinguishable will—he flew, reaching wildly for the toppling ladder.

And if his leap had lasted just a moment longer—and Harold often reflected on this, long after the fact, pausing sometimes in the most ordinary task—if he had followed through on his original, unconsidered arc, he would have grasped only air. For he had misjudged the distance. Another moment and it would have been clear to the crowd that his was a wild and unconsidered leap.

But the ladder came down heavily against his shoulder, shifting his path, staggering him toward the edge. And still he reached wildly past it toward the boy, who was silently invested in the slow arc of his own fall, gradually separating himself from the tumbling ladder, drifting free like a man in space.

Then Weland glimpsed out of the corner of his eye the hanging mural. The bright image of his greatest triumph. And surely it must have called out to him on a level far beyond the simply utilitarian. How could a man be thinking clearly during those hectic seconds? But surely that elemental feeling of wanting it, of yearning to latch onto all that had been so important, was bright in his mind. So that while his brain occupied itself in the terrible certainty of all that was about to be lost, his hand reached out and fastened onto the slender edge of mylar.

At the same moment he grabbed a handful of the boy's shirt. But his grip wasn't strong enough. Perhaps his desire for the falling boy was not as intense as that feeling for all that he had once had. His hand slipped. The clawed fingers ran skidding down the slender chest. And in one final grab, they hooked themselves fiercely onto the boy's belt. They fell together, twisting in the air, levitating up over the low parapet. Until the heavy plastic of the photograph straightened, stretched, and pulled taut just for a moment before it tore. The grommets dragged loose from their screws one and then another, like the seconds counting down, until the third, fourth, no, fifth one held and drew them in, bright in the searchlight, bouncing hard against the low brick barrier, all grace vanishing in the thump and judder of re-entry into the world of physical things as they tumbled down onto the dark and shadowy roof.

Silence. As if even the air had frozen into place. Then it started to thaw. Voices, cries, a soaring tumult as Weland, Adam in his arms, rose up into the light. The boy was limp and broken—a blow to the head, a terrible crack to his arm and the largest bone in his leg—but he lay back, graceful for all that. That's what would strike viewers all across the country when the picture went out on the morning wire. The beauty of the pose and the force of Weland's expression. Fierce, exultant, like some ancient hero. As if in the face of every opportunity for mischance he could not stop succeeding. As if triumph didn't so much drop from the sky as tumble, and Weland in his incontestable hunger, simply could not help but catch it.

D. K. Smith is the author of three
previous novels, *Nothing Disappears,*
Missing Persons, and *Bunny, a romance.*
He and his wife divide their time
between the American heartland and
their island in Canada.

* 9 7 9 8 9 8 5 1 9 4 1 1 1 *